DISCARD

COMPANION TO THE BESTSELLING
RANGER'S APPRENTICE

BROTHERBAND

BOOK 5
SCORPION MOUNTAIN

JOHN FLANAGAN

PHILOMEL BOOKS - An Imprint of Penguin Group (USA)

ALSO BY JOHN FLANAGAN

BROTHERBAND CHRONICLES

THE RANGER'S APPRENTICE EPIC

For my son Michael, once more.

PHILOMEL BOOKS

Published by the Penguin Group | Penguin Group (USA) LLC
375 Hudson Street, New York, NY 10014

USA | Canada | UK | Ireland | Australia | New Zealand | India | South Africa | China
penguin.com
A Penguin Random House Company

Copyright © 2014 by John Flanagan. Illustrations © 2011 and 2014 by David Elliot.
Map copyright © by Mathematics and Anna Warren.
Penguin supports copyright. Copyright fuels creativity, encourages diverse voices,
promotes free speech, and creates a vibrant culture. Thank you for buying an authorized
edition of this book and for complying with copyright laws by not reproducing, scanning,
or distributing any part of it in any form without permission. You are supporting
writers and allowing Penguin to continue to publish books for every reader.
Library of Congress Cataloging-in-Publication Data
Flanagan, John (John Anthony), author.
Scorpion Mountain / John Flanagan.   pages cm.—(Brotherband chronicles ; book 5)
Summary: Princess Cassandra of Araluen has already survived one assassination attempt, but when a
second attempt proves that the deadly Scorpion Cult is involved, Hal, his Heron Brotherband crew,
and the Ranger Gilan are dispatched to ensure her safety by launching a preemptive strike against
Scorpion Mountain and its cult of assassins.   1. Quests (Expeditions)—Juvenile fiction.
2. Seafaring life—Juvenile fiction. 3. Assassins—Juvenile fiction. 4. Attempted assassination—Juvenile
fiction. 5. Adventure stories. [1. Adventure and adventurers—Fiction. 2. Seafaring life—Fiction.
3. Assassins—Fiction. 4. Fantasy.] I. Title. II. Series: Flanagan, John (John Anthony). Brotherband
chronicles ; bk. 5.   PZ7.F598284Sc 2014   823.92—dc23   2014028703
Printed in the United States of America.
ISBN 978-0-399-16356-2
1   3   5   7   9   10   8   6   4   2

American edition edited by Michael Green.   Design by Amy Wu.   Text set in 13-point Centaur.
The publisher does not have any control over and does not assume any responsibility
for third-party websites or their content.

A Few Sailing Terms Explained

Because this book involves sailing ships, I thought it might be useful to explain a few of the nautical terms found in the story.

Be reassured that I haven't gone overboard (to keep up the nautical allusion) with technical details in the book, and even if you're not familiar with sailing, I'm sure you'll understand what's going on. But a certain amount of sailing terminology is necessary for the story to feel realistic.

So, here we go, in no particular order:

Bow: The front of the ship, also called the prow.

Stern: The rear of the ship.

Port and starboard: The left and the right side of the ship, as you're facing the bow. In fact, I'm probably incorrect in using the term *port*. The early term for port was *larboard*, but I thought we'd all get confused if I used that.

Starboard is a corruption of "steering board" (or steering side). The steering oar was always placed on the right-hand side of the ship at the stern.

Consequently, when a ship came into port it would moor with the left side against the jetty, to avoid damage to the steering oar.

One theory says the word derived from the ship's being in port—left side to the jetty. I suspect, however, that it might have come from the fact that the entry port, by which crew and passengers boarded, was also always on the left side.

How do you remember which side is which? Easy. *Port* and *left* both have four letters.

Forward: Toward the bow.

Aft: Toward the stern.

Fore-and-aft rig: A sail plan in which the sail is in line with the hull of the ship.

Hull: The body of the ship.

Keel: The spine of the ship.

Steering oar: The blade used to control the ship's direction, mounted on the starboard side of the ship, at the stern.

Tiller: The handle for the steering oar.

Yardarm, or yard: A spar (wooden pole) that is hoisted up the mast, carrying the sail.

Masthead: The top of the mast.

Bulwark: The part of the ship's side above the deck.

Belaying pins: Wooden pins used to fasten rope.

Oarlock, or rowlock: Pegs set on either side of an oar to keep it in place while rowing.

Telltale: A pennant that indicates the wind's direction.

Tacking: To tack is to change direction from one side to the other, passing through the eye of the wind.

If the wind is from the north and you want to sail northeast, you would perform one tack so that you are heading northeast, and you would continue to sail on that tack for as long as you need.

However, if the wind is from the north and you want to sail due north, you would have to do so in a series of short tacks, going back and forth on a zigzag course, crossing through the wind each time, and slowly making ground to the north. This is a process known as **beating** into the wind.

Wearing: When a ship tacks, it turns *into* the wind to change direction. When it wears, it turns *away* from the wind, traveling in a much larger arc, with the wind in the sail, driving the ship around throughout the maneuver. Wearing was a safer way of changing direction for wolfships than beating into the wind.

Reach, or reaching: When the wind is from the side of the ship, the ship is sailing on a reach, or reaching.

Running: When the wind is from the stern, the ship is running. (So would you if the wind was strong enough at your back.)

Reef: To gather in part of the sail and bundle it against the yardarm to reduce the sail area. This is done in high winds to protect the sail and the mast.

Trim: To adjust the sail to the most efficient angle.

Halyard: A rope used to haul the yard up the mast. (Haul-yard, get it?)

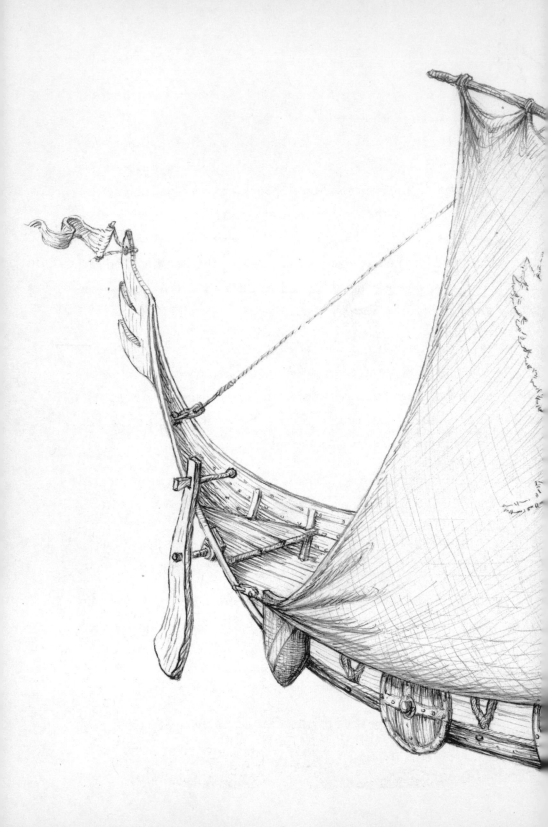

PART ONE

CASTLE ARALUEN

"Whoa there, Tom! Steady on, fellow!"

Tom was a plow horse, well past middle age and resigned, like most of his placid breed, to the constant task of plodding up and down, hauling a plow that carved consecutive furrows in the rich earth of Halder farm. He wasn't accustomed to being stopped in mid-furrow and he turned his shaggy head to look at his owner, Devon Halder.

Devon, like his horse, was well past middle age. And the smock that he was wearing was liberally daubed with patches of drying mud. Later that night, when he was asked in the local tavern what led him to stop and and turn around, he couldn't really recall. Perhaps he had heard the slight sounds of creaking leather and rope, or the rustle of a sail in the brisk wind.

Whatever it was, it was enough for Devon to halt Tom and turn to face the river behind him. When he did, the sight that met his eyes sent a sudden jolt of panic through him.

Barely forty meters away, gliding smoothly up the river, was a ship.

His first thought was that she was a wolfship, and Devon was old enough to remember when the sight of a Skandian wolfship on the river was a prelude to a sudden, savage attack. He tensed his muscles to run and spread the alarm in the nearby village. But he paused at the last second.

The days when Skandians used to raid the coastal and river villages of Araluen were well in the past now. And besides, on second glance, this was no wolfship.

She was similar in style and shape, sure enough. She was slim waisted and had a look of speed about her. She didn't have the broad, capacious lines of a cargo hull. But there was no large square sail such as a wolfship would use. Instead, this ship was rigged with a triangular sail that was mounted fore and aft along the line of the ship, supported by a long, gracefully curving spar that swept up high above the hull.

She was smaller than a wolfship. Also, at her bow post, there was no carved wolf's head, with raised hackles and snarling teeth. Instead, there was a carving in the shape of a bird's head. And there was a motif of a seabird in flight on the sail—a graceful bird with wings spread wide. A heron, Devon realized.

But the four circular wood-and-metal-reinforced shields arrayed down the starboard bulwark were unmistakably Skandian in design, although he noticed that a fifth shield, set level with the helmsman's position, was shaped like a triangle.

The crew, those he could see, were dressed in Skandian fashion—with leather and sheepskin vests and leggings held secure by crisscross bindings. Yet he saw none of the horned helmets for which the Skandian sea wolves were well known, the sight of which would strike fear into any honest farmer's heart. Instead, several of them wore dark woolen watch caps, rolled down to cover their ears against the cold.

As he watched, the figure at the helm raised a hand in greeting. Devon shaded his eyes to look more closely at the helmsman. He appeared to be quite young, and relatively slim for a Skandian. The person beside him was more like a typical sea wolf, Devon thought. He was bulky, with wild gray hair blowing in the wind. As Devon watched, he realized that the second man had a wooden hook in place of his right hand.

Definitely a sea wolf type, he thought. But then the man made a similar gesture of greeting. Devon returned the wave cautiously—his suspicions were still raised. Small as she might be, this was definitely a cruiser, a raiding ship. She was fast, lean hulled and potentially dangerous. And, as the shields arrayed down her bulwark attested, her crew were fighting men. He watched her closely as she sailed past, gradually pulling out into the center of the river to round the approaching bend. The helmsman and his companion lowered their hands and seemed to lose interest in the elderly farmer and his plow horse.

"That'll give him something to talk about in the tavern tonight," Thorn said with a grin. "Probably the most exciting thing that's happened to him since his plow got stuck on a tree root five days ago."

Hal raised an eyebrow. "Us? Exciting?"

Thorn nodded, scratching his rump with the blunt end of his wooden hook.

"He was a graybeard. He'd remember the times when the sight of a Skandian ship meant a raid. I'm surprised he didn't go pelting off to raise the alarm when he saw us." Thorn had no idea how close the farmer had come to doing just that.

As they rounded the bend and the farmer and his horse disappeared from sight, Kloof planted her forepaws onto the starboard bulwark and gave out a single bark. Then, content that she had asserted her superiority over all things Araluen, she dropped back to the deck, slid her front feet and flumped down onto the planks. For a few seconds, she watched Hal out of one eye, then she sighed and settled back to sleep.

Hal cast his gaze over the tilled fields and green forests that lined the banks of the river. It was attractive country, he thought.

"Did you ever raid in Araluen, Thorn?" he asked.

The old sea wolf shook his head. "Erak preferred to raid the Iberian coast, and sometimes Gallica or Sonderland. And now that I've seen Gilan in action with that bow of his, I'm glad he did. Maybe Erak knew something. Imagine facing half a dozen archers with Gilan's skill and speed."

"Facing one would be bad enough," Hal agreed.

Stig was sitting on a coil of rope several meters away, idly putting an edge on his already razor-sharp saxe knife as he listened to their conversation.

"D'you think Gilan will be at Castle Araluen yet?" he asked.

Originally, they had planned to leave Cresthaven Bay at the

same time as the Ranger, who was riding overland back to the capital. But they'd had a long, hard voyage south to Socorro and Hal wanted the *Heron* in tip-top shape for her first appearance at Castle Araluen. There were some sections of running rigging that had frayed and needed splicing and repairing, and there was a large, splintered gash in one of the planks on the waterline, where they had nearly run aground pursuing Tursgud's renegade ship *Nightwolf* through the shoals. It took half a day to plane that smooth and repaint the timber so there was no sign of the damage.

In addition, Edvin wanted to replenish their stores and fresh food and suggested that they should do it at Cresthaven, where the village was contracted to supply their needs as part of the duty ship agreement.

"No point spending our money elsewhere when they'll provide it for nothing here," Edvin had said, and Hal agreed.

As a result, they sailed out of Cresthaven and headed north to the river mouth some two days after Gilan had ridden off, waving farewell as he topped the rise above the bay where they were moored.

"He should be," Hal replied to Stig's question. "It's a little over a day's ride and I'm told those Ranger horses cover ground at a prodigious rate."

"He can have the welcome committee ready for us then," Thorn added. "Maybe this king of theirs will come down to the jetty to greet us."

Hal smiled sidelong at his old friend. "From what I've heard of kings, they don't stand around on windy jetties waiting for rough-neck sailors to arrive."

"Do you consider yourself a roughneck?" Thorn asked. "I've always thought of you as quite sophisticated."

"I may be. But you're roughneck enough for all of us," Hal told him and Thorn grinned contentedly.

"Yes. I'm glad to say I am."

Farther forward, in the waist of the ship and with no responsibilities to attend to during this current long reach of the river, the twins were bickering, as they were wont to do. They had been silent for some time, much to the crew's relief, but that was a situation too good to last.

"You know that brown-eyed girl who was sitting on your lap at the welcome-home feast?" Ulf began.

Wulf eyed him suspiciously, before replying. "Yes. What about her?"

Ulf paused, smiling quietly to himself, preparing to throw out his verbal challenge. "Well, she fancied me," he said.

Wulf looked at him, eyebrows raised. "She fancied *you?*"

Ulf nodded emphatically. "So you noticed too?"

Wulf snorted in annoyance. "I wasn't agreeing," he said. "I was querying you. That was why I raised my voice at the end of the sentence. It signified that I was saying, *What do you mean, she fancied you?*"

"I mean she found me attractive—actually, very attractive. It was obvious, after all."

Wulf paused for several seconds. "If it was so obvious that she fancied you—that she found you attractive—why was she sitting on *my* lap?"

Ulf waved his hand in a dismissive gesture. "That's what makes it so obvious. She wanted to make me jealous, so she played up to you. She was playing hard to get."

"Well, she played it very well. You certainly didn't get her," his brother told him, with some heat in his voice. He had noticed Ulf admiring the girl early in the evening and had swooped, successfully, before his brother could act.

Lydia, who was leaning on the bulwark several meters away, groaned audibly as the exchange continued.

Ulf laughed. "I could have if I wanted to. She was overwhelmed by my devilish good looks."

"Devilish good looks? You're as ugly as a mange-ridden monkey," Wulf told him. But his brother was already shaking his head.

"It's odd that someone as unattractive as yourself would say that," he replied. "That was why she chose to sit with you when she planned to make me jealous. She chose the most unattractive person she could see."

"Then obviously," Wulf retorted, "she couldn't see you."

Of course, what made this discussion puzzling for the rest of the crew was that Ulf and Wulf were identical in every respect. For one of them to call the other ugly was for him to call himself ugly as well. But they never seemed to grasp that fact.

As they continued speaking, their voices, at first lowered, rose in volume so that the entire crew could listen to their meaningless drivel. Hal decided that enough was enough.

"Ingvar?" he called.

The massively built boy was sitting forward of the mast, leaning back against it, his long legs splayed out on the deck before him. He turned and peered back toward the steering position.

"Yes, Hal?"

"Would you say that sailing down a river counts the same as being at sea?"

The rules of the ship were that if the twins carried on one of their idiotic arguments at sea, Ingvar was within his rights to throw one of them overboard. In fact, some of the crew felt, he was *obliged* to throw one overboard. Usually, a reference to this fact was enough to stop the mindless discussions they enjoyed so much.

Ingvar shrugged. "Eh? Oh, I don't know. I suppose so."

His voice was distracted and flat. Lydia, a few meters away, noticed this and turned to look at him, frowning. Hal mirrored the expression. Usually Ingvar was good tempered and cheerful. Now he sounded listless and bored. Hal wondered if something was on the big boy's mind.

Ulf and Wulf fell instantly silent. These days, they were never quite sure how much rope Hal would give them before he ordered the huge Ingvar to toss one or the other, or even both, overboard. Discretion was the better part of valor in such a case.

Hal noted that they had stopped arguing, and he nodded in Ingvar's direction. But the young giant wasn't looking his way anymore. He had resumed his seat against the mast, and Hal heard him give vent to a loud sigh. Hal looked at Stig, who was also watching Ingvar curiously.

"Have you noticed Ingvar's been acting strangely for the past few days?" Hal asked his first mate.

Stig nodded, a slightly worried look on his features. "Something definitely seems to be on his mind. I've been wondering . . ."

Whatever it was that he had been wondering was forgotten as

the ship swept past a high bluff. In the near distance, set among tailored and carefully tended parkland, stood the majestic, beautiful Castle Araluen, a mass of graceful spires, soaring turrets, flying buttresses and fluttering pennants.

"Gorlog's earwax!" Jesper said. "Will you take a look at that!"

The castle stood on rising ground half a kilometer from the river. It was surrounded by an area of open ground. In the intervening space was a narrow belt of forest—naturally occurring trees of a darker, wilder green, rather than the carefully planted and positioned ones that surrounded the castle.

The castle itself glittered golden in the sunlight. It was huge, but its size did nothing to diminish the grace and beauty of the building. Quite simply, it was like nothing the crew of the *Heron* had ever seen. They stood transfixed, staring at the castle with something approaching awe.

"It's amazing," Stefan said quietly, and the others murmured agreement—all except Ingvar.

"What is it? What are you all talking about?" he asked, the

irritation obvious in his tone. Lydia turned to him and placed her hand on his arm in a gesture of apology.

"It's Castle Araluen," she explained. "It's absolutely beautiful. It's huge, but so graceful, and it gleams in the sun and there are all these colorful flags and pennants and—"

She stepped back in surprise as Ingvar shook her hand from his arm and scowled out in the direction of the castle. To him, it was nothing but a blur. In fact, he couldn't even be sure that the blur he was he was looking at was the castle.

"All right. You've made your point," he said brusquely. "It's beautiful. I suppose I should be mightily impressed."

For a moment, Lydia was too shocked to reply. This was so unlike Ingvar—gentle, good-natured, helpful Ingvar. She looked around uncertainly, to see if the others in the crew agreed with her. She caught Hal's eye and the skirl shook his head in a warning gesture. He thought he was beginning to understand the reason for Ingvar's recent depression.

Lydia looked back at Ingvar, standing scowling out at the countryside. With an effort, she made her voice light and friendly.

"Of course. Forget I spoke," she said.

Ingvar snorted disdainfully. "If we must," he said, and moved forward to stand alone by the covered shape of the Mangler.

An awkward silence settled over the small craft, eventually broken by Thorn.

"Personally," he said, "I don't find it so impressive. It's not a patch on Erak's Great Hall."

Stig let out a snort of laughter. "Erak's Great Hall?" he repeated. "That's nothing more than a log shanty compared to this!"

And he was right. Erak's Hall was an impressive building by Hallasholm standards, but compared to this vision of wonder, it was little more than a log cabin.

Thorn refused to give ground. "Look at it!" he said scornfully. "All towers and flags and fancy folderol! Imagine what it takes to heat it in winter! At least the Great Hall only needs one big fireplace."

"And it's drafty and smoky with it," Edvin said.

"But think of the cost of heating that . . . pile of masonry," Thorn persisted.

Hal smiled quietly to himself. Thorn's interjection had taken the crew's minds off the awkward scene between Ingvar and Lydia. It wasn't the first time the old one-armed warrior had done something like this. The young captain realized that he could learn a lot in man management from his shabby friend.

"I imagine Duncan can afford the heating bills," Hal said mildly. "He is a king, after all. Kings usually have a pile of money stored away."

"Hummph!" Thorn sniffed. "Provided by their long-suffering subjects, no doubt."

"Well, you pay taxes to Erak," Stig pointed out.

Thorn gave him a withering look. "Not if I can avoid it," he said in an undertone.

The discussion could have continued indefinitely, but Stefan, standing on the bulwark for'ard of the mast, pointed to the bank.

"There's a landing stage there, Hal—and a crowd ready to welcome us."

Hal assessed the position of the substantial wooden jetty, then glanced quickly at the wind telltale on top of the boom. They'd be heading directly into the wind as they steered toward the jetty.

"We'll go in under oars," he decided. Then, raising his voice slightly, he called, "Down sail. Stow the boom. Man the oars."

The crew hurried to obey his orders. Jesper and Edvin cast loose the sheets while the twins brought the mast and sail sliding down to the deck. The four of them quickly bundled the sail up and stowed mast and sail along the line of the ship. Then they hurried to their rowing positions, sliding their white oak oars out through the rowlocks.

Stig and the others were already in position, Stefan having slipped down from the rail and dropped onto his rowing bench. Thorn and Lydia stood close by Hal at the steering platform. Ingvar, Hal noticed, remained in the bow, staring moodily across the river. The young captain shrugged. Ingvar usually didn't take an oar for ordinary maneuvers. His massive strength tended to unbalance the thrust on the ship.

"Ready?" called Stig, and the six oars rose slightly in preparation.

"Stroke!" he called and the oars went back, then dipped into the placid surface of the river. As the rowers heaved on their oars, Hal felt the ship drive forward, and the tiller came alive in his hand. He swung the ship toward the jetty on the southern bank of the river.

As Stefan had noted, there was a considerable crowd—perhaps fifty people—on the jetty and the riverbank beside it. A small group of three, presumably the official party, stood apart from the others. Two of them were clad in the now-familiar gray-and-green cloaks of the Ranger Corps. The third was far more lavishly dressed. Jewelry and decorations glittered on his doublet, catching the sunlight in a series of little flashes.

"There's Gilan," Lydia said quietly, as one of the cloaked figures stepped forward and raised a hand in greeting. Hal returned the gesture.

"There's another Ranger with him," Hal noted. He studied the third figure in the small group. "And someone who's very fancily dressed."

As they glided closer to the jetty, Hal could make out the rich accoutrements on the third man's doublet, and the fur trim on his red velvet-lined cloak.

"Maybe it's the King," Thorn joked.

Hal grinned at him and shook his head. "Kings don't stand out on windy jetties to greet common sailors."

Thorn raised an eyebrow at the description. "Common sailors?" he repeated. "I rather see myself as a sophisticated world traveler."

Kloof, sensing the interest that they were showing, advanced to the bulwark and reared up on her hind legs, her massive forepaws on the railing.

Kloof! she said. There were several dogs among the group onshore and they quickly replied, in a chorus that ranged from high-pitched yips to deep-chested baying.

"Looks like she's found some friends." Lydia smiled. The big dog remained in her position, her ears pricked. Lydia then indicated the wider group on the shore. "Who do you suppose all the others are?"

Hal shrugged. "Rubberneckers," he replied. "Come to see the

savage men from the north." He allowed himself a sidelong glance at Thorn. "Along with the sophisticated world traveler."

"Can't blame them," Thorn replied expansively. "I'm a fascinating sight for stay-at-homes like these."

As they had been talking, Hal had automatically been gauging the distance and angle to the jetty. He called now to the oarsmen.

"Easy all! In oars!"

Stig and the others instantly stopped rowing and raised their oars to the vertical. Then, in one movement, they lowered them, dripping with river water, into the ship, stowing them along the line of the hull beneath the rowing benches.

With the last of the way on her, Hal swung the little ship so that she came alongside. Jesper and Stefan took bow and stern lines and scrambled up onto the jetty, making the ship fast and hauling her in against the timber pilings so that the fenders on her side creaked.

There was a momentary silence, then Gilan stepped forward.

"Welcome to Castle Araluen," he called cheerfully. "Come ashore."

Hal and Thorn stepped up onto the jetty, followed by Stig and Lydia, then the other crew members.

Gilan shook hands with Hal. "Good to see you again," he said. He indicated the richly dressed man standing a few paces back. "This is Lord Anthony, the King's Chamberlain. Lord Anthony, meet Hal Mikkelson, skipper of this year's duty ship."

The Chamberlain was short and stout. As Hal had noted on the approach to the jetty, he was dressed rather flamboyantly, his red velvet doublet decorated with precious stones and chains. Anxiously, Hal cast a quick glance over his shoulder to make sure Jesper was out of pickpocket reach. Then he shook hands. Lord Anthony's grip was firm, but the hand was soft, not calloused and hardened like a warrior's. Hal guessed he was the King's administrator. He noted, however, that the man's eyes were intelligent and observant, casting a quick, appraising glance over the assembled crewmen.

"Welcome to Araluen, on behalf of King Duncan," the Chamberlain said, in a raised voice. "If you need anything to improve your comfort, please let me know."

"Thank you . . . Lord Anthony." Hal stumbled over the title. He wasn't sure how one addressed someone called "Lord." But he seemed to have got it right.

Anthony nodded and smiled, then stepped back. "I'll return to the castle and make sure your rooms are ready for you," he said.

Hal gave a half nod, half bow, then the Chamberlain turned away, swirling his cloak around him as he did, and strode off the landing jetty to where his horse was tethered.

"Anthony's a bit stuffy, but he's a good man," Gilan told Hal. "Now come and meet Crowley, the Commandant of the Ranger Corps—and my boss," he added, with a grin.

The other Ranger was a little shorter than Gilan, and as he pushed back the hood of his cloak, Hal could see that his sandy hair and beard were liberally sprinkled with gray. His eyes were blue and had a mischievous light to them. Hal found that he instinctively liked the older man.

"You must be Hal," Crowley said, stepping forward to shake hands. Then those cheerful eyes turned on Thorn. "And you could be nobody else but the redoubtable Thorn."

Gracefully, he switched hands to shake hands with Thorn in his turn, doing it left-handed.

"Don't know about redoubtable," Thorn said. "But I am a sophisticated world traveler."

"You certainly have the look of one," Crowley replied smoothly, then, as Hal introduced Stig, he looked up to meet the young man's gaze, taking in the broad shoulders and well-muscled physique. "I imagine you'd be a handful in a fight."

Stig grinned. "I try to be."

Crowley, however, had already moved on to the slim, beautiful girl beside Stig. "And you, no doubt, are Lydia, the deadly dart thrower. Our Princess Cassandra is keen to meet you."

Lydia flushed. She'd spent most of her early life alone in the forests hunting and she wasn't good at social occasions. She shook hands with Crowley and mumbled something inarticulate along the lines of *pleased to meet you*. Crowley sensed her awkwardness and favored her with a friendly grin.

"Don't know what you're doing with this rough crowd," he said and she smiled in return. Crowley had a natural charm to him and he was expert at putting people at their ease.

"I try to keep them in line," she said and he released her hand, patting it with his free hand first.

Crowley moved on as Hal introduced him to the rest of the crew. Hal was glad to see that Ingvar had joined them and seemed to be over his disconsolate mood. Crowley raised his eyebrows slightly at the size of the young giant but, perhaps wisely, didn't comment. He raised his eyebrows even farther as they came to the twins.

"And this is Ulf and Wulf," Hal said.

Crowley looked from one to the other. "Which is which?"

"I'm Ulf," said Wulf.

"I'm Wulf," said Ulf.

The Ranger Commandant frowned thoughtfully at them. "Why do I think you're not telling the complete truth?"

The twins looked crestfallen that he had seen through their ploy so easily. Hal grinned. It wasn't often that someone got the better of the twins. Perhaps Gilan had warned his Commandant of the twins' propensity to play practical jokes.

"Doesn't matter which is which," he said cheerfully. "They're both idiots."

Crowley nodded, then gestured to the stunning castle that stood on the hill behind them, visible above the belt of trees in the near distance. "Let's get you settled into the castle then. We have horses here if you'd like to ride."

He didn't quite succeed in hiding his smile as he said it. Hal glanced quickly at Thorn before replying.

"I think we'll walk."

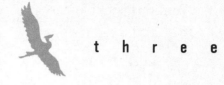

In spite of his earlier comments, Thorn couldn't fail to be impressed by the size and beauty of the castle as they drew closer. They strode across the drawbridge and under the portcullis, their footsteps echoing on the flagstones of the large courtyard before the keep, and Thorn craned his head back to peer up at the soaring towers above him.

Lydia nudged him with an elbow. "Better close your mouth before a bird uses it as a toilet," she muttered.

He glared at her, realizing that his mouth had indeed dropped open as a result of his craning back to look at the higher reaches of the castle. He clamped it shut now and said nothing. Sometimes, he thought ruefully, there was just no comeback clever enough. Lydia had scored a point in their ongoing battle of words.

The two Rangers led them into the massive keep building directly into the vast reception hall. Thorn wasn't the only member of the crew to be staring around, marveling at the rich furnishings and tapestries.

There were beautiful, and no doubt expensive, artifacts in wall niches and displayed on polished wood cabinets and small tables around the walls. A huge tapestry on the wall facing the entrance depicted a boar hunt. Hal studied it critically. The weaver may have exaggerated the size of the boar, he thought.

Gilan noted his interest in the work and said quietly, "It's a depiction of a hunt from King Duncan's younger days. The boar gets bigger in the telling every year."

Hal nodded, embarrassed that Gilan had obviously sensed his thoughts. To cover his slight unease, he turned and caught Jesper's eyes. The former thief was casting an appraising gaze over the items on display in the room.

"Keep your hands off," Hal said in a warning tone.

Jesper raised his eyes, spread his hands innocently in a "who, me?" gesture and smiled back at his skirl. "Off what?" he asked disingenuously.

"Off everything." Hal knew Jesper never actually kept anything he took, but the Araluens didn't, and things could get nasty before he had a chance to explain. Jesper's skills were incredibly useful when it came to breaking in to slave markets and dungeons. They weren't so desirable in the richly decorated halls of an ally.

There was a bustle of movement from the side of the room and Lord Anthony appeared, followed by a group of people who were, from their attire, castle servants. They carried bundles of linen and clean towels.

"Welcome once more," he said as he crossed the marble floor to meet them. The servants moved with him, staying several paces back in strict formation. "The King is ready to receive you"—he nodded to Hal—"and your senior officers. The servants here will show the rest of your men to their rooms."

"And the lady," Hal said, inclining his head toward Lydia.

Lord Anthony nodded apologetically. "And the lady, of course. Naturally, she'll have a room to herself."

He consulted a list he was carrying and clicked his fingers at the servants.

"Right, let's get these guests settled." He glanced at Ingvar and frowned, turning to one of the men servants. "We may need a larger bed for . . ." He consulted the list again. "Ingvar, I assume?" He added the last two words as a question to Ingvar, who nodded.

"That's me."

"Hmmm," said Anthony, frowning at the list in his hands. "Didn't realize you were quite so tall. Never mind, we'll tend to it, won't we, Arthur?" This last was addressed to the balding servant.

"Of course, my lord," the man named Arthur replied gravely.

Watching proceedings, Hal realized that Gilan must have provided the Chamberlain with a list of the crew's names and brief descriptions of each of them. It also struck him that, Castle Araluen being the national capital, Anthony and the servants must be kept busy providing for foreign guests with a wide range of requirements and in a wide range of sizes and shapes.

He realized that Anthony was hesitating, waiting for Hal to nominate who should accompany him to meet the King. "Stig, Thorn, you come with me," he said.

Anthony nodded briskly, proving that Hal's supposition was correct, and ushered the rest of the crew, and the attendant servants, toward a curving staircase on the eastern side of the room.

Hal turned to Gilan and Crowley, and jerked a thumb in the direction of his disappearing crew. "I assume we'll see them again?"

Crowley nodded easily. "Anthony hasn't lost a guest in nearly a week now," he said, his eyes alive with a sense of mischief. He made a bowing motion and gestured toward a matching staircase on the western side. "Shall we go?"

The five of them strode across the tiled floor of the hall. The Skandians' sealskin boots made virtually no noise on the hard surface and Hal noticed that the Rangers also wore soft-soled shoes. There was the barest whisper of footsteps to mark their passage. The stairs were stone, and the risers were well worn, with a slight dip in the center of each where most of the traffic passed.

"The King's apartments and offices are on the third floor," Crowley told them as they strode up the curving flight of stairs to a landing. "Your quarters are on the fifth floor."

"Sounds cozy," Thorn said, although Crowley's statement hadn't called for any comment.

They crossed the landing and took another flight of stairs to the next floor. This flight wasn't as ornate as the first. The stairs were narrower as well. Hal noted that the stairs ascended spiraling to the right, as was the custom. A defender on the stairs would only have to expose his right arm and shoulder to someone coming from below. Whereas an attacker would need to expose his entire body to bring his right hand, or his weapon hand, into play.

The idea, of course, Hal mused, would be to have an army of

left-handed swordsmen. As far as he knew, nobody had ever tried to assemble such a group.

They went up another flight and found themselves on a floor where corridors stretched away to the left and right, with a third corridor behind where they stood. The wall facing the stairs was blank stone, but Hal was willing to bet there was a concealed passage behind it, and observation points where a watcher could see who came up the stairs.

Crowley gestured to the right-hand corridor. "This way."

They passed several doors—heavy wooden doors without ornamentation of any kind, but with solid brass fittings. Eventually, Crowley stopped by one that seemed no different from its fellows and rapped with his knuckles on the center panel. From within, they heard a muffled voice.

"Come in."

The door was obviously heavy, and reinforced by brass strips and fittings. But it swung open smoothly and silently as Crowley twisted the circular door handle and pulled it toward him.

A small detail but an important one, Hal thought. An attacker couldn't simply batter the door open with a ram or a heavy log. It closed onto the solid stone frame, which supported it on three sides, and hinged outward.

Crowley ushered them in and followed just behind.

"My lord," he announced, "meet Hal Mikkelson, Stig Olafson and Thorn . . ." He hesitated and turned to Thorn, saying in a lowered voice, "I don't think I heard your second name?"

Thorn grinned wickedly. "Hookyhand," he said.

Crowley was about to repeat the name when he realized what

he was on the verge of saying. Instead, he amended to say: "And Thorn the Mighty."

Thorn wagged his head from side to side. "Prefer Hookyhand," he murmured. "It's less pretentious."

"Gentlemen," Crowley continued, talking over him, "his majesty, King Duncan of Araluen."

King Duncan rose from behind the table where he was sitting, studying a sheaf of papers. He was an impressive man, Hal thought. He was tall and broad-shouldered and although there was some gray in his blond hair, his face was still youthful and his movements were easy and athletic. Unlike his Chamberlain, this man *was* a warrior.

The three Skandians strode forward in step and stopped before the table, facing the King. Duncan eyed them calmly, suppressing a smile. He was used to dealing with Skandians. He'd met with Erak on several occasions over the years and he was aware of the Skandian spirit of equality and lack of regard for inherited titles.

"Greetings, gentlemen," he said, his voice deep and resonant. "It's a pleasure to meet more of our allies."

None of the three were quite sure how to reply to that. They all mumbled something incomprehensible, and that seemed to serve.

"I'm told you've done my Kingdom a great service, rescuing a dozen of my subjects from the Socorran slavers," Duncan continued, singling out Hal. The young skirl shifted his feet, a little embarrassed. He still hadn't decided how he would address the King. It was fine for Thorn to airily declare that he would simply call him "King." Now that he was in his presence, though, Hal wasn't so sure that was a good idea. There was a definite air of authority and command about the tall man facing them. It seemed to demand more respect than the simple sobriquet of "King." He decided to compromise.

"It wasn't all my doing, King Duncan. Stig and Thorn here disabled the prison guards."

Duncan eyed Hal's two muscular companions—one tall, lean and wide shouldered, the other equally tall, but heavier and more solidly built. His eye flicked over the wooden hook on Thorn's right arm. Gilan had told him about the old sea wolf's lost hand, and the various ingenious devices Hal had created to replace it.

"I imagine they did," he said, with a ghost of a smile.

Thorn returned it with a wide, easy grin. "Your man Gilan also lent a hand, King," he said easily.

Duncan glanced sideways at Gilan, who remained expressionless. "Yes. He's a capable fellow." The King returned his gaze to Thorn's bluff, open face, still with a trace of a grin in the corners of his mouth, and frowned thoughtfully. "I've met your Oberjarl Erak on several occasions," he said. "You remind me of him."

Thorn shrugged. "Well, I did serve with him. As a matter of fact, at one stage I was his right-hand man."

"And what happened to change that?" asked Duncan, sensing a story.

"He cut off my right hand," Thorn said, delighted that the King had fallen into his trap.

Crowley and Gilan both laughed. Duncan tilted his head and regarded Thorn for several seconds without expression.

"Thorn, mind your manners," Hal cautioned. Thorn looked at him, all wide-eyed innocence.

"Just a joke, Hal," he said. "I'm sure King here can take a joke."

Duncan finally smiled. "If I can't, I should never have signed up to be King." He indicated a low table set by the fireplace, with half a dozen comfortable-looking armchairs set around it.

"Let's sit and get down to business."

Lydia had spent some time inspecting her room—or rather, the suite of rooms that had been allotted to her. There was a large, airy sitting room, comfortably furnished, with a fireplace and with a wide double window that over-looked the wall and battlements of the castle, and the green park-land beyond.

In addition, there was a spacious bedroom, furnished with a canopied bed, with velvet curtains that closed to keep out cold drafts—and in a castle like this, there were always cold drafts. A small privy with a water closet was discreetly positioned off the bedroom.

She had already unpacked her belongings, putting her small collection of clothes into the capacious closets provided. Her atlatl and dart quiver were hanging on what appeared to be a hat stand.

Having no hat other than her black Heron watch cap, Lydia had co-opted the hatstand as a weapons rack. For the moment, though, she retained the wide leather belt that supported the scabbard for her long-bladed dirk.

There were several armchairs and she tried each one in turn, finally settling on the most comfortable—a carved wooden chair furnished with thick, soft cushions. She leaned back in it, placing her booted feet on the windowsill and crossing her hands in her lap, and smiled contentedly.

The rooms were nearly as large as the house in Limmat where she had grown up with her grandfather. At the thought of him, her smile faded. He had been killed when Zavac's pirate crew had invaded the town and at times like this, when she was alone, she still missed his calm presence and gentle sense of humor. She shook off the momentary sadness.

"Don't mope," she said. "You've got plenty to be thankful for."

And indeed, she did. She had always been an outdoor type, fond of hunting, tracking and adventure. Now, as a member of the *Heron* crew, she saw plenty of that. In addition, she had a solid group of good friends around her. She knew she was valued as a member of the brotherband and had been totally accepted into it. She smiled at the thought.

"I guess I'm a sister of the brotherband," she mused. It was like being suddenly provided with eight older brothers, all of whom were intent on looking after her—particularly Ingvar, she thought, and the smile faded again. Something was bothering him. It had started shortly after they escaped from Socorro and sailed north, she realized. He had become withdrawn and morose. At the celebratory feast when the slaves had been returned to their village, he had stayed a little aloof, not really taking part in the festivities.

His outburst earlier in the day, when they had sighted Castle Araluen, had surprised all of them. She wanted to talk to him about it but she sensed that now wasn't the time. She'd bide her time until an opportunity arose. He was too good a friend for her not to try to resolve whatever was bothering him.

The concept of good friends led her thoughts to Stig and Hal. While all the Herons were her friends, these two were something special—although how special, she wasn't quite sure yet. Both young men were attractive, each in his own way. And Stig, she knew, would leap at any chance to make their relationship closer.

As for Hal, she wasn't sure. At times she felt there was a special bond between them. Then, at others, he seemed a little stand-offish.

That might be part of being skirl, she thought. As captain of the ship, Hal had to retain a little distance between himself and the crew. He was their friend, but he was also their commander, and he had to make sure that friendship didn't undermine his authority. As their captain, he had to know that his crew would instantly obey any order he issued, without hesitation or argument.

That was where Thorn played such an important role for his young skirl, she realized. The shaggy old warrior had a knack of placing himself between Hal and the crew when necessary, thereby diverting the crew's attention from problems or concerns. He had done it just prior to their battle with Zavac's pirate ship in the waters off Raguza, when he'd hurled his old horned helmet into the sea and donned a Heron watch cap instead. And he'd done it again earlier today, she realized, when he'd distracted the crew from Ingvar's outburst. She admired the old warrior for his battle skills and his man management skills. She just wished he'd stop teasing her all the time. Still, it was a small price to pay for the life she was now leading, and enjoying.

There was a light tap at the door.

"Who can that be?" she said. Long hours spent hunting alone in the woods had accustomed her to talking to herself. Occasionally, she even answered herself, as she did now.

"One way to find out. Open the door and see."

She was expecting to see one of the other Herons outside her door. After all, she didn't know anybody else in Araluen. She opened the door and was somewhat taken aback to see a young woman standing there, smiling at her. She was several years older than Lydia. She was petite and very beautiful, with shoulder-length glossy blond hair.

Her clothes gave no hint as to her position or rank. She was dressed neither as a servant nor as one of the castle's ladies. Instead, she was dressed pretty much the same way Lydia was, in a thigh-length soft leather sleeveless jerkin over a white shirt, with tight leggings leading to knee-high brown leather boots. The jerkin was belted at the waist and, to her surprise, Lydia could see the hilt of a saxe knife sheathed on the woman's left hip.

"May I come in?" she said. "I've been dying to meet you."

Lydia stepped back and motioned for the woman to enter. She was beginning to get an idea as to who her unexpected visitor might be. The woman's next words confirmed it, as she held out her hand in greeting.

"I'm Cassandra," she said. "I'm the princess in this pile of bricks. You must be Lydia?"

Lydia wasn't sure how to behave in front of a princess. She had never met anyone of such an exalted rank. Briefly, she wondered if she should curtsy. She'd heard somewhere that was what you did when you met a princess. But Cassandra seemed so easygoing and informal that Lydia sensed that wouldn't be the correct procedure. Just as well, too, she thought, as she had no idea what a curtsy was or how to do one.

Instead, after another brief moment of doubt, she took the proffered hand and shook it. Should she maybe kiss it? But the handshake seemed to do the job. Cassandra's grip was firm and strong. She obviously wasn't the sort of princess to sit meekly around the castle doing petit point and crochet—whatever they were.

Cassandra was looking around the room, as if making sure it was up to standard.

"This is nice," she said. "I was worried they might put you all in the ground-floor rooms. They're too small and pokey and so dark. But this . . . this is good."

She walked to the armchair Lydia had just vacated but, seeing the indentations in the cushions, she pulled another one around to face it and plumped herself in it. For a second, Lydia was struck by the ludicrous sight of the princess's feet not quite reaching the ground. She really was quite tiny. Then Cassandra wriggled her bottom around in the seat cushion and managed to plant her feet properly.

"Let's chat, shall we?" she said, indicating the other armchair.

A little mystified as to why she'd been singled out by the princess, Lydia took the chair facing her. She waited for the other girl to begin. Cassandra looked out the window to the green park and forest below them and indicated it with one hand.

"So, how do you like Araluen?" she asked brightly.

Lydia hesitated a moment, then answered. "It's very beautiful," she said. "It seems a lot more"—she searched for the right word—"gentle than Skandia."

"Yes, I think that's true," Cassandra replied. "Did you know I spent some time in your country?"

"I'm actually not Skandian," Lydia said. "Although I've made my home there now."

Cassandra studied her more closely. "Yes, I didn't think you had the coloring of a Skandian," she said. "They tend to be blue eyed and blond, don't they?"

Lydia, of course, was olive skinned and had black hair and hazel eyes. She nodded. "Skandian women are very beautiful."

Cassandra frowned slightly. The girl facing her was stunning, but obviously had no idea that this was the case. Cassandra changed the subject.

"Of course, in Skandia, I'm better known by the name I use when I'm incognito." She saw Lydia's eyebrows contract at the term and explained, "That's the name I use when I'm traveling and don't want to be recognized as a princess."

"Why would you do that?" Lydia asked. If she were a princess, she'd want everyone to know.

Cassandra shrugged. "Sometimes, it can be awkward if people know you're a princess," she explained.

"Awkward? In what way?"

"Well," Cassandra said, smiling, "in Skandia, if the Oberjarl had known my true identity, he would have had my head lopped off."

Lydia was shocked. She knew Erak well and she couldn't imagine him having such a vital, cheerful woman executed.

"Erak?"

Cassandra waved that idea aside. "No. Erak is a darling. I'm talking about his predecessor, Ragnak. He hated my family. Erak actually saved my life. He helped us escape. We hid out for the winter in a little cabin up in the mountains above Hallasholm."

A suspicion was forming in Lydia's mind. "What was the name you used then?" she asked.

"Evanlyn," Cassandra replied. "A lot of people still call me that."

Lydia leaned forward in her chair. "I saw that name! It was carved into the wall in a hunting cabin I stayed in up in the mountains!" she said excitedly.

Cassandra's eyes lit up with pleasure. "You stayed there?"

Lydia nodded eagerly. Why she found it so fascinating she wasn't sure. But she had looked at that name on the wall and wondered about the woman who had carved it. Now she knew who it was.

"Yes. I was hunting." She considered for a moment. "Must've been a few months ago. I left in a hurry because there was a bear wandering round looking for trouble. But I definitely saw your name there."

"Well, isn't that fascinating! I remember carving my name into the wall one day when I was feeling bored and lonely. Somehow it's comforting to know it's still there. Do you hunt often?" Cassandra added.

"Whenever I can. I grew up in the woods around Limmat. That's my hometown."

Cassandra nodded and indicated the quiver of atlatl darts on the hatstand. "And you use those darts and some kind of throwing stick?" She rose and moved to the hatstand, half withdrawing one of the darts, then pausing. "May I?"

"Of course," Lydia replied. "The thrower is called an atlatl. That's it beside the quiver."

Cassandra studied the beechwood atlatl, its surface worn smooth from years of handling, then withdrew the dart from the quiver, feeling its weight, and testing the razor edge of its broadhead with her thumb.

"I imagine this would get the job done all right," she said. "I'd love to see you using it. We should go hunting while you're here."

"Do you hunt?" Lydia asked, although it was fairly obvious from her mode of dress that the princess did.

Cassandra nodded enthusiastically. "I use a sling," she said. "But maybe I could switch to one of these. I'll get you to show me how to use it."

Lydia rose now and moved to the window, looking out to the green parkland, then the darker green forest beyond it.

"Looks like there could be deer in that forest," she said.

Cassandra grinned. "And plenty of them. That's because only certain people are allowed to hunt them."

"Oh," said Lydia, disappointed. But the princess continued to grin.

"And of course, I'm one of them—as are my guests. I'll organize it, shall I?"

C an I offer you something to drink?" Duncan asked, once they were all seated. "Ale or wine, perhaps?"

He thought the skirl and his first mate looked a little young for alcohol, but one never knew. They both shook their heads. Thorn hesitated. The thought of a mug of cool ale was a very tempting one. But these days he limited his drinking, and finally he shook his head as well.

"Coffee?" Gilan said, with a slight smile. On the trip to Socorro, the Skandians had plundered his supply of coffee beans. They obviously had a taste for the beverage. Their hearty agreement to his suggestion confirmed the fact.

Duncan picked up a small silver bell from the table and rang it. Almost immediately, the door to the corridor opened and a liveried servant entered. The King ordered coffee for all of them and the servant departed.

"Perhaps you'd like to explain the mission you have in mind for Hal and his crew, my lord?" said Crowley.

Duncan glanced at the Commandant and nodded. He took a second or two to muster his thoughts, then began.

"Several years ago, my daughter, Cassandra, helped rescue your Oberjarl Erak from a renegade tribe in Arrida." The King noticed that Hal and Stig both nodded. The affair had been kept quiet while the rescue was under way, but once Erak returned to Skandia it became common knowledge.

Thorn was frowning thoughtfully. Erak's kidnapping and rescue had happened at a time when he saw most things over the rim of a brandy tankard. He vaguely remembered talk of Erak's capture and subsequent rescue, but he was hazy on the details.

"In the course of that rescue," Duncan continued, "she had reason to use her sling against the leader of the renegades—a man named Yusal. The stone from her sling hit him in the head. It didn't kill him, but it might have been better for him if it had. He was badly injured. He lost his memory and the capacity to speak or think. He was reduced to a state where he would hobble around, his mind blank, doing little more than drooling and mumbling nonsense."

He paused, then added, "And from what I've heard, it was a fate he richly deserved."

Hal raised his eyebrows at that. But Duncan was continuing.

"Unfortunately, Yusal had a brother, Iqbal. This brother took over control of the tribe." He glanced at Gilan. "What was their name again?"

"The Tualaghi, my lord. They're brigands and killers."

"Quite so. But apparently, this Iqbal feels the ties of family quite strongly. He was determined to avenge his brother and he decided to exact this revenge on Cassandra. At her wedding last year, he sent a pair of Genovesan assassins to kill her."

Hal and Stig exchanged a quick glance. This was a serious matter they had become involved in.

"Genovesans!" Thorn spat the word contemptuously. "They're a pack of cowardly, sneaking murderers."

"Indeed they are. But their attempt was foiled by one of my Rangers—Will Treaty." He scanned the three Herons. "I believe he's quite well known in your country."

Hal shrugged. "I've heard the name."

"Be that as it may. He and one of your countrymen, by the name of Nils . . ." He hesitated over the name, but Gilan supplied it.

"Ropehander, my lord," he said quietly and Duncan nodded.

"That's it." Duncan cocked his head at the three Skandians. "You people have some strange names, don't you?"

Thorn smiled. "Nothing strange about Hookyhand, King."

"I suppose not," Duncan replied. "It's certainly appropriate. In any event, Will Treaty and this Ropehander fellow stopped the two Genovesans in their tracks. Killed one and captured the other."

"And you're concerned that the Genovesans will try again?" Hal inquired.

Duncan shook his head. "Not according to my spies. The Genovesans are pragmatists. They lost two of their best men in this attempt and they don't plan to lose any more. They returned half of Iqbal's fee and took themselves out of the game. He blustered and threatened, of course, but then they pointed out that they could just as easily mount an assassination attempt against him if he continued to do so. He shut up rather smartly, I'm told."

"So the problem is solved?" Stig asked.

Duncan regarded him for a moment. "That particular problem is solved. But we're hearing rumors that Iqbal may be trying another tack. We've had a message from a friend of ours in Arrida, a man named Selethen, that Iqbal has found another group to continue the attack. Apparently, he's sworn an oath to kill Cassandra for what she did to his brother and these people don't take such oaths lightly."

"So what's the new plan he's got in mind?" Thorn asked.

Duncan screwed up his mouth in consternation, making an uncertain gesture with his hands, both palms upward . "That's the problem. We don't know. Selethen was able to give us only vague details—something about a cult of killers who are based in a place called Jabal Akrab—in their language, that means Scorpion Mountain."

Hal raised an eyebrow. "Sounds ominous."

Duncan nodded agreement. "It does. But we can't get any hard information about them. There are a lot of rumors, but nothing concrete."

"And you want us to go find out more about this cult and stop them?" Thorn asked.

"No. That'll be Gilan's task. You just have to transport him to Arrida, where he'll meet with Selethen to get more information. Then he can work out a way to stop this plot once and for all. I'll buy them off, if necessary. They're mercenaries, after all."

Hal looked at Gilan, whose face remained impassive. "Sounds like a big task for one man."

"He won't be alone," Duncan said. "I'll be sending a troop of cavalrymen with him. Normally, I'd assign this to a Special Task Group I formed some time ago. It consists of Will Treaty, who I mentioned before, a senior Ranger called Halt and Horace, the Kingdom's foremost knight. Coincidentally, he's Cassandra's husband. But unfortunately, they're in Hibernia at the moment, helping King Sean put down an insurrection. And I don't want to waste any more time getting this affair settled. My daughter's life is at risk."

"One point I'd like to raise, my lord," said Gilan, leaning forward. "This is the first I've heard of any cavalrymen. I'd prefer to work alone. I'll be able to move around more easily and I'll attract a lot less attention if I don't have a bunch of heavy-footed horsemen clanking around after me."

They were interrupted by a tap at the door. A servant entered, bearing a tray of cups and a coffeepot. Duncan held up a hand to Gilan warning him not to talk about the mission while the servant was in the room.

It was a wise move, Hal thought to himself. Secrets aired in front of servants had a habit of becoming non-secrets and this mission was definitely a confidential one. Conversation halted while the coffee was served. Then, when the servant had departed, Duncan continued.

"I thought you'd say that, Gilan. But this is Cassandra we're talking about and I'm not taking any chances with her safety. My judgment is you'll need a substantial force to back you up."

"Perhaps, my lord. But I still think—"

Once again, Duncan held up a hand to stop him. But this time the gesture was more peremptory. "It's not up for discussion, Gilan. You'll do as I say."

Hal had been watching the two of them carefully. He saw Gilan's jaw set into a tight line. He glanced at the Ranger Commandant and saw that Crowley agreed with his younger colleague. The sandy-haired Ranger spoke now in support of Gilan.

"I think Gilan knows his own abilities, my lord," he said in a reasonable tone. "And I agree with him. Blundering around Arrida with a troop of cavalrymen isn't the way to get this done. It's not the way Rangers operate."

Duncan flushed. Hal guessed that he wasn't used to debating his ideas. He also guessed that the Rangers were quite used to doing just that with him. He decided to intervene.

"Right or wrong, it's academic," he said. And when the three Araluens turned their attention to him, he continued, "We don't have room on board for a troop of cavalry. Our ship is too small."

"Too small? Your wolfships have carried extra men before, and horses as well!"

Hal shrugged. "You could fit them on a normal wolfship. But the *Heron* is much smaller. And this will be a long trip. As for horses, there's definitely no way we could fit them." He caught Gilan's eye and shrugged. "Sorry."

"No problem," Gilan said. "I'll borrow a horse from Selethen if I need one. Those Arridan horses are fine animals, and they're accustomed to conditions in the desert."

"And if Gilan needs to use force, we can provide it. My crew are all experienced warriors. We just proved that in Socorro," Hal added.

But now, Duncan was angry, and not just because Gilan, Crowley and Hal were contradicting his plan. "This ship of yours, you say it's not a normal wolfship?"

Hal nodded. Before he could elaborate, Duncan continued, his voice rising. "So you're telling me that Erak has fobbed us off with a second-rate vessel to act as the duty ship this year? That is totally unsatisfactory. It's an insult to me and to Araluen."

They were all startled by a roar of fury from Thorn, matching Duncan's raised voice. The old warrior erupted from his chair and shook his wooden hook at the King.

"Second rate? *Second rate?* Where do you get off your high horse calling the *Heron* second rate? I'll have you know, King, she is the finest vessel in the Skandian fleet and you're lucky to have her!"

But now Duncan was on his feet as well, leaning forward to threaten Thorn. "How dare you speak to me like that? I am the King, do you understand?"

"Hah!" Thorn snorted derisively.

"And don't go pointing that . . . thing at me!" Duncan roared, indicating the polished wood hook on Thorn's right arm. Thorn was unabashed, although he did lower his voice somewhat.

"Then don't you go insulting our ship and our skirl. Our *second-rate* ship has just rescued a dozen of your people from the Socorran slavers. How second rate was that? Now you will apologize to our ship and our skirl or we'll just walk out of here and sail back to Skandia," he said.

"Thorn, sit down," Hal said, standing and placing a hand on Thorn's arm. The old sea wolf looked at him angrily, but his regard for Hal, both as a person and as his skirl, made him sit down again. Hal turned back to the King, but now Gilan was on his feet as well.

"My lord, could I have a word, please?" He indicated a door leading to another room. Duncan, his face red with anger, glared at

Thorn, who glared back, then, tight lipped, the King nodded and led the way to the other room.

Once they were in private, Gilan spoke before Duncan could say anything.

"My lord, I've just spent the past three weeks with this ship and this crew, and believe me, there is nothing second rate about them. She may be small, but *Heron* is fast and highly maneuverable. She'll outsail any normal wolfship."

"Well, that may be . . . ," Duncan began, a little mollified by Gilan's obvious sincerity. The King had a quick temper but he was, at heart, a fair man. That was why he allowed his Rangers to dispute with him if they thought he was in the wrong.

"As for the crew," Gilan continued, "I couldn't ask for better help if it comes to a fight. Young Stig there is every bit as good as Horace himself. He's fast and agile and deadly. And Thorn is even better."

"Better than Horace? That shabby one-armed man?"

"That shabby one-armed man was the premier warrior in Skandia for three years in a row," Gilan told him. Lydia had filled him in on Thorn's background while they were in Socorro. "Nobody else has ever achieved that. And the rest of the crew are all seasoned fighters as well. Thorn's trained them himself. Even the girl, Lydia, is a warrior. She's an absolute dead shot with her atlatl darts."

He paused, watching Duncan's breathing settle and the red flush of anger drain from his face.

"I know them, my lord. I've fought beside them. They'll be better than any troop of cavalry."

"Well . . . all right. If you say so."

"I do, my lord. Trust me."

Duncan groaned. "Why do I hate it when people say that?"

Gilan waited. Finally, Duncan came to a decision.

"All right. Let's go back in there. But I'm not apologizing to that one-armed ruffian," he added. Gilan allowed a ghost of a grin to touch his lips.

"That's all right, my lord. I'm sure he doesn't plan to apologize to you."

While the King and Gilan were absent from the room, Hal spoke urgently to Thorn.

"Thorn, for pity's sake, will you settle down? You can't go around ranting at the King like that. He's the King, after all."

Thorn looked at him, unrepentant. "So? I'd speak to Erak that way. And I respect our Oberjarl more than any foreign king. He insulted our ship and that insults all of us. And he accused Erak of trying to break the rules of the treaty."

There was a brief silence between them. Crowley took a sip of his coffee and regarded them evenly. "If you ask me, Thorn had every right to say what he did," he said.

The three Skandians all looked at him, surprised, and he grinned. "Perhaps not quite as forcefully as he did. But his passion only serves to emphasize his sincerity. You and your crew have just done a great service for this country and it was right to remind Duncan of the fact. He had no call to disparage you or your ship— which Gilan tells me is a remarkable craft."

He set his cup down and leaned forward to speak to them in a more confidential tone.

"Duncan is a fair man. But he is a king and kings don't like to be contradicted. To his credit, that's why he keeps us Rangers around. We argue with him all the time if we think he's wrong. You can bet that Gilan is in there now straightening him out."

Hal frowned. The thought of the young Ranger "straightening out" the angry monarch was hard to accept.

"How will he take that?"

"He'll listen to reason—eventually. Bear in mind, he's mad with worry about his daughter. And the uncertainty of the whole thing makes that worry even worse. If he had a clear idea of who's involved and what they're planning, it would be a lot easier. But he's worried and he's lacking hard intelligence on this Scorpion Mountain place. Just give him time and he'll come round. He's a good man at heart."

Stig grinned and leaned over to clap Thorn on the shoulder. "So you get back in your box, Thorn, and stop trying to disrupt the treaty."

Thorn snorted indignantly. "All very well, Stig, but he insulted you too, you know."

"And I'm big and ugly enough to take exception to that myself, if need be," Stig told him. "But Crowley's right, the man obviously has a lot on his mind and he's got a kingdom to run as well. Let's give him a little slack, shall we?"

Hal nodded his thanks to Stig. His tall friend had come a long way in the past year and a half. The old Stig was always willing to flare up at any slight—real or imagined. This measured approach to the situation was something new.

I suppose we're all growing up, he thought. Except maybe Thorn.

They looked up as the door to the inner room opened and Duncan and Gilan emerged. Gilan, slightly behind the King, made a reassuring gesture with his hand. Hal and the others stood, Thorn a little reluctantly. Duncan cleared his throat before speaking.

"Gilan has pointed out that I spoke without full knowledge," he said. "I understand now that your ship, the *Heron*, is not in any way inferior to the wolfships that have been stationed here before. In fact, he tells me it's possibly superior to them."

Thorn grunted noisily. Hal turned to him and raised a warning hand. The gesture wasn't lost on King Duncan, who eyed the recalcitrant Thorn for a few seconds before continuing.

"So let me say, I regret any offense I may have caused—to you, your ship and its crew, or to the Oberjarl himself." He paused again then looked directly at Thorn. "That is not to say that I am apologizing. I regret any offense caused but I am *not* apologizing."

Thorn stuck his jaw forward pugnaciously. "That's just fine, because neither am I!" he said, with equal force.

Hal raised his eyes to heaven and went to step forward to appease the King. To his surprise, after a few seconds, Duncan began to laugh. It started as a deep chuckle, then spread until his shoulders were shaking uncontrollably. Hal glanced at Crowley, who shrugged his shoulders and raised his eyebrows.

"Ah, Thorn," said the King, "it's good to have someone like you around. Someone who has absolutely no respect for me."

Thorn tilted his head thoughtfully. He was grinning at the King now. "That's true," he said, and Duncan laughed all the louder.

"You really do remind me of your Oberjarl Erak. He always managed to puncture my dignity for me. I need that, you know. Kings don't take kindly to people disagreeing with them. We get accustomed to thinking we're always right just because we are kings. That's why I have these reprobates serving me." He indicated Crowley and Gilan.

Crowley smiled. "We do our best to keep you in line, my lord."

Duncan, who seemed now to have totally adopted Thorn as a friend and trusted confidant, slapped him on the shoulder and pulled him a little closer.

"And if you think these two are bad, you should see Halt. He's a senior Ranger and he shows no respect for me at all."

"That's not quite true, sir," Gilan interjected. "He has enormous respect for you, so long as you agree with him."

"Yes. That's true." Duncan released his grip on Thorn's shoulder and took a second or two to collect himself.

"All right," he said at length, "let me think about what we've discussed here." He looked at Gilan. "I'm still inclined to the idea of sending you with some reasonable force."

Gilan shrugged. "That's all right, sir. You'll soon see the light of reason."

Duncan sighed. "I suppose so." He looked keenly at Stig now, taking in the wide shoulders, the muscular build and the easy, athletic grace with which the young Skandian moved.

"And you say this lad is as good as Horace?" He addressed the question to Gilan.

"Without a doubt. Different weapons and technique. But there's nothing to choose between them."

"Hmmm. Pity Horace is in Hibernia. It'd be good to see a practice match between them." He came back to the matter in hand, and said briskly, "Very well. Let me give this some consideration and I'll give you my decision tomorrow."

He waved them toward the door. Crowley and Gilan gave slight bows of the head. The Skandians contented themselves with coming loosely to attention. As they passed through the door, Stig slipped up beside Hal.

"Who's this Horace that I'm a match for?" he asked.

Hal managed to keep a straight face as he replied. "He's a one-legged, half-blind old beggar who suffers from uncontrollable flatulence."

"Flatulence? What's that?" Stig asked. Words of more than two syllables sometimes confused him.

"He farts," Thorn put in.

Stig thought about it, then nodded his head. "Yeah, well, I can do that."

Hal and Thorn both answered simultaneously.

"We know."

The three Herons split up and went to their rooms to unpack and familiarize themselves with their new surroundings. Like Lydia, they had little in the way of luggage or belongings and the unpacking took only a few minutes.

As the skirl, he'd been given a large suite to himself. There was a jug of water on the table in the sitting room, along with several beakers. He poured himself a glass and sipped it. For a minute or two, he prowled restlessly around the room, picking up items to examine them before putting them down again. After weeks in the close confines of the ship, never more than a few meters from other members of the crew, it felt strange to be on his own. He drained the last of the water from his glass and hitched his rump up onto the sill of the open window. Below him, and beyond the castle walls, the green parkland stretched out to the forest. He could see several people—couples walking in the sunshine, children playing. And of course, there were guards patrolling around the perimeter of the castle, their helmets, armor and spear points occasionally catching the sunlight.

He studied the surrounding land. The ground around the castle was landscaped with small shrubs and isolated trees. The grass was mown short and he realized that, beautiful as the grounds were, they were also highly practical. There was no cover to conceal any attacking force. The trees of the forest were at least a kilometer away and there would be no way an enemy could stage a surprise attack. Any attackers would be sighted long before they came within bowshot. He craned out and looked upward. The turrets and spires of the castle were decorative. But they were also practical. Jutting out at each corner, their crenellated tops provided positions from which archers could sweep the ground below, close to the castle walls. And of course, any attacker trying to find shelter there would have had to cross the moat first.

Castle Araluen might be a spectacularly beautiful building, he thought, but it would also be a remarkably tough nut to crack. He glanced down into the courtyard, where a group of servants were drawing water from a well in the middle of the cobbles. With an internal water supply, it would be able to withstand a long siege.

There was a knock at the door and he shoved off the window-sill and crossed the room to open it. The heavy wooden door was perfectly balanced. It swung easily and silently on its oiled hinges to reveal Ingvar standing in the corridor outside.

Hal was momentarily taken aback. He had half expected Stig or Thorn to be there, ready to discuss the meeting with Duncan. But he smiled and gestured for the massively built boy to come in.

"Ingvar," he said. "Good to see you. Come on in. How's your room? Did they get you that bigger bed they promised?"

A half smile touched Ingvar's face, then quickly disappeared.

"Yes. Yes, they did. It arrived only a minute or so after I moved in. They whipped the other one away and set up the new bed for me in a few minutes. They're very efficient here."

"I guess that's the way things are at a royal residence," Hal said. "So what can I do for you?"

For a moment, Ingvar was silent. He fidgeted with his hands, shifting his feet constantly. Hal could tell he was embarrassed and ill at ease. But when he finally spoke, the words hit the young skirl with the force of a thunderclap.

"Hal, I've decided I want to leave the brotherband and go home to Skandia."

Hal was so startled by Ingvar's words that he actually recoiled a pace. For several seconds, he was speechless. Ingvar—solid, reliable, powerful, loyal Ingvar. The idea of the Heron Brotherband without him was unthinkable. He had always been there when Hal needed him. Immensely strong, with a quiet wisdom and a gentle sense of humor. Above all, Hal realized, it was the fact that he was so utterly dependable—a constant in their dangerous world—that made him so invaluable. Finally, he found his voice.

"Ingvar, what is it? Is it something I've done? Has someone in the crew said something to insult you? I can't believe what you're saying!"

But Ingvar was shaking his head at the suggested reasons for his wanting to leave.

"No, no, Hal. On the contrary, you and the rest of the brotherband have given me a sense of worth and a sense of purpose. Since I've been a Heron, I've realized that I'm not totally useless. I can actually contribute."

"Of course you can!" Hal said. He gestured for Ingvar to take a seat at the table by the window and joined him there, leaning forward to appeal to him. "After all, ask that girl you carried back to the ship in Socorro. And you're the only one with the sheer strength to load the Mangler. How would we have managed the fight against Zavac without you? Or the escape from the harbor in Socorro?"

Ingvar listened patiently to Hal's list of his achievements. When his skirl finally fell silent, he spoke again, calmly and sadly.

"The problem is, Hal, as I've become more confident, and learned to appreciate my own worth, I've realized how limited that worth is, compared to the rest of you. You're all leaving me behind."

Hal frowned. He felt a sense of panic. Ingvar seemed determined on his course and Hal could think of nothing to say that might change his mind. And if he couldn't find the right words, the Herons would be left with an unfillable hole in their ranks.

"I don't understand, Ingvar. You're part of the team. Part of the crew. We've been together since the very start. What can I say to change your mind?"

Ingvar smiled sadly and shook his head. "There's nothing to say, Hal. I've loved my time with you and the others. But in Socorro, I realized that I would always be limited."

"But—" Hal began desperately, only to subside as Ingvar held up a hand.

"All the things you mentioned, Hal, they all boil down to one thing. I'm big and strong. That's it. And that's all I'll ever be. The rest of you are growing and developing your skills and abilities. You're an expert navigator and helmsman, and you can plan a raid like the one on the slave market.

"Stig is becoming a more skilled warrior every day. And he's a perfect first mate for you. Even Ulf and Wulf are becoming better fighters. So is Edvin, and he's the smallest of all of us. And he's becoming a good helmsman too.

"As for Thorn—well, I doubt that there's anything he can't do. He's fast, agile, powerful . . . No wonder he was the Maktig for three years.

"Then there's Lydia! She can track. She can hunt. She's deadly with those darts of hers. And she's totally fearless. She can even shoot the Mangler now as well as Stig can.

"The point is, Hal, all of you are developing and growing. I'm not. I've reached my limit. I'm big and strong. I'm a dumb pack animal and that's all I'll ever be. I feel I'm not pulling my weight as part of the crew and it hurts to feel that way. I'd rather quit."

Hal shook his head slowly. He'd had no idea that this feeling had been building in Ingvar. He'd realized that the massively built boy had been somewhat out of sorts for the previous few days . . . but this! He felt a deep sense of shame that, as Ingvar's skirl, he'd allowed this situation to develop and hadn't noticed it.

"Of course you're pulling your weight!" he said. "What will we do without you?"

Ingvar smiled that sad little smile again. "You'll manage. Two of the others can learn to load the Mangler. Or you could extend the cocking levers so one person could do it. I was thinking, you could fashion a tube of some kind, make two of them and slip them over the cocking handles. The extra leverage will make it possible for one person to do the job."

Hal made a helpless gesture. "There you are! You're a thinker! You've just come up with a way to improve the Mangler! How can you possibly say you're not pulling your weight?" He paused, trying to think back over the preceding weeks. "Has something happened to make you feel this way?"

Ingvar nodded. "There are a couple of things. Do you realize that when you shoot the Mangler, I can't even see what's happened? Someone has to tell me. *Oh, Hal hit the helmsman and the ship has swung off course,* or *The bolt hit the guard tower and set it alight.* Can you understand how frustrating that is?"

"Yes, of course. But—"

"But even worse than that: When we were making our way back to the ship in Socorro, with the released prisoners, remember how we came face-to-face with a platoon of Mahmel's guards?"

Hal frowned uncomfortably. He thought he could see where Ingvar was heading with all this, where the problem lay.

"Yes. I remember."

"Do you remember what you said to me?"

Hal spread his hands dismissively. "Oh, come on, Ingvar. You can't have let that get you to this state—"

But Ingvar gently overrode him. "You said 'Stay back, Ingvar.' Remember?"

"Yes, but that was just because . . ." Hal stopped, not wanting to proceed. But Ingvar finished the thought for him.

"Because I can't see. Everything beyond a few meters is a blur for me."

"That's not your fault!" Hal protested and Ingvar placed a hand on his arm to calm him.

"No, it's not. And it's not your fault either. It's just the way things are. I know why you said that and you were right. With my eyesight, I'd be a danger to the rest of you. I might accidentally hit one of you without realizing. Worse, I might put you in danger because someone would have to watch out for me, and they might be hurt while they were doing it."

Hal opened his mouth to protest, then shut it without saying a word. Ingvar was right. And he knew he was right. If Hal argued against the fact, Ingvar would know he was lying.

Ingvar noted his skirl's silence and nodded. "Thanks for not trying to tell me I'm wrong. And the problem is, Hal, I'll always be a burden to the rest of you when it comes to a fight. You simply can't depend on me."

"But we don't care!" Hal said.

"I do," Ingvar replied. And there was no answer to that, Hal knew. "There are only a few of us in the crew," Ingvar continued. "We're not a big wolfship with a crew of twenty to thirty warriors. There are nine of us. We can't afford passengers when it comes to a fight. Worse, you can't afford to have someone who'll distract another crew member and may leave him vulnerable in a battle."

Hal dropped his gaze. Ingvar was right, he realized. But he was also wrong—so wrong.

"Ingvar, you're part of our brotherband. We accepted you for what you are—and as you are. If you pull out, you'll be destroying something very valuable."

"You can always find someone to replace me, Hal. There are plenty of big, strong boys out there. And, as I said, strength is the only thing I bring to the *Heron*. But I couldn't live with myself if someone was injured, or even killed, trying to look out for me. To tell the truth, I'm weary of being told to stand back whenever there's a fight brewing. And there are going to be more and more occasions when we're called upon to fight. Best if I make a clean break now."

"Oh, Ingvar." Hal felt a prickle of tears on his eyes. "You are so, so wrong. You bring so much more than just brute strength to the brotherband. You bring a sense of loyalty and humor and wisdom. In a way, you personify the very spirit of the brotherband. Can't you see that?"

The minute the last four words left his mouth, he regretted them. Ingvar smiled that slow, sad smile again and shook his head.

"No, Hal. I can't. I can't see and that's the whole point. This is hard for me. Please don't make it harder by arguing."

Hal slumped back in his chair and covered his face with his hands for a moment or two, his brain racing. Then he lowered his hands and sat up straighter once more.

"All right. I've heard what you've said. I can see your point. But I think you are underestimating yourself and your value to me and the crew. Please don't do anything about this for a day or so. Let me think. There must be something I can do."

"You can't make me see any better, Hal."

Hal set his jaw in a determined line. He stood and gestured for Ingvar to do the same, then led him to the window.

"Look out there and tell me what you see," Hal said. He

watched Ingvar closely as the big boy shrugged, then leaned forward to peer out the window.

"I can see a green sort of blur in the foreground. I imagine that's the park you've all talked about. Farther out, the green becomes darker." Ingvar looked at Hal, a question on his face.

"That's the forest. It's a darker green." Hal gestured out the window again. "Can you see anything else? Can you see any people?"

He watched closely as Ingvar leaned forward and squinted his eyes almost shut.

"I can see water," he said, looking at the moat, "and is that a bridge just there?"

He was pointing to the drawbridge below them and to their left. Hal nodded eagerly.

"Yes! That's the drawbridge and the castle moat!" he told his friend. "Can you make out the sentry at the far end of the bridge?"

Ingvar sighed and squinted even harder. "I can see something," he said doubtfully. "Might be a sentry. But it's just a shape . . . Wait! He's moving! Yes, it's a sentry."

He stepped back from the window and spread his hands in a defeated gesture.

"See? It's hopeless. Even with your prompting me, I couldn't tell that was a sentry until he moved."

"But you did see him?" Hal asked.

"I did. But I didn't know what he was."

Hal rubbed his chin thoughtfully. "When I asked if you saw him, you were squinting. Why do you do that?"

Ingvar thought about it and shrugged. "I don't really know. I guess when I narrow my eyelids like that, things become a little clearer. But I can't walk around squinting all the time."

Hal's mind was racing, vague possibilities forming in his brain. He felt the old familiar rush of excitement as an idea hovered, not fully formed yet just out of reach.

"I suppose not," Hal said distractedly. He thought for several seconds, then spoke again. "Ingvar, give me a day or two before you decide, all right?"

"I've already decided, Hal. But I'll give you a day or two before I tell the others."

Hal patted the boy's massive hand. "That's fine," he said. "I can't ask for more than that."

"Are you hoping to change my mind? It won't happen."

"We'll see," Hal said.

Ingvar snorted softly. "I doubt it," he said. "That's the problem, after all."

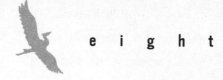

The following day, Hal remained in his room, speaking to nobody, having his meals brought to him. The crew wondered what he was up to and several asked Stig, assuming that he'd know.

The young warrior simply shrugged. "I have no idea what he's doing," he told them. "He gets like this when he's planning something."

There was one exception to this isolation. Stig, Thorn and Hal had a further meeting with the King and the two Rangers. As Crowley and Gilan had predicted, Duncan reluctantly agreed to Gilan's plan of action.

"I suppose you know best how to handle a situation like this," he told the tall young Ranger. "But if you need any extra force, ask Selethen to provide it."

"I will, my lord," Gilan replied, smiling. "But I'm sure that between us, the *Heron's* crew and I can handle things. We did pretty well in Socorro, after all. Isn't that right, Hal?" He smiled at the young skirl sitting beside him.

Hal seemed to start awake. His mind was miles away. "Eh? Yes. Fine, I'm sure."

Thorn frowned, wondering what was distracting his friend.

"So, when do you plan to get under way?" Duncan addressed the question to Hal. Once again, the skirl needed a moment to gather his thoughts.

"What? Oh, sorry. I've got something on my mind. Let's see, we'll need to provision the ship. It's a long voyage, after all. That'll take a day or so."

They had restocked the ship in Cresthaven, but it was always wise to top up their store of perishables like fresh vegetables, bread and water at every opportunity. He continued, his mind now on the question of getting *Heron* back to sea. The river that ran past Castle Araluen was tidal and that would influence his decision. He didn't want to have the crew rowing against the tide. Or to leave in the dark.

"I'd like to go out in daylight, and with the ebbing tide. That means . . ." He thought about it. A good skirl was always aware of tide timetables. You never knew when you might want to leave in a hurry, after all. "The day after tomorrow at the earliest."

Stig smiled. "That's ideal."

Thorn turned an inquisitive eye on him. "What are you so happy about?"

"Princess Cassandra has invited us on a hunt tomorrow," Stig said. "I think she wants to see Lydia in action with the atlatl."

Duncan inclined his head thoughtfully. "Wouldn't mind seeing that myself," he said. "I might join you."

"What do you say, Hal?" Stig urged his friend. "Would you like to get a little hunting in?"

But again Hal's mind was miles away. Stig prompted him sharply. "Hal? What do you say?"

Hal looked at his first mate, frowning. "About what?" he asked and Stig explained, speaking slowly and carefully, making sure he had Hal's attention.

"A hunt. We're . . . going . . . on . . . a . . . hunt . . . tomorrow. You could use your crossbow."

"Oh. No. Not me. I've got something I have to work on," Hal replied.

Stig spread his hands in a helpless gesture and smiled at the King. "He's not always as vague as this. Sometimes, you'd swear he was almost intelligent."

Duncan nodded knowingly. "I suppose a skipper has a lot on his mind before a long voyage."

Stig nodded, unconvinced. "Yes. I suppose that's it."

So, while the others prepared for the hunt, Hal remained in his room. Stig made one further attempt to persuade him to join them. He knocked on the door to Hal's room, heard no reply and went in anyway.

Hal was standing by the window, holding a sheet of parchment close to his face. There was a long, narrow slit in the parchment. He was totally unaware that Stig had entered. For a few seconds, he peered at the slit parchment, then threw it down in disgust.

"No. That won't do. Too floppy."

"Too floppy for what?" Stig asked cheerfully.

Hal looked round, startled to see him. "Oh . . . just something I'm working on. But it's got to be more rigid."

"I'm sure it has," Stig agreed. "Rigid is always better."

Hal didn't seem to notice the irony in his friend's tone. "Yes. I need something else. Something thin like parchment but not as floppy."

"Floppy is definitely not what you want," Stig agreed. But again, Hal appeared to take no notice. Finally, his patience exhausted, Stig said forcefully, "Hal! Snap out of it!"

"Eh? What's wrong, Stig? What do you want?" Hal was obviously irritable—irritable and distracted. Stig had seen it before.

"Are you coming on Princess Cassandra's hunt? We're leaving in an hour."

Hal shook his head. "No. I'm busy. But you go, by all means."

"I planned to," Stig said, rolling his eyes. And Hal nodded several times, reaching down to finger the slit sheet of parchment, holding it up, then putting it down again.

"Yes. Fine. Have fun. Catch a fish for me."

"We're hunting. Not fishing," Stig said.

"Oh, well, good. Then best if you don't catch a fish," Hal said.

Stig raised his eyes to heaven. "Maybe we'll catch a dragon in a tadpole net."

"If you say so," Hal replied.

Stig sighed heavily, then turned and left the room, closing the door behind him.

"Have a good time," Hal said. Then he looked up and realized Stig had gone. "Oh . . . where did you go? Well, never mind."

He tapped the sheet of parchment once more, then angrily shoved it aside. It fluttered off the table, caught the breeze from the window and settled gently to the floor, sideslipping back and forth as it descended.

He propped his feet up on the table and sat for several minutes, his fingers steepled under his chin, lost in his thoughts. Then a tap at the door distracted him. He looked at the door irritably.

"What is it?" he called. Then he added, "Come in."

The door opened to admit one of the serving girls, bearing a tray with a pot of coffee and a cup on it. There were also several of the sweet cakes he had grown to enjoy. She stood just inside the door, hesitating at his tone. Hal realized it wasn't fair snapping at a servant.

"Come in," he said in a more friendly voice. "That looks terrific. Set it over here on the table."

The girl moved quickly across the room, glancing at him surreptitiously. She'd always heard that Skandians were big and loud and hairy—and a little frightening. But this young man was slim and well built. Generally, he spoke quietly . . . and he was very handsome, she thought.

She set the tray down and indicated the coffeepot.

"Shall I pour you a cup?" she asked. He smiled at her. Very handsome indeed, she thought. And he was a ship's captain, and so young.

"You'd better watch the cup," he said, smiling.

She realized she'd been about to pour the coffee on the table, as she was looking at him. She flushed and lowered her eyes to the task in hand. He took his feet off the table to give her room, then frowned as he noticed the amulet she was wearing. He waited till she set the pot down, then pointed to it.

"What's that?"

She was puzzled for a moment. She donned the amulet every morning as a matter of habit. As a result, she was unaware that she was wearing it now and it took a few seconds for her to realize what he was talking about. She looked down, then held it out so he could inspect it more closely.

"It's just an amulet," she said. "It's not very costly but my dad gave it to me and he's dead now, so it's precious to me."

"May I see it?" Hal asked. He held out his hand.

She hesitated, reluctant to give him the piece of jewelry. He might be young and handsome, but he *was* a Skandian, after all. And Skandians had a reputation for *liberating* jewelry. She'd heard the other servants talking about another one of the *Heron* crew, who delighted in removing their bangles, necklaces and even earrings without their noticing. Then, he would return the purloined article with a beaming smile. But this young man had an honest face, she thought. So she shrugged the suspicion aside and handed it to him, passing the leather thong over her neck.

Hal frowned as he studied the pendant itself. It was a thin, light material. Some kind of shell. It was exactly what he was looking for.

"What is this?"

"It's just tortoiseshell. It's not worth much. It's not precious or anything."

"It's perfect," he said. "Where would I get something like this?"

She shrugged. "There's a jeweler in the village across the river.

He'd have supplies of it. He makes a lot of cheap jewelry for the villagers."

Hal handed her back the amulet and a smile lit up his face. Her heart missed a beat or two and she curtsied, feeling the warmth rise up in her cheeks.

"How do I find him?" he asked and she made a deprecating gesture.

"He's right on the main street. His name is Geoffrey. Geoffrey the goldsmith."

"I suppose that sounds better than Geoffrey the tortoiseshell smith," Hal said and she smiled and giggled. She was glad she had been assigned to look after the ship's captain.

Hal rose from his chair. It was apparent that he was planning to go out and she gestured to the coffee tray.

"Did you want more coffee?" she said, although in truth he hadn't drunk any. He'd become engrossed with her amulet before he could do so. He looked at the tray in surprise, as if seeing it for the first time.

"Eh? Oh, no thanks. Sorry you bothered with it. You may as well take it away." He paused, then held up a hand to stop her and scooped three of the cakes off the plate. "I'll take these, however. Geoffrey, you said his name was?"

"That's right, sir. Although I'm not sure he'll want any cakes."

"I'm not sure he'll be getting any," Hal told her, and crammed one of them into his mouth, smiling blissfully at the sweet honey taste as it spread across his taste buds. "Thank you . . ." He hesitated, realizing he didn't know her name.

She supplied it, and curtsied quickly again. "Milly, sir."

"Well, thank you, Milly. And never mind the 'sir.' My name is Hal."

She smiled at him. She was pretty, he realized, and the smile really lit up her features.

"I'll remember that, sir. I mean . . . Hal," she said. Then, blushing again, she preceded him to the door, balancing the tray with the ease of long practice.

H al was whistling cheerfully as he strode through the landscaped parkland in front of the castle, heading for the river and the village. He thought he could see a way to solve Ingvar's problem, or at least alleviate it. The stumbling block had been finding the right material for what he had in mind, and Milly's necklace had provided the answer to that.

Preoccupied with his thoughts, he didn't notice the sentries at the outer end of the drawbridge as they came to attention when he passed. One of them, an older man, shook his head and spoke lugubriously to his companion.

"Still seems odd to salute Skandians. I recall when we used to salute them with a shower of rocks and a cauldron of hot oil. Somehow, that seemed more fitting."

His companion was a younger man who hadn't known the old days, when Skandian raiders were regarded with fear and suspicion the length and breadth of Araluen.

"Still, it was a Skandian who helped save the life of Princess Cassandra on her wedding day, wasn't it?" the younger sentry said.

The older man snorted. "That may be. But saving one princess hardly makes up for centuries of raiding and looting, does it?"

"I bet it does if you're the princess." The younger man smiled, but his senior refused to concede the point.

"Well, I'm not, am I?" he said truculently.

"No, you're not. You don't have the legs for it." The older guard's legs were noticeably bowed. "Long and shapely, hers are."

"Don't be disrespectful!" snapped the older man.

The young sentry shrugged. "No disrespect to the princess in admiring her looks."

"I don't mean her. I mean me!"

They continued their idle bickering as Hal strode across the neatly mown grass of the castle park. It was soft and springy underfoot. The mowers had been out that morning with their scythes, and the smell of newly cut grass was strong in his nostrils. He enjoyed the sensation. It was such a . . . land-bound smell, he thought. He was more used to the fresh salt air of the sea, but this made a pleasant change.

A fifteen-minute walk took him to the bridge that spanned the river. The last fifty meters were through the dim, cool shade of the forest. Then he was on the bridge itself, pausing to look at the *Heron*, moored alongside the landing stage. Edvin was on board, supervising a group of locals who were carrying small casks and nets of fruit and vegetables onto the ship. Edvin looked up, saw his skirl watching and waved a hand. Hal returned the greeting before continuing on his way. He could never resist an opportunity to stop and admire his ship when he came upon her like this. He felt a deep surge of pride when he studied her clean lines. She was his, totally, and he felt a pride not just of ownership but of creation. He had helped build her in the first place, when she was intended as a pleasure craft for a retired sea wolf. Then Hal supervised the re-rigging after her owner died unexpectedly and the opportunity arose to buy the hull cheaply from Anders, the senior shipbuilder in Hallasholm.

As he crossed the bridge, he noticed that its center section was removable. If the village came under attack, the inhabitants could retreat to the safety of the castle, removing the middle section of the bridge to slow down their attackers. He sighed softly to himself. The castle, and its parks and gardens and woodlands, were all beautiful and peaceful. But that could change in a moment, he knew. They were living in potentially dangerous times, and it was wise to take precautions in case that potential became a reality.

A hundred meters from the bridge, the path he was following widened and formed into the main street of the village. Shops, craftsmen's workshops and private homes lined either side. They were a mixture of building styles. Some were the wattle-and-daub construction he'd seen in Cresthaven village. Others were more substantial buildings, constructed of logs, reminding him of the houses in Hallasholm. And finally, there were others made from sawn timber. They all shared the same form of roof—a sweeping pitched roof made from thatch, with the straw bundled tightly to repel rain. The eaves swept down low, so that they ended below head height. A visitor had to stoop to enter one of the doors.

It was a neat village, well planned and well maintained, without the accumulation of rubbish that so often spoilt the appearance of places like this. There was a fresh smell of wood smoke, and as he proceeded down the main street, another smell became apparent.

It was the mouthwatering smell of roasting meat—meat that had obviously been spiced and seasoned before it was placed over the glowing coals of a fire. He looked to one side and saw a building, larger than its neighbors, with a covered verandah facing onto the street, furnished with half a dozen tables and chairs. A dark-haired woman was sitting at one of them. Judging by her apron and the flour on her hands and arms, she was the cook. She became aware of his scrutiny and smiled a greeting.

He nodded in return and continued moving, studying the buildings either side for sign of the jeweler's workshop.

He spotted it without any trouble. The house had a solid timber door, reinforced with iron bands. And a sign hung over it, depicting a yellow vertical half circle—the common symbol for gold. He walked to the door, raised the heavy knocker and brought it down onto the iron striker plate several times.

There were no windows either side of the door. He assumed this was for security purposes. The occupant would almost certainly have stocks of gold, silver and precious stones on the premises and it would be foolish to make entry to the house too easy.

He reached for the knocker again, but stopped as he made out the sound of shuffling footsteps inside the house.

There was the rattle of a bolt on the other side of the door but, instead of the door opening, a carefully fitted panel swung open in the door at eye height. Framed inside it, he could see a portion of a face, and two rheumy blue eyes staring out at him.

"What do you want?"

The voice was old, but firm. And it was decidedly unwelcoming. Hal assumed that a jeweler would be suspicious of any stranger—and particularly if that stranger happened to be dressed as a Skandian. He smiled at the thought. A mistake, he realized.

"What are you smirking at? Who are you and what d'you want?"

The tone was quite peremptory now. Hal hurriedly rearranged his features and did his best to look ingenuous—although exactly how that might be accomplished, he wasn't quite sure.

"I'm Hal Mikkelson," he began. "I wanted—"

"Skandian, are you?" the voice challenged.

Hal nodded. "Well, yes." It was too hard to explain his mixed parentage. And besides, he thought of himself as a Skandian these days.

"Don't hold with Skandians," said the old man, who, Hal assumed, was Geoffrey the goldsmith. "Your lot stole a gold ingot from me."

Instantly, the smile was wiped from Hal's face, replaced by a frown of anger. I'll kill Jesper, he thought. But aloud, he said: "When? When did they do this?"

Geoffrey wrinkled his forehead in thought. "Fifteen year back. No, closer to sixteen now, I think."

Hal breathed a sigh of relief. Then realized Geoffrey was still talking.

"No. Maybe it were seventeen year. That's more like it. Seventeen."

"Well, I'm sorry to hear it. But I actually wanted to buy something from you. I need some tortoiseshell and I was told you might be able to supply it."

"No," said Geoffrey and Hal made a moue of disappointment. "You don't have any?"

But Geoffrey was shaking his head. "No. It were more like fifteen year. I remember now."

"But you do have tortoiseshell?" Hal pressed. He saw Geoffrey's hand wave dismissively behind the spy hole.

"Oh yes. Got plenty of that. You're buying, you say?"

"That's right," Hal said.

Geoffrey nodded once or twice, then said: "Wait here. And take that big knife off. Leave it by the gatepost."

The hatch swung shut and the footsteps receded again. Hal quickly unbuckled his saxe and hung the belt and sheath on the gatepost. A minute passed, then he heard the rattle of a larger bolt and the door eased open a crack. When Geoffrey ascertained that Hal had removed the knife, the jeweler swung the door open wider, gesturing him inside.

Hal entered, finding himself in a long, dimly lit hallway. As his eyes adjusted to the low light, he heard the door shut solidly behind him. Then Geoffrey pushed past him and beckoned him to follow. They emerged into a workroom, where the light was considerably brighter. There were large windows in the side wall and a skylight directly above the work table. That made sense, Hal thought. If Geoffrey was shaping and designing his pieces here, he'd want as much light as possible. The skylight was constructed from wooden slats that could be opened and closed depending on the weather.

The windows were secured by heavy bars. That made sense as well.

Geoffrey gestured to a wooden tray set out on the work table in the center of the room. "Here are some of my samples of tortoise-shell."

It struck Hal that, when the jeweler had left him at the front door, he had gone to fetch these samples from some hidden strong-box where he kept his gold, silver and other materials.

The young skirl bent over the tray, moving the pieces slightly with his forefinger so he could see them more clearly. Finally, he selected two—roughly circular pieces about six centimeters in di-ameter, both thin and dark brown in color.

Geoffrey grunted. "Not very pretty," he said, leaning down to peer more closely at them.

"I'm not after pretty," Hal said. Then, as he watched the jeweler stooping over the table, a thought struck him. "You're shortsighted?"

Geoffrey looked up at him. "Comes of spending my life work-ing hunched over tiny pieces," he said.

Hal nodded. "Would you mind trying something for me?"

Geoffrey grunted assent. He was still suspicious of this Skan-dian, but he was interested to know why the young man would want these two fairly unattractive pieces. Most people, if they chose tortoiseshell, wanted the pieces to be light and translucent. These were dark and opaque. He was quite pleased to be able to sell them at all. He'd planned to cut them into smaller pieces and use them as highlights in a design.

Hal picked up one of the discs and pointed to the center of it.

"Could you bore a tiny hole here in the center?" he asked. "I'll buy the piece, of course."

Geoffrey shrugged. "Why not?" He picked a small auger from

the clutter of tools on the table and held it up for Hal to see. "This small enough?"

Hal examined the tiny drill and nodded. "That should be fine. Drill it right in the center."

It took only a minute for Geoffrey to comply. Then he looked questioningly at Hal, who motioned for him to hold the disc in front of one eye. "Hold it over one eye, close the other eye and look out the window," Hal said.

Geoffrey, shaking his head in puzzlement, did as he was asked. As he looked out the window, however, Hal saw his shoulders stiffen in surprise.

"That's remarkable." The jeweler took the disc away from his eye, looked out the window, then replaced the disc and looked again.

Hal leaned forward eagerly. "What happens?"

"I can see things much more clearly when I look through this tiny hole. It seems to bring things into focus."

A wide smile spread over Hal's face. "That's just what I wanted to hear. Now, how much do I owe you?"

The hunting party assembled outside the castle, on the outer side of the drawbridge. Stig, Thorn, Ulf, Wulf and Lydia emerged, and stood waiting for the princess to join them.

Ulf and Wulf in particular excited comment.

"Wonder how their mother tells them apart?" said one of the sentries. His companion shrugged.

"Wonder how they tell themselves apart?" he replied. "They're like two peas in a pod, they are."

The other member of the party who excited comment was Kloof. Stig had her on a short leather leash that was hooked to her collar. She pranced a little, pleased to be out in the fresh air after her time in the castle. But after a few minutes, she settled down.

"No need to go hunting, really," said the first sentry. "They've brought their own bear."

Lydia had looked askance at the big dog. "She's likely to scare off the game," she said skeptically.

Stig shrugged. "If she plays up, I'll bring her back to the castle."

Before Lydia could comment further, Princess Cassandra emerged from the gatehouse and crossed the drawbridge. She was dressed for hunting, in dark green tights and knee-high boots, with a leather over-jerkin that came to mid-thigh. A wide leather belt held the jerkin in at the waist, with a sheathed saxe and a heavy-looking shot pouch on either side. She wore a long peaked hat with a green feather in it and had her sling hanging around her neck.

Two muscular bodyguards, armed with swords, daggers and crossbows, marched a few paces behind her.

"Good morning, everyone," she called cheerfully. "Sorry I'm late."

Thorn and Stig mumbled a reply. Princesses were obviously allowed to be late.

Lydia frowned slightly. In her book, nobody should be late when there was hunting to be done, princess or not.

Kloof whined and strained at the leash until Stig allowed her to advance a few steps to greet the princess. He noticed that one of her companions dropped a hand to his sword hilt as the dog came closer. Then the guard saw the massive tail wagging and relaxed.

"Hullo, beautiful!" said Cassandra. She stretched out a hand to Kloof, knuckles upward, and let the dog sniff it. She was so petite that Kloof's head came up past her waist. Kloof sniffed, then allowed the woman to fondle her chin and ears and the ruff at her neck. The huge dog closed her eyes with pleasure at the touch and sank to her haunches.

Cassandra looked up at Stig, smiling. "Why, she's just a big old friendly pussy cat, isn't she?"

Stig inclined his head. "If she likes you. If not, she's a big old rampaging monster."

Cassandra wiped her hand on her tights and held it out to Stig. "We haven't met. I'm Cassandra."

He shook hands with her and grinned. "I'm Stig. I'm the first mate of the *Heron*."

Cassandra nodded and turned to Thorn. "And you must be the famous and redoubtable Thorn."

Thorn grinned easily. "I can't deny it," he said. He wasn't sure what *redoubtable* meant but it was coupled with famous so he thought it must be good.

Cassandra turned to Lydia. "Morning, Lydia." She nodded at the dart quiver slung over the dark-haired girl's shoulder. "Can't wait to see that in action."

Lydia nodded, a little more deeply than she might have normally. It was her concession to a curtsy. "Morning, Princess," she said.

Cassandra smiled, waving the formality aside. "Please. Call me Cassandra. Or better still, Cassie," she said. "After all, we're hunting partners." Her gaze fell on Ulf and Wulf and her eyebrows went up. "And I've heard of you two. All the servants are talking about you."

The twins regarded her, their mouths slightly open. She was beautiful, they thought. Small, with a neat figure and blond hair that came down to shoulder length. But, above all, her face was alight with the joy of living, and the sheer pleasure of being out in the sunshine on a pleasant day like this. Ulf and Wulf were smitten. All thoughts of the practical jokes they had planned to play on the Araluen princess were forgotten. They stared at her in mute admiration.

She stepped forward, prompting them. "And you are . . . ?" she said to Ulf.

He shook his head. "Ulf," he finally managed to mutter incoherently.

Cassandra inclined her head to one side, puzzled. "I beg your pardon?" she asked. It sounded to her as if the Skandian had something caught in his throat. But Ulf continued to gape at her like a love-struck schoolboy.

Finally, Thorn explained. "That's his name. Ulf."

Cassandra made a small moue with her mouth. "Remarkable," she said, then turned to Wulf. "And what do I call you?"

Wulf was a little more composed than his brother had been. After all, he was expecting the question.

"I'm Wulf, your highsomeness," he said, confusing the correct term of address for a princess.

Cassandra affected not to notice. "Ulf and Wulf?"

They both nodded dumbly, their eyes fixed on her. She grinned and added, "And are you two related by any chance?"

They both snot sniggered with delight and nodded enthusiastically. Cassandra turned to the other three Herons and grinned at them.

"Oh, these two are fun!" she said. "Can I keep them?" She was taken aback by the instant chorus of assent from Thorn, Stig and Lydia.

"Please!" they all said at once, and even Kloof joined in, barking. Ulf and Wulf looked at their friends, insulted. But then they turned their adoring gazes back to Cassandra and the goofy smiles reappeared on their faces.

"Well," said Cassandra, "I suppose we should be . . ."

She didn't finish the sentence. There was a clatter of hooves and a squad of a dozen armored cavalrymen trotted out under the raised portcullis and across the drawbridge, forming up in a loose cordon around the group.

Cassandra frowned at them. "And what are you planning?" she asked.

The lieutenant in command of the squad saluted, his right hand touching his helmet. "We're your escort, your highness," he explained.

Cassandra snorted in disdain. "Who says I need an escort?"

The lieutenant shifted uncomfortably in his saddle and looked toward a tall figure who was striding across the drawbridge.

"I do," said Duncan. "I was going to join you but something's come up. So I've ordered an escort for you."

"But I don't need an escort," Cassandra protested. "I've got Cedric and Farrer here." She indicated her two guards, who both stiffened to attention. "And four fierce Skandian warriors to protect me. And anything they can't handle, Lydia and I can take care of." She grinned at Lydia, who gravely nodded agreement. To her way of thinking, all of the others were superfluous.

But Duncan wasn't impressed.

"Cassandra," he said, "just humor me until we find out about this new threat from Iqbal. I don't want you taking risks."

"I'm not taking risks, Dad. I'm going hunting with my friends, and I'll be perfectly safe. I'm not going to be a captive in my own home just because of some vague threat from Arrida. Please tell the lieutenant and his men to stand down."

There was a long silence between them. Her brow tightened into a frown and she said, with extra emphasis, *"Please."*

Duncan hesitated a few more seconds, then capitulated. He'd spent his life trying to protect his freedom-loving daughter and, not for the first time, he realized he couldn't keep mollycoddling her as if she were a baby.

"All right," he said. "Lieutenant, take your men back to the barracks."

"Yes, sir!" said the cavalry leader, saluting once more. At his brisk command, the troop wheeled and trotted back into the castle.

Duncan shrugged philosophically. "Happy now?"

His daughter beamed at him as she stood on tiptoe to kiss his cheek. "Delighted—although I'd be happier if you could join us."

He shook his head. "I've got dispatches in from Halt. Horace is fine, by the way," he added as an aside and she nodded.

"I know. I had a letter from him by the same courier."

"So there you have it. I have work to do, while the crown princess traipses off into the forest with a crowd of wild northmen."

"And woman," Cassandra added, indicating Lydia.

Duncan bowed slightly in her direction. "Forgive me. And a wild northwoman."

Lydia shifted her feet awkwardly. She knew from his tone that he was joking but she was never completely sure how to respond to jokes. That was one of the reasons she found it difficult to deal with Thorn's teasing.

Duncan swung his gaze over the small party. "Have a good hunt," he said. "And keep an eye on my daughter."

"With pleasure!" Ulf and Wulf chorused as one, and their shipmates all turned to look at them in surprise.

"Let's be off then," Cassandra said briskly. "We're wasting daylight."

As the small party walked down the slope toward the dark line of the woods, Duncan stood watching them depart. Eventually, he sighed and turned, heading back into the castle and his paper-laden desk.

He wasn't sure whether he was sighing out of concern for his strong-willed daughter, or over the fact that he'd rather leave the papers to take care of themselves and go hunting.

Sometimes, he thought, it wasn't so great to be the King.

T hey soon left the close-mown grass close to the castle for the wild, more unkempt area leading to the forest. The grass was knee-high and rougher here, and clouds of grasshoppers fled from them, skipping with whir-ring wings into the air at their approach, settling again, then taking flight once more as the party came closer.

Cassandra was examining one of Lydia's darts, turning the meter-long missile over in her hands, admiring the neat workman-ship that bound the three vanes to the shaft, and the razor-sharp edges of the warhead.

"You make these yourself?"

"All except the broadheads," Lydia said. "I have a smith make them. But I sharpen them and bind them into place. That way I can be sure that every dart will fly the same way."

Cassandra nodded. She knew that Will and Halt made their own arrows and attended to the fletching themselves. The castle archers tended to let the armorers make their arrows for them. But the castle archers didn't approach the accuracy that the Rangers could achieve.

She tested the double-edged broadhead with her thumb. "Isn't this a bit . . . extreme for small game like rabbits?" she asked.

Lydia nodded immediately. "Oh yes. A dart like this would tear a bird or a rabbit to pieces. There wouldn't be enough left to eat. For smaller game I use one of these." She drew another dart from the fleece-lined quiver and handed it over for Cassandra's inspection.

The princess examined it curiously. "There's no broadhead at all," she said. And she was right. In the place of the leaf shaped iron broadhead was a bulbous length of hard blackwood, carefully shaped and polished.

"It's a blunt," Lydia explained. "The blunt head knocks out the bird or animal without tearing up the carcass. And if I cast at a bird roosting in a tree, I don't lose my dart."

There was a rueful sound to her voice and Cassandra looked up, smiling. "I take it that has happened to you?"

Lydia nodded. "At one stage the trees around my hometown were riddled with darts stuck in the trunks and branches, way out of reach."

Cassandra weighed the two darts in her hands experimentally. "They're the same weight and balance," she observed, handing them back to Lydia.

"I make sure of that. They all have to have the same flight

characteristics. Of course, the blunts are a little slower because the head is bigger and there's more resistance as it flies through the air. But they're as close as I can get them."

She carefully replaced the darts in her quiver.

"If you two ladies have finished nattering, Kloof seems to have spotted something," Stig said quietly. The two girls looked up, startled. Kloof was standing rock steady, one forepaw raised from the ground, staring intently to their left. A low rumble sounded in her throat.

Following the direction of her intent gaze, Cassandra saw a large, fat hare in the long grass, staring fixedly at them.

"I think Kloof might have done this before," Stig said quietly. Of course, nobody knew too much about Kloof's life prior to the time she had "discovered" Hal on the mountainside near Hallasholm. But it was apparent that she had been trained for hunting.

Lydia and Cassandra exchanged a glance, trying to decide who should shoot at the hare. Lydia made a "go ahead" gesture with her left hand.

"You're the princess," she said and Cassandra didn't need a second invitation. Quickly, she fitted a shot into the pouch of her sling, made sure it was settled securely, then began to swing the weapon round her head at ever-increasing speed. The loaded pouch hummed softly in the air and she saw the hare tense suddenly as it became aware of the alien sound.

Quickly, she released, casting the shot at the small animal.

Too quickly, as it turned out. The shot was thirty centimeters high and off to the right. The *whiz* of its passage through the air finally alerted the hare of their presence, turning his nervous curiosity into panic as he skittered away, zigzagging wildly through the long grass.

"Hern's breath!" Cassandra said, invoking a most un-princessly curse. "That was terrible! I'm out of practice."

Lydia shook her head reproachfully. "If you're going to use a missile weapon, you have to practice constantly," she admonished.

Cassandra glared at her. She might be egalitarian and friendly, but no princess likes being lectured to—particularly by a younger woman. Her cheeks flushed with annoyance, then she forced herself to calm down. Lydia was simply stating the situation as she saw it, Cassandra realized. She wasn't lecturing or even criticizing. She was just stating a fact.

And of course, she was also right.

Cassandra took a deep breath, then said, "Sorry I spoiled that chance. You take the next one."

But the next shot went to Stig, as it turned out. Lydia had wondered how he planned to hunt. He wasn't carrying a spear or a javelin. He was armed only with his saxe, and that was hardly suitable for hunting.

But earlier that morning, Stig had walked to the river and filled his pockets with smooth, round river rocks. He'd spent his boyhood years hunting rabbits and birds in the woods around Hallasholm and had developed an uncanny accuracy. Now, when a partridge broke cover twenty meters from them, he dropped Kloof's leash, whipped out a rock and sent it whizzing at the plump bird. The partridge fell to the ground, limp and lifeless.

Stig clicked his fingers at Kloof, who had remained motionless, and the giant dog took off at a run to retrieve the dead bird. Stig grinned at the two girls, patting Kloof on the head as he took the partridge and pushed it into his game bag.

"Good girl, Kloofy. Good dog."

Thorn looked at the dog admiringly. "You're right. She has done this before," he said. Then he added, "By the way, that was a great throw."

Cassandra smiled at Stig. "I agree. No fancy equipment. Just a good arm and a dead eye."

Lydia said nothing, but caught Stig's eye and nodded slowly in approval. He smiled, pleased with the praise, and pleased with himself.

Then Kloof barked sharply, three times.

The Heron crew members had heard her bark like that before. It was Kloof's danger signal. Kloof had stayed silent through the hunt, as her long-ago training must have taught her. But now she broke that silence and they sensed that she would only do so if danger were imminent. Instantly, they all scanned the surrounding countryside. They were close to the forest now where the shrubs and trees grew more thickly, with patches of deep shadow where an attacker might lurk.

Thorn saw him first. "There!" he shouted, pointing.

A figure was rising from behind a small shrub forty meters away. The shrub was so small that it seemed almost impossible for it to conceal a grown man. But it had. Now, with the dog's warning bark, as the man realized he had been discovered, he stood clear of its branches.

He was dressed in a light brown flowing robe over a white shirt and billowing white trousers. On his head, he wore a turban, the kind favored by the inhabitants of the hot, dry deserts of Arrida.

He held a short, single-handed crossbow, with thick, stubby limbs and a bolt in position ready to release. As he stood, he raised the bow, aiming it unwaveringly at the Araluen princess, steadying the hand that held the bow by clamping his other hand around the bow-hand's wrist.

There was an ugly *SMACK!* as the bow released, and the short, stubby quarrel flashed across the intervening space, straight at Cassandra. Frozen by the sudden turn of events, she stared, open-mouthed, as she saw death bearing down on her.

Then Thorn threw his right hand up, into the path of the hissing messenger of death.

Thock!

The quarrel struck the hardwood of Thorn's wooden hook and stuck there, the force of the impact jerking his arm violently back. Thorn staggered a pace, and Cassandra went pale as she realized he had intercepted the deadly quarrel a bare meter from her face.

Then the little tableau, seemingly frozen in place for seconds, erupted into sudden movement. The would-be assassin, seeing his shot intercepted, turned and ran. Ulf and Wulf set off after him—a faint hope seeing that the man had a forty-meter start on them and was just a few meters from the forest proper. At the same moment, Stig released Kloof's leash and pointed at the fleeing figure.

"Get him, Kloof!" he ordered and the dog bounded away in pursuit.

But Lydia reacted fastest of all. She had whipped a shaft from her quiver, fitted the notched end into the atlatl, and cast. It was so smooth and practiced, it seemed like one continuous movement.

"Don't kill him!" Thorn shouted. "We need to—"

But it was too late, the dart was already on its way, closing the distance between Lydia and the fleeing assassin in seconds.

They heard the ugly smack as it hit him, saw him throw his hands in the air and fall face downward into the long grass.

Thorn turned a disgruntled look on Lydia. "We needed to question him," he said, completing the sentence he had begun just as she cast her dart.

She returned his annoyed look, perfectly unperturbed. "He's not dead," she replied calmly. "I used a blunt."

Thorn had been about to unleash a torrent of abuse at her. Instead, he closed his mouth, opened it again, then looked at the prone figure in the grass. Kloof had just reached him and was standing over him, growling deep in her chest.

"A blunt," he repeated, finally, and Lydia nodded.

"A blunt. He's unconscious. He'll have a massive headache when he wakes up."

Stig grinned at the two of them. "He'll have a massive fright when he wakes up. How would you like to come to and have Kloof's jaws just a few centimeters from your face?"

"Not a pretty sight," Thorn agreed. He gripped the crossbow quarrel close to the end that had penetrated his wooden hook and started slowly working it back and forth to release it. Finally, he jerked it clear and studied the broadhead. There was an ominous dark stain around the tip.

"Poisoned," he said, glancing at Cassandra. "Just as well my timber hand got in the way."

Cassandra was staring, wide-eyed, at the three of them. She had grown up around Rangers and warriors. But she had never seen faster reactions than the Herons had just shown. Thorn's feat in intercepting the quarrel was near miraculous. And Lydia's shot with the dart—easily fifty meters as the would-be assassin gathered speed—was exceptional.

"Thank you," she said quietly, finally throwing off the shock that had frozen her. There had been a time, she thought regretfully, when she might have reacted as quickly as her companions. But she had spent too much time in the castle, attending to the duties that befell a royal princess, and too little time in the field. Like using a sling properly, she thought, it all required practice.

The three of them brushed aside her thanks.

"I don't suppose Kloof can fetch *that* piece of game back here," Stig said cheerfully. "We'd best go and collect him."

Ulf and Wulf were already standing by the figure of the assassin. He stirred, then rolled over onto his back. As he opened his eyes, his vision was filled with the sight of Kloof's slavering, snarling jaws. The man screamed in sudden fright and tried to rear back. But of course, he was lying on the ground and there was nowhere to rear back to. Then he shifted his vision to the twins, both angry and vengeful, both with saxes drawn and ready. He called out in alarm.

The others were hurrying across the grass to secure him.

Stig snorted. "Probably thinks he's seeing double after that crack on the head."

"If he is," Thorn put in, "he may well be seeing four of them."

"What a terrible thought," Lydia said.

Thorn smiled at her. "That was one heck of a shot," he said.

She looked at him suspiciously. Thorn's compliments were all too often barbed.

"And . . . ?" She waited for the sting in the tail.

Thorn shrugged innocently. "And nothing. It was a great shot." However, he couldn't resist adding, "Just as well you accidentally pulled a blunt out of your quiver."

Lydia threw her hands in the air. "I knew it!" she said. "You can't resist having a snipe at me, can you?"

Thorn turned away to hide his smile. He reached down and got hold of one of the man's arms. "Let's get this beauty back to the castle. Get away, Kloof."

The dog reluctantly backed away, still growling deep in her chest as Thorn heaved the man to his feet. He swayed clumsily, rubbing his head where the dart had struck him.

Stig gestured to the back of the man's right hand. "Thorn, look."

There was a tattoo on the man's hand—a depiction of a scorpion, with its stinger raised threateningly.

Thorn whistled softly. "Well, what do you know," he said. The fierce sea wolf smiled at the semiconscious man. It wasn't a pleasant smile.

"Let's see what you can tell us about this Scorpion Mountain business," he said.

G eoffrey sat back and admired his handiwork with a satisfied smile. Hal, who had sat quietly for the past hour watching the artisan at work, leaned over his shoulder to look at the finished product.

"Wonderful," he said, and Geoffrey turned the smile on him.

"Yes. Even if I do say so myself," he replied. "But let's see if it works."

The old jeweler, fascinated by the improvement in vision afforded by the tiny hole in the tortoiseshell disc, had offered to make a device to hold two of the discs in place in front of Ingvar's eyes. He created a wire frame to hold the two pieces of tortoiseshell side by side, and about a centimeter apart. In the space between them, he fashioned a padded rest that would sit on the wearer's nose. At either side, he soldered sprung wire arms that stretched back at right angles to the discs, angled in so they would sit firmly against the wearer's head, resting on the top of the ears.

He picked up the device now and moved to the side window of the house. Bending the side arms slightly apart, he slipped them on, one either side of his head, and settled the discs in place in front of his eyes. The nose rest held them firmly in position.

Then he peered out the window at the countryside behind his workshop.

Hal heard his sudden intake of breath, and his excited exclamation.

"They work?" the young Skandian said hopefully, and Geoffrey turned his gaze on him. It was a somewhat disconcerting sight. The two tortoiseshell discs suspended in front of his eyes gave him a sinister appearance, looking like the eyeholes in a skull. But no skull ever smiled so contentedly as Geoffrey did now.

"It's amazing," he said. "The holes definitely help focus my vision. I can see much more clearly." He slipped the device off, shaking his head a little sadly as he reverted to his normal shortsighted vision. "The extra holes were a good idea."

Once he had determined that a tiny hole would improve the focus of a shortsighted person, Hal decided to experiment. He purchased a third piece of tortoiseshell from Geoffrey and had the jeweler pierce it once in the center, then another dozen times in a circle around the original aperture. The result was a big improvement. The small holes still focused Geoffrey's sight, but the greater number widened his field of vision as well. The two collaborators smiled at each other now. It had been a fruitful morning's work. Hal reached for the coin purse hanging at his belt.

"How much do I owe you?" he asked. But Geoffrey reached out

one gnarled hand and closed it over Hal's, stopping him from opening the purse.

"No charge," the older man said. When Hal went to remonstrate, he spoke more firmly.

"I'll be making myself a pair of these," he said. "And I have you to thank for the idea. So there's no fee to be paid. You've already paid me with improved sight."

His sincerity was obvious and Hal withdrew his hand from the purse, inclining his head gratefully.

"You're sure?" he said. "You've spent the best part of the morning working on the frame."

"I'm sure," Geoffrey said. He took the wire frame and wrapped it carefully in a piece of chamois cloth, then handed it to Hal. "Now go and show it to your friend."

Hal placed the wire frame carefully into one of his side pockets and followed Geoffrey as the older man led the way to the front door.

Geoffrey held out his hand and they shook. "Good-bye, young Hal. If all your ideas are as good as this one, you've a bright future ahead of you."

Hal smiled diffidently. "Unfortunately, they're not. I've had my share of disasters. I'm just glad this wasn't one of them."

"Me too," Geoffrey told him. "Now get going. I want to get busy making myself a pair of . . ." He hesitated. "What exactly do we call this idea of yours?"

Hal shrugged, thinking. "How about *viewing discs?*" he suggested, but Geoffrey made a disapproving face.

"That's a little prosaic," he said. "After all, the improvement in vision is quite spectacular."

"Well then," Hal said slowly, "if that's the case, how about *spectacles*?"

Geoffrey thrust out his bottom lip. "That's not a lot better."

"That's the best I've got," Hal told him. "I'm going with *spectacles*."

But the jeweler shook his head gloomily. "Can't see it catching on," he said.

Inevitably, when Hal reached the castle and went looking for Ingvar, the big lad was nowhere to be found. He wasn't in his room, or in the large common room that had been set aside for the *Heron* crew to relax in as a group. Edvin and Stefan were there. The re-provisioning of the ship was completed and Edvin wasn't required at the jetty any longer.

Jesper was prowling the corridors, examining the locks on the many doors with a professional interest that Hal found disconcerting. He came upon the former thief crouching by a heavy lock that secured a door on the second floor. The lock was far more formidable than the relatively simple ones on the bedroom doors.

"Just forget it, Jes," Hal said, startling his crewmate.

Jesper looked up and grinned disarmingly. "Have you ever noticed," he said, "that when people have something that's valuable, they tend to advertise the fact by using bigger and stronger locks on the door where it's kept? If they'd just put a normal lock on this door, I'd take no notice of it at all."

"Which is what I want you to do," Hal told him firmly. "Have you seen Ingvar around?"

Jesper shook his head. "Haven't seen him all morning."

Hal turned away. He had gone a couple of paces when he turned back. Jesper was still contemplating the locked door. "How strong is that lock?"

"Oh, it's quite solid," Jesper replied. "It'd take me at least a minute to get it open."

Hal rolled his eyes to heaven and walked away. He continued his search of the massive castle and its grounds and finally discovered Ingvar sitting on a wooden bench in a sunny corner of the battlements, his back leaning against the sun-warmed stone, his face turned up to the sun, eyes closed.

"Come to talk me out of it, Hal?"

Hal stopped a few meters away, surprised. "How did you know it was me?"

Ingvar's eyes were still closed against the sun's brightness. The big boy smiled. "I've got to know your footsteps. You have a distinctive gait. You seem to be always in a hurry to get where you're going."

Hal nodded thoughtfully. He'd heard that when people had restricted vision, their other senses, such as their hearing, took on an increased keenness. Apparently that was the case with Ingvar.

Hal sat down beside him on the bench. "Good spot," he said.

Ingvar nodded. "It's warm and sheltered from the wind. And there's a young girl in one of the rooms along there who was singing a little earlier. Nice voice she had too."

Hal looked around. The battlements were higher than the floor where they had been quartered. They looked out over the outer wall and down to the forest. From this height, however, one could see the roofs of the buildings in the village.

"Nice view too," he said.

Ingvar's smile faded. He opened his eyes to look directly at Hal. It wasn't like his old friend to be so tactless, he thought.

"I'll have to take your word for that."

Hal shrugged elaborately. "Maybe not." He reached into his pocket and produced the spectacles, wrapped in their protective layer of chamois. He carefully unwrapped them and held them out toward Ingvar.

Ingvar frowned. Close up like this, he could see them with reasonable clarity. But he had no idea what they were, or what their purpose might be.

"What have you got there?" he asked. Ingvar sensed Hal's feeling of excited anticipation. Hal had been the same when he'd built the Mangler and they'd tested it on the beach many months ago, on the far side of the Stormwhite Sea.

"Just try these on," Hal said. "Hold still, and close your eyes."

Carefully, Hal spread the wire arms and slid them onto either side of Ingvar's face, setting them to rest on his ears, and then releasing them so they held firmly in place.

Ingvar flinched slightly at the unaccustomed touch of the nose pad between the two discs as Hal settled it into position. "What is it? What are you doing?" he asked.

"Just wait. You'll see," Hal said—and realized belatedly how prophetic those words were. "Keep your eyes closed and stand up."

He took Ingvar's arm and steadied him as he rose from the bench. Then he placed his hands on the big boy's wide shoulders and turned him to face the view below them.

"Open your eyes," he said.

It took several seconds. Then Ingvar uttered an incomprehensible grunt of surprise. He shook his head, turning it from side to side.

"Gorlog's eyebrows!" he said, his tone a mixture of surprise and delight. "I can see!"

He pointed to the dark line where the forest began. "I can see the trees!" he said excitedly. "I could only see a dark blur before. But now I see trees! And look there!" he continued, pointing down to the parkland, where a squad of soldiers were drilling. "There are people down there. I can see them!"

"What kind of people are they?" Hal asked quickly. He was eager to know how much the spectacles improved Ingvar's vision. Ingvar leaned forward.

"They're soldiers," he said. "I can see their shields and spears. And the sun is glinting off their armor. Oh, by my sainted auntie's mustache, this is just amazing!"

"Your sainted auntie had a mustache?" Hal asked and Ingvar nodded.

"That's how we told her from my uncle," Ingvar replied. "He was clean-shaven." He looked around excitedly, peering up at the pennants fluttering from the towers above them, seeing them as more than a blur of movement for the first time.

"Flags!" he said in delight. "Yellow and blue and purple flags! They're beautiful."

Hal looked at them and frowned. "They're just flags," he said, but Ingvar shook his head emphatically.

"To you, maybe. But to me, they're beautiful!" His head darted from side to side as he sought new sights. "Oh, this is just too wonderful for words! How did you ever come up with this idea? It's one of your very best ever!"

Hal shrugged. "You know, I'm not sure. I started to think when you said that if you narrowed your eyelids, things became clearer. Then I just sort of . . . experimented, I guess."

Ingvar shook his head. Reaching up, he carefully removed the wire frame, with its two glossy back discs, and looked at it in wonder.

"How can I ever thank you?"

A slow smile spread over Hal's features. "Just stop this nonsense about leaving the brotherband."

There was a bustle of commotion at the drawbridge when the hunting party returned, with their captive secured between Ulf and Wulf. The twins had a firm hold of an arm each. They held the would-be killer so that he was forced to stand on tiptoe, and frog-marched him up the grassy slope to the castle. Kloof pranced beside the three of them, moving around them in circles, emitting deep, threatening growls at the stranger.

At the drawbridge, the commander of the sentry detail approached and saluted Cassandra.

"What's this, your highness?" he asked.

"This," Cassandra stated, "is a man who tried to kill me. Would you send a messenger for my father, please?"

As the commander hurried to comply, several of the sentries

stepped forward and relieved the twins of their burden. The man was quickly tied, with his hands behind his back. His feet were secured as well, with only a short length of cord between them, so he could do no more than hobble. He cried aloud in pain as the bonds around his hands and elbows were pulled tight.

The sentries ignored him. Cassandra was a popular figure among the palace guards and the thought that someone had tried to harm her made them boil with rage.

Duncan arrived within minutes. He had descended the stairs from his quarters three at a time. As Cassandra explained what happened, and how the Skandians protected her, there was a further angry growl from the guards nearby.

Bad enough that someone had threatened the princess's life, they thought. But compounding that was the thought that she had been protected and saved by a group of foreigners. Their professional and national dignity was affronted and they jostled the man roughly as they led him inside.

"Take him to the guardhouse," the King ordered. Castle Araluen didn't have dungeons as such—Duncan considered such an idea inhumane. But the guardhouse was a secure area with cells where prisoners could be held securely.

They reached the guardhouse—a rather utilitarian room furnished with a large wooden table and a dozen straight-backed chairs where the duty sentries took their meals and breaks in between patrolling. Off to one side, a heavy, reinforced wooden door led to a passageway where half a dozen cells were situated. There were three guardsmen present when they arrived. They reacted with surprise at the sight of the King—he wasn't a frequent visitor—

and they scrambled to set their uniforms and equipment to rights.

Duncan indicated a heavy wooden chair set against the wall. "Put him there," he told the two sentries who were supporting the prisoner.

The sentries shoved him roughly into the chair and the assassin glowered around him. Duncan hooked another chair forward with his foot, placed it a meter in front of the prisoner and sat facing him, leaning forward. Cassandra and the Herons ranged around him, along with the guard commander. Stig held Kloof on her leash again. The big dog strained to reach the prisoner, who eyed her warily. Everyone else, he viewed with contempt.

"Send for Crowley and Gilan," the King told the guard commander, without taking his eyes from the assassin.

"And Hal," Thorn added. The commander nodded and hurried from the room.

Duncan turned and looked at Cassandra. "Perhaps you should leave us. This might get a little unpleasant."

But the princess shook her head, her cheeks flushed with color. "This piece of garbage tried to kill me and he would have succeeded if Thorn hadn't caught the quarrel. I want to know who sent him."

Duncan's eyes widened. This was the first he'd heard of that detail. He regarded Thorn with amazement.

"You *caught* the crossbow quarrel?"

Thorn nodded in a matter-of-fact manner. "No big thing," he said. "Sometimes a wooden hand can be useful."

Duncan shook his head. Gilan had told him of the shabby northman's skill and ability. He tried to imagine the dexterity and reflexes that had been necessary to catch a speeding quarrel.

"No big thing *indeed*," Duncan said. He looked back at the prisoner. "Where do you think he came from?"

"From his clothing and complexion, I'd say somewhere in Arrida," Cassandra replied.

Thorn noticed that the man's eyes flicked to her inadvertently when she said the word *Arrida*. Then he quickly regained control of his features and settled back into a masklike stillness.

The door opened to admit Crowley and Gilan. The two Rangers took in the scene and regarded the prisoner with surprise. The messenger who had reached them hadn't given them any details. In fact, he hadn't known any. The guard commander had simply told him to summon the two Rangers to the guard room.

"What's going on?" Crowley asked. But Duncan held up a hand to stop him.

"We'll explain when the Skandian captain gets here," he said. "No point in going over it all twice."

As he spoke, the door opened again and Hal hurried in. Like the Rangers, he frowned at the sight of the stranger tied up in the chair. Before he could ask the obvious question, Duncan spoke.

"Right. Now we're all here. There's been an attempt on my daughter's life. This man here"—he indicated the prisoner, although the others had quickly assumed that he was the would-be killer—"tried to shoot her with a crossbow." He looked at Hal. "Apparently, your man Thorn caught the quarrel in mid-flight."

If he expected a surprised reaction from Hal he was disappointed. The young skirl simply looked at Thorn and nodded approval.

"Good work," he said quietly. Thorn shrugged.

Duncan raised an eyebrow. The fact that Hal wasn't surprised or particularly impressed by Thorn's amazing feat told him a lot about these Skandians. Gilan had said they were a capable lot. It seemed the young Ranger was correct.

"Where did it happen?" Crowley asked. It was Stig who answered.

"We were just short of the forest. He was concealed in the undergrowth but Kloof here spotted him and gave the warning."

Kloof! said the huge dog, in response to her name. Hal, who was watching the prisoner closely, noticed that he flinched when the dog barked. Then he quickly rearranged his features again into a contemptuous sneer.

"So he was lying in wait for you?" Gilan asked. "It wasn't a chance encounter?" He addressed the question to Cassandra and she replied thoughtfully.

"No. He seemed to know we were coming. Mind you, the hunting trip was no secret. Lots of people knew about it and knew where we'd be heading, both here and in the village. We'd arranged to hire beaters later in the day, so word would have got around."

"What does he have to say for himself?" Crowley asked, jerking a thumb at the prisoner.

Duncan turned back to him, his face grim. "So far, not a lot. Thought we'd wait till everyone was here." He leaned forward and addressed the man now, their faces only a meter apart.

"Who are you and who sent you?" he demanded. The man sneered and looked away to one side. Duncan's hand shot forward, seized his chin and turned his head roughly so that he was facing him once more.

"I said, who are you?" he repeated.

The man gave a sniff of disdain. He tried to turn away again but Duncan's grip was like iron.

"I'm a civilized man," Duncan said, his tone low and dangerous. "But I'm also a father, and you attempted to kill my daughter. I warn you. Do not press me too far."

The man finally made eye contact with Duncan. "You can do nothing to me," he said with a noticeable accent. "My life is dedicated to the goddess Imrika and she will protect me."

They all exchanged puzzled looks. The name Imrika was unknown to them. Duncan turned back to the man.

"Tell us about this Imrika," he said but the man shook his head.

"You're an infidel. I will not talk of the Scorpion goddess to the likes of you."

Duncan breathed heavily. "You *will* talk or I will have you tortured."

He had no such intention. Indeed, he had nobody who might carry out the order to torture the man. But his voice gave no inkling of the fact and his eyes were determined. The Arridan sneered at him.

"You cannot harm me. Imrika will ensure I feel nothing."

Thorn stepped forward suddenly and slapped the man hard across the cheek. The chair rocked under the force of the blow and the assassin cried out in pain.

"Looks like she's not on the job," Thorn said. "You felt that all right. Next time I'll use my right hand." He held up the polished wood hook for the man to see.

"That's enough!" Duncan snapped angrily. "I won't have you hitting a helpless man."

"Suit yourself," Thorn said. "But he's a murderer and I don't see any reason to treat him with kid gloves."

Duncan glared at him and Hal stepped in. "Leave it, Thorn," he ordered, and Thorn turned away, muttering. Hal continued to the King, "I think I have an idea, your majesty. Can I have a word with you?"

They stepped away from the prisoner, retreating to the farthest corner of the room.

"He's not afraid of us," Hal said. "And he's sensed that you won't use torture on him."

Duncan shrugged. "I don't hold with it."

"Fair enough. But I've been watching him and there's one thing that might shake his tongue loose." He gestured to the dog, standing a few meters from the prisoner, straining against her leash.

"The dog?" Duncan said.

Hal nodded. "Every time she moves, he flinches. He tries to hide it, but he can't help himself. Let me ask him a few questions."

Duncan considered the suggestion, then nodded. "Go ahead," he said. "You can't do any worse than I have so far."

"Let's see what I can do," Hal said. He returned to where the others stood around the prisoner, Duncan following a pace behind him. He took the leash from Stig's hand and led Kloof closer to the bound man. The huge dog growled, a low rumbling sound in her chest. Hal was watching the prisoner, whose eyes were now riveted on Kloof. He saw them widen with fear.

"Up, Kloof," he said quietly, making a gesture to reinforce the order. Kloof reared up onto her hind legs, placing her massive forepaws on the man's shoulders, so that her face was a few centimeters from his. Hal saw a sheen of sweat break out across the man's brow as he strained back as far as he could from the dog.

"Speak," Hal said to Kloof. He gave the order in Skandian so that the man didn't realize that that was all he'd told the dog to do.

Instantly, Kloof began baying. Her hackles rose around her neck so that she seemed twice as large as before. The barking was deafening and her huge teeth were only centimeters from the cringing man's face.

The effect was instant.

"Stop! Stop!" he cried, terrified by the proximity of the seemingly crazed animal. "Call off the dog!"

Hal let her bark a few more times. The prisoner had his face turned away from her as far as it would go and his eyes were screwed tight shut in terror. Finally, Hal signaled for Kloof to stop.

"Down, girl," he said and she dropped back onto all fours. Quickly, he began shooting questions at the man before he could realize he was no longer in danger.

"Your name?" he snapped and the man answered, his voice shaking.

"Ushir," he said.

"What is the Scorpion cult?" Hal demanded.

"We serve the goddess Imrika."

"And who's she?" Hal maintained the pace of the questions, giving the man no time to think or relax.

"She is the goddess of death. The Scorpion goddess."

"So the Scorpion cult is a band of assassins?" Hal asked, and the man shrugged.

"We serve the goddess Imrika," he repeated. "If she tells us to kill, then we do."

"And why did she tell you to kill the princess?" He gestured toward Cassandra. Like the others, she was standing, fascinated, as the answers poured out of the man.

The would-be assassin glanced at her and licked his lips. For a moment he said nothing and Hal looked down at Kloof, raising his hand to command her. Instantly, Ushir began talking again.

"No! No! Leave the dog, I beg you. There is a *tolfah* against the princess."

Hal exchanged a quick glance with Crowley and Gilan. Both of them shrugged. He turned back to Ushir.

"What is a *tolfah?*"

The man hesitated, then looked at the dog again. Fortuitously, Kloof chose that moment to growl, and raised the hackles on her neck again.

"It is a compact with the goddess. Once it is in place, she demands the death of the object of the *tolfah*," he said, the words almost tumbling over themselves.

"So how do we cancel this compact?" Duncan asked.

Ushir turned to face him, a small amount of his self-confidence returning. "You can't," he said.

Then he closed his mouth and stared straight ahead, refusing to speak further. It was obvious that, dog or no dog, he had said as much as he was going to. Hal stepped back and the small group exchanged worried glances. Then Thorn broke the silence.

"Well, that could be awkward," he said.

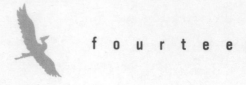

chapter   fourteen

I've sent a message by pigeon relay to Selethen," Duncan said. "I've asked him to find out more about this Scorpion cult. He'll be watching for you when you pass through the Narrows of Ikbar. Stay close to the Arridan coast and he'll signal you."

They were gathered on the jetty where *Heron* was moored, with the crew already on board. Hal and Thorn remained on the jetty with the King, Cassandra, Crowley and Gilan. They had learned nothing more from the assassin. Once he had time to think, Ushir apparently realized that if Duncan were reluctant to torture him, he was unlikely to allow the huge dog to savage him, so he had clammed up.

"This *tolfah* thing is a nasty business," Gilan said. "I never like it when religion gets mixed up with killing."

Crowley nodded agreement. "It's always difficult dealing with fanatics. You may have to destroy the cult itself."

Gilan shrugged. "Easier said than done."

"See if you can buy them off first," Duncan said. "Offer a donation to this Imrika. Build her a shrine or a temple or something."

"I'll try. But I don't think it'll be that simple," Gilan said.

Duncan nodded gloomily. "Neither do I. But try it anyway. And if you need to use force, ask Selethen for men. I'm sure he's not happy about this murderous cult operating within his borders."

Thorn tossed a small twig onto the surface of the river and watched as it circled aimlessly in the water beside the ship, drifting neither up nor downstream.

"Slack water," he said. "Tide'll be running out soon."

Hal nodded to him. "Time we were going," he announced. He shook hands with Duncan, Crowley and Cassandra.

"Wish I was coming with you," Cassandra said.

"Me too," Hal lied. He had no wish to have a high-ranking passenger on board. That sort of thing blurred the lines of command.

In fact, the previous night, Cassandra had argued in vain with her father over the fact that she wanted to accompany the expedition. But this time, Duncan would not be persuaded. He had let her have her own way over the hunting expedition and it nearly cost her life. He flatly refused to let her sail with the Herons.

"Some people get to have all the fun," Cassandra said reluctantly. "Travel safely, Lydia."

She had grown to like the serious-minded Limmatan girl in the brief time they had known each other. Cassandra respected and admired capable people and Lydia definitely fitted that mold.

Lydia simply nodded acknowledgment.

"Let's get on board," Hal said and he and Thorn stepped across the narrow gap onto the bulwark of the *Heron*, dropping lightly down to the deck. Gilan followed them, stepping more carefully. It seemed every spare inch of space was festooned with supplies: nets of bread and vegetables, extra water casks and joints of meat. Duncan hadn't stinted in supplying them with fresh food and Edvin had taken full advantage of it.

"Take in the bow line," Hal said and Stefan moved to comply. Held only by her stern line, *Heron* began to pivot out from the jetty as the wind took her. There was no need to fend her off. She was moored port side to, facing downriver, and the wind was from the north.

"Starboard sail," he ordered. Stefan and Jesper had been awaiting the command—the starboard yardarm and sail soared up the mast, catching the wind and bellying out. Ulf and Wulf, ready on the sheets, looked at Hal, but he held up a hand for them to wait.

"Stern line, Stig," he said. His first mate hauled in to gain a little slack. Then, before the line could tauten again, he flicked it with practiced ease, causing the looped end to leap free of the mooring bollard. *Heron* was now unleashed. The sail flapped noisily in the wind as she drifted out onto the river.

"Sheet home," Hal ordered. The twins obeyed and instantly the little ship was under power and surging away downstream, sped on her way by the wind and the tide, which had now turned, flowing toward the sea.

The small group standing on the jetty receded in their wake with remarkable speed until they rounded a bend in the river and Duncan, Crowley and Cassandra were lost to sight.

Hal held the ship in a narrow zigzag course, staying on a broad reach with the wind from the port side, obviating the need for constant changes of tack.

As the crew settled down for the journey, Ingvar reached into his side pocket and produced his spectacles, wrapped in the chamois cloth. He unwrapped them deliberately and slid them over his face, beaming in delight as he scanned from one side of the river to the other.

"This is fantastic!" he exclaimed. "Look! Trees! And a small hut! And there's a haystack—isn't it?" He added the last a little doubtfully.

Stefan reassured him, grinning. "It's a haystack right enough."

Ingvar looked at him gratefully. "Thought so," he said. "But I've never really seen one before, have I?"

The crew had learned of Hal's gift to Ingvar the previous day, while Hal and Thorn and Stig had been involved in questioning Ushir. They were all genuinely delighted for their big shipmate and they joined him in his impromptu game of "I spy."

"What's that, Ingvar?" Ulf said, pointing.

Ingvar leaned forward to peer in the direction Ulf indicated. "A farmer plowing his field."

"What about that?" This was Stefan, pointing to the opposite bank.

"A watermill. Is that what a watermill looks like?" This last was said in a tone of genuine wonder. Stefan laughed and clapped his big shipmate on the shoulder. Lydia stepped up closer to the steering platform and placed a hand on Hal's arm.

"That's a wonderful thing you've done for him," she said quietly.

Hal smiled at her. He was always pleased when one of his ideas worked. But this time it was doubly pleasing because he could see how much it meant to Ingvar. He shook his head as he thought how close they had come to losing him as a crewmember.

"Good to see him enjoying himself," he said.

And in fact, the novelty of clearer vision didn't seem to tire for Ingvar. He stood by the bulwark, his hand on one of the stays supporting the mast, his face lit up by the beaming smile as he named the objects they sailed past.

After several minutes of this, Thorn dropped down into the rowing well and produced a long, narrow bundle wrapped in canvas. "I've got something for you, Ingvar."

Ingvar turned curiously as Thorn moved toward him with the bundle.

"I figured you'll be taking a more active role in combat now that you can see who you're hitting," Thorn said. "And since it's a little late for you to start picking up the finer points of swordsmanship, I thought this might be a more useful weapon for you."

He unwrapped the canvas and dropped it on the deck. In his hand, he held a long weapon that looked like a cross between a heavy spear and a long-handled ax. The shaft was blackwood, almost as hard as iron, and the head combined a spear point at the end with an ax blade on one side and a curved, sharp-edged hook on the other.

Ingvar took the weapon as Thorn offered it and tested the weight and heft of it in his hands. "It's quite well balanced," he said thoughtfully. "I would have expected it to feel awkward and clumsy."

He moved it through the air in an experimental thrust, then

raised it above his head and performed a slow downstroke. As he had said, the weapon, seemingly clumsy in appearance, felt light and responsive in his hands—although a smaller person might have found its weight made it a little clumsy to handle.

"Yes," he continued, holding it out and admiring it. "I think I could do some damage with this."

"And to the right people," Stig put in, smiling.

Ingvar grinned at him. "I can almost hear you all breathing a giant sigh of relief," he said and there was a low murmur of laughter from the crew. "Where did you get it, Thorn? And what's it called?"

"I found it in the armory at Castle Araluen," Thorn told him. "After my amazing feat of plucking a speeding arrow from the sky and saving their princess, the armorers were only too happy to let me have it. It's called a voulge."

"Odd name," Ingvar said.

Thorn shrugged. "Well, you can call it anything you like, really. Call it a sticker-chopper if you want to. It's a versatile weapon." He took it back from Ingvar. "If you're fighting someone, you can chop 'em, stick 'em, hook 'em or pull 'em."

He demonstrated the various strokes as he listed them. In his hands, the voulge was obviously a weapon of considerable menace.

Edvin nodded, impressed. "That's very poetic, Thorn. You should consider putting that to music. Chop 'em, stick 'em, hook 'em or pull 'em. Has a definite ring to it."

"People say I've got a poetic bent," Thorn said, with false modesty. "I've composed more than one love song in my time."

"Well, I hope you didn't use 'chop 'em, stick 'em and pull 'em' in any love song," Stig declared, and nobody could really argue with that.

They made good speed down the river. The wind remained constant from the north, which boded well for their passage down the Narrow Sea. In mid-afternoon, the river widened noticeably, the banks receding to either side until they were low green headlands in the middle distance, and they sailed out into the ocean proper. As the *Heron* lifted beneath their feet to the first real roller, Hal let out a small sigh of contentment.

They were back at sea, and it felt vaguely like coming home.

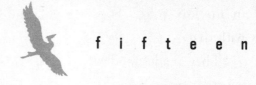

They made good speed down the east coast of Araluen. Occasionally, as the Narrow Sea lived up to its name, they could sight the coast of Gallica as well, out to the port side. Then the straits would widen and the low gray line that marked the land would recede into the distance again.

Thorn passed the time drilling Ingvar in the use of the voulge, and those members of the crew who were off duty gathered to watch.

Thorn stood facing Ingvar, with a long wooden shaft in his hand to simulate the voulge. He made sure he stood well out of Ingvar's reach, however, as he demonstrated the various attacking and defensive strokes in a drill sequence—a sequence that became progressively faster.

"Thrust! Parry! Back! Advance! Overhead! Side stroke! Parry! Butt stroke!"

He called the moves in a random pattern, never repeating the same pattern twice, demanding a different sequence of moves each time.

"Stay on your toes, Ingvar!" he called. "Remember the net!"

"Who could forget it?" Stefan grinned. In the early days of their pursuit of the Magyaran pirate Zavac, Thorn had made them practice their fighting moves while standing knee deep in a large rope net. Strangely, Ingvar had proven to be quite adept at this, particularly when Thorn told him to close his eyes and imagine the net in place.

Ingvar nodded. His brow was creased with concentration above the dark brown circles that hid his eyes.

"Parry! Parry! Parry! Back! Thrust! No, use your legs when you thrust, not just your arms!"

"His arms are pretty powerful," Stig said in mild protest.

Thorn turned to face him. "Maybe so. But if you put the strength of his legs behind that spear thrust, nothing could stop it. He could knock over a horse."

"That's not so easy," Stig said skeptically.

Thorn raised an eyebrow. "I've done it."

His tone of voice left no room for discussion. Stig held up a hand in surrender and fell quiet while Thorn went back to drilling Ingvar, performing the moves himself with speed, precision and a deceptive smoothness.

"How did Thorn get so good with a voulge? You people don't use them, do you?" Gilan said softly to Hal, who was at the tiller.

The young skirl shrugged. "It's a weapon. He's good at weapons."

After forty minutes, Ingvar was soaked with perspiration and panting with exhaustion. Thorn finally took pity on him.

"All right. That's enough for today. But keep practicing."

Ingvar, his face scarlet, his shoulders and chest heaving, nodded. He didn't trust himself to speak. He slumped down on the deck, his feet in the rowing well, and held the voulge between his knees. Thorn had given him a leather head cover for the weapon, which would prevent the salt water gathering on it and rusting it. He rewrapped the cover and laid the long weapon down.

"How did the spectacles work out?" Hal called to him. Ingvar looked up and grinned tiredly.

"They're great. It really helps when I can see what I'm doing. One thing, though . . ." He hesitated, not wishing to criticize Hal's brilliant invention. Hal gestured for him to speak up and he continued, a little reluctantly. "It's just that, when I get hot and sweaty, they slip down on my nose. And several times, I thought they might even fly right off my face."

Hal nodded. It was a sensible comment and one he thought he should have foreseen.

"I'll attach laces to the earpieces so you can tie them firmly in place," he suggested.

Ingvar smiled, glad the solution was so simple. "Yes. That should fix it."

"Let me have them when I've finished this spell on the helm," Hal told him. He glanced at Thorn, who had moved to join Hal, Stig and Gilan by the steering platform.

"He's not bad at all," Hal said, nodding in Ingvar's direction.

"He's good," Thorn told them. "Ingvar has always been good. He's fast and well coordinated, particularly for someone his size. His problem has always been confidence. His lack of confidence, and his poor vision, have always made him clumsy. Now that he can see what he's doing, his natural abilities are coming to the fore."

He glanced around the small group. "Anyone else for a bit of weapons drill?"

"I'm on watch for another hour," Hal said quickly. Practice sessions with Thorn were exhausting, and often painful, even with the wooden drill weapons they carried. Especially with those, he amended, as Thorn tended not to hold back when he was using them. With real weapons, he was a little more accommodating.

"I wouldn't mind a workout," Gilan said casually.

They all looked at him with interest. Lydia had told them how he had fought several guardsmen at once when they were retreating from the gold market in Socorro.

Thorn gestured now to the stack of wooden weapons by the arms chest. "Pick out a sword and get ready."

Gilan took off his cloak and folded it carefully. Then he tested two or three of the swords, swishing them experimentally through the air until he found one whose weight and balance seemed right. He unclipped his sword and scabbard from his belt and rested it against the railing. He'd lost a sword in the fight at the gold market, throwing it at one of the attackers in order to gain time to escape through the ceiling. Upon his return to Castle Araluen, he'd taken the opportunity to replace it.

Now he looked at Thorn and raised his eyebrows. "Ready?"

But Thorn shook his head. "I think we might see a match between you and young Stig," he said. "It'll be good experience for him."

Gilan looked at the strapping first mate and smiled. "Sounds good to me." He took up one of the padded practice jackets and slipped into it, then donned a heavily padded gauntlet.

Stig grunted agreement. He donned a padded jacket and gauntlet as well, then selected a practice wooden ax from the weapon stack. Then he unhooked his round shield from its spot on the bulwark and slid his left arm and hand through the straps.

"You going to use a shield?" he asked Gilan.

The Ranger shook his head. "A sword will do for now."

They both looked expectantly at Thorn. The crew had gathered a little closer to watch. A few of them were calling encouragement to Stig.

"Away you go," Thorn said mildly.

Stig reacted instantly, driving forward and aiming a massive overhead blow at the Ranger, expecting him to leap back, off balance, to avoid it. But Gilan stood his ground and flicked his sword at the descending ax, deflecting it so that the wooden blade thudded into the deck planks. Then, in the blink of an eye, he responded, thrusting the sword at Stig's unprotected chest.

Only to feel a jarring sensation in his arm and wrist as the heavy wooden shield came round to block his thrust.

"Oh, nice work, both of them," Thorn muttered to Hal. Stig was every bit as fast as Gilan, although he sensed the Ranger might have the edge in experience and technique.

Now the Ranger began a lightning-fast series of strokes at the Skandian youth. Backhands, forehands, overheads and straight thrusts. Stig gave ground slowly, but each blow was blocked by either his ax or his shield. At one point, he caught the descending sword in the narrow gap between the wooden blade of his ax and the shaft. He twisted his wrist violently, trapping the blade, nearly wrenching it from Gilan's grip. The Ranger leapt back hurriedly to disengage, sliding his sword free in the nick of time. He grunted in admiration and nodded to Stig, acknowledging a good move.

But Stig wasn't looking for praise. As Gilan withdrew, he leapt forward once more and slammed his shield into the Ranger's left shoulder, sending him flying across the deck and crashing to the planks.

Stig followed up with a huge downstroke but Gilan avoided it just in time, rolling away. As he did, he kicked Stig's legs from under him and brought the first mate thudding to the deck beside him.

Catlike, they both regained their feet at the same moment and faced each other again. Gilan was the first to reengage. He drew back his sword for a downward cut, then, with bewildering speed, flicked it to his left hand instead. The move was totally unexpected and Stig felt the light touch of the wooden tip against his chest.

Several of the crew groaned as they realized their man had been defeated. They had never seen that happen before.

Jesper quietly cursed to himself. He should have taken bets on this, he thought.

"That's it!" Thorn called, and the two of them stepped back, breathing heavily.

"Nice move," Thorn said to Gilan.

Stig nodded his agreement. "I never saw that coming," he said. "I'll be careful of that in future."

"Like to try another bout?" Thorn said.

Gilan realized that the old sea wolf had donned his fighting hand—the massive club that Hal designed for him to replace his missing right hand and forearm. He nodded, his eyes narrowed. It would be an interesting weapon to face, he thought. In his left hand, Thorn held a small, bowl-shaped metal shield.

They shaped up to each other. Jesper, furious, realized it was too late to organize bets once more.

"Call time, Hal," Thorn said, his eyes fixed on the slim young Ranger.

"Time!" Hal called and the bout began.

Gilan was expecting the massive club to be used in a downward or sideways arc. Consequently, Thorn's opening gambit caught him by surprise. Thorn jabbed forward with the club, sliding inside Gilan's guard and thudding into his ribs. The old sea wolf pulled the thrust at the last minute but Gilan realized that, if this had been a real fight, he would be crippled, with several ribs fractured. It had taken his shaggy-haired opponent a matter of seconds to deliver a winning blow, he realized. He shook his head in new admiration of the old fighter, then shaped up again.

"Let's keep going," he said and, before he finished speaking, he darted his sword forward in a series of rapid thrusts, his right foot stepping and stamping to deliver more power to the attack.

Thorn withdrew, blocking and deflecting with his small shield, the club-hand always in readiness to exploit any gap in Gilan's defense.

But there was none. Gilan's thrusts were fast and economical. He was never out of balance, never allowing an opportunity for Thorn to exploit.

At the same time, Gilan realized that his series of rapid thrusts were causing Thorn no problem at all. The sea wolf parried or blocked each one, the small shield seeming to form an impenetrable barrier that was always in the right place at just the right time. The bearded warrior's reflexes were fantastic, Gilan realized.

Time to try something else, he thought. He withdrew a pace, and they eyed each other carefully, waiting for the next move. It came from Gilan. He threw up the sword for an overhand stroke. But at the last second, he flipped it sideways to his left hand, just as he had done with Stig.

It never reached his left hand.

Somewhere on the way, Thorn's club flashed up and struck it, sending it spinning high in the air, over Gilan's head. Stig reached up and caught it just before it disappeared over the side into the sea.

The crew cheered Thorn's success. One hand or not, he was one of the greatest fighters they had ever seen. One of the greatest Gilan had seen too, the tall Ranger realized.

"Thought you'd try that sooner or later," Thorn said.

Gilan smiled ruefully. "I should have remembered. You're the man who can pluck speeding arrows out of thin air."

Thorn nodded. "True. But you're giving that move away," he said.

Gilan's smile turned to a look of surprise. "What am I doing?" he said. "Is it my eyes? What?"

Thorn shook his head. "Just before you do it, you flex the fingers of your left hand, ready to catch the sword. I saw you do it with Stig and I was waiting for it."

Gilan looked down at his left hand now. "I never realized," he said softly. "Thank you. That's a habit I'll have to break."

"I'd advise it," Thorn said.

Gilan regarded him with new-found respect. Very few warriors would have noticed that minimal movement when he had fought Stig—or been able to see it again in the heat of battle. Gilan realized that Thorn had possibly saved his life in some future combat. He nodded his gratitude to the old warrior. Thorn recognized the nod for what it was—an honest and heartfelt gesture of thanks. He turned to the rest of the crew.

"Anyone else fancy themselves against the great arrow catcher?" he challenged with a grin. The Herons hurriedly looked away, avoiding eye contact and calling their refusals.

All except Lydia.

"I'll take you on, old man," she said and Thorn raised his eyebrows in surprise.

"But we'll do it onshore, fifty paces apart. And we'll see how many of my darts you can pluck out of thin air before I skewer you."

This time, Jesper realized he had time to get organized.

"Taking bets now!" he shouted eagerly. "Two to one Lydia. Even money Thorn!"

Thorn regarded him quizzically. "I think you're selling her short," he said. "I'd take two to one on her anytime."

everal days later, they turned east, and sailed through the gap that was known as the Narrows of Ikbar. The two headlands, one marking the southernmost extremity of Iberion, the other the northernmost of Arrida, were visible on either horizon.

As they entered the Narrows, the constant wind from the north, which had accompanied them down the coast of Araluen, became fluky and sporadic, as it was masked by the Iberian headland. The sail surged and flapped and Hal was contemplating setting the crew to the oars when the gap widened, the wind stabilized and they sailed into clear air again.

"Do you think this Ikbar person was really thin?" Ulf said, with mock innocence, trying to recommence the nonsense dialogue they had snared Gilan into on the previous occasion when they had passed the Narrows. But the Ranger wasn't falling into that trap again. He eyed the twins steadily until they realized he wasn't going to bite.

Instead, Wulf searched for a new point of contention.

"It's a strange language, this Arridan, isn't it?" he said. His brother had no idea where he was going with this, but he sensed another leg pull and agreed instantly.

That, in itself, was sufficient to warn the others that the two had something up their sleeves. Ulf and Wulf never agreed on anything, unless they were seeking to make fun of a third person.

"Very strange," Ulf said emphatically.

His brother continued. "I mean, look at the lack of variety in their names. We're hunting a man called Iqbal, and this demi-semi-wemi god, or whatever he was, that they named the Narrows after, was called Ikbar."

"I see your point," Ulf replied promptly, although he most certainly didn't. His brother continued to expound.

"Wouldn't you think they could have come up with two names that weren't so similar? I mean, there's only two letters difference between Ikbar and Iqbal. That's very odd, I think . . ."

"Very odd indeed," Ulf agreed.

Stig and Hal exchanged a glance, waiting to see if any of the crew would bite. But Lydia squashed the debate conclusively.

"That's rich," she said, "coming from two people called Ulf and Wulf."

Several of the crew laughed. Ulf and Wulf were taken aback by her logic. For a moment, neither of them could think of a reply. Then Wulf said:

"That's totally different. It doesn't matter that our names are so similar."

"That's right," said Ulf, nodding emphatically, and looking to his brother for a further explanation.

"Because nobody takes any notice of Ulf, so who cares if his name is a poor cousin to mine," Wulf concluded. In the absence of any discussion with the rest of the crew, he was content to start yet another argument with his brother. Ulf, predictably, rose to the bait.

"Nobody takes any notice of me?" he said indignantly. "What brings you to say that?"

But Wulf said nothing, looking through his twin as if he wasn't there.

Ulf's face reddened with anger. "Did you hear me? Explain yourself!"

Wulf jumped, in mock surprise. "Oh, I'm sorry," he said. "I wasn't taking any notice of you, just like the rest of the world."

"Ingvar?" There was a warning tone in Hal's voice. The big boy was seated amidships and he looked up now.

"Yes, Hal?"

"Have you ever wondered what it looks like when you throw one of these idiots overboard?"

Ingvar nodded. "As a matter of fact, I have," he said. "The sound of the splash is quite edifying but I've always wanted to actually see one of them hit the waves."

"This could be your lucky day," Hal said. "Put on your spectacles."

Ingvar reached into his side pocket and produced the wrapped spectacles. He slipped them on, then took a minute or so to tie the restraining laces that Hal had fitted to them. He looked up, glanced around and beamed. He was still enjoying the novelty of being able to see his surroundings in greater detail.

"Ready, Hal," he said. But Ulf and Wulf had wisely fallen silent, retreating back to their post by the sail trimming sheets, as if to remind Hal of their importance when it came to maneuvering the ship.

"Maybe later, Ingvar," said Hal, hiding a smile. Ulf and Wulf busied themselves making minor and totally unnecessary changes to the sail trim.

Lydia laughed softly. "Look at them," she said. "Just as quiet as two little mice—until they get another stupid idea through their heads."

"Sail!" called Edvin, who was the duty lookout. He'd been standing in the bow of the ship, scanning the horizon in a hundred-and-eighty-degree arc to either side. Now he was pointing to port, at a point halfway along the ship. As the strange ship continued to move west, the point changed to farther astern.

"Going about to port!" Hal called. He could see the ship now. Her sail was a small white square on the horizon. The crew moved to their sailing stations and he brought the ship through the eye of the wind and onto the opposite tack, so they were heading toward the other ship. Edvin hauled himself up onto the bulwark, steadying himself on a stay, and shaded his eyes for a clearer look at the newcomer.

"Can you see what she is, Edvin?" Hal called. There was a pause, then Edvin shook his head.

"Not very big, Hal. I'd say she's probably a fishing boat."

"Not a fighting ship then?" Hal asked. In these waters, the ship could be anything from an innocent trader or fishing smack to a vicious corsair, crammed with men, ready to overwhelm any passing ship.

"She looks like a coastal trader. There only appear to be half a dozen men on deck."

"Could be more hidden below, of course," Hal said. He wasn't unduly worried. If the approaching ship turned out to be hostile, he was confident his crew could take care of any mischief they might be planning. "Stig, Ingvar, ready the Mangler, please."

The two moved forward and unlashed the canvas covering over the Mangler—the massive crossbow mounted in the ship's bow. Ingvar opened the ammunition locker behind the weapon and selected a standard bolt. He stood ready with it. Stig, meanwhile, had dropped onto the operator's stool and was swiveling the Mangler to bear on the approaching ship, walking it round in a small arc with his feet.

"Lydia," said Hal, "stand by to give them a hand."

She nodded and touched the flights of one of the darts in her quiver, reassuring herself that it would fall easily to hand if she needed to load. "I'm ready, Hal."

"This is great!" they heard Ingvar call, as he traversed the Mangler to keep it trained in the direction of the unknown ship. "It's so much better when I can see what's happening." In the past, of course, he'd had to rely on directions from Stig or Lydia to keep the Mangler even roughly on line with its target.

Stig turned and grinned at him. "Just remember to obey directions when we get close," he warned and Ingvar nodded enthusiastically.

"Should we load?" Stig asked.

Hal hesitated, glancing at Thorn. "What do you say, Thorn?"

The old sea wolf pursed his lips thoughtfully, then shook his head.

"I wouldn't bother," he said. "They look harmless enough and if they do try to start something, Lydia can teach them a lesson with the atlatl."

"I might take a hand in that as well," said Gilan. The Ranger had unslung the massive longbow he carried over one shoulder and was standing close to the port bulwark, an arrow nocked, ready to draw and shoot at a moment's notice.

"As you say," Thorn said. "Between you two, they should get a very nasty surprise."

Then any doubts they might have had as to the strange ship's intentions were dispelled.

"She's letting her sheets fly!" Edvin called. Instantly, the regular white rectangle that was the vessel's sail was transformed into a fluttering shapeless mass as her crew cast loose the ends of the ropes that held it in place against the wind. It was a sign of surrender, or of peaceful intentions. The boat was no longer under way and couldn't maneuver to attack them—or to avoid any attack they might make. A figure in the stern stood on the railing and waved a greeting.

"Looks like they want to talk. I'll come up alongside her," Hal said. "Stefan, get ready to throw a line across to her."

Stefan waved a hand in acknowledgment and moved to the rail as the *Heron* slid smoothly toward the other craft, aiming to come close alongside. Ulf and Wulf were poised, ready to de-power their own sail when the moment came.

As Hal judged the moment to be right, he called a rapid series of orders.

"Let go the sheets! Down sail! Send a line across, Stefan!"

The sail lost its shape and the yardarm came sliding down as Jesper, assisted now by Edvin, cast off the halyards and let it fall. Ulf and Wulf helped them gather in the billowing, flapping canvas as Stefan stood poised by the rail, the weighted end of a line in his hand, letting it swing idly back and forth, gathering momentum.

"Now, Stefan!" Hal called and the line snaked across the gap between the two craft, curving down in a smooth arc to land on the other boat's foredeck. Two of her crew, which Hal could now see comprised only five men, hauled it in and made it fast.

The way came off *Heron* as she slid alongside, then Ulf, Wulf, Edvin and Stefan bent their backs to the line and hauled the two ships together, until their wicker fenders were grating and creaking as the two hulls alternately crushed then released them.

Hal tied off the tiller to stop it slapping back and forth with the sea's motion, and strode a few paces forward.

"What boat is that?" he called. His counterpart, at the tiller of the other ship, cupped his hands round his mouth to reply.

"We're the *Gerbil*," he called. "We have a message for the Araluen Ranger Gilan, from *Wakir* Seley el'then."

Hal glanced curiously at Gilan.

"That's Selethen's full name," Gilan informed him.

Hal nodded and called back to the *Gerbil*. "Come aboard and pass your message." Out of the corner of his mouth, he muttered to Lydia, "Stay alert, Lydia, in case this is a trick. If I give you the word, skewer him."

He liked the sound of that word—Lydia had used it when she challenged Thorn a few days earlier. It seemed an appropriate description of what happened when one of her darts found its mark. Unobtrusively, she clipped a dart into the atlatl.

The *Gerbil's* skipper made his way forward on his own craft to the point where the two hulls met. The Arridan boat was much smaller than *Heron*. He stepped aboard and nodded to Stig, who was in the bow. Stig indicated Gilan and Hal. The other skipper strode easily aft to the stern to meet them. The uneven pitching and surging of the two hulls tied together caused him no problems. He was an experienced sailor, Hal noted.

He stopped as he came to Hal, glancing quickly to either side and taking in Thorn, Lydia and Gilan—a somewhat disparate group that left him slightly confused. Being a captain himself, his natural instinct was to address the ship's skipper first.

"I am Kav al Bedin," he said, "master of the craft *Gerbil.*" He touched the fingers of his right hand to his lips, forehead, then lips again in the traditional Arridi greeting. Hal declined to try to mirror the greeting, choosing instead to incline his head slightly, as befitted the captain of a larger vessel.

"I am Hal Mikkelson," he said, "skirl of the vessel *Heron*. And this"—he indicated Gilan, who was standing half a pace behind him—"is the Araluen Ranger Gilan, the man you are seeking."

Kav turned to Gilan and repeated the ritual greeting. "My lord Seley el'then sends you his greetings, Ranger." Gilan, like Hal, responded with a slight inclination of his head. Kav continued. "He has important news for you about the brigand Iqbal and wishes you to meet with him in the township of Al Shabah."

Gilan turned to Hal. "Al Shabah is a small town about thirty kilometers along the coast. It's where Erak was taken prisoner by the Arridi."

Hal raised an eyebrow. "Do you think there's anything significant in that fact?" he asked suspiciously.

But Gilan shook his head. "No. It's a convenient place to meet with him. It's the nearest town of any size in this part of the coast. I doubt he's planning any treachery. He's a trusted ally these days."

Hal nodded. "Then we'd best get under way and see what this important news is."

PART TWO

TABORK

The entrance to Al Shabah's harbor was narrow and there was a tricky crosscurrent running along the coast, so Hal chose to enter harbor under oars.

Heron slipped smoothly between the moles on either side of the harbor entrance. *Gerbil*, whose captain was familiar with the conditions, was under sail some forty meters in her wake. As they came to the wider, calmer waters within the breakwater, *Gerbil*'s skipper signaled for his sail handlers to sheet home more firmly and accelerated to come alongside the *Heron*.

He pointed to the long wharf directly opposite the harbor mouth. A green flag stirred lazily in the breeze on a tall flagpole set back from the wharf.

"Go alongside the wharf, captain," he called. "Seley el'then's men will meet you there."

Then he waved farewell, leaned on his tiller and sheered off, heading for a side channel in the harbor.

Gilan looked around the busy little port. There were trading ships of all shapes and sizes crammed inside the protective breakwaters. The long government wharf, however, had been left free for the *Heron.*

"Look familiar?" Thorn asked him, noticing the Ranger's gaze wandering round the harbor. Gilan, of course, had visited Al Shabah before, as part of the delegation that had come to ransom Oberjarl Erak from the Arridi.

"Pretty much," Gilan replied. Then he frowned slightly. "There's a good many more ships here than last time."

Thorn shrugged. "Maybe trade is good at the moment."

Hal brought the ship neatly alongside. The mooring lines were passed to men on the stone wharf and fenders tossed over the side of the ship to protect the timbers and paintwork from the rough stone. The *Heron*'s deck lay well below the level of the wharf. A ladder was passed down and lashed into place.

Hal turned to Gilan and gestured to the ladder. "This is your show," he said. "Who do you want with you?"

Gilan considered for a second or two. "For the moment, I think you and Thorn will be enough," he said. Hal glanced round to see if Thorn had heard.

The one-armed sea wolf nodded. "Wouldn't want to overwhelm them."

Hal turned to Stig, who was supervising the crew as they stowed oars, yardarm and sail.

"Take charge here, Stig," he said. "We're going ashore."

Stig nodded briefly, then turned back to the task of furling the sail tightly. When they had lowered it before entering harbor, the sail handlers had simply bundled it up and thrown a line around it to secure it.

The crew paused briefly in their various tasks as Gilan mounted the ladder, followed by Hal and Thorn. Then a curt command from Stig brought them back to their duties. As first mate, he was the jealous guardian of *Heron*'s appearance. It wouldn't do to have her looking untidy or slipshod in front of a bunch of foreigners. He demanded that everything be neat and shipshape when they moored in a new port.

Gilan stepped onto the crushed stone that covered the surface of the wharf and moved to one side, waiting for Thorn and Hal to join him. He raised his eyebrows as he saw a tall, thin figure striding across the wharf to greet them. A file of ten soldiers stood at ease behind him, their armor and accoutrements highly polished and gleaming in the bright sun.

"Here's an honor for you, Thorn," he said quietly. "You're about to be greeted by Seley el'then himself."

The tall Arridi nobleman reached them and bowed slightly at the waist, touching his hand to lips, brow and lips in the traditional manner. Then he straightened and his narrow, swarthy face and dark beard were split by a wide smile of genuine pleasure.

"Friend Gilan," he said. "It's good to see you again."

"And you, Selethen," Gilan replied and, stepping forward, he embraced the Arridan. Although Gilan was relatively tall for a Ranger, Selethen towered over him. They released each other and stepped back.

"Selethen, let me introduce Hal Mikkelson, the captain of our ship, and his battle leader, Thorn."

Selethen bowed gravely to them, appraising them keenly.

"Welcome to Al Shabah, gentlemen," he said.

"Good day, *Wakir* Selethen," Hal replied. Gilan had coached them in the correct greeting for Selethen, which, in recognition of Skandian custom, consisted of his title and name. Skandians were not big on addressing people as "your honor" or "your lordship."

"Morning, *Wakir*," Thorn said cheerfully.

Selethen eyed him closely. One hand missing, but a hearty and confident manner. There was no sense of self-pity about the man. He obviously wasn't one to sit around bemoaning his loss. And the polished wood gripping hook that replaced his right hand was a fascinating object, obviously fashioned by a master craftsman.

"Thorn," Selethen mused. "Is it just Thorn, northman? Or do you have a second name?"

Thorn's grin widened. "Some call me Hookyhand, your *Wakirship*."

Selethen found his own severe features creasing into a grin in response. There was something essentially likeable about this shabby, shaggy warrior.

"Behave yourself, Thorn," the young captain said and, instantly, the older man nodded deferentially.

"Whatever you say, Hal," Thorn replied.

Selethen nodded. That was interesting. The younger man was barely more than a boy, yet he obviously had the respect and loyalty of the one-handed Thorn. He looked at Gilan again.

"As ever, friend Gilan, you are surrounded by interesting people," he said.

Gilan smiled in return. "You have no idea how interesting, Selethen."

"I've arranged for you to be quartered in the guesthouse you used last time you were here."

Gilan nodded his thanks. "That will be most suitable. Is there room for the entire crew?" On his previous visit, the crew of *Wolfwind* were kept confined on board ship. But times had changed and the Arridans no longer viewed Skandians as enemies.

"That will pose no problem," Selethen said. "I'll have one of my officers escort you there. You can bathe and change and I'll have food brought to the house. Then we'll meet to discuss matters. There's been a development that I think you'll find significant. Iqbal is quite close to hand."

He clicked his fingers and a young officer stepped forward from the squad behind him, his boots grating on the crushed stone.

"Lieutenant Samur, please see our friends and their crew to the guesthouse and make sure they have everything they need."

The young officer slapped his right palm across the silver breastplate he wore with a resounding smack. "Yes, my lord."

Selethen nodded to Gilan. "Rest, relax and refresh yourselves. Then we'll talk. The lieutenant will bring you to the *khadif* in two hours."

Rested, relaxed and refreshed, the *Heron*'s party presented themselves at the *khadif*, Selethen's official residence, the equivalent of a customshouse in Araluen or Erak's Great Hall in Skandia.

It was a graceful two-story building, with a wide colonnaded front that provided shade from the hot Arridan sun. Lieutenant

Samur led them through the massive front doors, then through a large anteroom and into the vast official hall itself. Their soft boots whispered on the blue tiled floor. The room was long and high ceilinged, with the second story consisting of galleries around three sides, where the town's officials worked. Al Shabah was the capital of the province and Selethen was the *Wakir*, or local ruler, answerable to the *Emrikir*, Arrida's paramount ruler.

Halfway down the hall, Samur directed them to one of the many rooms that lined either side, set beneath the upper galleries.

"Lord Selethen will meet with you in his private office," he explained. The four visitors, for this time Hal had suggested that Stig should join them, followed him as he led the way to an ornately carved door and knocked. Selethen's voice bade them enter and Samur held the door open, deferring to them as they went in, with Gilan leading the way.

It was a comfortable room, with a breeze coming through large windows screened by stone latticework that kept out the glare of the sun. There was a low table, with plump, soft cushions around it and a brass coffeepot and tiny cups set on it.

Selethen rose easily from his seat on one of the cushions and gestured for them to make themselves comfortable. Then, after Samur had poured them all coffee—and excellent coffee it was, Gilan thought—Selethen came straight to the point.

"Good news and bad news," he said. "The renegade Iqbal is currently in the town of Tabork, a fortified town some forty kilometers down the coast."

"I take it that's the good news. What's the bad?" Gilan said.

"The bad news is that it *is* a fortified town. It's secured by a wall and he has several hundred soldiers with him. The *Emrikir* has tasked me with winkling him out."

"The *em-who-rir*?" Thorn asked, frowning.

Selethen shifted his gaze to the old sea wolf. "My immediate superior. Similar to your Oberjarl."

"Then we'd best go and start winkling," Stig said. "If it's forty kilometers away, we can be there in half a day."

"It's not so simple," Selethen said. "As I said, it's a walled town and I have only cavalry at my disposal. I have no heavy siege weapons, nor enough men to lay siege to Tabork."

"I take it the harbor itself is well defended?" Hal said.

"Very well defended. And besides, your little ship couldn't carry enough men to stage a surprise raid, if that's what you were thinking."

Hal nodded. "The idea had crossed my mind."

"Well, it gets worse. Iqbal has joined forces with a Hellenese corsair named Philip the Bloodyhand. He has a large war galley in the harbor. As a matter of fact, they've been disrupting coastal traffic for some weeks now, dashing out to snap up any trader foolish enough to pass by." He spread his hands. "You may have noticed how many ships are in our harbor. Their captains are unwilling to go farther east until the situation is resolved."

"Why don't they just go farther out to sea and bypass Tabork?" Hal asked.

"There's a problem with that." Selethen rose and moved to where a large chart of the Constant Sea was displayed on one wall. "This is Tabork," he said, indicating a town set on the coast. "To the north, there's a relatively narrow passage of clear water, close to the coast. Then there's a huge range of small islands, reefs and shallow water, reaching almost a hundred kilometers to the north. It's a dangerous, treacherous stretch of water, known as the Lion's Teeth."

"Very poetic. We've had our share of shoals and reefs recently, thank you," said Thorn. During their recent voyage to Socorro, they had blundered into shoal water off the Araluen coast, nearly losing the *Heron* in the process.

"To make matters even more difficult," Selethen continued, "the prevailing wind is from the north. If a merchant ship tries to beat into it to work its way round the shoals, Philip's galley can easily run them down and capture them. That's why he and Iqbal took the town in the first place. It's an ideal base of operations for them. They've taken over fifty ships in the past few months."

"Tell us about this galley," Hal said.

Selethen paused. He wasn't a sailor and he needed to muster his thoughts before he described the galley to the Skandians.

"She's called the *Ishtfana*—that means Sea Leopard. She's big, probably three times the size of your ship, and she has twenty oars a side. She has a small mast and she can mount a sail, but her main motive power comes from her oars. She's long and very narrow. And the captains of ships in harbor here say she's very fast."

"But probably not very seaworthy in bad weather," Thorn said. Long, narrow galleys rarely were.

Selethen shrugged. "That I couldn't say. In addition to her rowers, she usually carries a fighting crew of about twenty men."

"What about the oarsmen? Will they fight?" Stig asked. But the *Wakir* shook his head.

"They're slaves. They're kept chained to the oars."

"That's a relief," said Thorn. "We'll only be outnumbered two to one."

The three Skandians exchanged glances.

"Sounds like a tough nut to crack," Stig said.

"Tough, but not impossible," Thorn replied.

Hal said nothing. He was deep in thought. Gilan watched him closely. He had an idea that the young skirl was hatching a plan.

"You're thinking you can fight *Ishtfana*?" Selethen asked.

Hal looked up at him. "I'm thinking we might be able to use her."

T he others pressed him for details but Hal begged off saying more.

"It's just a rough idea at the moment," he said. "Let me sort out the details and I'll tell you. Give me an hour or so."

Hal requested a copy of the map of the Arridan coast, and another of Tabork, if one was available. Selethen sent a servant to fetch both charts, and when they arrived, the visitors drained the last drops of their coffee. Selethen noticed Gilan's longing gaze on the coffeepot, which was still a quarter full.

"There is coffee at the guesthouse, friend Gilan," he said with a smile and Gilan nodded his thanks.

They made their farewells to Selethen and rose to leave, with Lieutenant Samur ready to escort them back to the guesthouse. As they left the room, Hal glanced back and saw that the *Wakir* was already engrossed in a series of reports and lists of figures. There was a lot of detail work in being a *Wakir*, he thought.

Back at the guesthouse, Hal went to his room and shut himself in. The others made themselves comfortable in the large sitting room, recounting to the rest of the crew what had taken place at the *khadif*.

"What's this Selethen like, Gilan?" Lydia asked. She knew little of the inhabitants of the countries that ringed the Constant Sea and, knowing nothing, she had deep suspicions of them. Gilan paused before answering.

"Brave, loyal and a man of his word. Absolutely trustworthy. And he's an excellent warrior and leader. Quite frankly, we couldn't ask for a better man to be helping us."

Lydia was surprised at his unstinting praise of the Arridan nobleman. But she knew Gilan well enough to trust his opinion. He wasn't a man who was easily fooled. Nor was he the type to praise someone for the sake of being polite. If he said Selethen was a man to be trusted, Lydia knew she could believe him.

Around the middle of the day, the house servants set up a charcoal grill in the inner courtyard of the house and began grilling skewers of seasoned lamb meat. The delicious smell permeated the house, even drawing Hal out from behind his closed door to join them. The Herons sat on low benches in the courtyard, shaded from the sun by striped canvas awnings, while the servants passed around plates of sizzling lamb, topped with soft fried onions that had been prepared on a hot plate over the coals. There were also bowls of a green, leafy salad, dressed with a mixture of olive oil, pepper and lemon juice, and another salad, which consisted of cracked wheat, chopped parsley, mint, and finely diced tomatoes. Stig tasted it on a piece of warmed flat bread and nodded his approval.

"That's great!" he said enthusiastically. "What's it called?" he asked one of the serving staff.

"It's called tabouleh, lord," the man told him, and Stig filed that information away for future reference.

If the tabouleh was good, the lamb was positively heavenly. Marinated in lemon juice and oil, it was pink and tender and delicious, particularly when sprinkled with more lemon juice. There were platters of flat Arridan bread that had been warmed over the coals. The Herons slid the lamb off the skewers and onto a round of bread, then heaped piles of tabouleh and green salad onto it, rolled it into a cylinder and ate. And if some of the delicious lamb juice happened to run down their hands and arms during this process, nobody really cared. It was a simple matter to lick one's hands to clean them.

For the most part, the crew had been silent while they ate. The food was too good to waste time in idle chitchat. But now, sitting back and patting his stomach, Thorn emitted a low burp and addressed his skirl.

"Got the plan sorted out yet?" he asked.

Hal nodded, slipping a last chunk of lamb from a skewer and placing it in his mouth. He chewed for a few seconds, unable or unwilling to talk. Then he swallowed, sighed contentedly and replied.

"Pretty much. There may be a few details I've missed," he added quickly. He had a reputation for occasionally missing the odd important detail in a plan and he wasn't about to let Thorn remind everyone about it. Instead, he decided to place the onus on his old friend. "I'll rely on you to see where I've missed something and point it out."

"So, let's hear it," Stig said eagerly. He admired his friend's ability to see an opportunity that everyone else had overlooked, and create a plan to take advantage of it. What really fascinated Stig was, once the opportunity or idea was pointed out, it was so blindingly obvious that one had to wonder how everyone else had missed it in the first place.

But Hal shook his head. "We'll wait for Selethen," he said. "In the meantime, let's have coffee."

They applied themselves enthusiastically to the coffee. It had become a favorite drink among the *Heron* crew and it was usually in short supply as a result. It made a welcome change to have it available in such liberal amounts. With the coffee, they enjoyed a dessert of a delicate pastry, cut in small squares, whose pastry layers were filled with a concoction of crushed walnuts and pine nuts, and soaked in honey.

"This is a great cake," Ulf said contentedly. "After you've eaten it, you can keep enjoying it by licking the honey off your fingers."

For once, Wulf didn't automatically disagree with his brother. But that could have been because he was too busy licking honey off his fingers. Instead, he made several contented grunting sounds.

More servants entered, bearing copper bowls of warm, scented, clear liquid and clean linen towels. Stefan eyed the bowl set in front of him with suspicion.

"Isn't it a bit late to serve soup?" he asked.

"It's water," Gilan told him. "It's a finger bowl to clean your hands—although in your case, you could possibly keep going until you reach your armpits."

And indeed, most of them were busily wiping honey and pastry flakes from their hands, their mouths, their cheeks and, in some cases, their foreheads. They were young men and they had enjoyed the food with the gusto and enthusiasm that young men so often display.

Thorn disdained using the finger bowl, cleaning his one hand by the simple expedient of wiping it on the front of his tunic and the leg of his breeches. His hook was also liberally smeared with honey and he licked that clean, then wiped it with the linen napkin the servants had provided.

Lydia looked at him, shaking her head. "Are you always so disgusting, old man?"

He gave her a beatific smile. "No. I'm doing this solely for your benefit. I'm usually very civilized."

They were saved from further discussion along these lines by one of the servants, who now appeared in the doorway and addressed Gilan.

"Lord Gilan, the *Wakir* is here for you," he said.

Gilan glanced at Hal. "Ready to talk?"

When Hal nodded, the Ranger heaved himself to his feet with a small groan. He had eaten one too many lamb skewers, he realized. Lamb grilled over coals was always his weakness.

Selethen was waiting for them in the large sitting room. As they all trooped in, he rose and made his usual greeting. Hal indicated the rest of the brotherband.

"I thought the crew should sit in on this," he said. "It'll save me having to brief them separately, and they might see a few spots where we can improve the plan." He introduced the other crew members to Selethen. Predictably, the *Wakir* was particularly interested in Lydia, noting the long dirk at her waist and her no-nonsense style of dress. Seeing his interest, Hal expanded a little on her introduction.

"Lydia joined us last year," he said. "She's an expert hunter and tracker. And she's a dead shot with her dart-casting atlatl."

Selethen inclined his head, looking impressed. "You Skandians and Araluens seem to have a tradition of warlike women," he said. "I recall that the Araluen princess was also a deadly shot —but with a sling."

Hal thought they'd spent enough time on small talk. He cleared his throat meaningfully and looked down at the chart he'd spread on the table. Selethen made a graceful gesture for him to proceed.

"All right," the young skirl said. "This is the chart of the coast you showed me." The others moved forward slightly to see more clearly. He indicated Al Shabah, then Tabork, farther to the east.

"We're here, and Iqbal is here, with"—he paused and looked up at Selethen—"how many men?"

"Perhaps two hundred," the *Wakir* said. Hal made a note.

"Very well. You have one hundred and fifty cavalrymen, but no siege equipment." He glanced round the other Herons, who hadn't been present at the earlier meeting. Then he unrolled the second chart, which was a more detailed map of Tabork itself. "The town is fortified, with a high wall around it. The main gate is on the landward side."

"What about the harbor?" Edvin asked. "How strongly is that

defended?" Being a sailor, he thought in terms of attacking from the sea, and the harbor was a potential weak point.

"There's a boom—a heavy chain that can shut off the entrance. And the two moles are manned with troops. The entrance is narrow and any ship passing through is within bow and javelin range of the moles." The chart Selethen had provided had been accompanied by detailed notes on the town and its defenses.

"So we can't get in that way," Stefan said. Hal looked up at him.

"We can't *force* our way in," He said. "But there might be another way."

He felt a stirring of interest in his crew. Selethen remained impassive. Unlike the Herons, he hadn't been privy to Hal's previous successful plans and stratagems. But he saw the reaction in the others, particularly Thorn, who nodded expectantly, waiting for Hal to reveal his idea. This is a young man worth watching, Selethen thought.

"Iqbal is in league with a Hellenese corsair called Philip Bloodyhand," Hal continued.

Jesper gave a scornful snort. "Bit overdramatic, isn't it?"

"Hellenes are like that," Lydia replied. "Besides, you'd hardly expect a corsair to call himself Philip Pussyfoot, would you?"

Jesper grinned at her. She had said the words with a perfectly deadpan expression.

"I suppose not. I would guess a corsair would want a more warlike . . ." Jesper became conscious that Hal was regarding him with his head slightly to one side, waiting for him to be quiet. "Sorry, Hal," he said. "Please continue."

"Thank you," Hal said, with just a hint of irony. "Philip has a war galley, the *Ishtfana*," he said. "When trading ships pass by Tabork, he's ideally positioned to dash out and capture them. That's the main reason he and Iqbal have occupied the town."

He placed one foot on the low table and rested his elbow on his knee, leaning forward to address them all.

"Now, my idea is this. We'll rig *Heron* to look like a trader. We still have the square sail we used in Socorro. We'll sail along the coast and lure the galley out. Then we retreat to the northwest, with old Philip Pussyfoot following us." He drew his saxe and lightly traced a path on the map, tapping a spot some ten kilometers out to sea. "Once we're out of sight of the town, we'll lose the square sail and re-rig with our own sail. Then we'll turn on the *Ishtfana*."

Thorn pursed his lips, staring at the chart as if he could actually see the two ships there, twisting and turning about each other. "She carries twenty men, right?"

"She has a fighting crew of twenty," Hal replied. "And forty slaves on the oars."

"Hmmm. Twenty fighting men. Twice our numbers. We'll need to whittle them down."

Selethen glanced quickly around the line of Skandian faces, all intent on the chart and their leaders. None of them, he noticed, seemed daunted by the prospect of taking on a larger ship with twice as many crew members as their own. Then he remembered, Skandians were born fighters.

Hal was nodding agreement. "That'll be up to Stig and Ingvar on the Mangler," he said. "And Lydia and Gilan. We'll have surprise on our side. And these corsairs rarely find themselves facing a real fighting crew."

Selethen nodded quietly at that point. But all the same, he had raised a hand and was frowning curiously. Hal looked at him.

"Yes, *Wakir*?"

"What is this . . . Mangle . . . you mentioned?"

He saw the smiles lighting up the faces of the young crew.

"The Mangler," Hal corrected him. "It's our equalizer. It's a giant crossbow we've mounted in the bow of our ship. It shoots a heavy bolt about this big." He held his hands about a meter apart. "It'll smash through the bulwarks of the galley—and its men." He glanced at Stig. "I want you, Stig, to concentrate your shots on the helmsman and the tiller. Try to smash and disable it. Then we can slip behind her and board her over the stern."

Selethen raised an eyebrow. It was a day of surprises and revelations, he thought.

"Forty oars," Thorn said. "She'll be fast."

Hal nodded agreement. "Initially, yes. But we'll be heading upwind once we change sails and the rowers can't keep up full speed for too long. And we should be able to out-turn her."

Thorn looked doubtful. "A galley can turn in its own length."

Hal was speaking again almost before he had the words out. For once, this was a detail that he had taken into account, he thought, smiling grimly.

"It can. They back one set of oars and go forward on the other so the ship pivots on the spot. But to do it, they have to come to a virtual standstill, then accelerate again. We can turn without losing speed. I'm confident we'll run rings around her."

"And if you can't?" Selethen said.

Hal grinned at him. "I'm confident he'll sink us."

"So, let's assume we shoot her crew full of holes, board her and take her," Thorn said. "Then what?"

Hal used the point of his saxe to tap a spot on the coast between Al Shabah and Tabork.

"Selethen will be waiting at this bay with twenty-five of his men. We'll bring the *Ishtfana* inshore, load his men aboard her—there'll be plenty of room for them—and head back to Tabork, with *Heron* in tow behind her. The defenders will assume she's captured us, rather than the other way round. They open the boom, we sail in to the wharf and storm ashore."

Edvin raised a hand. Edvin was a thinker, Hal knew.

"What if they have some password or signal for them to open the boom?" he asked.

"That would be a problem," Hal admitted. "But why should they? They know the *Ishtfana*, they're used to her coming and going. Why bother with a secret signal?"

Edvin thought about the answer and nodded. "Fair enough."

Hal continued, addressing Selethen directly. "With thirty-five of us, and the element of surprise, we should be able to fight our way through to the main gate." Again, he tapped the map with the point of his saxe to indicate the spot. "And open it for the rest of your men." He looked at the Arridan nobleman. "I assume you're confident that you can handle Iqbal and his troops once you get inside the walls?"

Selethen smiled grimly. "Just get us inside," he said. "We'll do the rest."

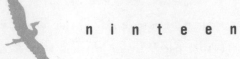
Heron was wallowing along the coast of Arrida under the makeshift square-sail rig Hal had designed as a disguise when they had sailed into Socorro weeks previously.

This time, however, the square sail and yardarm were attached so they could be quickly discarded and her usual triangular sail raised in its place.

As before, Hal grimaced continually as the inefficient square sail alternately filled and half emptied, causing the ship to move with an awkward surging motion as the wind spilled out of the bellying sail. The motion was so different from *Heron*'s normal smooth and powerful action that it grated on him.

Lydia, who was standing by the steering platform, asked a question that had been bothering her for some hours.

"Why are we bothering with the square sail?" she said. "After all, nobody here has seen the *Heron* before. It's not as if we need to disguise her."

Hal winced as the ship plunged into a shallow trough between waves and tried to head stubbornly downwind. He dragged her back on course with a savage heave on the tiller.

"That's true," he replied. "But I want us to look like easy prey, and this sail rig definitely achieves that. Fore-and-aft-rigged sails aren't unknown in the Constant Sea, and I'd rather Philip Tinky-toes didn't get any idea of our true performance."

Selethen had decided to accompany the Herons on this mission—partly because he wanted the chance to settle with Philip and partly because he wanted to see the young warriors in action. Now he smiled quietly at Hal's comment. Philip Bloodyhand was a name feared along this stretch of the Constant Sea, yet it held no fears for this cheerful crew of young Skandians. So far, he had been dubbed Philip Pussyfoot and Philip Daintyfinger. Now Hal had added another sobriquet to the growing list. Selethen had no doubt the bearded, and purportedly foul-tempered, Hellenese corsair would be furious to hear himself described in such dismissive tones.

They were running over a shallow sand bottom and the water around them was a brilliant green. Farther out to sea, the color darkened into deep blue as the bottom shelved away temporarily. Once it reached the area known as the Lion's Teeth, however, the *Wakir* realized it would lighten to this beautiful green once more. Beautiful, he thought, but potentially treacherous.

Hal glanced at the coastline slowly passing by them. He was

looking for a landmark he'd noted down earlier, after studying his charts. Now he saw it—a headland that was split in the middle by a landslide many years ago. The two halves of the headland reared up like the arms of a giant V. He gestured to Lydia.

"We're getting close. Slip up to the masthead lookout."

She nodded and went forward, climbing easily onto the bulwark and from there into the standing rigging, where she climbed nimbly upward until she reached the crosstree a meter above the top of the sail. She sat easily upon it, shading her eyes as she stared at the coast.

"Let me know the minute you see a ship leaving the harbor," Hal called. She waved a hand in acknowledgment. Normally, Stefan was the chosen lookout for the ship but Lydia's eyes were even keener than his, and on this occasion there was no need for his greater seagoing experience. There was only one thing to look for—the galley emerging from the harbor mouth—and Lydia could manage that easily.

"What happens when we sight *Ishtfana?*" Selethen asked. He knew the general idea that Hal had described but he wanted to see how it played out in practice. Hal pointed to the north.

"The wind's on our port side," he said. "So we're making reasonable speed—well, as reasonable as this sail will allow. Once we sight *Ishtfana* we'll have only one choice. We'll go about and head back toward the northwest, pretty much the reverse of the course we're on now."

"We can't just run north?" Selethen asked.

Hal shook his head. "We can't point up into the wind. We could do it under oars, but *Ishtfana* has four or five times as many as we have and they'd soon run us down. West of northwest will be the best heading we can make."

Thorn, who was nearby, added, "Until we raise our normal sail. Then we'll be able to show Philip Fancyfingers a thing or two about sailing."

Again, Selethen suppressed a smile. Another title to add to the list.

"So," said Hal, "we'll trail our cloak past Tabork and see if Philip bites." He frowned at the words. He seemed to have mixed his metaphors there, he thought.

Edvin seemed to agree. "Who'd bite a cloak?" he asked, grinning.

"Kloof would," Ingvar said heavily. He was stitching a rent in his sea cloak that Kloof had made only the day before. The huge dog looked up as she heard her name.

Kloof! she said. Ingvar curled his lip at her.

"Oh, shut up, you idiot dog."

But, in the contrary way of dogs when they're being roused on, Kloof thumped her tail on the deck at him and inched forward on her belly so that her massive chin rested on his thigh. Then she turned adoring eyes up at him.

"Fleabag," he said. But he was smiling when he said it.

"I can see the town!" Lydia called from the crosstree. All eyes went up to her. She was clinging to the mast with her left arm wrapped around it, shading her eyes with her right hand. As they looked, she pointed her right arm toward the shore. From deck level, the town was still out of sight.

"Any sign of *Ishtfana?*" Hal asked, although he knew that lookouts in the town would only just have caught sight of the *Heron*.

Lydia leaned forward slightly. "There's a red flag going up on the harbor mole!" she said. "And there's a group of men doing something at the end of the mole."

"The red flag will be the signal that we've been spotted," Selethen told Hal. "And I'll wager those men are opening the boom."

Hal glanced around the little ship. The crew were already in position and now they tensed, like racing dogs waiting for the start. They all had specific tasks in the coming minutes and it was vital that they carried them out smoothly to achieve the transition from their clumsy square rig to the graceful, speedy *Heron* rig in as short a time as possible. Several minutes passed, in expectant silence, then—

"She's coming!" Lydia shouted, her voice cracking with excitement. She scrambled higher, to stand on the crosstree, giving her a better sight of the harbor mouth.

Sure enough, a long, narrow hull was emerging from between the gray stone moles at either side of the entrance. As she emerged, Lydia could make out the twin banks of oars, rising and falling in unison, looking almost like a bird's wings beating, the blades catching the sun as they turned flat when they emerged from the water, then turned ninety degrees to the vertical again before they plunged back in.

There was something implacably ominous about that measured, synchronized movement, something that seemed to belie any human involvement, and she felt the hairs on the back of her neck prickle as the ship moved out into the open sea.

"Time to turn?" Stig asked. His hands were clenching and unclenching on the battleax shoved through the ring on his belt.

Hal shook his head. "We'll give them a minute or so," he said. Again, he glanced around the ship at his crew. Only Thorn was relaxed, leaning one elbow on the windward bulwark. As Hal's gaze fell on him, he smiled encouragingly at his skirl. Hal felt the tension drain out of him. Thorn had the ability to do that in times of stress, he thought.

"Stand by to go about!" he called and felt a tremor of movement from the crew as they moved closer to their action stations.

"Wear ship!" he shouted, and put the helm over so that the ship began to turn to starboard, with the wind continuing to drive the sail through the turn.

Stefan, Jesper and Edvin heaved on the braces to bring the yardarm around. Ulf and Wulf released the sheets momentarily, then hauled in again as the ship came onto its new course, paralleling their previous direction, with the yard and sail now on the port side of the ship.

A stray wave hit her starboard bow as she came round onto the new course, sending a brilliant shower of spray over the decks. Selethen raised an arm to cover his face. The Herons ignored the sudden shower of water. Even with the clumsy square sail, she came round well enough and settled on her new course.

Lydia, who had used both hands to cling to the mast as the yardarm rotated a meter or so beneath her position, now took a more relaxed stance and resumed her scrutiny of the *Ishtfana*.

The twin banks of oars were continuing their remorseless rhythm. It all looked so smooth and mechanical, she thought, although she knew that, hidden from sight, the sweat-streaked oarsmen would be straining muscles and gritting teeth against pain and weariness to maintain that nonstop momentum. As she watched, the rowing rate increased, and the oars moved up and down, up and down, more quickly.

"They're rowing faster!" she called down to the deck. She glanced down and saw the crew's faces upturned to her.

"Are they gaining on us?" Hal called.

She looked again at the galley, shading her eyes once more to focus her vision. She could see the ship in greater detail now. There was a short, stumpy mast on the fore part, but no sail was rigged. She was traveling under oar power alone. She could make out the black dots of men's heads along the bulwarks, and a small group of figures in the stern, gathered around the helmsman.

"Yes," she said, and sensed a stir of movement and nervousness among her shipmates.

"Let me know when you can't see the town anymore," Hal called back. When he switched sails, he didn't want anyone onshore seeing the changeover. On deck, he couldn't see the town, but that didn't mean they wouldn't be able to see the mast and sail higher up.

"There she is!" Stig shouted, pointing over the stern. All eyes swiveled to follow the direction he was indicating as the galley slowly appeared over the horizon.

"Get ready!" Hal called. The sail handlers were all briefed and everyone knew what his role was in the coming maneuver. "We need to move fast, but don't overdo it. No mistakes in the change-over, all right?"

There was a low growl of agreement from the crew assembled in the waist. Stefan, Jesper and Edvin glanced aloft at the square sail, billowing and relaxing as the wind alternately filled it, then spilled from the sides. Stig and Ingvar stood ready to haul the port fore-and-aft sail up in its place, as soon as it reached the deck. Ulf and Wulf stood by the trimming sheets, ready to switch from one set to another.

Selethen, an interested bystander, moved a pace closer to Gilan and nodded his head toward the young skirl, who was half turned to watch the approaching galley.

"He's a cool one," he murmured and the Ranger glanced round at him, nodding.

"I doubt you'll find cooler," he said. "And he knows what he's doing."

"I gathered that, from the way the crew look up to him," Selethen replied.

A third voice interrupted their conversation.

"He's the finest natural helmsman I've ever seen," Thorn said quietly. He'd moved a little closer to them. He had no specific role in the upcoming maneuver. His brief was to watch, ready to lend a hand anywhere he was needed. "He feels the ship. He knows what it's going to do, how it's going to react. You can't be taught that. You're either born with it or you never have it. Wait till you see how he throws the *Heron* around once we have our normal sail hoisted."

They weren't going to have to wait too long, Selethen realized. Lydia's voice came to them from the masthead.

"Town's out of sight! *Ishtfana* is still gaining."

Hal looked up at her. "Get down here and get your atlatl ready," he called. He glanced at Gilan. "You too, Gilan. We're going to need your bow." Then he turned back to his waiting crew, as Lydia scampered down the rigging, reaching the deck in a matter of seconds.

"All right, Herons. Let's ditch that square sail and send up our own! Go!" As he added the last word, the waiting crew exploded into action.

"Clear!" Ulf shouted as he and Wulf cast off the trimming sheets on the square sail and it flew up in the wind. Instantly, Stefan, Jesper and Edvin cast off the rigging that secured it and allowed it to fall from the masthead, sliding down, just keeping it under control with tension on the braces, gathering it in a rough bundle as it came. The moment it touched the deck, Stig yelled to Ingvar.

"Up port!"

The two powerful youths put their backs into it, sending the slender yardarm soaring aloft to clunk home into the bracket that secured it. Barely had this happened than the twins were heaving on the trimming sheets. The sail made a *whumping* noise as the wind filled it, then they sheeted home, trapping the wind, and the *Heron* surged forward with increased speed and purpose, her prow swinging to the north as Hal leaned on the tiller.

The sudden increase in speed caught Selethen by surprise and he staggered a pace or two, then recovered. He raised an eyebrow at Gilan.

"Who built this ship?" he asked.

Gilan grinned and nodded toward the intense figure at the helm. "Who do you think?"

The room was on the second floor of the former harbor master's building in Tabork. It was high ceilinged, and the wide-open arches that led onto a deep veran-dah overlooking the harbor admitted the sea breeze to cool the interior. The floor was tiled, the tiles forming a geometric pattern that was pleasing to the eye. The furnishings were mini-mal—several blackwood chests and a long wall table, and plush cushions on the floor to provide seating around a low table.

Simple as the furnishing might be, the room was a big improve-ment over the goatskin tent that was Iqbal's normal residence in the desert. He had appropriated the second-floor premises when his men had overrun the town. Its former occupant, the harbor master, a minor official of the *Emrikir,* was killed in the brief, savage battle that had marked the seizing of Tabork. Iqbal's men had stormed the inland wall at night, while Philip's corsairs launched their attack from the sea. After years of peace and prosperity, the town had neglected to deploy the heavy chain boom across the harbor mouth—much to their misfortune. In the same lackadaisical fashion, the watch on the walls that protected the town had grown careless and inefficient.

Iqbal stood with his back to the verandah, the strong glare of the sun behind him. He was facing one of his subordinates, a fierce and cruel fighter named Dhakwan, who was the leader of a *Khumsan*, a company of fifty riders. Dhakwan, in deference to his tribal chief, had dispensed with the blue veil that normally covered the lower half of his face. Iqbal's head was bare, exposing his shaven skull to Dhakwan's view.

"When will your men be arriving?" Iqbal asked. His voice was harsh and demanding. Iqbal valued Dhakwan as a fighter and a leader of men. But there was no affection between them. In fact, there was no affection between Iqbal and any of his men.

"They're ten kilometers away, in camp," Dhakwan told him. "I thought it better if they arrived in darkness. I assume you don't want the tyrant Selethen to know we have extra men in the town?"

Iqbal grunted. What Dhakwan assumed or didn't assume was unimportant to him, although the man was correct. Selethen had one hundred and fifty cavalrymen outside the walls of Tabork, and he knew that Iqbal's force numbered two hundred. The addition of another fifty fighting men would come as an unpleasant surprise if the Arridan leader decided to attack the walls. And Iqbal knew that Selethen was being goaded by his overlord, the *Emrikir*, to retake the town and send Iqbal in chains to the capital. Although how the fat, lazy ruler in the far-off city of Mararoc thought his local commander could achieve this was beyond Iqbal. Selethen's men were already outnumbered. The walls of Tabork were high and in good condition and the *Wakir* had no siege equipment or artillery.

It was all very well for the *Emrikir* to make demands and grandiose statements about the need to destroy Iqbal and his Tualaghi nomads—but the *Emrikir* had never so much as raised a sword in anger, or faced an opponent more dangerous than a roast guinea fowl. Selethen was the one who was tasked with achieving the impossible. And, capable as he might be, the task assigned to him was impossible—and had just become even more so.

"Bring them to the east gate by the cliffs," he told Dhakwan. That was the most inconspicuous entrance into Tabork. "And make sure there is no noise and no sign of light."

"Of course," Dhakwan replied. His lip curled slightly in disdain. There had been no need to tell him that. He imposed an iron discipline on his men. But sometimes Iqbal seemed to believe that he knew everything and his subordinates knew nothing. He was an arrogant and boastful man, but he had been an effective leader, bringing large amounts of booty to his followers. Gold made up for a lot of arrogance, Dhakwan thought.

"I saw our Hellenese friend leaving port when I arrived," he said, with that thought in mind. If he was present when the *Ishtfana* captured a ship, he would share in the profits. "Where was he off to?"

Iqbal looked sharply at him. "Is there any reason why you should know that?"

Dhakwan met his gaze evenly. "Is there any reason why I shouldn't?"

The two men eyed each other for several seconds. Iqbal was aware that he was leader only by dint of his ability to keep his subordinates in control. And that meant keeping them content. He had to walk a fine line between harsh discipline on one side and unpopularity on the other. If too many of his men began to believe that he was out of his depth, his term as leader would be over. As would his life.

And Dhakwan was known as a strong leader and a good fighter. He had a lot of friends among the upper echelons of the Tualaghi band. He was not a man to alienate. Finally, Iqbal shrugged and gave in, gesturing vaguely to the harbor mouth beyond the shaded verandah.

"Philip is still here," he said. "He sent his first mate, Kyrios, to bring in a small trader that we sighted." He frowned and stepped out onto the verandah, peering into the glare that bounced off the blue waters of the Constant Sea. "I'm surprised they're taking so long about it," he said. "I would have thought they'd be back by now."

"Maybe one of the ship's crew was armed with a knife," Dhakwan said sarcastically. His opinion of the Hellenese corsairs and their fighting abilities was decidedly low. Iqbal looked at him and nodded in understanding.

"Perhaps they're not the boldest of allies," he said. "But they've brought in a lot of booty since we've been here. We couldn't have done it without them and their ship."

Dhakwan snorted dismissively. "And they wouldn't be here without us," he pointed out. "Do you think those overdressed fops could have taken this town on their own?"

Hellenes were renowned for their fondness for colorful clothing and excessive jewelry. And none more so than the corsairs who crewed Philip's galley.

Iqbal shrugged. "Nevertheless, they're our partners and we need them," he said. He glanced at the ocean again. Kyrios certainly seemed to be taking an inordinately long time about capturing that one small trader, he thought.

"What are they doing?" Hal asked. Lydia was balanced on the stern bulwark of the Heron, keeping an eye on the galley behind them.

"They're gaining on us," she said.

Hal nodded. "I expected that. They'll row their hearts out at first. But we'll keep them heading into the wind and they'll soon tire."

If Philip was like most slave owners—and Hal had no reason to think otherwise—he would be unlikely to look after his rowers too well. They'd be poorly fed. Good food cost money, and corsairs didn't like throwing that away.

He wanted a fraction more speed, so he allowed the ship's head to fall off a little to port. Ulf and Wulf re-trimmed the sail without being told to, and *Heron*, with the wind now more abeam, moved faster through the water. He glanced over his shoulder. The galley was visible on the horizon, and as he watched, he saw her turn to match his heading, the oars rising and falling in their constant rhythm.

"They're still coming," Thorn said. He had joined Lydia at the stern rail and was peering at the pursuing ship, using a reference mark on the sternpost to measure their relative positions as the minutes passed. Hal looked to confirm the fact, then edged the ship north again, causing the *Heron*'s speed to drop off.

"Got to keep them on the hook," he said, after a few minutes. He frowned. By now, he had expected the rowers to be losing rhythm and power.

Lydia spoke almost simultaneously. "They're closing again!"

Hal looked at the sun, still high in the sky to the west. There were hours of daylight left—plenty of time to wear out the *Ishtfana*'s rowers. He looked at the ship behind them once more. He saw that the oars were still moving smoothly and powerfully and amended his earlier thought: plenty of time for them to catch the *Heron* and sink her, if they could keep this up.

He drummed his fingers on the tiller. Surely they couldn't maintain this pace much longer?

Stig moved a few steps closer to the steering platform. "I thought they'd be slowing down by now," he said, in a low voice that the rest of the crew couldn't hear.

"They will be soon," Hal said, feigning a confidence he didn't feel. He was beginning to worry about the inexorable pace of the galley. If he was going to outmaneuver the other ship in a close-in fight, he needed the oarsmen to be exhausted and their efforts clumsy and uncoordinated. So far, there was no sign that they were. They simply kept coming.

And gaining ground.

"They're closer," Lydia said, shading her eyes to peer at the galley. "Didn't you think they'd be tired out by now?" She hadn't heard Stig's almost identical comment.

"They will be soon," Hal repeated, irritation obvious in his tone. He edged the *Heron* to port again, for a little more speed. Looking over his shoulder, he saw the *Ishtfana* match the movement. His heart lurched as, this time, he was sure he saw the beat of the oars actually increase.

"They're gaining on us again," Thorn said.

Hal glared at him. People seemed to enjoy passing on bad news, he thought. "They can't keep it up all day," he said, as much to bolster his own confidence as that of the crew.

"They don't need to," Thorn replied in a matter-of-fact tone. "They just need to keep it up till they've caught us."

Again, Hal reflected on the pleasure people took from imparting bad news. The stamina of the *Ishtfana's* rowers amazed him. If he could bring the wind abeam, he'd be able to outpace them. The problem with that idea was that, once they realized they were outmatched, they might well abandon the pursuit. He had to keep them on the hook by heading upwind. But under those conditions, they were able to match his speed, even exceed it. And since they didn't need to tack continually, they could take a direct path, unlike the zigzag track the *Heron* had to follow.

Maybe I miscalculated, he thought. Perhaps it was yet another case of overlooking a small detail, of missing some important fact in the mix that had thrown his plan into disarray. He racked his brains, trying to see what he had overlooked. The two ships raced on, with the larger vessel astern slowly drawing closer.

What Hal couldn't know was that he had misjudged the slaves' physical condition. With the cessation of the shipping trade along the coast, marked by the number of ships in harbor at Al Shabah, the *Ishtfana* hadn't put to sea for several weeks. As a result, her rowing crew were well rested, which was why they had been able to maintain this killing pace for so long.

But it had to tell eventually. Rested they might be, but they were still ill fed and in poor physical condition, and their overseers had been keeping them at maximum speed now for far too long, enforcing their demands with whips.

Thorn saw it first: a hesitation in the beat of those implacable banks of oars as first one rower, then another, missed a stroke. *Ishtfana* staggered sideways and the old sea wolf allowed himself a satisfied smile.

"They're faltering," he said and Hal immediately turned to view their pursuer.

Now it was more obvious. The twin banks of oars were no longer moving in smooth cohesion. He saw one oar on the starboard side miss a stroke completely, throwing up a fountain of spray as it caught the water at the wrong angle. The crew of the *Heron* let out a spontaneous cheer and Hal realized how much the *Ishtfana*'s relentless progress had been preying on their minds. He felt a wave of relief sweep over him.

"Now," he said quietly, looking steadily at the galley, "let's see how you handle my ship and my crew."

H al craned out over the bulwark to peer at the galley plunging along in *Heron's* wake.

Now three of the galley's oars weren't moving in concert with the others. They dragged lifelessly in the water beside the ship. As he watched, another suddenly lifted from the water, then dropped again, splashing uselessly alongside the ship's narrow hull.

Thorn had noticed the movement too.

"They're losing rowers," he said. "The men are collapsing."

Three of the motionless oars were on the starboard side of the ship and Hal could see the galley's bow swing to starboard under the uneven thrust. The helmsman hastily corrected the movement and brought the galley back on course. But Hal could see she was in trouble. She had lost that purposeful, implacable air. She was struggling. The oars were out of the perfect synchronization that had seen them rising and falling as one when they first sped out of the harbor.

"I think it's time," Thorn said quietly.

Hal nodded agreement. Then he filled his lungs and bellowed his orders to the sail handlers. "Stand by to tack starboard . . . Tack!"

The port sail slid down the mast as he hauled the ship's bow around to the right. She left a perfect curved wake in the sea behind her as she swung up through the wind, then began to turn away from it. There was a rattle of canvas and the usual rasping squeal of ropes through the blocks as Edvin, Stefan and Jesper sent the starboard sail sliding up the mast. Then it filled and the twins heaved on the sheets to bring the sail taut, and *Heron* was speeding back downwind toward her pursuer.

"Ulf, Wulf! Ease off a little!" Hal shouted. He expected *Ishtfana*'s skipper to head for him, cutting across his course to ram him, and he wanted to keep some speed in reserve. He felt the urgent thrust through the water decrease slightly as Ulf and Wulf obeyed his order.

"Stig, Gilan, Lydia!" Hal shouted. "Get for'ard. I'm going to go down his starboard side. As soon as you're in range, start shooting. Stig, aim for the tiller."

Stig nodded, and he and Ingvar scrambled forward to the Mangler. Gilan and Lydia moved to the starboard side, level with the mast. With the port sail driving the ship, they had a clear view of the galley bearing down on them. As she rose and fell on the waves, they could see the black, iron-shod ram set low in the bow as it emerged from the waves, then dipped under again. It reminded Lydia of the beak of an evil bird of prey.

The galley's helmsman continued to turn the long, narrow ship, keeping it pointed directly at the center of *Heron*'s hull as the smaller ship crossed her path. Hal watched, eyes slitted, counting seconds to judge the moment exactly. The ram was less than a hundred meters from them and coming inexorably toward them, in spite of the increasingly ragged action of the rowers.

Now! he thought, and yelled his command at the twins.

"Sheet home!"

They leaned back against the strain on the ropes, tightening the sail against the stiff breeze from the north. *Heron*'s deck heeled to port and she accelerated through the water, evading the galley's clumsy thrust.

As *Ishtfana* tried to match her maneuver, Hal kept the little ship turning, swinging inside the arc of the galley. The wind was now well abeam, *Heron*'s most efficient point of sailing, and she was moving with increasing speed toward *Ishtfana*'s starboard side. He could hear the galley's crew yelling abuse and threats at the little ship as it evaded them, then had the gall to approach so close to its pursuer.

Then Gilan and Lydia began to shoot.

Gilan got away five arrows. Lydia managed three darts from her atlatl. All eight missiles sailed across the narrow gap between the ships, wreaking havoc on the men clustered around the command post.

Lydia's first dart hit the helmsman, killing him instantly. He reeled back across the deck, releasing the tiller, then crashed to the planks. Two of the crew standing by him stared at their companion, momentarily frozen in place. Then they looked back to the ship approaching them and, in rapid succession, were struck down by Gilan's arrows.

Lydia's second dart missed. She had been aiming at one of the men Gilan had just shot and he fell to the deck as her dart whizzed over his head. Her third hit another corsair in the leg and he fell to the deck, yelling in pain, looking in horror at the iron broadhead that had gone through his calf and out the other side.

Kyrios, after a moment of stunned disbelief, had the presence of mind to drop to the deck, beneath the cover of the timber bulwark. He looked up and saw the tiller banging aimlessly back and forth as the ship drove on under the erratic thrust of her oars. He shouted to one of his crew, who had also had the good sense to take cover, and pointed to the tiller.

"Matlos! Take the helm!"

The man looked at him, wide-eyed with terror, and shook his head. Kyrios mouthed a string of terrible curses and threats at him, then, still crouching below the bulwark, began to move toward him, drawing a curved knife from his belt. Matlos looked at the first mate, then at the untended tiller. The storm of arrows and darts seemed to have abated. Carefully, he rose to a crouch and moved toward the tiller, his eyes riveted on the fierce, unforgiving features of the first mate, and the wickedly gleaming knife in his right hand.

He rose tentatively, peering over the bulwark. The little ship was barely forty meters away now. Exposing no more than the top of his head, he reached up for the tiller.

At that precise moment, Stig's first shot from the Mangler slammed into the pine railing that topped the bulwark, centimeters away from the tiller itself.

The iron warhead smashed through the timber, sending a storm of splinters flying. Matlos lurched away from the railing, his forehead lacerated by a flying piece of pine eight centimeters long.

He yelled in pain and fright. Kyrios stared at him, aghast, wondering what sort of weapon could cause such damage.

One thing he knew, he wasn't about to put his head above the railing to find out. He cowered on the deck.

Farther forward, in the waist of the ship, the fighting crew continued to yell curses and threats at the *Heron.* So far, the missiles from the little ship had concentrated on the steering position in the stern, and the rest of the crew were untouched. One of them, emboldened by this fact, seized a heavy spear and stepped up to the bulwark, his arm drawn back to throw it, his eyes searching for a suitable target. He made out two figures crouched over what appeared to be a massive crossbow in the bow of the other ship. He half turned toward them, taking his arm back a few more centimeters to get the maximum power behind his throw.

He never managed it. An arrow suddenly thudded into his chest. The spear fell from his nerveless fingers, clattering on the deck. Another crew member turned toward him. The movement saved his life, as another arrow from Gilan's bow struck him in the upper arm. A second earlier and it would have pierced his heart.

Even so, the shock and the pain were unbearable. He dropped to his knees, holding the wound and sobbing in pain.

Stig's second shot, from point-blank range, smashed into the twisted birch ropes that held the tiller in place, severing most of them so that the tiller dropped to one side, loosely attached by only a few remaining fibers. A few seconds later, the third and final shot severed the remaining fibers and the tiller fell overboard, into the *Ishtfana*'s wake.

On board *Heron,* Hal saw the tiller drop into the sea. "Oh, good shot, Stig!"

The galley could only be steered by the oars now, and the rowers were in a totally disorganized state. He could see no sign of anyone taking control on the stern. Farther forward, as Gilan and Lydia concentrated their barrage of arrows and darts on the rest of the crew, men were falling and crying out in pain.

He came to a sudden decision. Now was the time to take advantage of all this confusion.

"Tack to starboard!" he yelled, and saw the faces of the sail handling crew turn toward him, understanding on their features. "Now!"

He swung the helm, bringing the ship spinning on its heel to starboard. Watching the other ship, he sensed rather than saw the *Heron*'s port side sail come sliding down, the starboard sail whipping up. He heard the *WHUMP* of the sail filling and felt it through the soles of his feet as it reverberated through the deck planks.

In a matter of seconds, the little ship had turned through one hundred and eighty degrees, pivoting on the fin keel that gave her a solid grip on the water, and a fulcrum about which to turn.

Gilan and Lydia had shifted to the port side and were ready to let fly at anyone who showed themselves above the bulwarks. Nobody had been sufficiently foolhardy to do so for the past few minutes. None the less, Gilan sent an arrow humming just above the bulwark to keep their heads down.

The *Heron* gathered speed and Hal turned to Thorn, standing ready a few meters away. "I'm going to take out their starboard side oars."

Thorn nodded understanding. Rudderless, the galley was out of control. Her only way of steering now would be with the oars. If Hal could disable some of them, it would make that task much more difficult. Besides, there was another opportunity. The galley's officers and crew were disorganized and demoralized.

This was the perfect time to board.

As Hal angled the *Heron* in toward the starboard bank of oars, Thorn dashed forward and seized a grappling iron and a length of rope from under the rowing benches. He stood poised beside Lydia and the Ranger.

"Hang on to something," he warned. "Hal's going to hit her."

They could see it coming, although the *Ishtfana's* crew, cowering out of sight, had no idea what was about to happen. Hal arrowed the *Heron* in at an angle, sending her strengthened bow post slicing into the starboard side oars like a giant ax blade.

There was an ear-splitting crash of wood shattering as the oars split and splintered under the impact. Oar shafts and blades spun up into the air as the bow smashed through them. Splinters flew in a further deadly storm. *Heron's* crew were ready for the sudden impact and crouched down undercover as their ship plowed its way through the rearmost six rows of oars.

On board *Ishtfana*, the rowing deck was in chaos as the butt ends of the oars were suddenly jerked and smashed in all directions, hurling rowers off their benches to send them sprawling on the deck, breaking bones and bruising limbs. The slave master, who had bent to peer out through an oar port to see what was going on, was caught across the jaw by one of the leaping oar butts. He fell senseless to the deck. Two of the rowers, seeing their chance, leapt on him, drawing the long knife from his scabbard. The rowing master had whipped too many slaves in his time.

He would never do it again.

On deck on the *Heron*, Thorn felt the ship come to a momentary halt, her bow wedged at an angle against the galley, with the surface of the water between them littered with broken oar shafts and blades.

He swung the grapnel line up and over, letting it slam into the wood at the galley's stern, then heaved hard on it to set it tight.

As Hal called for Ulf and Wulf to loosen the sheets, *Heron* began to drift astern. Thorn quickly measured the distance with his eye and took a turn around one of the *Heron*'s bollards with the grapnel rope. The rope came up into a straight line, then, with a jerk, *Heron* began to move forward, towing in *Ishtfana*'s wake. Amazingly, some of the forward rowers were still at work, sending the ship crabbing through the water. Thorn gestured to Stefan and Jesper, then pointed to the rope.

"Haul us in!" he yelled. "We'll board her!"

Hearing the call, Stig and Ingvar left the Mangler and scrambled for their weapons. Thorn glanced round and saw Selethen standing ready a few paces away. His curved sword was still in its scabbard. But now he had a small, spiked shield on his left arm. Thorn gestured to him.

"You coming, your *Wakirship*?" he asked, with a savage grin.

Selethen returned the grin with a smile on his narrow, hawklike face. He had a score to settle with the skipper of the galley.

"Just don't get in my way, northman," he said.

chapter   twenty-two

A s the crew hauled in on the grapnel rope, Thorn leapt up onto the bulwark beside the bow post. He had donned his fighting hand, and carried his small shield in his left hand.

The bow bumped against the stern of the *Ishtfana*, and as Ulf and Wulf made it fast, Thorn leapt up onto the bigger ship's rail.

"Come on!" he roared.

Stig was close behind him and they dropped lightly to the deck, turning to meet the group of men charging aft to defend their ship. The first to reach them drew back his sword, yelling a curse at them.

It was the last sound he ever made.

Stig's ax cut the cry short and the man stumbled before falling over on his side, a shocked look on his features. Thorn parried another man's sword with his club-hand, then slammed his small shield into his attacker's face, sending him flying across the deck.

Selethen swarmed over the railing behind them, his attention falling instantly on Kyrios, who was slinking toward Stig and Thorn from slightly behind them, a heavy-bladed cutlass in his right hand and his knife in his left.

Kyrios was suddenly aware of Selethen's gaze. The *Wakir*, taking in the other man's ornate garb—he was dressed in a white silk shirt and wide-legged red trousers of fine linen, with a broad-brimmed felt hat adorned with a long peacock's feather—mistook him for the corsair captain.

"Philip!" Selethen shouted. "Throw down your weapons!"

Kyrios made no reply, but he lunged forward, swinging the heavy sword down in an overhead stroke that would have split Selethen to the chin.

Had it landed.

The *Wakir* contemptuously flicked the blade aside with his shield, then swung his scimitar in reply, in a bewildering combination of strokes.

Side cut, back cut, overhead. The flashing blade seemed to come from several different directions at once. Kyrios blundered back in panic, barely managing to evade the lightning strokes of the master swordsman. With the dim thought that he should try to turn defense into attack, Kyrios attempted a clumsy lunge at his tall opponent. His sword slid along Selethen's, the blades rasping together. Then, with a twist of his wrist, Selethen deflected Kyrios's cutlass, leaving the first mate open to his riposte. The curved scimitar blade darted forward and back like a snake's tongue.

But, unlike a snake's tongue, the scimitar bit, and bit hard. Kyrios barely felt the impact. But he looked down in wonder at the spreading red stain on his shirt.

"I'm . . . not Philip," he managed to croak, although he wasn't sure why he felt that needed to be said. Then his legs gave out under him and he fell to the deck.

With the threat from behind eliminated, Selethen turned his attention back to Stig and Thorn, and the rest of the corsairs.

The latter stood uncertainly in a ragged semicircle facing the two Skandians. Two of their number were already out of action, and the remainder had witnessed the incredible speed and power of the Skandian warriors as they dealt with that first attack. They had also seen the ease with which Selethen defeated Kyrios. As a result, none of them was willing to be the first to face fighters such as these.

A deep growl began to form in Thorn's chest. He hated indecision and delay. He knew momentum was everything in a fight like this, where he and his companions were outnumbered. He was on the brink of launching an attack at the hesitant Hellenes. Behind him, he heard Ulf and Wulf scramble over the rail and drop onto the deck. That made five of them on board now and that, thought Thorn, was plenty to take on these overdressed popinjays. He tensed his muscles, singling out the first man he would strike down with his fearsome club-hand.

The he heard rushing feet behind him, and a huge voice roared: "Clear the way!"

Next minute, Thorn was shouldered aside by a heavy body and Ingvar, spectacles firmly lashed in place and his voulge held across his body in both hands, surged past him to attack the *Ishtfana*'s crew.

Ingvar swung the voulge horizontally to the left, allowing his right hand to slide down from its position halfway along the shaft until it was adjacent to his left hand, on the butt end, adding immense leverage to the stroke.

The ax blade of the long weapon came round with a deadly hissing sound, like a scythe cutting into barley.

And, like a scythe, it cut down three of the *Ishtfana*'s crew, sending them sprawling and their weapons clattering to the deck. The first stroke was barely completed before Ingvar reversed the movement, snagging the shoulder of another corsair's leather breastplate with the hook on the back of the voulge and jerking the man forward, off his feet. As he hit the deck, Ingvar jerked the hook free and lunged with the spearhead of the voulge at a fifth crewman.

This one had a shield and he tried desperately to block Ingvar's stroke. But the big boy had lunged forward, stamping his right foot for extra power, and putting the force of his legs behind the thrust, as Thorn had taught him in their long hours of drilling as they sailed down the Iberian coastline.

As Thorn had predicted, with the force of his legs behind the thrust, Ingvar's attack was unstoppable. The wood of the shield split and the spear point went through as if there were no resistance at all. It took the corsair in his left shoulder and he cried out, releasing the shield, leaving it dangling awkwardly on the end of Ingvar's voulge. Then, clutching his shattered, bleeding shoulder, the Hellene turned and ran.

Enraged by the broken shield impeding his weapon, Ingvar got rid of it in the quickest way possible. He whipped the voulge back and forward in a violent movement that dislodged the splintered shield and sent it hurtling into the group of men facing him, knocking another to the deck, unconscious.

And that was enough for the rest of them. Terrified by the awesome figure with the shining black circles for eyes and the deadly long-handed triple weapon, they turned and ran.

Ingvar roared again and set off after them.

"Let's get 'em!" he bellowed to the others. As Stig, Selethen and the twins surged forward after him, Thorn paused and leaned back, more than a little affronted.

"I'm supposed to say that," he said indignantly.

Hal, having turned over the helm to Edvin, found Thorn standing, decidedly discontented, on the rear deck of the galley, glaring forward as the others surrounded the beaten corsair crew. As the latter let their weapons fall to the deck in a shower of swords, knives and spears, the shabby warrior gestured at the scene with his club.

"He stole my fight," he said resentfully. "Ingvar stole my fight out from under my nose."

Hal grinned. "He had plenty of room to move then," he said. Then, shaking his head in wonder as he saw his massive friend terrifying the cowed galley crew, he added, "I guess the fight's over." He patted Thorn's shoulder and the two of them started forward to join their victorious friends.

But the fight wasn't over. Not completely. Three of the galley's fighting crew, the first to turn tail and run, had made their way

down through a hatch to the rowing deck below. The lines of rowers, chained to their oars, glared at them with hatred. With no one
to command them, they had finally stopped sweeping their oars
back and forth and the ship rocked in the even swell. The first of
the corsairs, a man named Davos, looked at the angry eyes surrounding them. The rowers were chained, but how long they would
remain that way was anyone's guess. He saw the slumped figure of
the rowing master on the catwalk between the rowing benches.
Somewhere on his body was the key that would release the rowers.
Perhaps they had already found it. It wasn't a healthy place to be
for too long.

"Let's get out of here," he muttered.

"Where?" One of his companions was wide-eyed with panic.
He looked from side to side, seeing the hatred that surrounded
them.

"We'll go aft and out a rowing port," the leader decided. "We'll
take their ship and cut her loose. There can't be more than two or
three people left on board her. And they'll be sailing crew, not
fighting crew."

Which showed how little he understood the composition of a
Skandian crew. On a Skandian ship, *everyone* was a member of the
fighting crew.

They ran aft, crouching under the low headroom, their progress marked by muttered curses from the rowing benches. But, in
addition to the fact that the rowers were constricted by their chains,
the three men were all armed with swords and none of the slaves
was ready to confront them.

They reached the aftmost oar port on the starboard side. Here was the point where *Heron*'s ramming had caused the most damage. Several men were lying awkwardly on their benches and the oars themselves were splintered and foreshortened.

"Come on!" said Davos. The slave on the bench was huddled over, clutching a broken forearm, moaning in pain. The corsair jerked him roughly out of the way and leaned his head and shoulders out the oar port. The oar, shattered by the collision with *Heron*, was no longer in place to impede him.

He gave an exclamation of satisfaction as he saw the bow of the other ship no more than a few meters away, surging up and down on the waves, snubbing against the hawser that connected her to the galley.

He sheathed his sword and hung his upper body out the oar port again, gripping the railing above him with both hands. Then he kicked his feet clear of the port and worked his way, hand over hand, along the rail until he could grip the rope. He transferred his weight to the rope, feeling it sag under his weight, then swung himself across to the other ship.

His companions were close behind him. The three of them dropped lightly to the *Heron*'s deck and took stock of the situation.

There seemed to be only two crew members left aboard the little ship. One of them, Davos saw with a grunt of satisfaction, was a girl. The other was a youth. He was wearing a sword but he was small and slimly built. So far, neither of them had noticed the three corsairs who had just boarded the ship. Their attention was focused on events happening on the galley.

"Easy meat," muttered Davos to his friends. He took a pace forward.

And froze.

The growl was deep and threatening. So deep that he knew it must come from a massive chest. And presumably that massive chest would have a massive head with massive teeth to match. He dropped his hand onto his sword hilt.

The growl came again, even louder and more threatening this time. Where was it? Davos cast his gaze back and forth around the raffle of sails and ropes that littered the forward deck.

"What is it?" asked one of his companions. It was Patrokos, the one who had shown signs of panic a few minutes earlier.

"It's nothing," Davos told him, although from the way the hairs on the back of his neck had risen, that was obviously a lie. "Just a—"

"Dog," said the third member of the party, as Kloof emerged from the far rowing well and paced deliberately over the untidy folds of the hastily lowered sail.

Her lips were curled back from her huge teeth. Her hackles were raised, making her appear even larger than she was. And her eyes had a manic, dangerous light in them. She advanced on the three men, her head low, her stride deliberate.

At the stern, Lydia and Edvin became aware of the situation on the foredeck.

"Where did they come from?" Lydia asked, reaching for a dart from her quiver and clipping the atlatl to it. Edvin laid a hand on her arm.

"Careful. You might hit Kloof," he said. Then, as he saw the withering glance she turned on him, he added awkwardly, "I mean, if she moves suddenly, or jumps at them, you could . . . accidentally, of course . . ."

He trailed off but she nodded reluctant agreement. Relieved, he added, "Besides, she seems to have things pretty well in hand."

Davos chose that moment to try to draw his sword. As soon as he moved, Kloof leapt at him, hitting him with all her weight and sending him crashing back to the deck. She stood over him, her tail lashing furiously, snarling and snapping those massive jaws just centimeters from his face. Relinquishing his grip on the sword, Davos raised both his arms to cover his face in a vain attempt to stop the furious, snarling dog.

His two companions backed away from the scene, but neither one made any attempt to draw a weapon. They had seen what happened to Davos.

"What do we do?" asked Patrokos, his voice high pitched and whining with fear. His friend nodded his head toward the sea behind them.

"Jump," he said. But Patrokos looked at the water, looked at Kloof, and shook his head.

"I can't swim," he bleated. The other man shook his head in disgust.

"This would be a good time to learn," he said. Then he grabbed Patrokos's arm and dragged him over the side into the sea.

Under Stig's direction, the remaining members of *Isht-fana*'s crew were lying belly down on the deck, menaced by Stig's, Selethen's and Ingvar's weapons, while Ulf and Wulf moved quickly among them, lashing their hands behind their backs. Jesper and Stefan, who had boarded behind Hal and so had taken no part in the fight, hurried to lend a hand. In a few minutes, the Hellenes were all securely tied.

Thorn, the aggrieved look still on his face, stepped up to Ingvar, who turned to him, smiling.

"You stole my fight," Thorn accused.

The huge youth shrugged. "Didn't see your name on it," he replied. But Thorn shook his head and repeated himself.

"You stole my fight. And you said my thing."

Ingvar frowned at that. "Your thing?" he said. "What thing would that be?"

"My tactical plan. My battle order," Thorn said, glaring. Still Ingvar showed no sign of understanding, so he added, *"Let's get 'em. That's my battle plan."*

"That's a battle plan?" Selethen put in, smiling.

Gilan, who, like Jesper and Stefan, had boarded too late to take any part in the fight, grinned in return. "It's about as complex as Skandian battle plans seem to get."

Selethen considered this and nodded sagely. "Simple plans are the best. There's less that can go wrong."

"Exactly," Gilan agreed. "Once you've said, *Let's get 'em,* you've said it all, really." Thorn turned to the two foreigners and gave them a withering look. Selethen and Gilan smiled easily at him, remaining decidedly unwithered.

"I'll thank you," said Thorn, "not to disparage Skandian tactics." Gilan and Selethen both made disclaiming gestures.

"Far be it from us to disparage," Selethen said.

Gilan hurriedly agreed. "It was more a case of discussing than disparaging."

Thorn eyed them for a few seconds longer, then shrugged. "Very well then." He turned back to Ingvar. "And you should know, Ingvar, that I am the battle leader. When it's time for someone to say, *Let's get 'em,* I will be the one doing the saying. You will be one of the boys who does the getting. Clear?"

"Absolutely, Thorn. My apologies. I got carried away, I'm afraid. Blame Hal. He's the one who fixed it so I can see what I'm doing." Ingvar touched his hand to the tortoiseshell spectacles strapped over his eyes.

Hal stepped forward and put a hand on his massive shoulder. "All the same, Ingvar, you should be careful. What if someone had slashed you across the face and you lost the spectacles? You'd be helpless."

Ingvar grinned. "Think about that, Hal. What if someone slashed you across the face? Spectacles or no, you'd be pretty helpless too."

And Hal had to admit that he was right. The young skirl turned to Thorn with a rueful smile. "You can take some of the blame too, Thorn. You were the one who taught him how to wield that enormous bargepole."

"Did you see him, Thorn?" Stefan chimed in. "It was just like you said. He chopped, he stabbed, he hooked and he chopped again. It was like poetry." He stepped forward to slap Ingvar on the back in congratulation. The big boy shuffled his feet, embarrassed at being the center of attention and admiration.

Thorn finally lightened up. "You did well, Ingvar," he admitted.

Ingvar looked up and beamed at him. Thorn's praise wasn't easily come by—particularly for someone who had just usurped his position in a fight.

"Thanks, Thorn," he said.

Stig, who had finished supervising the binding of the prisoners and, with the twins' help, had dragged them into a line along the bulwarks, rejoined the group.

"If we're finished with this mutual love fest," he said, "what do we do now? How do we get this ship to go where we want it?"

Hal acknowledged the question and gestured to the hatch leading to the rowing deck.

"Good point," he said. "Let's go talk to the rowers. Stig, Thorn, come with me. The rest of you keep an eye on the prisoners." He remembered his manners and looked apologetically at Selethen, realizing that he had just told the nobleman what to do rather abruptly. "If that's all right with you, *Wakir*?"

Selethen gestured graciously for him to go ahead. "Perfectly all right, Captain Hal. I'm here to obey orders." A sly grin touched his lips. "Particularly if someone yells out, *Let's get 'em!*"

"Everyone's a comedian," Thorn grumbled. Then he and Stig followed Hal through the hatch to the rowing deck below.

They went down a short companionway, momentarily blinded by the dimness belowdecks after the bright sun outside. Even before they could see clearly, the smell assaulted their nostrils. It was the smell of dozens of unwashed, sweating bodies, kept cramped in the badly ventilated space of the rowing deck, and of the dirty, foul-smelling water that washed back and forth in the bilges farther below.

As their eyes became accustomed to the darkness, they saw row after row of dirty, bearded faces regarding them. There was neither friendliness nor hostility in the eyes that turned toward them. The three Herons paused at the bottom of the ladder, crouching slightly under the low headroom of the rowing deck, taking stock of the situation. In spite of Davos's earlier fear, the rowing master, whose body could be seen sprawled on the catwalk aft, had made it a practice never to carry the key to the slaves' chains on him. That would have been placing temptation too close to their hands. Instead, it hung on a peg by the aft hatch, well out of the slaves' reach.

As a result, the slaves were still held firmly in place, chained to their oars below the level of the central catwalk. Hal moved a few paces aft and thirty-odd pairs of eyes turned to watch him as he went. Toward the stern, he noted several men collapsed over their oars or slumped on their benches, nursing injuries.

"Fetch Edvin," he said softly to Stig. "And tell him to bring his healer's kit. We've got wounded men here."

The fact that they had been wounded by his own action in bringing the *Heron* slamming alongside was all too obvious to him. The least he could do was have Edvin patch them up as best he could. He stepped a few further paces, stopping about a third of the way down the catwalk. He looked around those unwavering eyes, looking for some glimmer of trust, finding none.

"We need your help," he said, after a pause.

Nothing. No reaction. No buzz of conversation. He looked quickly at Thorn, who shrugged, then he continued.

"I'm Hal Mikkelson, skipper of the Skandian ship *Heron*. We've captured the *Ishtfana* and imprisoned her crew. You'll probably be glad to hear that her captain is dead. He was killed in the fight."

"That wasn't Bloodyhand," a voice from a bench close to him growled. "It was his first mate, Kyrios. Bloodyhand didn't come on this voyage."

Hal made a small moue of interest. "Well, that's news to me. Nevertheless, we've killed or captured Bloodyhand's crew. But we have no wish to keep you imprisoned here. I plan to set you all free."

That created a stir of interest. A low muttering ran along the benches as they heard that magic word *free*—a word none of them had hoped to even think about for the rest of their lives. Hal held up a hand and silence gradually fell.

"But, as I said, we need your help. We plan to drive Iqbal and his Tualaghi bandits out of the town of Tabork, and we need to use this ship to do it. We'll set you free, feed you and clean you up if you wish. But we'll need you to row the ship back to Tabork for us."

Again, there was muttering on the benches. This time, he sensed a darker reaction. He hurried to reassure them.

"There'll be no whipping, no ramming speed, no force used. We don't even want you to fight for us. Just get us to Tabork and you're free to go."

He paused, looking around, waiting for a reaction. He saw uncertainty in some eyes, agreement in others, hostility and distrust in a minority.

One of the rowers spoke up. "What if we say no?"

Hal spread his hands in a gesture of defeat. "We won't try to force you."

Then Thorn stepped forward and spoke. "But we won't unchain you, either. You can stay here, locked to your oars, while we find another way to get into Tabork. In other words, if you won't help us, we won't help you."

Hal glanced at his old friend. It was a harsh threat, he thought, and one that he wouldn't have made. Yet he saw the sense in it. Thorn was simply promising to pay the rowers in their own coin. *Don't cooperate with us and we won't cooperate with you.*

In fact, it wasn't a threat that Hal would carry through. If necessary, they'd tow *Ishtfana* behind the *Heron* to the rendezvous point on the coast. Once there, they'd have plenty of men to row the ship to Tabork. But it would take time, and Hal knew that the sooner they got back to Tabork, the better it would be. The longer they took, the greater the chance that Iqbal would be suspicious on their return. Their entire plan could collapse if the slaves didn't agree to one more journey at the oars.

The silence in the dim rowing deck seemed to stretch on for minutes. Hal heard footsteps on the companionway and turned to see Edvin descending into the rowing deck, wrinkling his nose in distaste. He had his healer's kit slung over his shoulder in a canvas satchel. Hal pointed to the injured men in the stern.

"Down there," he said. "See what you can do for them."

Edvin hurried aft along the catwalk, stopping at the sternmost oar, where the rower slumped against the hull, nursing an obviously broken arm. His face was lacerated and bloodstained. The slightly built healer stepped down onto the rowing bench beside him and began to mop gently at the gash on his forehead—caused by a splinter from the shattering oar.

He worked quickly, but with a light touch that caused as little discomfort as possible. And he spoke in soft, encouraging tones to the man as he worked. The other rowers had swiveled on their benches to watch.

Edvin finished cleaning the wound, smeared it with a healing paste and quickly bound the man's head with a clean linen bandage. His deft touch, and his caring manner, impressed themselves on the watching slaves.

Gently, he pried the man's left hand away from his broken right forearm, inspecting the injury with critical eyes.

"Stig," he called, "I'm going to need you to straighten this arm."

The tall first mate hurried down the catwalk and stepped down onto the bench. Edvin showed him where he wanted to grip and pull the arm back into position.

"When I give you the word," he said, "do it firmly, but don't jerk it. Just pull smoothly and keep going until it's straight. Then I'll splint it." Stig nodded, licking his lips nervously. Edvin touched the wounded man on the shoulder, and leaned close.

"This will hurt," he said. "It will hurt very badly. But it will only be for a minute. And we have to do it if you don't want your arm to be bent for the rest of your life. Understand?"

The man nodded, sweat breaking out on his forehead in anticipation of the pain to come.

"Yell long and loud if you want to," Edvin told him.

The man looked up into the steady eyes of the healer and trusted what he saw there. "Do it," he said.

Edvin prepared himself with two wooden splints and a roll of bandage, then nodded to Stig. "On three," he said. "One, two, three."

Stig gripped and pulled steadily, stretching the arm against the tendons and muscles that wanted to keep it crooked and crippled. Edvin had chosen Stig deliberately. He was young and his muscles were hardened by long hours of rowing and weapons practice. He was stronger than anyone on board, except perhaps Ingvar, and strength was what was needed to put that arm back into a straight line. Thorn, of course, would have been stronger, but with only one hand, he would have been incapable of pulling the two halves of the bone back into position.

The rower screamed in agony, his cries echoing down the length of the rowing deck, the other rowers wincing and turning away as they heard it. Then the arm was straight, the bone was back in line and Edvin quickly wrapped the splints in position, one on either side, whipping the linen bandage round and round to hold them firmly in place and keep the arm straight and supported. The man stopped screaming, his breath coming in ragged gasps.

"You can let go now," Edvin said. Stig released his grip on the man's arm and stood erect. His brow was covered in sweat too.

"Thank you . . . ," the rower gasped. He put his filthy left hand up to touch Edvin in a gesture of gratitude. "Thank you, my friend."

There was a collective release of breath from the rowing benches. Then the man who had queried Hal spoke up.

"We'll row you to Tabork."

chapter twenty - four

Butrus ibn'Shaffran leaned on his spear, gazing out over the dark ocean, and yawned quietly.

The sun had set several hours earlier, plunging into the bloodred western waters of the Constant Sea in a spectacular display of light. As yet, there was no sign of the moon and the sea was black, glistening occasionally with reflected starlight, or where a wavelet toppled over and broke into white foam.

Aside from the muted sounds of the ocean, there were the sounds of the desert behind him as the heat of the day departed. The coast here was hard, rocky ground, but there was a belt of sand dunes half a kilometer wide just inland from the beach, and the sand constantly emitted a low-level whisper of sound as the grains cooled, contracted and shifted closer together. Butrus was a town dweller, not a desert nomad, and the sound was alien to him—

alien and a little disconcerting. But now, as most of the heat dissipated into the clear night air, it was dying down.

He estimated that he had another two hours on watch and yawned again. Behind him, the camp was sleeping. They had eaten early, before sunset, and the men had promptly spread their sleeping blankets close to the cook fires and turned in. They were experienced campaigners and took any opportunity to snatch a few hours, or even minutes, of sleep. Only Butrus and five other sentries remained awake and on guard—along with the troop sergeant major, who seemed to need no sleep and had a disturbing ability to materialize out of the dark, virtually without warning, to check that his sentries were all awake and alert.

"Anything moving?" The sergeant major's hoarse whisper came from just behind Butrus and startled him out of his thoughts. He was sure he actually jumped several centimeters in the air, then brought his spear and himself to the correct vertical position, stiffening to attention as he did so.

"No, Sergeant Major," he said, managing to keep his voice low in spite of the shock. The forty-odd men sleeping on the beach wouldn't thank him for waking them with a shouted reply.

"Then what in the name of the Crimson Djinn of Djebel-Ran is that?"

The sergeant major appeared beside him, grabbing his shoulder and jerking him around so that he was facing to the half right and out to sea. And there, sure enough, was the faintest sign of a bow wave—indicating that ship, a large one, was only forty meters off the beach. Butrus groaned inwardly. That slipup would cost him a week's fatigue duty, he knew.

"It's a ship, Sergeant Major," he said in a dejected tone.

"A ship. So it is. Were you planning on reporting it to me?"

The voice was laced with sarcasm and Butrus ground his teeth in frustration and a sense of unfairness. After all, the sergeant major had *already* seen the ship. He had pointed it out, in fact. It seemed somehow excessive to now tell him what he already knew. Nevertheless, he was the sergeant major.

"There's a ship, Sergeant Major, approaching the beach. Looks like the corsairs' galley."

"Well, I know that," the sergeant major replied. "I told you, didn't I?"

"Yes, Sergeant Major," the hapless sentry replied. There was no other possible answer.

The sergeant major nodded several times. "But were you planning on reporting the other ship as well?"

And, a moment before he said it, Butrus was aware of a smaller ship emerging from the darkness, thirty or so meters astern of the galley.

"There are two ships, Sergeant Major," he said miserably.

The grizzled veteran stared hard at him, shaking his head scornfully. What was the army coming to, he wondered.

"Idiot," he said. "Go and wake the captain. Tell him there are two ships here. I assume it is only two ships?" he added sarcastically.

Butrus actually leaned forward to peer into the darkness again. "Yes, sir. Two ships. Just two."

The sergeant snorted derisively and started to head down the beach toward the spot where the ships would run ashore. Butrus hesitated a moment, then set off at a run toward the captain's small

tent, his equipment and mail armor jingling in time with his hurried footsteps.

"Stop rowing. In oars," Hal called down the companionway. On
the deck below him, he heard Thorn repeat the order and the long
ash-wood oars rose up from the water to lie parallel to the surface
for a count of three. Then, with a slithering clatter of wood on
wood, they slid inboard to be stowed.

Ishtfana, with way still upon her, glided the last twenty meters in
to the beach, her bow nudging into the coarse sand. Hal glanced
over his shoulder and saw *Heron* slipping alongside, to ground her
own bow five meters away.

He tied off the spare oar they had rigged as a makeshift tiller
and nodded to Selethen. "Let's get your men on board."

The tall *Wakir* was already striding forward to where the bow
of the ship rested on dry land. Hal followed him, seeing a small
group of men standing on the beach ready to greet their leader.
Farther up the beach, he could see dark shapes stirring as the
junior officers woke their squads preparatory to boarding the
ship.

Hal slipped down the aft companionway and looked along the
twin line of rowers. Small lanterns at bow and stern cast an uncertain light over them but he could see more than half of the men
were clean and clad in fresh clothes. On the trip to pick up Selethen's men, he had allowed groups of five to clean themselves and
take new clothes from the corsairs' quarters in the bow. He had
also allowed them to eat—food from the corsairs' supplies, not the
vile muck that had been kept for them as slaves. Edvin, who had

finished patching up the rest of the injured men, had supervised them, making sure they didn't eat too much, too fast. A sudden excess of rich food after months of near starvation could make them violently ill.

"Thank you," Hal called along the lines of rowers. "Just a few more hours and you never need to touch an oar again."

Hal couldn't resist a smile as he looked at the men on the rowing benches. For months they had spent their time clad only in filthy loincloths. Occasionally, the crew would "bathe" them by hurling buckets of water over them as they sat chained to their oars. Now those who had already cleaned themselves up, washing in buckets of seawater on the main deck, were dressed in the corsairs' finest clothes, and as has been noted, the Hellenese pirates tended toward the flamboyant when it came to fashion. The rowing benches now were a mass of scarlet, yellow and bright blue silks and satins. Shirts with ridiculously wide sleeves gathered at the wrist were very much the order of the day. Hal doubted if anyone had ever seen such an exotic group of rowers. He shook his head and made his way back to the main deck.

Already, the first of Selethen's twenty-five soldiers were clambering over the bow, carrying their weapons and equipment. They stared about them curiously as they came. Many of them were desert cavalrymen, and the odds were, none had ever seen a ship close up, let alone been on one, before. They were shepherded aft by the twins. That was another point of fascination for the Arridans. Several of them gawked openly at the two identical sailors who were urging them to keep moving.

Finally, Wulf reacted to the constant staring and head-shaking.

"What are you looking at?" he demanded of one young soldier—a youth barely out of his teens. The cavalry trooper pointed to Ulf, who was a few meters away.

"That man," the trooper said. "You look just like him."

Wulf scowled at his brother, then at the young Arridan. "No I don't," he retorted crisply. "He looks like me." Then he added darkly, if not logically, "And he'd better stop doing it if he knows what's good for him!"

Thoroughly confused, the trooper continued aft, stumbling over a coil of rope as he turned to look back at the two identical figures.

Hal waited until a dozen of the Arridans were gathered in the stern of the ship, then addressed them. "You can stay on this deck while we're heading up the coast. Once we get closer to Tabork, you'll have to go below and stay out of sight. But for the moment, enjoy the fresh air."

He had visions of the troopers, unaccustomed to the sea and to the overpowering atmosphere of the rowing deck, being violently sick all the way to Tabork. Better to let them stay on the upper deck for as long as possible, he thought. Once they went below, they would crouch on the catwalk, between the rowers. But that would only be for a relatively short time and he hoped the confined space, the rank air and the evil smell from the bilges wouldn't have too debilitating an effect on them.

Leaving the first group to pass on the word to their comrades, he strode forward and climbed down onto the beach, where Selethen and Gilan were talking. From the deck of the *Heron*, Stig had seen him going ashore and hurried now to join them.

"Ready to go aboard, *Wakir*?" Hal asked. But Selethen surprised him by shaking his head.

"I won't be traveling with you to Tabork," he said. He turned to a small group of officers waiting nearby and beckoned one of them over. "Captain Rahim! Would you join us, please?"

A stockily built man in his early thirties came toward them. He had obviously spent his life as a cavalryman, Hal thought with a smile. His legs were slightly bowed from years in the saddle, and as a consequence, he rocked slightly from side to side as he came. He stopped and performed the traditional Arridan salute to his *Wakir*, touching his fingers to lips, brow and lips, and bowing slightly.

"*Wakir*?" he said, waiting for orders. Selethen turned to Gilan and Hal, introducing them to the captain, who bowed to them in turn. Rahim's keen eyes assessed the two foreigners and Hal could almost hear his thoughts: *This one is young. I hope he knows what he's doing.*

"Captain Rahim will command the landing party," Selethen continued. "I'll travel overland to Tabork and resume command of the main attack." He took two long bundles from another of his subordinates and handed them to Gilan.

"These are signal arrows," he said. "The heads contain a substance that is highly flammable and that, when confined, explodes in a large puff of white smoke. When you're in position, light the fuse on one and shoot it vertically into the air. As soon as I see the signal, I'll launch the attack on the main gate. Then, if you hit Iqbal and his men from behind, you should be able to drive through them and open the gates for us."

"So long as everything goes according to plan," Hal put in.

Gilan smiled grimly. "Which it rarely does."

Selethen raised an eyebrow, acknowledging the fact that the best-laid plans usually fell in a heap once the actual fighting started.

"Well," he said, "if you have any trouble, just let friend Ingvar loose on the Tualaghi with his ax on a stick. I'm sure he'd frighten the hardiest desert bandit."

"I'm sure he would," Stig said. "He frightens me plenty."

chapter twenty-five

P hilip the Bloodyhand came awake to a discreet knocking on the door of his room. At least, the knocking started discreetly. When the initial attempts failed to rouse the corsair captain, the servant at the door progressively increased the volume until the sound pierced the wine-sodden consciousness of the gross man inside.

Philip was sprawled on his stomach on the bed. He went to rise, putting his hand down to push up from the soft mattress. But he was lying crosswise, where he had collapsed the night before. His hand missed the bed, he lost his balance and rolled off onto the floor. Fortunately, the bed was a simple pile of thick cushions laid on the tiled floor, so he didn't have far to fall. But his temper flared as he rolled onto the tiles, then struggled to a sitting position.

"What is it?" he shouted angrily, and instantly wished he

hadn't. His hand flew to his pulsing forehead in a vain attempt to stem the sudden pain there. His tongue was thick and his mouth was dry. And there was that sullen pulse of pain behind his eyes. Several empty wine flasks and jars scattered around the room bore mute testimony to the source of his discomfort.

The door opened a crack and one of his servants leaned a cautious head around it. Philip had been known to hurl objects—often pointed ones—at people who woke him.

"Captain, the ship is back. With a prize," the servant said nervously. At least the second part of the statement should allay any serious display of bad temper, he thought.

Philip grunted and rubbed his eyes. He swallowed several times and scowled at the man at the door.

"Get me wine," he said, then thought better of the idea. "No. Wait. Get me water—cold water. And squeeze some lemon juice into it."

"Yes, captain," said the servant, taking the order as permission to leave. He scurried away while Philip looked blearily around for his clothes. It took a few seconds for him to realize that he was still wearing them. They were the usual gaudy mixture that Hellenese corsairs were so fond of. His trousers were wide bottomed and bright blue, held in place by a scarlet sash. His shirt was buttercup-yellow satin, stretched across his large belly, and his calf-high boots were soft red Socorran leather.

The visual effect of the bright colors was somewhat spoiled by the food and wine stains that were all too apparent on them, but such matters were below Philip's notice. He looked around for his red bandanna, cursing as he failed to see it. Someone had once told him that wearing a red bandanna was the sign of a feeble mind but Philip was inordinately fond of his, perhaps proving the point. After scowling around the room, he realized that it was on his head, cocked to one side. He straightened it and heaved himself off the floor, moving to the open archway that led onto his second-floor terrace, overlooking the harbor.

He winced at the sun reflecting brilliantly off the white buildings and sparkling waters of the harbor, narrowing his eyes to see against the glare.

Yes, there was the *Ishtfana*, rowing steadily toward the harbor entrance, with a smaller ship in tow behind her—the prize his servant had mentioned. Shading his eyes, he peered at the twin moles and saw the boom crew were busy releasing the massive chain that barred entrance to the harbor, allowing it to sink below the surface so that *Ishtfana* could enter unhindered.

He heard the door of the room open and his servant was back, bearing a tray that held a jug of water, a mug and several lemons, cut in half. He seized the jug and drank greedily from it. The sharp taste of the lemon juice already lacing the water cut through the thickness that clogged his mouth. He upended the jug, water spilling round the sides of it and soaking his shirt front. Then he lowered it, took a deep breath, belched and dropped it onto the bed cushions. The servant hurried to retrieve it.

"Tell Lord Iqbal the *Ishtfana* is back," he said curtly, and strode toward the door. His curved sword hung from a peg by the door. He took it down, shoved the scabbard through the yellow sash round his waist and went out, tugging on the single red gauntlet that he wore on his right hand as a reminder of his nickname—Bloodyhand.

"He's already been informed," his servant replied. But Philip was gone.

He lumbered down the stairs and out into the hot sun. He was a tall and grotesquely overweight man, given to the pleasures of the flesh. He had barely gone twenty paces before his face was running with perspiration.

He grunted with the effort of walking in the heat, and with the dull pain that still thumped behind his eyes, as he made his way onto the wharf. He could see Iqbal already there, waiting by the water's edge, watching the galley make its way through the harbor entrance. In contrast to the corsair, the Tualaghi chief was a tall, ascetic person, his dark blue robes seemingly in defiance of the heat of the sun. The lower half of his face was covered with the traditional blue veil of the Tualaghi. Philip had only ever seen his face uncovered in private. He knew that beneath the headdress and veil, Iqbal was bald—his head carefully shaven daily. His nose was a hooked shape, reminiscent of a bird of prey's beak, and his eyes were dark and penetrating—again like those of a hawk or an eagle.

Those dark eyes turned now onto the stained and lumbering figure of the pirate captain, viewing him with obvious distaste. Philip was sure that beneath the veil, Iqbal's thin-lipped mouth would be curled in a sneer. Philip couldn't care less. Iqbal's opinion on Philip's personal habits meant nothing to him. They were allies, bound together by convenience, not friendship or mutual admiration. For his part, Philip considered Iqbal to be a cold-blooded, joyless desert lizard.

"I see she took the trader," Philip said, gesturing toward the smaller ship bobbing obediently in *Ishtfana*'s wake.

The Tualaghi leader raised an eyebrow. "It took her long enough," he said. "It would seem your second in command isn't very good at his job."

Philip shrugged. The small trader had appeared to be a slow sailer when she was sighted the day before. He wondered why Kyrios took so long to secure her and bring her back. Iqbal was right. His first mate wasn't the most reliable or the most intelligent of men. As a corsair captain, Philip had always made sure that the men beneath him were capable, but not outstanding, in their jobs. That way, there was a smaller chance that one of them might try to usurp him. Knowing Kyrios as he did, he assumed that the first mate had kept the rowers at maximum speed for too long, exhausting them far too early in the chase so that their quarry had gained ground on them.

But he wasn't about to let this camel-riding oaf denigrate his ship or his crew.

"Easy to criticize when you know nothing of the problems facing a sailor," he said truculently.

"She's here now. That's all that matters to me," Iqbal said dismissively. He turned on his heel and strode away from the edge of the wharf. There was nothing to be gained from standing watching the ships come alongside. He would be informed of the trader's cargo in due time, and he knew Philip wouldn't dare to cheat him or short change him. Iqbal's own men would keep a strict eye on the unloading of the cargo.

As he crossed the wharf, heading for his own accommodation, he caught sight of Dhakwan and three of his men striding onto the wharf. Dhakwan's *Khumsan*, or squad of fifty, had entered Tabork the previous night under cover of darkness. They were quartered close to the harbor, in a disused warehouse. It occurred to Iqbal that Dhakwan's men would be a suitable group to oversee the unloading of the captured ship. He beckoned to the leader, who approached him, performing a perfunctory version of the traditional salute.

"My lord?"

Iqbal jerked a thumb at the two ships moving across the harbor. "*Ishtfana*'s taken a prize. Rouse your men out and take charge of the unloading. Make sure that fat, greasy Hellene doesn't try to spirit any of the cargo away."

"As you command," Dhakwan said. He turned to one of his companions and issued orders for the *Khumsan* to be roused and paraded on the wharf.

"Armed, sir?" his lieutenant asked.

Dhakwan eyed him steadily. "Of course I want them armed," he said. "I'm not taking them on a picnic. Now move!"

His assistant accepted the rebuke philosophically. Dhakwan was a sarcastic commander. He'd known that when he elected to join his band years ago, working his way up through the ranks to become one of his trusted deputies. A little sarcasm never really hurt, once you learned to ignore it, and Dhakwan had been a successful leader, helping his men win large amounts of gold and silver and jewelry over the years. He hurried back through a narrow alley, leading to the large building one street back from the wharf where the *Khumsan* was billeted. As he came within hearing, he began shouting for the men to assemble.

On the wharf, Philip was peering blearily at the rapidly approaching ship. Something wasn't quite right, he thought. He scanned the small group standing around the steering platform. None of them looked familiar. In particular, he searched for Kyrios's distinctive and colorful figure—but without success. He frowned. The foredeck was empty. Normally, the fighting crew would be gathered there, drinking and celebrating a successful pursuit. But there was nobody.

And the group in the stern bothered him. None of them were dressed in the bright colors that he expected to see. They were in drab browns and grays. One of them was wrapped in a gray-and-green cloak. And he appeared to be armed with a longbow.

And surely that slim figure to one side was a girl!

Suddenly, Philip realized that they had been tricked. This was not his crew bringing the *Ishtfana* alongside. He had no idea who they might be, but they weren't his men. He turned desperately. There was a harbor guard standing nearby, armed with a heavy horn bow. Philip ran to him, snatched the weapon, then dragged several arrows out of the man's back quiver, nocking one to the string and turning back to face the ships.

"Sound the alarm!" he shouted. "We're being attacked!"

The man stared at him in surprise for a second or two, then he saw the corsair leader drawing the arrow back and taking aim at the incoming ship and was galvanized into action.

"Alarm!" he shouted to the two lookouts in a tower above the wharf. "Sound the alarm! We're under attack!"

He heard the deadly thrum of the bow as Philip released.

The corsair captain was fat, debauched and unpleasant. But he had excellent weapon skills. Without them, he wouldn't have lasted a week at the command of his band of cutthroats. The arrow flashed across the intervening space, aimed unerringly at the helmsman holding the tiller.

Gilan saw it coming, heard the shouting on the wharf. He grabbed Hal and dragged him down just in time, as the arrow hissed overhead, through the space the young skirl had just occupied.

"Thorn!" the Ranger shouted. "Get those men up here now!"

He could see the gaudily clad figure on the wharf nocking another arrow and reached for his own quiver. But his hand fell on one of the two signal arrows that he had carelessly placed in there the day before. He cursed and fumbled for a normal shaft.

But Lydia was quicker. She too had seen the archer on the wharf. And she took note of the red gauntlet on his right hand, guessing the significance.

"Well, well," she muttered. "It's Philip Pattyfingers himself."

With the speed of totally instinctive movement, drilled into her muscle memory by years of practice and thousands of shots, she selected a dart, clipped it onto the atlatl, sighted and cast in a matter of seconds.

Philip was drawing back the second arrow when he felt a massive impact against his chest. The bow and arrow fell from his grip and he looked down, puzzled, to see the long dart that had just transfixed him. He felt no pain at first. The impact was like a hard punch but the area was numb.

Then the pain came. Huge waves of it.

Then the bright sunlit day turned black and he collapsed to the wharf like a rag doll.

chapter   twenty-six

Ishtfana's bow bumped against the wharf at an angle and grated along it as the ship slewed in parallel to the stone wall. Stefan and Jesper hurled mooring ropes over the bollards set along the wharf's edge and, with Stig and Ingvar helping, hauled the ship alongside. All four of them had their weapons ready and, with the exception of Ingvar, their big round shields slung over their backs.

Led by Thorn, the first of the Arridan cavalrymen surged up the companionway onto the deck, then leapt up onto the wharf itself. They were joined by the Herons, with the exception of Edvin, who was on board the *Heron,* steering her behind the galley. Kloof remained with him, just in case there was a repetition of the flanking attack that had happened the previous day. With Kloof remaining on the ship, it would have to be a bold Tualaghi who dared to try and board *Heron.* Or a foolish one.

Hal was the last to step ashore, held up by the surge of cavalry-men as they clambered awkwardly onto the wharf, hampered by their knee-high riding boots. He slipped his own shield, the blue Gallican kite-shaped one, over his left arm and drew his sword from its scabbard.

Briefed by Thorn on the journey up the coast, the Arridan troops formed two lines behind the Skandians, who were in their traditional wedge shape, with Thorn at the apex, flanked by Stig and Ingvar, who was reveling in the fact that he could take an active part in the fight. The dark brown, opaque circles over his eyes gave him an ominous, skull-like look.

There was a small group of harbor guards facing them, perhaps nine or ten men. They began backing cautiously away from the new arrivals, their eyes darting nervously along the line, bristling with weapons.

Then the whole picture changed.

There was a rattle of boots on stone and a jingle of mail and equipment and a file of blue-clad Tualaghi emerged from a side alley, running quickly onto the wharf and forming up in a single line in the shape of a shallow crescent. The harbor guards, their confidence boosted by the unexpected reinforcements, fell into place with them.

Thorn estimated their numbers. Close to sixty, he thought. And most of them would be hardened desert warriors, not fat, under-trained garrison troops.

"This could be a problem," he muttered.

Gilan had shouldered his way through to stand beside him, one of the signal arrows ready on his bow. Lydia stood with a flint and steel ready to light the fuse.

"Should I send up the signal?" he asked.

Thorn hesitated, then came to a decision. "Do it. If we wait any longer, Selethen won't be in position in time."

Gilan half turned and held the cloth-wrapped arrow tip out to Lydia. She struck her flint against steel, and the sparks caught the oil-soaked fuse, setting it spluttering and hissing as it burned its way toward the explosive powder wrapped in the cloth. Gilan swung the bow up to near vertical, drew back and released. The arrow soared upward, trailing an almost-invisible thread of gray smoke behind it.

All eyes swung up to watch it. All except Thorn's. His eyes were slitted as he watched the Tualaghi facing them, waiting for the moment when the exploding arrow would distract them.

"Ready . . . ," he growled.

It came. The arrow, almost at the apogee of its flight, suddenly burst in a cloud of white smoke. A second later, they heard the dull *crump* of the chemicals erupting.

There were exclamations of surprise from the men facing them, and in that moment, while their attention was on the drifting cloud of smoke, Thorn gave his time-honored command.

"Let's get 'em, boys!" he yelled, and charged full tilt at the half circle of Tualaghi facing them.

The flying wedge of Skandians slammed into the center of the enemy line, driving half a dozen of the Tualaghi back, leaving four of them on the stone surface of the wharf. Axes rose and fell, shield smashed against shield, swords flashed a· ¹   And, in the center, Thorn's terrible club-ha·nd rose   ⸱ from side to side ⸱·   ·ng bones ⸱   ⸱g ⸱·⸱   ·ying

                              ·un   ·e Skandian

force on either side, to be met in turn by the Arridan troops arrayed behind them. The fighting became general, with men on either side seeking an opponent and hacking and thrusting and shoving at him.

Gilan and Lydia stood back, one on either side, watching to see if a sneak attack might threaten one of their comrades. Gilan's bow and Lydia's atlatl were both loaded and ready. But in the confused mass of fighting, shoving troops, it was too difficult to single out an enemy. The odds of hitting one of their own were too high.

It was the Skandian wedge that made the difference, as was so often the case. Thorn's club, Stig's ax and Ingvar's thrusting, hacking voulge took a terrible toll of the defenders. The defensive line wavered, then broke as the blue-robed warriors began to retreat. At first they went a step at a time, still facing their attackers. Then, as more of them fell to that dreadful trio of weapons at the head of the wedge, they began to move more quickly.

Then they were running for the shelter of an alleyway behind them, leading away from the wharf.

"Come on!" yelled Thorn, leading the charge after them. But as the group surged forward, he roared another order. "Don't break formation! Maintain the wedge!"

It was the wedge formation that gave them the strength to break the line, with each man in the wedge capable of supplying support and assistance to the men beside him. If they broke that pattern, they could be isolated and picked off as individuals by their more numerous enemy.

Accordingly, Thorn slowed the pace of their advance to a fast walk, with the wedge still in place and the Arridans supporting either side.

And it was this delay that gave Dhakwan the chance to rally his men and launch a counterattack.

The lieutenant shoved his way to the head of the jostling mob as they struggled through the narrow alley. By the time the retreating Tualaghi emerged into a small plaza at the end of the alley, he was in position to confront them. He stood before them, arms spread wide to contain them, his scimitar gleaming a threat in his right hand.

"Stop!" Dhakwan screamed. He dragged the blue veil down from his face so that they would recognize him. "You're running like women! Now stop. Turn and face the enemy!"

Gradually, the panic began to seep away. The warriors looked at the men either side of them, shamefaced. Seeing their returning confidence, Dhakwan seized the opportunity.

He pointed to another, narrower alley leading out of the plaza, on the far side. "We'll make a stand there!" he shouted. "At the far end of that alley is another plaza. We'll meet them there where they're restricted in the alley and we have room to move. And we will annihilate them!"

He pointed with his sword at the dark entrance to the alley across the plaza. From the far end of the one his men had just taken, he could hear the steady tramp of feet as the Skandian wedge, supported by the Arridans, advanced.

The Tualaghi began to stream across the plaza. Again, Dhakwan's booming voice, echoing off the buildings surrounding them, nipped any incipient panic in the bud.

"Move quickly. But steadily!" he shouted. "Hold your formation. Rear ranks, turn to face the enemy. Those in front, steady them as they march."

Obediently, those in the rear of the Tualaghi force turned to face their pursuers. The men in front of them placed hands on their shoulders to guide and support them as they walked quickly backward to the alley.

They had just plunged into the second alley, moving at a steady pace, when the Skandians emerged from the first. Thorn glanced around, saw the last of the defenders drifting back into the shadows of the second alley, and motioned his men forward.

"Come on!" he shouted. "At the double!"

The Skandian wedge, followed by the Arridans, double-timed across the small plaza. From upper windows, veiled women and curious children peered out at the two groups of foreigners engaged in a battle for their town.

Thorn plunged into the shadows of the alley. At the far end, he could see the Tualaghi force emerging into the sunlit open space of yet another plaza. Slowing down a little more, to make sure their formation remained intact, he led the combined force forward.

"This is all taking too long," he muttered. It had been some time since Gilan had shot his signal arrow. Selethen and his men must now be engaged at the main gate, with no sign of any help from within. He had hoped to scatter the Tualaghi defenders who faced them, sending them running in panic at his sudden, unexpected attack. But the alarm had been raised too soon and he could see that the leader of the enemy group had his men well in hand, and was staging a carefully controlled retreat.

On top of that, he estimated that they were facing nearly sixty men—out of a reported force of two hundred. Iqbal could hardly manage to commit such a large proportion of his available troops away from the main attack. Somebody must have got the numbers wrong, he thought grimly. There were more Tualaghi in the harbor town than they had been led to believe.

He reached the end of the second alley and stopped. In the sunlit plaza outside, the Tualaghi had stopped retreating and were formed up in a crescent line again, facing their pursuers.

"Shields!" Thorn bellowed, as the line facing him surged toward him, swords swinging, spears thrusting. Instantly, he found himself engaged in a desperate battle. He had nearly thirty men behind him but no more than half a dozen could force their way out of the alley at any one time.

Fortunately, that half dozen was made up of some of the finest warriors he had ever served with. Stig and Ingvar hacked and thrust and stabbed at the surging line of Tualaghi. Hal fought with his usual controlled ferocity and skill, deflecting attacks and darting his sword forward in lightning thrusts that sent enemy soldiers reeling or sprawling to the cobblestones. The four of them forced their way forward and Ulf and Wulf emerged to widen the line, facing out on either side at the warriors who were trying to envelop them. As the Herons fought their way forward, more of the crew joined the battle, slowly forcing the enemy line back.

Then the Tualaghi came at them with renewed energy and desperation, and they were forced to give ground. Behind them, confined in the alleyway, the twenty-five Arridans shouted in frustration, desperate to get into the clear and join the battle.

Gilan and Lydia, unable to take part in the battle without endangering their own men, met at the rear of the force.

"We should have taken a dozen men down one of the parallel alleys," Lydia said. "That way, we could have launched a flanking attack on them." But Gilan shook his head.

"There are too many of them. We'd need a bigger force to make that work. A dozen men attacking from the flank would be cut down in short time. We'd need thirty or forty and we don't have them."

Lydia frowned, then looked up at him. "I think I know where I can find them."

She turned and, running lightly, headed back across the plaza for the wharf.

chapter twenty-seven

S elethen saw the white cloud of smoke blossom over the town, then heard the muted *thump* of the exploding chemicals. He drew his sword and turned to one of his lieutenants.

"They're in the town," he said. "It's time for us to go. Make sure the riders with the ladders are close behind us."

His subordinate turned in his saddle and checked the line of riders ready to follow the *Wakir* into battle. Devoid of any heavy siege towers or assault machinery, Selethen's men had constructed three light ladders to aid their attack on the walls of Tabork. Each one was supported between two riders. He made eye contact with the ladder carriers now and received their nods of confirmation. They were ready.

"Stay close!" he called.

Selethen's plan was a simple one. They were currently hidden from sight on the reverse slope of a shallow hill some two hundred meters from the southern gate—the main access way into the town. On his command, the troop would gallop across the open space to the town, trusting to their speed to minimize any losses from missiles shot by the defenders. Once at the walls beside the main gate, they would dismount and turn their horses loose. The three ladders would be placed against the wall, and with a little luck, some of them might reach the top and give cover to their comrades below. The Skandians, reinforced by twenty-five of Selethen's troopers, would hopefully fight their way through to the gate from the opposite direction, taking the defenders by surprise and opening it to admit the bulk of Selethen's men into the town. Success depended on speed and surprise, catching the defenders from two sides.

"Stay close to the walls!" Selethen called to his men. He'd already dinned this into them. If they stood out from the walls, they would be easier targets for the defenders above. Huddled close in the lee of the fortifications, they would be protected, unless the Tualaghi leaned out through the battlements to shoot at them. And when they did that, they would be exposed to return shots from the attackers' short but powerful bows.

"Ready!" He raised his sword, then swept it down to point straight ahead. "Charge!"

He jammed his heels into his stallion's ribs and the horse leapt away, going from a dead stop to full speed in a matter of a few meters.

Behind him, he heard the thunder of hooves as his men followed him, spreading out in a ragged line, their pennants and headscarves streaming behind them in the wind. This wasn't an ordered cavalry charge, where each man and horse had to maintain a strict position in the line. This was a matter of crossing the open ground between them and the walls in as short a time as possible. Out to his right, he saw a trooper overtaking him, forging ahead.

Then the man went down, his horse somersaulting beneath him and sending him flying headlong into the rocky ground. A cloud of dust obscured them and Selethen had no idea whether it had been the man or the horse who had been hit by an arrow.

He could hear the arrows buzzing past his ears now as the Tualaghi singled him out as the leader and tried to pick him off. He swerved his horse violently and a salvo of arrows flashed through the space he had just occupied. One of his riders had unslung his own bow and was fitting an arrow to the string, controlling his horse with only his knees. Selethen shouted to him.

"Save your arrows! We'll need them at the wall!"

Accurate shooting from a plunging, galloping horse would be virtually impossible, he knew. Better to wait until they were at the base of the wall. An arrow tugged at his sleeve, jerking him around in the saddle. He saw another two riders go down, then saw a spear striking sparks off the rocks as it hit and rebounded.

If they were within spear range, there were only seconds to go. He looked up at the wall, towering above him. He could see the blue-veiled heads of the defenders peering over it, and from time to time, a defender was visible from the waist up as he stepped into one of the crenellations for a clearer shot.

A platoon commander a few paces ahead of him reined in, drew back his arm and cast his spear at one such Tualaghi. The blue-robed figure staggered back from the wall, transfixed by the heavy spear.

Then Selethen was sliding his horse to a stiff-legged halt, clouds of dust billowing around him as his men did the same. Throwing his leg over the pommel, he released the reins and dropped to the ground, instantly breaking into a run as he dashed for the walls.

All around him, horses were neighing and whinnying as they kicked up extra storms of dust and their riders dismounted. The horses, no longer under control, trotted aimlessly as their riders scrambled for the vestigial shelter at the base of the walls.

The dust and the blundering horses served an unforeseen purpose, providing cover for the dismounted men, distracting and unsighting the Tualaghi on the walls. Selethen saw two of the ladder carriers running forward to the wall. He went with them, beckoning to a group of five troopers to follow.

"Bows!" he shouted to them. "Clear the top of that wall while I go up. Then come after me!"

One of them, a corporal with years of battle experience, nodded his understanding. As the ladder crashed against the top of the wall, bouncing out once, then settling again, he mustered the other four men to its base, bows ready.

"Go on, lord!" he shouted to Selethen. "We'll cover you."

At that moment, a blue-veiled face appeared above the wall as its owner tried to shove the ladder back. Three of the bows thrummed loudly and the Tualaghi screamed and fell back. Two of the shafts had found their mark. Two more would-be defenders were picked off and Selethen realized he was wasting time. He leapt for the ladder and ran lightly upward, feeling the springy wood bending and flexing under his weight as he ascended. An arrow from below hissed just over his head, and he heard a cry of pain from the battlements above him.

Then he was at the top. He felt the ladder vibrating as one of his men began to follow him up it. A defender to his left raised a spear, then dropped it as an arrow took him in the armpit. Another came at Selethen from the right, thrusting with a spear. Selethen deflected the heavy weapon with his sword, then chopped back at the enemy, the razor-sharp curved blade cutting into the man's shoulder and neck. The *Wakir* snatched his sword free as the man fell, then vaulted over the battlements onto the catwalk behind them. Three more defenders rushed at him and he stood firm, parrying their blows with an iron wrist, then, when one of them over-reached, darting the tip of his sword forward like a striking snake. Behind him, he heard two more of his men coming over the wall, dropping onto the catwalk with him. A third was less fortunate. A Tualaghi archer standing back from the fight felled him with an arrow. The man hung over the empty space at the top of the ladder for a moment, then toppled back down onto the hard ground below.

Now there were more Tualaghi archers running onto a redoubt that stood out from the wall thirty meters away, allowing them a clear shot back at the men at the base of the wall and any who tried to mount the ladder.

"Shields!" Selethen yelled to his men below. "Shield wall and roof! Now!"

The men bunched together, the front rank dropping to their knees and raising their shields into an angled wall facing the archers. Those in the second rank crouched to take cover, and brought their own shields up over their heads. The group now presented a protective steel barrier to the archers. They were relatively safe behind the shield wall and roof, but they couldn't go anywhere without being shot. They were trapped.

Selethen brought his attention back to his immediate situation—and not a moment too soon. A Tualaghi swung a murderous two-handed stroke at him with a huge scimitar. Selethen swayed to one side to evade the blow and cut at the man's upper arm.

His sword bit through the chain-mail shirt the man was wearing over his blue robe, and sliced through the flesh and muscle, cutting to the bone. The desert raider screamed in pain as the sword fell from his hands. He stumbled away, doubled over, trying desperately to stanch the blood flowing freely from the wound. Selethen grunted in satisfaction. He was out of the fight, just as surely as if the *Wakir*'s blow had killed him. Selethen parried another sword, jabbed back at his attacker's eyes, visible above the blue veil, and sent him reeling back in panic.

"Get your backs to the wall!" he shouted at his two comrades, and the three of them slowly gave ground until the rough stone of the wall was against their backs. With their rear safe from attack, they faced out at the remaining three sides, defending desperately, attacking when they had the opportunity. Selethen noted that one of the other troopers had blood running down his right leg.

"Hurry up, Gilan," he muttered under his breath. "We can't hold out here for long."

Lydia ran onto the wharf, her soft-soled boots making a grating noise on the crushed gravel that formed the surface. Edvin was now aboard *Ishtfana*. He waved to her and she headed gratefully for the galley. Since they had been gone, he had hauled the *Heron* alongside the larger ship and tied them together. Kloof, seeing him wave, stood up on her hind legs to peer over the bow of the galley and barked a cheerful greeting to Lydia.

Kloof!

Lydia clambered up onto the ship, then stepped down onto the foredeck, absentmindedly patting Kloof's huge head as she did so.

"What's the rush?" Edvin said. "Is there some kind of trouble?"

"There's plenty of trouble," she told him. In spite of her run back to the wharf, she wasn't even breathing heavily. Lydia was in excellent condition and, as a hunter, she had spent years running down fast-moving prey. "There are a lot more defenders than we were told and we're badly outnumbered. The crew are bottled up in an alley by about sixty men and can't make headway. If we don't get them moving, Selethen's force will be wiped out."

Before she had finished speaking, Edvin had clambered back aboard the *Heron*, where he retrieved his sword belt and shield. He rejoined her now, a doubtful look on his face.

"Well, I'll come back with you. And we can take Kloof. But I'm not sure we'll make much of a difference."

"I was thinking of enlisting the rowing crew," Lydia said. "There are over thirty of them and if we can make a flanking attack, that should turn the tide. Are they still on board?"

He nodded. "They're below. I guess they're used to it there and they didn't see much point in going ashore into the middle of a battle. Do you think they'll fight?"

Lydia shrugged and ran to the hatch leading to the rowing deck. "If they don't, they'll be slaves again in less than an hour."

There was a low buzz of conversation on the rowing deck. As

she came down the companionway, the noise ceased and thirty-five pairs of eyes studied her curiously.

"We need your help," she said bluntly.

"Again?" It was the rower who had originally questioned Hal when he had asked them to row the ship to Tabork. Lydia singled him out and nodded.

"Again," she said. "The battle is going badly. Our men are outnumbered. There are far more Tualaghi in the town than we'd been told. If we don't break through them, and soon, the attack will fail. Selethen's men are already outnumbered and they won't have any way of getting into the town. They need Hal and the others to fight their way through and get the gates open."

"And how is that our problem?" another man asked, and his companions' eyes all turned briefly to him, then back to Lydia.

"If we lose," Lydia told him, with a grim note in her voice, "Hal and the others will be killed." She saw the man beginning to shrug, and added quickly, "And what do you think will happen to you then?"

The man's head came up and several of the others began to mutter as they realized the implications of what she had just said. She rammed home the point.

"D'you think Iqbal is going to shake your hands, pat you on the head and send you on your way?" she asked sarcastically. She paused, then added the obvious answer to her question. "You'll be chained up and pulling those oars again before you have a chance to think."

"We could take the ship ourselves," the man said. "We could escape to sea."

"And how would you get past the boom?" Lydia asked him, and saw the sudden light of hope in his eyes fade. "You're stuck here, and unless you help us, you'll remain here."

"I knew we shouldn't have helped you!" a third man said.

She glared at him. He was the sort, she felt, who would always whine about his lot.

"Well, you did," she told him harshly. "You're here now and there's nothing you can do to change that. But you can fight for your freedom."

She stopped. There was nothing more to say. This wasn't the time for a stirring call to action. Their choice was grim, and simple. Fight alongside the Heron Brotherband or be dragged back into captivity. After a long pause, the original speaker asked a question that set her heart racing with hope.

"What do we do for weapons?"

She heaved a sigh of relief, then gestured forward to the crew's quarters. "The crew had weapons," she pointed out. "You can use them. And if there aren't enough, you can shape some of the broken oars into clubs."

The man stood and turned to face his fellow rowers.

"She's right," he said. "We have no choice. So let's arm ourselves and finish the fight."

chapter   twenty-eight

It was a raggle-taggle mob that Lydia led away from the ship. She and Edvin were in the lead, with Kloof straining against the leash held by Edvin. Behind them straggled the former slaves. Some were dressed in the gaudy, but grubby, finery left behind by the corsairs. A few were still in the ragged, filthy clothes they had worn on the rowing bench for the past months.

The majority of them were armed with a selection of actual weapons—swords, axes, spears and maces. But half a dozen of them had to content themselves with clubs and staffs made from shortened oars. Looking at them, Lydia decided they would probably be just as effective as the other weapons in the hands of untrained men.

Normally, taking a group of ex–galley slaves into battle against the hardened troops commanded by Iqbal would be an almost certain recipe for failure. The rowers were hard muscled, admittedly. But they had been ill treated and malnourished for months and their reserves of energy and strength would be limited. Plus they weren't experienced warriors. The awkward way some of them held their weapons made that only too clear.

But her aim wasn't to defeat the Tualaghi defenders. It was to launch a surprise attack from the rear or the flank, distracting them, making them turn away from Hal and his men and so giving the latter a chance to break clear of the alley where they were hemmed in and drive the enemy back in confusion.

They reached the first plaza—the alley where the attackers were contained lay straight ahead. Lydia looked to either side and saw another narrow street leading off to the left, parallel to the alley. She gestured toward it.

"Come on!" she shouted, and set off at a jog, the irregular patter of the rowers' bare feet on the cobbles telling her that they were following.

Kloof let go a short, explosive bark and strained forward. It was all Edvin could do to contain her.

They entered the shady side street, their eyes unaccustomed to the dimness after the glare outside. As they ran along it, Lydia realized that it angled away from the alley where the Herons were fighting. Her heart pounded with anxiety. What if this street didn't connect to the same plaza? She looked ahead. The street was long and narrow and there was no sign of light at the far end, no sign that it led into the plaza. She was on the brink of turning the group around when they came to a narrow footway that ran off at right angles.

She stopped abruptly, the man behind her blundering into her. She cursed at him, shoved him away and studied the footway. It was barely wide enough for two men abreast. But she could see sunlight and an open space at the far end, and hear the clash of weapons and the shouts of men fighting.

"This way!" she ordered, and plunged into the dim, narrow space.

The sounds of fighting grew louder, but she could see no sign of the Tualaghi at the end of the walkway. That meant they had come past them and Lydia and the rowers would emerge into the square behind them—a perfect result.

Ten meters from the end, she held up a hand for the men behind her to stop. Mindful of the result last time she'd stopped, she kept going for a few paces, then came to a halt and turned. She could hear the sound of heavy, ragged breathing from the rowers. They really were in dreadful condition, she realized. But she hoped that adrenaline would see them through the few minutes it would take for them to perform a surprise flank attack on the Tualaghi. Adrenaline and an overpowering wish for revenge.

"When we get to the end, fan out either side so the men behind you can get out. Edwin and I will go forward a few meters, so form up behind us in one long line. Then, when I tell you, charge into them and hit them with everything you've got. All right?"

There was an angry growl of assent from the rowers—an almost primeval sound, she thought. After months and years of being brutalized and tortured while they sat helplessly in their chains, these men finally had weapons in their hand, and an enemy in sight. The Tualaghi may not have been the men who mistreated them, but they were allied to those men, and that was enough. She looked at them, saw the anger and determination in most of their eyes, and nodded.

"Let's go."

The mixed group of Skandians and Arridans had been pushed back until they were level with the end of the alley. They could deploy no more than three men at a time, so Thorn took advantage of this by constantly changing the men who were fighting, making sure there were always fresh warriors facing the Tualaghi. But the sheer weight of numbers was prevailing. Thorn himself refused to take a spell. He continued to lead the fight, smashing and jabbing with his club-hand, swinging his small shield like an oversized fist. He never stopped, never seemed to tire.

As Ingvar stepped back into the alley, Hal shoved forward to take his place. The defenders were now comprised of Thorn, Hal and Stefan. Ulf, Wulf and Jesper stood ready to take the next shift in the fighting, although it was doubtful that Thorn would relinquish his place.

Ingvar leaned on the shaft of his voulge, breathing heavily. Along with Thorn and Stig, he had borne the brunt of the fighting so far. Now he peered forward through his tortoiseshell spectacles, watching the progress of the fight as Hal drove forward at one of the Tualaghi, driving the man back until he stumbled, then following after him.

And going too far!

Ingvar realized that Hal, fresh to the fight, had lost his sense of where the small defensive line should be. He had gone several meters too far into the ranks of the Tualaghi, allowing one of them to get behind him, between him and the alley and his two co-defenders. Ingvar saw one of the Tualaghi sweep back a huge, straight sword for a horizontal stroke from behind his skirl.

"Hal! Drop!" he roared, his massive voice carrying over the sounds of fighting—the clash of weapons, the grunts and curses of the men.

Hal heard the call and didn't hesitate. He dropped to his hands and knees and felt and heard the massive blade whistle just above his head. Had the stroke connected, he would have been cut almost in two, he realized. He craned around to see his attacker. He was too close for a sword thrust, so he scrabbled out his saxe instead, preparing for a close-in stabbing thrust from below.

Then he saw the voulge, hurled with all Ingvar's massive strength, smash into the swordsman, shattering the links of his chain mail, plunging deep into his upper body.

The force behind the heavy weapon was so great that the Tualaghi was hurled back several paces, blundering into three of his comrades, bringing one of them down and scattering the other two like ninepins.

Hal took advantage of the confusion to regain his feet. He stepped back smartly into line with Thorn and Stefan. The old sea wolf glared at him.

"Keep the line," he growled. "You should know better!"

"Sorry," Hal said. He had no time to thank Ingvar as he found himself facing another two Tualaghi. He stabbed one in the thigh, sending him sprawling on the bloodstained cobbles, and disarmed the second with a bewildering circular motion of his sword, trapping the other man's blade with his own and twisting it from his grasp. The Tualaghi's eyes widened in fear as he realized he was suddenly defenseless. He dropped to his knees and scuttled back behind his companions.

Hal had no time to pursue him. He was immediately engaged by another attacker. His arm was aching already from the continual effort of thrusting and hacking and retrieving his blade, along with the jarring impacts as he parried the enemies' strokes.

Any minute now, he thought, and he'd call for Wulf to relieve him.

Then he heard a familiar sound, the deep-throated bark of a huge dog, infuriated and ready to fight.

"Kloof?" he muttered. "Where did you come from?"

And, suddenly, the men opposing him were facing away, turning in confusion to face a new and unexpected attack from behind.

A row of gaudily clad figures, mixed in with others wearing filthy, disheveled rags, was charging headlong into the rear ranks of the Tualaghi force, hacking and slashing with spears, axes and swords, swinging wildly with wooden clubs fashioned from galley oars. They hit the rear of the Tualaghi force with a resounding crash of metal and wood on metal, hurling men to either side as they smashed their way into the Tualaghi ranks.

Kloof seemed to be everywhere. The huge dog hit the enemy soldiers like a battering ram, hurling them aside, snapping and snarling and biting with those giant jaws, seizing weapon hands and shaking each one violently until the soldier released his grip on the weapon and it went spinning into the confused mass of his comrades.

The suddenness of the surprise attack from the rear splintered the Tualaghi force and the solid ranks in front of the Herons began to waver and disintegrate. Thorn, as a wise and experienced battle commander should, saw the moment for what it was: the opportunity to break the Tualaghi force once and for all.

"Come on!" he roared, and charged forward, his club swinging in terrible, controlled arcs, smashing men out of the way, driving them to their knees. Hal and Stefan, their tiredness forgotten, joined with him, and Stig and the twins came behind them.

The Arridan cavalrymen, finally freed of the constricting space of the alley, surged out like an unstoppable tide, scimitars rising and falling, shields ringing as they blocked the hopeless strokes of the blue-clad desert warriors.

Hal saw Edvin directing a group of enraged galley slaves toward a small knot of Tualaghi who had formed a defensive circle. The blue-robed men went down under the furious onslaught. To one side, he saw Lydia, casually picking off enemies who showed any sign of rallying after the attack. Her darts flashed through the air, sending men sprawling, staggering and screaming with the pain. Suddenly, Hal felt very tired. It was over, he realized.

But not quite.

"You! Northman!" A stocky Tualaghi man faced him, recognizable as an officer by the superior quality of his robes and veil, and the jeweled scabbard and sword belt around his waist. Although Hal didn't know it, it was Dhakwan, insane with rage over the total defeat and destruction of his elite *Khumsan*. He saw the young Skandian now as one of the agents of his defeat. He'd noticed him at the helm of the *Ishtfana* when she'd run alongside the wharf. Now, here he was, exhausted, sword down, its tip resting on the cobbles—at Dhakwan's mercy.

"Prepare to meet your gods!" the Tualaghi leader screamed. Hal began to raise his sword in defense, and realized he would never make it in time.

Then a sword flashed over his left shoulder, its point sliding into Dhakwan's exposed upper body. The Tualaghi officer's eyes showed first surprise, then pain. Then they glazed over as his knees buckled and he sank to the cobbles.

"Never shout out a threat like that in the middle of a fight," Gilan said calmly, withdrawing his sword and letting the dead Tualaghi officer topple to one side. "It's bad tactics and it gives your enemy time to defend himself. Or to kill you."

"I'll bear it in mind," Hal said. He looked at the Ranger with admiration. That sword thrust had been lightning fast and it seemed to have come out of nowhere. And it definitely had saved Hal's life.

Around them, the few remaining Tualaghi were throwing down their weapons or escaping into the narrow side streets that ringed the plaza. Thorn's voice boomed out, echoing off the buildings surrounding them, calling on the Herons and Arridi to re-form.

"Come on! We're not finished. Selethen will be in trouble at the gate! Let's go!"

"What about these men?" Edvin called.

Thorn looked around. There were a dozen or so Tualaghi standing weaponless, their hands raised in surrender, their faces shocked and numb at the sudden turn in their fortunes. Thorn gestured to the former galley slaves surrounding them.

"Leave them as guards. I'm sure they'll enjoy the irony of the situation. Now let's go!"

He led the way to one of the larger streets out of the plaza. This one headed south, which was the direction of the main gate and allowed the landing party to run four abreast. The Heron crew followed him. Behind them, the Arridan cavalry troopers ran, keeping up the brisk pace. Their weapons were blooded now and they were eager to fight again.

They encountered no opposition on the way. That was logical, Hal thought. The majority of Iqbal's men would be defending the gate, with the rest engaging the landing party. Both he and Thorn had studied a map of the town and the old sea wolf led the way unerringly to the main gate. As they burst into the large square facing it, the defenders turned to see them, assuming at first that they were reinforcements, then realizing that the enemy had some-how got inside the wall. They turned, too late, from their defensive positions at the gate, as the combined force of Skandians and Ar-ridan troopers surged forward.

As the two forces came together, Gilan looked up to the wall. He saw a group of half a dozen archers firing down at the attackers outside the walls. He unslung his bow and within half a minute the half dozen had become two, who turned and ran.

Selethen was still on the catwalk. His two companions had fallen and he had been fighting alone for several minutes. His nor-mally immaculate robe and burnished mail were stained with blood—his own and that of his enemies. As Gilan's shafts sliced into the archers on the redoubt, some of the *Wakir*'s men took ad-vantage of the fact and raced up the ladder to join their leader. He sank back gratefully against the battlements behind him. He raised his sword to his lips in salute to Gilan, standing in the square below.

"Just in time, my friend," he called.

Gilan inclined his head. It had been a close-run thing.

At that moment, there was a burst of cheering as Thorn, Stig, Hal and the twins led a final charge, battering into the defenders at the gate, sweeping them aside. Half a dozen Arridan troopers reached up and lifted the massive locking bar from its sockets and the gate, under the pressure from their comrades outside, swung inward to admit a howling, vengeful group of one hundred cavalry-men, all eager for blood.

They surged forward, sweeping the Tualaghi defenders back, trampling them underfoot. Some of the desert warriors threw down their weapons immediately, claiming mercy. But others stood in small, defiant groups and fought to the end.

Which wasn't long in coming.

Hal wiped his sword on a discarded Tualaghi veil and replaced it in his scabbard. Now it really was over, he thought. He had never felt so exhausted in his life.

Two of Selethen's men were helping the injured *Wakir* toward the ladder leading down into the courtyard.

Perhaps it was Lydia's hunting instincts that kept her alert. She was the only one to see a blue-robed figure rise from the pile of bodies around the spot where Selethen had held out for so long. The Tualaghi had lost his headdress and veil in the fighting. She could see he was totally bald, with a hook-shaped nose, reminiscent of a hawk's beak. He was badly wounded in the left arm, but his right held a gleaming scimitar and he raised it now against the *Wakir*'s unprotected back. Something alerted Selethen and he half turned to face the man.

"Iqbal!" he said. He hadn't recognized his enemy when they had been fighting earlier. Now he could see death staring him in the face.

Lydia's dart flashed past him and took Iqbal in the center of his chest, the force of the missile hurling him backward against the wall. He sagged down to the catwalk.

"That family don't have a lot of luck with women who throw things," Gilan observed.

Lydia turned to him, frowning slightly.

He shrugged. "Well, Cassandra walloped his brother with a sling. Now you've skewered him with a dart."

"He deserved it," Lydia said.

But before Gilan could reply, they were interrupted by a terrible wailing cry from the square in front of the gate.

Wulf was kneeling, tears streaming down his face, beside the still, white-faced body of his brother, Ulf.

Ulf was lying on the cobblestones, his head resting on his twin brother's knee.

His eyes were shut and he was barely breathing. His face was pale with loss of blood, and it continued to seep from a large wound in his side, soaking into his shirt and spreading in a pool on the ground. Wulf looked up at his friends as they gathered helplessly around. He was distraught, with the tears flowing unchecked and his words coming in ragged, disjointed phrases as they fought with the heart-wrenching sobs that burst from him.

"I couldn't get . . . to him . . . in time," he cried. "That coward had . . . surrendered to him and . . . thrown down . . . his sword." He indicated a Tualaghi warrior who was lying several meters away, staring up at the sky with unseeing eyes. "Then, as Ulf looked away . . . the treacherous swine drew a knife and . . . stabbed him in the side!" He bent over his brother, crooning wordlessly, his tears falling onto the blood-soaked shirt.

Edvin pushed through the small crowd and knelt beside Ulf, ripping open his medical pack as he did. He looked at the amount of blood on the ground and on Ulf's shirt and gave a small cry of despair. Then he cut the shirt away from the wound and began swabbing at the slowly seeping blood with a wadded-up piece of cotton.

"At least he didn't hit an artery," he said, more to himself than anyone else.

"How can he tell that?" Stig asked.

Hal glanced quickly at him. "The blood would be pumping if an artery was severed. It's just seeping out."

"Maybe, but a lot of it has seeped," his friend replied doubtfully, and Hal could only nod in mute agreement. Ulf had lost a lot of blood—and he was continuing to do so.

"Will Ulf be all right, Edvin?" Wulf asked, his voice breaking with fear and grief. "Can you fix him?"

Edvin, his head down, was cleaning the wound with a special salve. Then he packed a thick bandage pad against it. The blood continued to flow, rapidly staining the bandage red.

"I'll do my best, Wulf," he said. Until Wulf had mentioned his brother's name, he'd had no idea which of the twins he was treating. "But he's losing a lot of blood."

Selethen slipped through the ring of Herons surrounding their fallen brother. He took in the situation at a glance.

"I've sent for my *Tabibs*. My healers," he said, explaining the word. "They'll help you."

Wulf looked up quickly, his face a mask of rage. "No!" he shouted vehemently. "Nobody touches him but Edvin! Nobody!"

Edvin looked up from what he was doing, his hands keeping the bandage pad pressed hard against the wound in Ulf's side.

"Wulf, don't be crazy. Selethen's men are trained healers. Compared to them, I'm little more than a glorified bandage roller."

"I trust you," Wulf said. "I don't trust them. I don't know them!"

At that moment, two green-robed Arridans made their way through the growing throng to stand over Wulf and his fallen brother. From the fact that they were unarmed and unarmored, Hal deduced that these must be the healers. But Wulf dropped a hand to the hilt of his saxe.

"Keep back!" he warned. "Nobody touches my brother but Edvin!"

The older of the two ignored the threat. He went down on one knee beside Edvin, who looked round at him.

"He's losing blood," the Skandian said. "He's losing too much blood."

The Arridan nodded. He placed his hand over Edvin's, applying more pressure to the wound. The blood flow seemed to lessen. Wulf moved threateningly, half drawing the saxe. But as he saw the slackening flow of blood, he stopped and slid the big knife back into its scabbard, uncertain what he should do next.

"Can you help him, *Tabib*?" Selethen asked.

The healer looked up and nodded. "I think so, lord. We have a salve that can thicken the blood and slow the blood loss. That's the main problem. I'd like to get him to our hospital tent right away.

We need to check and see that no vital organ has been damaged. But it wouldn't appear to be the case."

Selethen leaned down and placed a hand on Wulf's shoulder. The young Heron went to shake it off, glaring resentfully at the tall Arridan. But Selethen maintained his firm grip.

"Wulf, the *Tabib* is a very wise and very skilled healer. And this is his student. They are two of the very best healers in my country. Please let them help your brother."

"Do it, Wulf!" Edvin urged. "I'm way out of my depth here!"

Still Wulf hesitated, his eyes flicking from Edvin to Selethen and finally to the *Tabib*. The latter's face was calm and composed and Wulf saw a depth of confidence and knowledge in his eyes.

Gilan joined the discussion. "Wulf, the Arridan healers are among the best in the world. They study in the east, in medical colleges that have been teaching for centuries. They've preserved the best of the old wisdom, and they're constantly discovering new ways—new salves and potions and healing compounds. I know of only one man in Araluen who might be their equal. Let them help you."

Again, Wulf's eyes flicked between the men gathered round him. As before, it finished on the older *Tabib*. The man was calm and composed still. He nodded reassurance to the young Skandian, and Wulf's irrational resolve faltered.

"Do it, Wulf," Edvin said quietly. "I'll stay with them. I'll watch over Ulf every step of the way. I promise. But you have to agree to it quickly. We're losing him here."

That seemed to do it. Wulf leaned back on his haunches, closed his eyes for several seconds, allowing the tears to course down his cheeks unchecked. Then he opened them and nodded slowly.

"Very well," he said. There was a collective sigh of relief from the people around him.

"Clear a path," the elder *Tabib* said, gesturing for the onlookers to move aside and allow two of his orderlies through with a litter. Gently, they lifted the stricken Heron onto the litter, with Edvin and the *Tabib* maintaining their pressure on the wound the whole time.

At the *Tabib's* count, they lifted the litter and began to move carefully toward the gate.

"Where are you taking him?" Wulf said, hurriedly rising. The younger *Tabib* held up a reassuring hand.

"We have our hospital tent set up outside," he said. "It's cleaner and better suited for healing than some dark, dirty room in the town."

Wulf nodded and fell into step with the litter bearers. The young *Tabib* walked beside him.

"Don't worry," he said. "My master will heal your brother. He has no equal in any country along the Constant Sea."

There was a certainty in his voice that did much to allay Wulf's fears, and calm the panic that had seized him when he saw his brother cut down. He looked at the young healer.

"Thank you," he said.

The young *Tabib* shrugged. "It is what we do," he said. "And none does it better than Master Maajid. His name means 'The Excellent One.'"

The rest of the group milled around uncertainly, not sure whether to follow the servants carrying Ulf's still form on the litter. When it came down to it, most of them were reluctant to—none of them liked being in a hospital or healer's tent. They lived a violent life and such places were too vivid a reminder of what could happen to each and every one of them at any time. Finally, Hal made the decision for all of them—which was only fitting.

"I'll go with them," he announced. "Thorn, Stig, organize the crew and help Selethen's men round up any Tualaghi who might still want to make an issue of things."

His two lieutenants nodded. Thorn touched the body of the dead Tualaghi with his toe. The man still clutched the blood-stained dagger with which he'd attacked Ulf and the old sea wolf gently nudged it out of his fingers.

"No sense in taking chances," he said. But Stig shook his head.

"He won't be attacking anyone again," he said. He looked around at the others. "Anyone know who settled his hash for him? I assume it was Wulf?"

Jesper shook his head. "Wulf was too far away. And when he saw Ulf go down, he was frozen to the spot. Ingvar took care of it for him. Now that he can see, he can really move like lightning."

Thorn and Stig exchanged a meaningful look.

"Hal's created a monster there," Thorn said, looking to where Ingvar was leaning on the shaft of his voulge, out of earshot. In fact, the two dark circles that covered his eyes made him seem like some apparition from another realm.

Stig nodded. "You didn't help, giving him that overgrown toothpick. He's a regular terror with that! Did you see him during the battle?"

"I did. Hook, chop, stab. And then some."

Thorn clapped the younger man on the shoulder, then began calling orders for the Herons to reform.

"Come on. We've still got work to do."

The interior of the medical tent was shady and cool. The sides were rolled up to allow fresh air in, although in the event of bad weather or wind-driven sand, they could be rolled down in a matter of minutes, keeping the interior clean and dust free.

Ulf was placed on a table covered with a white linen sheet and the two *Tabibs* began to go to work on him, standing either side of the table and speaking to each other in lowered tones and in their own language.

At least, Hal assumed it was Arridan. It may have been some secret healers' language. Wulf stood close by them, watching events like a hawk. From time to time, *Tabib* Maajid would pause and switch back to the common tongue to explain some point of procedure or the use of a salve or potion to Edvin, who took copious notes as they went.

"This is amazing," he said softly, on more than one occasion, shaking his head in wonder. The more they worked on Ulf, the more he realized that these were men of enormous skill and knowledge.

Hal noted that the blood was flowing less freely now, and when the healers changed the bandage for the third time, it no longer seeped through immediately. He assumed that was the result of the salve they had mentioned.

Or perhaps, more ominously, the blood flow was slowing because there was less blood in Ulf's veins.

They had been in the tent for twenty minutes or so when there was a commotion at the entrance and another litter was carried in. Its occupant was a tall Tualaghi warrior, recognizable by his blue robes, although without the headgear and face veil. Hal could see that his skull was shaved and his dark eyes burned in his face with an intense hatred. He was shouting incoherently and waving his arms and Maajid looked up in annoyance. His pupils left the table beside Ulf and moved quickly to examine the newcomer. After several minutes, he returned, caught his master's eye and shook his head.

"Nothing we can do for him," the *Tabib* said, and Maajid grunted philosophically. They were sworn to preserve life and ease pain, but sometimes there was little they could do to defy fate. As he went back to work on Ulf, the Tualaghi mustered his strength and called out to the orderlies around him.

"Get the Ranger!" he said. "Bring the Ranger to me! Tell him Iqbal bin Ha'rish has important information for him."

The orderlies stood uncertainly, not sure whether to obey the Tualaghi's command. But Hal, recognizing his name, moved toward the litter where the mortally wounded bandit leader lay.

"Do as he says," he told the orderlies. "He may have vital information for us, and we don't have a lot of time." One of the orderlies turned and ran out of the tent to find Gilan.

The assistant *Tabibs* had managed to remove Lydia's dart from Iqbal's chest, but the wound was a terrible one. The steel-headed shaft had penetrated Iqbal's lung and the damage was irreparable. There was a pink froth of blood around his lips and Hal knew that was never a good sign. He could see why *Tabib* Daanish had determined there was little to be done for the man.

Iqbal's gaze, wild and feverish, alighted on the young skirl as he stood by the litter. Recognition showed in the dark eyes.

"You . . . northman. You're one of them, aren't you? You're with the Ranger?"

"That's right," Hal said. He didn't really want to engage in conversation with the Tualaghi, but he thought that if he did keep him talking, it might prevent him from sinking into unconsciousness and death.

A horrible grimace twisted the dying man's face. "Why can't you people stay in your own country? Why are you always causing trouble in ours?" he demanded angrily.

Hal shrugged. "Seems like you were the one causing trouble here," he said. "You were the one who took out the *tolfah* against the Araluen princess."

Iqbal was seized by a fit of coughing and Hal was concerned to see more blood on his chin. Then he recovered, and a look of surprise crossed his features.

"So, you know about the *tolfah*, do you? Aren't you clever? Well, much good it will do you."

Even mortally wounded, Iqbal's manner was one of arrogance and superiority. It pricked Hal's anger. Even though he sensed he shouldn't antagonize the other man, he couldn't help it.

"Hasn't done you much good either, has it?" he said. "I'm not the one lying there with a gaping hole in my chest."

Iqbal's eyes darkened with anger. He was seized by another coughing fit. Then, when he recovered, he resumed his taunting, sarcastic manner.

"Nevertheless, you've lost," he said. "There's nothing you can do now to save your precious princess. The Scorpions will never give up. They will keep trying until they kill her. How does it feel to know you've lost, northman?"

Hal heard movement at the entrance to the tent and glanced up as Gilan entered. The Ranger looked around, saw Hal by the litter, recognized the dying man on it, and hurried across the tent to stand beside him.

"Why did you want to see me, Iqbal?" he said, keeping his tone neutral. Iqbal's lips curled in a sneer.

"Because I wanted you to know that you've lost. Your princess is doomed," he rasped, his voice strengthened by the venom of anger and malice that ran deep within him.

Gilan looked quickly at Hal, who shrugged, then he returned his gaze to Iqbal.

"So you wanted to gloat?" he said.

The bandit leader nodded vehemently, even though the movement obviously caused him pain.

"Yes. I wanted to see your face when you realized that all this has been for nothing." He waved a weak hand around the tent. "You may have killed me, but the Scorpion cult will kill your princess. Nothing can stop them. Nothing can save her. They'll keep trying and, eventually, they will succeed."

Gilan frowned, then said in a reasonable tone, "That hardly seems likely. After all, you'll be dead. Your compact with the Scorpions, and theirs with you, will surely die with you. Why should they continue losing men in their attacks on Cassandra? Why should they honor a compact with a dead man?"

And at that, Iqbal laughed. It was a genuine reaction, although it was full of derision rather than humor. The action obviously caused him pain and once again he was racked by a fit of coughing. More blood welled from the corner of his mouth.

"You really don't understand, do you?" he said scornfully.

"You've come all this way, had men killed or wounded, and you have no idea what you're up against, do you?"

Gilan said nothing. He was beginning to feel uneasy. Iqbal obviously knew he was dying, yet he'd wanted to see Gilan—wanted to gloat. If anything, Gilan thought, it should be the other way around. Iqbal had lost the battle and would soon be dead. What did he have to gloat about? What was it that Gilan and his comrades didn't understand about the *tolfah*?

Sensing the Ranger's uncertainty, Iqbal raised himself on one elbow, groaning with the pain that shot through his body as he did, and pointed one crooked finger at his own chest.

"You think the contract to kill your princess is between me and the Scorpions, don't you?"

Gilan shrugged. "Who else?" he asked and again Iqbal laughed, scornfully this time. The effort seemed to weaken him and he fell back on the pillow, his eyes closed. He was breathing heavily, trying to draw air into his savaged lungs. The two comrades could hear the rasping in his chest. Eventually, his eyes opened again and he fixed his gaze on Gilan. Looking at those dark, almost black eyes, Hal realized that the man rarely blinked. It was like looking at the eyes of an eagle—or, more fittingly, a vulture.

"I paid the Shurmel to take out the compact against your princess," he said. His voice was very low now and Gilan and Hal had to lean closer to hear him.

Gilan spread his hands in a dismissive gesture. "Then I'll pay him to cancel it."

Iqbal shook his head several times. That superior, taunting smile was back on his face. "You can't, because the contract is irrevocable," he said.

"A contract with a dead man?" Hal said bluntly. "I don't think so. Once you're dead, the contract's over and done with."

Iqbal's eyes flashed round to assess him for a few seconds. He shook his head dismissively. "You people are so ignorant of our ways. The compact cannot be bought off. Even I couldn't change it or cancel it now, if I wanted to. The compact isn't between me and the Shurmel . . ."

Gilan shook his head irritably. "Who is this Shurmel you keep mentioning?" he demanded, and Iqbal's gaze went back to him. Again, the bandit shook his head.

"As I say, you know so little about what you're facing. The Shurmel is the leader of the Scorpions—the sworn servant of Imrika, the goddess of destruction. I paid him to take out the compact, but not with me. It's between him and the goddess. Nobody can interfere with that now. Nobody can change it. Nobody can stop it. The contract remains in place for the lifetime of the Shurmel himself. Only death can cancel it—the death of your princess Cassandra."

Gilan felt a cold hand close over his heart as he heard Iqbal's words. They had been warned that the Scorpions were no ordinary cult of assassins. Their beliefs were based on a warped religious system, and their goddess Imrika was a pitiless taskmistress. He could see how the cult would continue to send men to kill Cassandra and he realized she was condemned to a life of constant watchfulness and fear.

The Ranger had hoped that Iqbal's death would dissolve the compact. Obviously, that wasn't the case.

Hal had been listening closely to the exchange. Now he could comprehend the tone of victory that had underpinned Iqbal's words, even though the bandit knew he was dying.

"So the contract stays in force for the lifetime of the Shurmel?" he said.

Iqbal turned to him. "Until the death of the princess. Finally, it appears you understand," he sneered. "There is no other way to end it."

"Unless we kill the Shurmel," Hal said slowly. And he had the satisfaction of seeing a momentary flash of doubt in Iqbal's eyes.

The bandit leader's eyes closed. His chest rose and fell for a few seconds, his breathing ragged and irregular. Then, without warning or preamble, it simply stopped and Iqbal, son of Ha'rish, leader of the blue-clad tribe known as the Forgotten of God, was dead.

"I've found out more about the Scorpion cult," Selethen said.

It was the evening of the battle for Tabork. Gilan, Hal, Stig, Thorn and Lydia were dining in Selethen's tent. Hal was interested to see that the tent was comfortably furnished, but not sumptuously. Selethen was essentially a soldier and tended to frown on excessive luxuries in the field. As he had said to them when he welcomed them to his tent, a good cook was more important than silk curtains and satin cushions. Instead, they sat on comfortable linen cushions around the low table. There was a carpet spread out on the desert sand, but it was a practical woolen weave, rather than a highly ornate design. It was functional rather than splendid.

His comments about a good cook were well founded. They had dined on tender young goat, minced and cooked with spices, and accompanied by hot flat bread. The delicious dish known as tabouleh was in plentiful supply, as was a salad of bitter green leaves with a tart dressing made from lemon juice and oil.

Now, as the servants cleared the plates away and set out bowls of sliced oranges and melon, and the Herons and Gilan helped themselves to the excellent coffee Selethen's staff had provided, the *Wakir* spread out a map of the Arridan coastline along the Constant Sea.

"One of Iqbal's lieutenants knew something of the cult and he was somewhat forthcoming in telling us about them—eventually."

Hal looked up at the last word. He didn't think it would be politic to ask what had brought about the Tualaghi's "eventual" willingness to discuss the Scorpions.

If Selethen noticed the reaction, he showed no sign of it. He tapped a table knife on a part of the coast at the eastern end of the Constant Sea. They all leaned forward to study the chart.

"Their headquarters are here, in the Amrashin Massif, a range of mountains just across the border between Arrida and Baralat. It's close to the entrance to the Assaranyan Channel, but about forty kilometers inland, to the southeast."

He looked up at them, seeing all their faces intent on the map, measuring distances and calculating times.

"It's a three-week ride from here, through some very harsh territory," he told them.

Hal scratched his chin thoughtfully. "Barely four days if we sail up the coast to this point." He indicated a spot on the coast level with the mountain range.

Thorn nodded. "Still a three-day march inland," he said. He tapped a town marked on the map at the point Hal had indicated. "What's this?"

Selethen shook his head. "It was a city—a big one. The Toscans colonized the area decades ago and this was their major trading port—Ephesa. They abandoned it forty years ago as their empire began to collapse. But there's a large oasis there. It'd make an ideal base for you—a good point to strike out inland. And as you say, it's a three-day march to the Massif. The ground is flat but the heat in the middle hours of the day is prohibitive. Your marching time would be limited."

"Pity we can't fit horses aboard the *Heron*," Hal said thoughtfully.

"Who says?" Thorn demanded.

"Who says we can't fit horses?" Hal asked.

Thorn shook his head emphatically. "Who says it's a pity? I'm content to do my own walking, thanks. I'd rather sore feet than a sore backside."

Hal smiled. Thorn's dislike for travel by horseback was well known. Still, he thought, it would be useful if they had some way of traveling more quickly across the desert than walking. He'd have to give that some thought.

Selethen continued. "Scorpion Mountain, which contains a complex of caves and chambers, is in the massif. Apparently, it's easily recognized. From a distance it looks like a scorpion, with three separate peaks. The two outer ones resemble the pincers of a scorpion and the middle one, the highest of the three, looks like the tail raised to sting. It's the headquarters for the Scorpion cult."

"Heavily defended?" Gilan asked.

Selethen shook his head. "The Scorpions maintain a force of several hundred troops, in addition to the assassins themselves. But getting in isn't a problem. After all, people have to be able to approach them to take out compacts like the one involving your princess."

"What about getting out?" Lydia asked.

Selethen looked at her for several seconds before answering. "That might not be so easy."

chapter thirty-one

Hal stooped to enter the hospital tent. The side flaps were rolled up for ventilation, but there was still insufficient headroom beneath them to walk straight in. He headed for the spot at the rear of the tent where canvas screens kept Ulf's litter private from the rest of the beds. The beds on either side of the long tent were occupied by Arridan troopers wounded in the fight for Tabork. He was pleased to see that there was only a small number of them. One section was guarded by armed cavalrymen. The beds there held Tualaghi wounded. Interesting, Hal thought. Many leaders would have left the enemy wounded to their own devices. Selethen was obviously a far more civilized man than that.

The roof of the tent bellied upward under a sudden increase in the wind. The wind was a constant here, he realized. You became so used to it that you rarely noticed it, unless a stronger than normal gust like this one disturbed the fabric of the tent. He stopped at the screen enclosing Ulf's bed and pulled it to one side. Wulf was sitting on a stool by his brother's side, his head bent over the still figure on the bed. *Tabib* Maajid was performing one of his regular inspections of the wounded Heron. He had his palm on Ulf's forehead, testing his temperature. Then he bent and, drawing back the bedclothes, sniffed carefully around the site of the bandaged wound. He looked up and saw Hal watching.

"Sometimes our sense of smell can give us the first warning of infection," he explained.

Hal gestured to the figure in the bed as Maajid returned the covers to their place. "Any sign there?"

The *Tabib* shook his head. "So far so good."

Wulf continued to bend over his brother, holding one of his hands in both of his own, his eyes riveted on Ulf's pale face. He showed no sign that he had noticed Hal's arrival.

"How is he?" Hal asked. Ulf had been under the *Tabibs'* care for several days now. Maajid considered for a few seconds before he answered.

"He's very weak. And he's very sick. There was internal damage caused by the knife. We were able to repair it and, fortunately, nothing vital was affected. If we can keep him clear of infection, I'm confident that he will recover. But it won't be tomorrow, or even next week. He'll need care for many weeks."

Hal frowned at that. "Will you be able to look after him for that long?" he asked. He assumed that Selethen and his force would be moving on in the near future. But Maajid smiled and nodded.

"We will be here for as long as it takes. I'm keeping him here, out of the town, because the air is cleaner. That way, there's less chance of infection. Lord Selethen has a lot to do here in Tabork, reestablishing the normal order of things. Many of the ruling council of the town were killed when Iqbal and his bandits took over. That has to be addressed."

"We need to sail east in a few days," Hal said.

Maajid nodded. He'd expected as much.

"He will be safe with us," he said calmly. "I would advise leaving him here. Moving him could be dangerous."

"I'll stay with him," Wulf said and Hal looked at him in surprise. It was the first sign he'd shown that he was taking any notice of what they were saying. The sail trimmer's eyes were red from weeping and his face was drawn. He'd eaten little since Ulf had been brought here, spending most of his time crouched by his brother's side. Hal glanced up at Maajid now, his eyes asking a question: *Is that wise?* The *Tabib* shook his head slightly.

"I need you on board," Hal said. He intentionally kept any note of pity out of his voice. It was an order from the skirl to one of his crew. Out of the corner of his eye, he saw Maajid nod approval.

But Wulf shook his head violently. "I can't leave him, Hal! He's my brother! He's dying . . . I can't—"

"He's not dying!" Hal snapped. "You just heard the *Tabib* say he would be safe here with them. And you can't do anything here for him."

"But he's my brother. I—"

"We're all your brothers, Wulf. I'm your brother. Stig's your brother. And Thorn and the rest of the crew. You swore an oath to every one of us when we formed this brotherband. We all depend on one another. I need you on board. The ship needs you. Your brothers need you."

"But if something happens to him—"

"If something happens to him, your being here will do nothing to prevent it. Do you think Ulf would want you to break your oath? Would he, if the situation were reversed? Would he betray his ship, his skirl and his brotherband?"

Wulf's eyes dropped. Tears rolled down his cheeks. Finally, he spoke, in a small voice.

"No."

Hal allowed his voice to soften. "Wulf, I need you. There's nothing you can accomplish by staying here. There's plenty for you to do on board the *Heron*. I need you more than ever now that Ulf is injured."

He let his hand drop onto Wulf's shoulder and squeezed it. Wulf looked up at him, studying his face. He saw compassion there. And friendship. And need. He saw the strength of the bond that tied the Herons together and he made his decision. And at that moment, Ulf stirred and his eyes fluttered open.

"Wulf?" he said, his voice weak.

Wulf turned back to his brother. Maajid hurried to crouch beside the bed, studying the wounded youth, placing a hand on his forehead to check his temperature, then placing a finger against the big artery in his neck. Sometimes, he knew, a sudden awakening like this could presage a crisis. But Ulf's temperature and pulse were normal.

"Ulf? What is it?" Wulf said. He was filled with hope as this was the first sign of consciousness or awareness that his brother had shown since he had been wounded. He grasped his hand again. Ulf nodded weakly, then opened his lips and tried to talk. For a few seconds, no words came. He moistened his dry lips with his tongue, then spoke deliberately.

"Don't . . . break your . . . oath. Don't."

For a second, Wulf felt pressure against his hand. Then Ulf's eyes fluttered closed again and his hand went limp. Panic rose in Wulf's chest.

"Ulf?" he said frantically. "Ulf? Are you all right?"

Maajid had been monitoring Ulf's vital signs and he nodded reassuringly.

"He's all right. He's resting. It took a lot of effort for him to say that," he added meaningfully.

Wulf tore his gaze away from his brother's face and looked up at Hal. "All right. I'll come with you. But if anything happens . . ."

Hal squeezed his shoulder a little harder. "*Nothing* is going to happen. Understand? In fact, it's going to be a lot more dangerous where we're going. If you want to worry about something, worry about that."

Wulf looked up at him and Hal grinned reassuringly. Wulf tried to grin in return. It was a faint effort, but it was something, Hal thought.

"Stay here with him until we're ready to leave," he said. "That won't be for a day or two so you may well see some improvement."

"Thanks, Hal," Wulf muttered.

The skirl took a deep breath, made eye contact with Maajid

and mouthed the word *thanks.* The *Tabib* nodded and Hal turned and left the hospital tent.

That evening, Hal strolled along the wall with Selethen and Gilan while they discussed plans for the voyage east.

"I'm sorry I won't be able to come with you," Selethen said. "I've got a lot on my hands here, trying to get the town back in order."

"Maajid said you'd be here for some time," Hal said.

Selethen looked at him. "How is your wounded man doing?"

Hal glanced out at the desert, past the lights of fires in Selethen's camp outside the walls, into the deep purple darkness to the south.

"Maajid is confident that he'll be all right," he said finally and the *Wakir* nodded in satisfaction.

"If Maajid is confident, then I'm sure he will be."

The wind, which had been constant all day, gradually died away. The rustling flags and awnings on the battlements lay still and undisturbed for a few minutes, then they began to stir again. But now the wind had shifted to the south. Hal, whose life depended so much on the wind, took notice. He turned around, facing the new breeze, smelling the hot, dry scent of the desert.

"Does it always do that?"

Selethen and Gilan looked at him in surprise.

"Does what always do that?" Selethen asked.

Hal gestured vaguely at the air around them. "The wind. It just backed to the south. It's been blowing from the north all day, and it just backed."

"Oh . . . yes. It does," Selethen replied. The wind wasn't as big a factor in his life. He was used to it and he accepted it. He frowned now as he tried to explain it.

"During the day, the sun heats the desert so the hot air rises. And the cooler air from the sea sweeps in. Then, at night, the desert cools and loses its heat. The air over the sea is relatively warmer and the breeze shifts."

"Every day?" Hal said, looking around with interest. His brow was furrowed.

Selethen nodded. "Every day. Sometimes, if it gets too strong, it whips up a *Khamsin*—a dust storm." He smiled at Gilan. "You remember what that's like?"

Gilan nodded emphatically. "Only too well." On his previous visit to Arrida, the mixed party of Skandians and Araluens had been caught in a devastating dust storm. "The sand was everywhere. You couldn't see your hand in front of your face."

But Hal wasn't listening to their exchange. He was continuing to look upward, turning his face to the south so that the steady breeze fell directly on it. The breeze grew stronger by the minute. *Heron* would make good speed under it. He frowned as the others continued to reminisce about the dust storm that had engulfed them some years previously. He barely heard them.

There was something significant about this breeze, he thought. Something significant about the constant, unvarying wind that blew throughout the day.

It seemed to him that there was a problem he'd been thinking about and that this factor might have something to do with it. He tried to summon up whatever it was that he had been thinking about but, as was always the case, the harder he tried, the more the idea receded.

Finally, he sighed with frustration. "I'm sure it'll come to me."

His two friends stopped and looked at him. He realized that he'd spoken the thought aloud.

"What'll come to you?" Gilan asked, but Hal shook his head and dismissed the question.

"Nothing. Nothing important," he said. But he sensed that that wasn't the truth.

PART THREE

EPHESA

They made good time sailing east along the coast, with the wind constantly blowing on their beam—their best point of sailing. *Heron* cut smoothly through the clear water—green colored now that there was a sand bottom barely ten meters below their keel. The system of reefs and shoals stretching north from Tabork into the Constant Sea presented no problem for them, as there was a clear passage close inshore.

The weather was good, the swell was smooth and the wind was abeam. It should have been a pleasant time. With no need for constant tacking and sail handling and with the kilometers rolling steadily beneath the keel, the crew should have been relaxing, enjoying the sun. But a strangely subdued mood had settled over the members of the brotherband. There was little conversation, other than what was necessary for the running of the ship.

Hal frowned as he and Stig stood by the steering platform. Stig had just taken over the helm and Hal remained close by. He wasn't tired and he knew if he stretched out on his blankets, he'd lie awake, worrying about his crew.

"They're very quiet," he said eventually.

Stig looked sidelong at him. "And you're complaining about that? It's a pleasant change from the bickering and nattering that they usually go on with."

Hal said nothing for a minute or two. He studied the crew carefully. None of them seemed interested in talking to one another. He could sense a feeling of unease.

"It's Ulf," he said finally. "They're worried about Ulf."

"Not surprising. No matter what the healers say, things can always take a turn for the worse."

Ulf was their first serious casualty since Ingvar had been struck down by an arrow in the fighting at Limmat many months ago. The fact that he was so seriously wounded hung over them like a pall. But on top of that, there was something else, Hal realized.

"It's more than that. They're worried about him, of course. But they're missing his constant wrangling with Wulf."

Stig looked surprised. "Who could miss that?" But then he realized that Hal was right. The twins, with their ridiculous arguing, provided a diversion for the crew during the long hours at sea. Plus there was the additional spice added by the fact that, at any moment, Hal could tire of them and order Ingvar to throw one, or both, of them overboard.

That was always something to look forward to, he realized. But without that continual distraction, the hours seemed empty and strangely lacking. If the weather would worsen, or the wind shift, they would have something to do, something to take their mind off things. But as it was, all they had to do was sit there with the ship trimmed to the wind, while she swooped gently over the swell on her way east.

"I think you're right," Stig said, at length. "And I never thought I'd say it, but I do actually miss all their nonsense."

Hal let his gaze wander over the crew.

Wulf was sitting disconsolately at his station by the trimming sheets. Usually, he would be accompanied by Ulf, but now, of course, he was alone. Jesper was in the bow, leaning on the bow post and keeping a bored lookout over the sea ahead and the coast-line to starboard. Stefan and Edvin sat opposite Wulf, ready at the halyards if there was a need to change sails. But there had been no such need for hours and Edvin was idly picking the stitches out of a woolen scarf he had been knitting. Apparently, he wasn't content with the result and was unpicking it to knit it again. Stefan stared at the deck below his feet, seemingly mesmerized by the planks.

Ingvar was leaning on the canvas-shrouded Mangler. He was wearing his spectacles and staring out at the sea. He spent a lot of time doing that these days. He never seemed to tire of the fact that now he could actually see the water surrounding them, and the coastline slipping by to starboard. Of all the crew, he alone showed any sign of animation or interest.

Even Kloof seemed affected by the atmosphere on board. She lay on her stomach in the bow, her forepaws thrust out and her massive head resting on them. Her tail, which usually stirred back and forth, warning of some form of mischief she had in mind, lay still on the deck behind her.

As he watched, Hal saw Thorn stir from his normal position

against the mast. The old warrior heaved himself to his feet with a sigh, cast a long look around the horizon, then moved a few meters to where Lydia was sitting in the stern rowing benches, idly running a sharpening stone over the blade of her dirk. She had been sharpening it for most of the morning, Hal thought. If she kept it up, there would be no blade left.

She glanced up suspiciously as Thorn settled onto the bench beside her. Lydia was all too conscious of the fact that Thorn was always ready to tease her about something. But that didn't seem to be the case today. Hal watched, unnoticed by either of them, as Thorn leaned closer to her and said something in a lowered voice. She looked at Thorn for a few seconds with a surprised expression on her face, then swung her gaze around the crew. Realizing she would be looking his way any moment, Hal hastily averted his gaze so that he appeared to be concentrating on the wind telltale on the mast above him. But he continued to watch the two of them out of the corner of his eye.

Eventually, Lydia's gaze returned to Thorn and she said something. He nodded, satisfied, and rose to return to his position by the mast.

Several minutes passed and Hal continued to watch curiously. Eventually, Lydia decided that the razor edge on her dirk couldn't be improved, and slid it back into its sheath.

She reached into the leather satchel where she kept her personal items and produced a wooden comb. Loosening the tie that held her long hair back from her face, she began to comb it, stroking the comb smoothly through its long strands.

Thorn appeared to notice her for the first time. "You're always doing that," he said.

She glanced up at him, her face an impassive mask. "Doing what?"

He made a combing motion over his own shaggy hair. "Combing that hair of yours. You're always doing it."

She raised an eyebrow at him. "I do it once a day," she replied. "But I suppose to someone like you, who combs his hair once a month, and does it with his wooden hook, it seems like I'm *always* doing it."

Stefan had looked up at Thorn's opening sally. Now, he gave a subdued snort of laughter at Lydia's retort. Thorn affected not to notice him.

"I'll have you know," he said with some dignity, "that I comb my hair more frequently than once a month."

"Is that right?" Lydia said, warming to her theme. "Then how come the last time you did it, a seagull flew out of it, with three hatchlings she'd been raising in there?"

Now there was a snicker of laughter from Edvin and Ingvar. Hal realized that the crew all had their attention focused on Thorn and Lydia. And for once, Thorn wasn't getting the better of the interaction between them.

"The crafty old devil," he said quietly to Stig. "He's doing this on purpose to take the crew's mind off Ulf."

Stig nodded silently, watching the two antagonists to see what was coming next.

"You should just cut it short," Thorn said and Lydia raised an eyebrow at him.

"Cut it short?" she repeated.

He nodded emphatically. "It'd be more stylish if you cut it short. More glamorous. Boys might take notice of you that way."

"Which boys might they be?" Lydia asked, her voice deceptively sweet.

Thorn shrugged. "No particular boys. Just boys in general. Rollond, maybe." He grinned as he said the name. Rollond was a boy back in Hallasholm who was totally smitten by Lydia. Unfortunately for him, she didn't return the sentiment.

Now all eyes on board were on the two of them, switching from one to the other as they followed the dialogue. At the mention of Rollond's name, a few of them leaned forward expectantly. Rollond's name was all too often like a red rag to a bull with Lydia.

"Let me make two things perfectly clear, old man," Lydia said, and now there was a steely edge to her voice. "One: I do not plan on taking hints on hair styles and grooming from someone who looks like he was dragged backward through a blackberry bush."

"That's a little harsh," Thorn said, trying to sound dignified. The attempt failed when a low snicker of laughter ran round the members of the crew. Even Wulf had a half grin on his face, Hal noticed.

But Lydia hadn't finished. "And two, I'm not interested having 'the boys,' be it Rollond or anyone else, take notice of me. Is that totally clear?"

Thorn shrugged. "Well, if you say. But I think it would be better if you cut it short. It would frame your face quite nicely."

"I'll frame your face for you, old man. I'll frame it with a leather bucket. How would you like that?" Lydia replied.

Thorn shook his head and sighed. "Whatever happened to femininity?" he asked, of nobody in particular. The only reply was a general round of laughter from the crew. Thorn shook his head huffily.

"Time was when people respected their elders," he said to nobody in particular.

He settled down, leaning his back against the mast once more, pulling his watch cap down over his eyes. Hal looked around the crew and took in the lightening of the mood on board. Nice work, Thorn, he thought to himself. Not for the first time, he realized how well the old sea wolf could read the crew's mood, and then change it in an instant. Their previous lack of interest, the sense of ennui, was now gone and several of the Herons were exchanging amused glances. Time to keep their minds engaged, he thought, before they slipped back into their previous depression.

"I don't like the look of that cape up ahead," he said to Stig, in a voice that could be heard by the rest of the crew. "I think we'll come a little farther to the north of it."

In fact, he could tell that they would pass the cape with plenty of sea room to spare. But he thought it might be a good idea to give the crew some work to do.

"Hands to sailing stations!" he called. "We're coming farther to port. Edvin, you can give Wulf a hand with the trimming."

Ingvar called from the bow. "I can do that, Hal."

But the skirl shook his head. "No. I want Edvin there. You'd probably pull the mast over."

There was a ripple of laughter from the crew, with Ingvar joining in. His massive strength was a byword on board. Whenever he took an oar, the ship tended to veer away from the side he was rowing.

"Besides," Hal called, "I want Edvin used to the job. If we go into action, I'll need you on the Mangler."

Ingvar nodded. That made sense. And Hal had another reason

for choosing Edvin. As the second substitute helmsman, he was developing an instinctive feel for the ship's movements and action—an instinct that would translate well to the task of sail trimming.

They brought the ship around to port, letting the sail out to accommodate the change of direction, then trimming it home. Wulf coached Edvin through the maneuver and Hal nodded to himself. It was good to see Wulf occupied, not brooding over his twin's injury.

After an hour on the new course, he brought the ship back to starboard, with plenty of sea room to weather the cape. Again, the crew settled down as the ship glided swiftly over the swell. But now the usual feeling of contentment was back and several of the crew exchanged snippets of conversation. After a while, Hal sensed someone was watching him and he glanced up to meet Thorn's amused gaze. The old sea wolf tapped his nose with one forefinger, and slowly slid one eyelid closed in an enormous wink. Hal grinned and shrugged.

But the change in mood stayed with them and the atmosphere on board returned to normal. They were all still concerned for Ulf, of course, but now they accepted that he was in good hands. After two days, Wulf brightened visibly. He turned to Edvin, who was leaning on the bulwark beside him.

"Ulf's going to be okay. He's awake," he said quietly.

Edvin regarded him with some interest. "How do you know?"

Wulf shrugged. "He's my twin. I can feel it—somehow." He was a little bewildered himself. He couldn't put it into words but he was feeling that strange communication that happens between twins. "He's hungry," he added, with the same sense of "how did I know that?" in his voice.

Edvin put a hand on his shoulder and smiled at him. "Good."

After that, the whole crew felt better about Ulf, content in the knowledge that he was on the mend.

On the afternoon of the third day, they sighted the buildings of Ephesa, shining white in the westering sun.

From a kilometer out to sea, Ephesa looked to be a thriving town.

Yet as *Heron* sailed in and moored alongside the open water stone jetty that jutted out from the shore, it became obvious that the buildings were derelict. The walls and ornate columns still stood, but the roofs, which had been terracotta tiles placed over wooden support beams, had long since collapsed, giving the town a sad, abandoned air.

The buildings were gleaming white—stone and mortar faced with marble—and they rose in ranks on one side of the town, following the natural slope of a hill on the west.

Some of them were large and decorated with columns and statuary. They had obviously been substantial dwellings, belonging to rich traders or government officials.

To the east, the ground was flatter, and more buildings were laid out in orderly rows. These were smaller, usually one story high. Houses, shops and manufactories, Hal guessed—the sort of mixture that would be found in any large town.

Toward the outskirts, the buildings became smaller and less ornate. The orderly rows that marked the rest of the town were missing. The buildings seemed to have been laid out anyway that suited the occupants, with narrow alleyways winding between them. Obviously, this was the poorer part of town, where the laborers and common people had lived.

Beyond the mean little buildings, and rising above them, a large walled structure could be seen. Hal viewed it curiously. It might have been a fort, but the walls rose steeply, with no openings until the top level, where large arched windows were in evidence. They seemed to be too big to form an effective fortification, he thought. Gilan saw the direction of his gaze.

"It's a hippodrome," he said, and when Hal looked at him blankly, he explained, "A racetrack. Horse races. Chariot races. The Toscans loved them. They built a racecourse just about any place they built a substantial town in their empire. A racecourse and a theater for the aristocrats."

"A theater?" Hal was impressed. Here, in this desert town, hundreds of miles from their homeland, the Toscans had taken the trouble to build a center for culture and drama, as well as a racetrack for less edifying pastimes.

"It'll probably be in the rising ground," Gilan said, gesturing to the western side of town, where there was a steep escarpment. "Their theaters were usually built into hillsides to give them the shape they needed for good acoustics."

Hal had never seen a theater, much less been in one. In Hallasholm the people were entertained from time to time by traveling mummers and jongleurs, but they usually performed in the Great Hall. A theater built specifically for such a purpose seemed somewhat exotic.

"So what did they see in these theaters?" Thorn asked. The crew had gathered around Gilan, who seemed to know a lot about Toscan customs and what they might expect to find in this abandoned imperial outpost. The Ranger looked at him.

"Plays, mostly," he said. "Sometimes an oration by a poet or a singer."

"What's a play?" Stefan asked. "Is that like a puppet show?" He'd seen a traveling troupe of puppeteers perform when he was a child.

Gilan twisted his lips thoughtfully. "It's a story written down and actors—players—take roles in it and act it out for the audience, bringing the story to life."

Stefan nodded. "So, it's like a puppet show then," he declared and Gilan, with a ghost of a smile, agreed.

"Pretty much," he said. Theatrical companies were not unknown in Araluen, and many of the performers showed the same sort of animation one might expect from a puppet—and, often, less intelligence.

"Where's the oasis?" Hal inquired. One of his constant concerns was topping up *Heron*'s supply of fresh drinking water. Gilan gestured to the southwest.

"It's outside the town limits," he said. They all turned to look in the direction he indicated and they could make out a few waving green trees in the distance.

"I would have thought they'd enclose it in the town walls," Hal said thoughtfully. But Gilan shook his head. He'd had an extensive briefing from Selethen on the history and layout of Ephesa before they left Tabork.

"It's too big," he said. "The fortifications here only enclosed the administrative buildings and the governor's palace. Besides, the Toscans thought they might antagonize the locals if they were seen to be taking control of the only water source in the area. They dug wells and built underground pipelines into the city so they would always have a water source for the inhabitants. But they left the oasis open to all comers to try to create a sense of hospitality and openhandedness."

"Did it work?" Ingvar asked. He was peering at the neat rows of ruined buildings that surrounded them on all sides. He was used to houses and other structures built in pinewood. The ranks of gleaming white marble housefronts fascinated him. Then again, now that he could see more clearly, most things fascinated him.

Gilan shook his head. "The locals—the Bedullin and the Tualaghi—never made the invaders feel welcome. They were constantly rebelling against them. They didn't agree with the Toscans that they were now part of the great empire. It was always a difficult outpost to maintain. Eventually, about forty years ago, the Toscan emperor gave up, and they gradually abandoned it."

"Let's take a look at this oasis," Hal said, and led the way to the southwest.

Somehow, he had pictured the oasis as a small grove of palms clustered around a single pool of dirty water in the dry desert ground. But as Gilan had said, this oasis was enormous. It was nearly as extensive as the town itself.

There were palm trees there, of course. But also half a dozen other species of trees that he didn't recognize. And there wasn't one pool. There were nearly a dozen, of varying shapes and sizes. The largest was fifty meters by twenty. Smaller ones were scattered around and the water was clear and clean. He knelt by one of the larger ponds and scooped a handful of water up to taste it. It was cool and refreshing. He jerked his head toward the pool.

"We'll get the water casks filled tomorrow," he told Stig, who nodded agreement.

Trees grew profusely, shading the area around the pools. Well-shaded paths led from one pool to another, with clear spaces by the larger pools that were obviously used as camping grounds by travelers.

By one pool, he noticed a thick grove of bamboos, the tallest of which were over ten meters in height, swaying gently in the ever-present wind.

"Are they native to this area?" he asked.

Gilan shrugged. "Maybe. But Selethen says the Toscans would have cultivated them here. They used big canvas sun awnings to shelter the audience in the hippodrome and they needed the bamboo to support the canvas."

Hal frowned. Something about the mention of bamboo and canvas stirred that errant thought that had been troubling his mind over the past few days.

"I can see why, in this heat," he said.

They retraced their steps to the town itself, returning for one last look at the hippodrome. It was a long, flattened oval in shape, with rows of stone seats overlooking the racetrack, which ran round the outer perimeter. The track itself was sand. Hal scuffed it with his boot. He stood in the center of the track, turning to look around him. He closed his eyes and imagined he could hear the thunder of the horses' hooves, the yelling of the crowd, the rattle and clatter of harnesses and chariots as they skidded through the turns at high speed.

"Hal!"

Stig's shout roused him from the daydream. He opened his eyes and found himself back in the deserted, half-ruined old racetrack. The rows of empty seats stared down at him. A few tattered remnants of the canvas awnings fluttered in the wind. It was desolate and deserted and silent. It was sad somehow, he thought. At one time, this must have been such a vibrant, exciting place, filled with yelling, enthusiastic humanity. And now it was left here to fall apart in the desert.

"Hal! Come here!" Stig called again.

The others were clustered around a large doorway leading under the empty grandstand. Hal walked across to join them, his boots squeaking in the fine dry sand. As he reached them, Stig gestured eagerly for him to go through the doorway.

"What is it?" he asked.

His friend caught hold of his arm and pulled him forward excitedly. "Look what we've found!"

As Hal's eyes accustomed themselves to the gloom, he found himself in a large, open room under the grandstand, measuring some twenty meters by ten. The rest of the crew followed him inside. There were three objects against the far wall and he walked forward, peering through the dimness to see what they were.

"Chariots?" he said. Then he repeated the word, answering his own involuntary question. "Chariots."

They were beautifully built vehicles. As a craftsman himself, he admired the fine carpentry that had gone into their creation. The rider's platform was enclosed by a curved railing on three sides—high at the front and sweeping down at the sides. The space between the railing and the chariot floor was plaited cane, presumably to save weight. In a racing vehicle, that would be all-important. The floor of the chariot was light pine planking—presumably for the same reason. He tested it with his finger. He wouldn't trust that dried-out old wood to support anyone's weight these days, he thought.

The yoke pole jutted out in front, a solid ebony pole with a T-shaped crosspiece at the end, fitted with harness points for two horses. The leather of the harnesses, and any other leatherwork on the chariot, had long since dried out and was brittle to the touch. It would crumble away if you tried to use it now, he realized.

But it was the wheels that drew his attention. They were solid wood—ebony again, he saw. They were designed with four thick spokes, beautifully fitted and with intricate carving on them. The rims were thick and heavy. Here, the need for strength took precedence over the need to save weight. He knelt down and inspected the points where the spokes fitted into the wooden rim. The workmanship was superb. He could barely see the join, even after years of neglect. He tapped the wood with his knuckles. It was sound.

"The dry air has preserved the wood," he said quietly. He ran his hand up one of the spokes to the thick wooden rim. Both spoke and rim were in excellent condition and he noticed with surprise that the iron tire binding the outside of the wheel rim was also preserved by the dry climate and the fact that the chariot had been under shelter all these years. The salt air from the sea hadn't been able to get at it. There was a little surface rust, but he drew his saxe and scraped some away. Underneath, the iron rim was sound.

He rose and moved to the other side of the chariot and checked the second wheel. He found it was in the same well-preserved condition. And he found his heart was beating a little faster as the idea that had been chipping away at the edges of his consciousness for the past three days began to take form. It was still dim and hazy. But it was coming closer to the surface. Long experience told him that in a few hours, it would appear to him in its entirety. He just needed to be patient. All the elements that had been drifting through his brain would soon come together. He rose and brushed rust from his hands, nodding his head several times as he looked down at the old racing vehicle.

"Pity we can't find some horses and harness them up," Stig said. "We could use these to get to the mountains."

But Hal shook his head. "The fittings and harnesses are dried out and rotten," he pointed out. "And you'd need to replace those floors as well."

"Besides," Gilan pointed out, "you can't just harness a horse into a chariot and drive off. It takes months to train a team. They race in pairs and they have to learn to work together. Like a brotherband," he added with a smile.

"Oh," Stig said, looking downcast. It had seemed such a good idea at first.

"Let's get back to the ship," Hal said. He never liked leaving the *Heron* for too long in a potentially hostile location, and night was drawing on. He didn't want to spend the night moored alongside the old pier, where an enemy force could approach unseen through the ruined buildings. He planned to anchor offshore for the night, where they would be safe from attack. Tomorrow, they could build a fortified camp on the beach.

They straggled back through the ruined buildings and the failing light. The columns and half-collapsed walls cast weird shadows across their path, strengthening his resolve to get back out to sea. He noticed that, as the sun went down, the wind from the south gradually died away. In several minutes, the evening sea breeze would begin to blow.

And in that moment, he realized how they were going to get to Scorpion Mountain.

They spent the night moored offshore, safe from any surprise attack. The sea was calm and Edvin was able to build a small cook fire on board, supported over a metal tray full of sand that caught any stray embers. He set charcoal smoldering, then glowing red hot, and grilled succulent lamb cutlets over the coals, serving them with the last of the tabouleh salad.

The night was clear, so there was no need to rig the tent-shaped canvas shelter they carried with them. After they had eaten, and swigged down mugs of coffee, the crew rolled into their blankets and settled for the night. With a clear sky like this, the desert heat would soon radiate away and the night would be cold. Hal organized a guard roster, leaving one person to watch the shoreline and the sea around them, and within a few minutes the huddled forms were sleeping almost silently. Almost, because the silence of the night was broken by the muted snoring from one of the group.

"Keep the snoring down, Lydia," Thorn called.

"Shut up, old man," Lydia replied tartly. Then, to her mortification, as she settled down again and was on the brink of deep sleep, she realized that it was indeed she who was snoring. Hastily, she turned onto her side, hoping to stop the rumbling noise. A few meters away, Thorn giggled softly.

"I rest my case," he said, to nobody in particular.

He always gets the last word, Lydia reflected. She racked her brain for ways to get the better of him in their ongoing verbal joust. Their clash two days ago didn't count, as they had quickly orchestrated it. In the middle of planning ways to leave him crushed and wordless she fell asleep.

In the morning, after they had breakfasted, Hal directed them to row to the western end of the narrow indent in the coastline off the town. There, a jumble of rocks would protect their back as they set up their camp, and fortified it.

"Why not camp in the oasis?" Jesper asked. "It'd save lugging water out here."

But Hal shook his head. "Too much cover for anyone looking to attack us. This way, we've got open ground all round us. If anyone is planning any mischief, we'll see them in plenty of time. Right, Thorn?"

The old sea wolf nodded agreement. "We can cut some of that thornbush and build a protective barricade around the camp with the sea at our back," he said. "Then, if we anchor the ship twenty meters offshore, the Mangler can cover the beach."

Hal studied the surrounding beach. It was flat and featureless. If anyone launched an attack, they'd be visible for several hundred meters. And they'd be forced to attack across the thick, heavy sand, which would slow them down. Thorn's idea for the barricade was sound. There was plenty of thornbush plant growing close by. On the down side, it *was* thornbush, which meant its thick creepers were covered in long, sharp spines. It was a painful and difficult material to work with.

"Can I leave you to set up the camp?" Hal said quietly to Thorn. "I've got something I have to take care of."

"Of course," Thorn replied. He was already mentally setting people to different tasks. Anyone who had annoyed him recently would be detailed to cut and drag in the spiky rolls of thornbush.

"I'll need Edvin to help me," Hal said, then, raising his voice, he called to him. "Edvin! You're coming with me."

"Right, Hal," Edvin replied briskly. He was pleased to be relieved from the heavy labor of building the camp.

Ingvar looked up at Hal, a little disappointed. Usually, he was the one the skirl chose to accompany him.

Hal saw the look and explained. "No heavy lifting today, Ingvar. But I need someone who's a good hand with needle and thread."

The disappointed look faded from Ingvar's face as he realized that Hal hadn't meant any slight by omitting him. He raised one finger to his forehead in an informal salute.

"That's definitely not me, Hal," he said

"We'll be in the hippodrome stables," Hal told Thorn. Then, collecting his tool bag, an ax and the roll of canvas they used as a shelter, he trudged off through the sand toward the hippodrome, accompanied by Edvin.

"What's he up to?" Stig asked Thorn. Hal had seemed preoccupied the previous night and both of them knew what that could mean.

"I'd say he's hatching one of his ideas," Thorn said, smiling. "Those chariots seemed to have him very interested."

Stig watched as his friend disappeared into the jumble of buildings, Edvin at his side. "What do you think he's got planned?"

But Thorn shook his head. "You know Hal. He'll never say. We'll see it when he's good and ready to show us."

Stig sighed. "I suppose so," he said. That was the way Hal always did things.

They worked solidly all morning, digging a curving trench to enclose their camp, then filling it with thornbush tangles. They piled more thornbush on the inner side of the ditch, and reinforced it with sharpened stakes driven into the ground and facing outward.

At one stage, Thorn consulted Lydia. "I thought we'd build an elevated mound for you in the center," he said. "We'll put it a few meters back from the front line. That way, you'll be able to see over the barricade and shoot into the enemy as they attack."

She studied the layout of the land and nodded. When it came to discussing matters of fighting, defense or deployment, she and Thorn rarely argued. That was left for less important matters.

"Good idea," she said eventually. "You might also give me a little protective cover—some boards or shields to crouch behind. Otherwise, I'll be exposed if they have archers."

"Hadn't thought of that," Thorn said. "I'll get it done. If we come under attack, you'll be our key weapon, along with the Mangler."

Stig strolled up to them as they spoke. He was wiping his forehead with a scrap of rag. He'd taken off his shirt and his shoulders were showing the effects of the sun.

"You'd better cover up," Thorn told him.

Stig nodded agreement. He leaned against a pile of timber and said casually, "Don't look too suddenly. But we're being watched. There's a rider on the western end of the oasis. And another on the escarpment overlooking the town."

Casually, Thorn let his gaze wander to the two spots Stig had mentioned. He could see the dark forms, sitting their horses and keeping watch.

"Who do you think they are?" Lydia asked.

Stig smiled at her, but it was a humorless smile. "I'll wager they work for this Shurmel character we've heard so much about. And the minute we set out for Scorpion Mountain, they'll ride lickety split to let him know we're on our way."

He was pulling his shirt on, glad that Thorn had reminded him to cover up. He could already feel the faint sting of sunburn.

"And since we'll be riding shank's pony, they'll get there long before we do," he continued.

Lydia frowned. "Who's Shank? And where is his pony?" she asked. She wasn't familiar with the expression.

"It means we'll be on foot," Stig explained.

Her frown deepened. "Then why not say *we'll be on foot* or *we'll be walking?*"

Stig shrugged. Sometimes, he thought, Lydia could be a little pedantic. Then he modified the thought. Sometimes she could be a lot pedantic.

"It's more poetic the way I said it," he replied and she snorted in derision.

"You? Poetic? When did that happen?"

Stig grinned at her. "I'm always poetic," he said. "I'm a big hit with the ladies back in Hallasholm."

"Not that I've noticed," she said. "The only poetry I've ever heard from you is bad limericks."

"I take it you're referring to my ode to the girl from the mountains?" Stig said.

"I'm not sure I've heard that one," Thorn interrupted.

"Oh, it's a classic of its kind," Stig replied, and placing one hand over his heart, he thrust his right foot forward in what he considered to be a theatrical, declamatory stance, then intoned the following:

> *There was a young girl from the mountains,*
> *who fell on her bum in a fountain.*
> *She said in high pique: "That's the third time this week."*
> *But her friend said, "The fourth. But who's countin'?"*

He spread his hands wide, as if expecting applause, and looked from Thorn to Lydia and back again. Slowly the expectant grin faded from his face.

"Oh, come on!" he said indignantly. "That's top-class stuff."

Thorn scratched his beard thoughtfully. "That's the sort of stuff you recite to the girls in Hallasholm?"

Stig nodded. "Yes. And that's just one of them. I have others that are nearly as good."

"That explains why you were on your own at the haymaking festival," Thorn told him and Lydia smothered a laugh. Stig's indignation grew.

"You two obviously know nothing about fine poetry," he said. "Nothing at all."

Thorn and Lydia exchanged a glance. Then the old sea wolf said, "And that makes three of us."

This time, Lydia didn't bother to smother her laughter. Stig drew himself up straight and looked down his nose at them.

"You're barbarians," he said. "Both of you."

"Perhaps we are," Thorn replied. "But we're barbarians with a ditch to finish. Let's get back to it."

He glanced up at the escarpment. The rider was still there.

"Then this afternoon, let's take a look at the theater Gilan was telling us about."

Lydia cocked her head sideways. She wouldn't have picked Thorn as a theater buff. "You're interested in drama?"

He shook his head. "I'm interested in getting a closer look at that rider on the escarpment."

Lydia looked to the east. The dark form was still evident on the skyline.

"I might come with you," she said. "I've just developed a sudden love for the theater myself."

chapter thirty-five

The camp was finished by early afternoon. Thorn inspected the defenses with a keen eye, pointing out several spots where the thornbush barricade needed thickening. But on the whole, he was satisfied with the work. The crew knew their jobs, he thought. They had become an experienced fighting band, with skills and abilities far beyond what one might normally expect of such a young group.

Edvin was busy with Hal, working on the mysterious project that the skirl had in mind, so there was no hot lunch. Instead, they scavenged through his supplies and found salted pork and flat bread. They toasted the latter over a small fire and wrapped the pork in it, along with generous helpings of pickles. It was a simple lunch, but after the exertions of the morning, it was nourishing and tasty.

Ingvar gestured toward the high walls of the hippodrome with a roll of flat bread and pork.

"I'd love to know what they're up to," he said. The others nodded agreement. Throughout the morning, they had seen Hal and Edvin going into the oasis and returning to the hippodrome dragging long, narrow trunks of bamboo behind them.

"We could sneak over and take a peek," Jesper suggested. He was a skilled thief and the idea of sneaking in where he wasn't wanted always appealed to him. But Stig shook his head.

"He'll have it covered with that canvas," he said. "Whatever it might be. And if he catches you sneaking in, you'll be on bilge bailing for the next week."

Even a well-found ship like the *Heron* took on water as she rolled and plunged and her seams opened slightly. The excess water would gather in the bilges under the floorboards, stagnant and evil smelling. From time to time, someone would be assigned to lift the floorboards and bail it out with a bucket. It was an unpleasant job and one that Hal saved for people who had displeased him. Jesper thought about it, weighing the possibility of getting caught against the obvious satisfaction of knowing what Hal was doing. He seemed to get more than his share of bilge bailing and it was a messy, smelly job that he abhorred.

"Probably wouldn't know what he was doing even if I could see it," he said. The others nodded.

"We'll find out when he's ready to tell us," Thorn said. He'd learned over the years that Hal wouldn't reveal his ideas until he was ready—probably because, in the past, some of them hadn't worked out so well.

"Did you want to take a look at the theater?" Gilan asked, sensing that Thorn was looking for a diversion from this talk of Hal and what he was up to.

The bearded warrior nodded. "That. And a look at that person who's been watching us all morning."

Involuntarily, they all looked toward the escarpment, where the solitary rider was still silhouetted against the bright sky. The other rider at the edge of the oasis was no longer in sight. But he may have retired into the shade and shelter of the trees there.

"Anyone not interested in a cultural outing to the theater?" he asked the group in general.

Jesper shrugged. He had no wish to study a group of crumbling stones. "Include me out," he said.

Gilan raised an eyebrow—a skill he had copied from his long-time mentor, a Ranger named Halt. "Interesting way of putting it," he said.

Jesper looked at him curiously. He saw nothing unusual in his statement.

Thorn gestured around the campsite. "Right. You keep an eye on things here. Keep Kloof with you." The big dog thumped her tail on the ground at the mention of her name. She was lying on a warm flat rock in the sun, her chin on her forepaws, her eyes constantly busy, watching them. "If there's any sign of trouble, blow that horn and we'll come running."

He indicated a battered ram's horn hanging from a pole inside the rough guardhouse-cum-shelter they had built inside the ditch, at the point where they had constructed a gate in the palisade.

"I'll blow to wake the dead," Jesper assured him with a grin.

Thorn was never comfortable when Jesper said such things. The former thief had a way of sneaking off and avoiding extra duties. Thorn was willing to bet that the moment they vanished into the town, Jesper would be flat on his back snoring. Still, he thought, Kloof would keep a good watch.

"If I come back and find you asleep," he said in an ominous tone, "you might not wake up yourself."

Jesper's grin widened. "Trust me, Thorn," he said.

Thorn raised his eyes to heaven. It was a statement that was almost exclusively said by totally untrustworthy people.

"How I wish you hadn't said that." He turned to the others. "All right, let's get moving."

They straggled out of the camp behind him. It was noticeable that, although nothing was said, they brought their weapons with them.

The mounted figure on the escarpment remained in place as they made their way through the derelict buildings of the town. When they began to climb the slope toward the theater, he slowly turned his horse's head and moved away, disappearing from sight. But they had managed to get close enough to make out some details.

"He's not Tualaghi," Gilan observed. "His head dress and cloak are red and black, whereas the Tualaghi's headdresses are blue."

"Maybe red and black are the Scorpion cult's colors," Lydia observed. "Do you want me to climb to the top of the escarpment and see where he's gone?"

Thorn shook his head. "It's a safe bet to assume he's out of reach. He's mounted and we're not. He'll just move away, staying out of bowshot and continuing to watch us."

Gilan was pacing the performance area enclosed by the steep

tiers of stone benches. He looked around, fascinated by the symmetry of the half circle of seats that rose steeply away into the side of the hill. Ingenious design like this fascinated the young Ranger. He had been in several Toscan theaters in the past and this one conformed to the usual overall design. He knew that the rising arc of seats provided an ideal acoustic setting for the actors who would have performed on the hard-packed sand stage—carrying their every word to each member of the audience. He gestured to the very top row of seats, some thirty meters above them, and said to Thorn, "Climb up to the back row and you'll hear how perfect the acoustics are."

Thorn frowned at him. "How will I hear that?" he asked. He didn't share Gilan's fascination with scientific matters. Hal might have, but Hal wasn't here.

"Well, I'll stay down here and say something. And you'll hear it."

"Why should I climb all those stairs when I'm right next to you now. What are you planning to say?"

The stairs were steep, and since they doubled as seating, each one was the best part of a meter high. Clambering from one to the next would be a considerable effort. But Gilan gestured in frustration. Thorn was missing the point—and Gilan suspected that he was doing so intentionally.

"I don't know. Nothing important."

"Then I'm not going to climb all that way for something that's not very important. If you want to say something to me, just say it now while I'm standing next to you."

"No. I want to demonstrate . . . ," Gilan began. But he saw a slight gleam of amusement in Thorn's eye and stopped.

"I'll go," Lydia said. Then, with a wicked smile in Thorn's direction, she added, "After all, those steps do look a little steep for a poor old dodderer like Thorn."

And having said that, she ran lightly up the steps, leaping from one to the next with speed and grace until she was at the very top. Thorn glared at her.

"Go ahead. Say something," she called. The acoustic properties of the theater were such that her voice carried clearly to the small group in the center of the stage.

Gilan opened his mouth, but as often happens at such times, his mind went blank and he couldn't think of anything to say. He shut his mouth again. He suddenly felt it was important that he didn't say something banal or meaningless. In times past, he'd seen theater assistants and actors testing the acoustics by saying "Two! Two! Two!" repeatedly. But he'd always felt that was vaguely mindless and he didn't want to say that now. So he hesitated, searching for inspiration.

Stefan was standing off to one side, an interested spectator. Over the past months, Stefan had begun to feel a sense of frustration. He was a skilled mimic and, growing up in Hallasholm, he had often caused confusion by mimicking important people like the Oberjarl or his hilfmann, or their instructors on the brotherband course. But it had been a long time since he'd had the opportunity to put his unique skill to use and he was missing it. Jesper, on the other hand, had been frequently called upon to employ his ability to open locked doors or padlocks and Stefan was feeling a little deprived by comparison. Now he saw an opportunity for mischief. He moved a few paces away from Gilan and Thorn, turned his back on Lydia high above him, and said, in a perfect imitation of Thorn's voice:

"You know, Lydia should lay off those honey pastries. She's getting a bit wide in the beam."

Lydia's head shot up as the comment was carried clearly to her by the curving amphitheater. She glared at Thorn, who was standing innocently beside Gilan. The comment was all the more pointed because Lydia *had* developed a weakness for the little layered squares of pastry, honey, walnuts and pine nuts since they had been introduced to them at the guesthouse in Al Shabah. At her request, Edvin had procured the recipe and barely a meal went by when she didn't help herself to two or three of the delicious treats. Or even three or four.

"You shut up, old man! I'll give you wide in the beam with one of my darts!" she shouted at him. Lydia, of course, was anything but wide in the beam. Even though she did indulge in the pastries, she was fit and active and kept herself in excellent shape.

Thorn looked up in surprise. He could hear the anger in Lydia's voice, and see it in the way she stood, hand on hips and feet apart, glaring at him. For a moment, he wondered what had set her off. Then he heard a muffled snigger. Stefan was a few meters away, his back turned and his shoulders shaking with suppressed laugher. Stealthily, Thorn moved toward him, measuring the distance to his backside and drawing back one booted foot.

"Owwwww!" Stefan howled in surprise and pain as a battering ram seemed to smash into his unsuspecting backside, lifting him half a meter off the ground and propelling him several meters across the open space of the stage. He turned and gave Thorn an injured look—injured in both pride and in body.

Thorn made an exaggerated bow in Lydia's direction.

"It seems our tame mimic had something he wanted to share, princess," he said.

Lydia transferred her angry glare to the hapless Stefan, who was rubbing his bruised posterior. "I'll settle with you later, Stefan," she threatened.

"No need, Lydia. I'm well and truly settled," he replied in a miserable tone. He flinched as Thorn stepped closer, but the old sea wolf was planning to speak, not give him a repeat dose of his boot.

"Next time you mimic me, boy, make sure you're not in kicking range."

A very subdued Stefan nodded his head several times. "I'll definitely keep that in mind, Thorn."

They trudged slowly back to the campsite. Thorn grinned to himself as he watched Stefan. The mimic was careful to stay well away from Lydia, who still eyed him from time to time with a scowl. At the same time, he contrived to keep a reasonable distance between himself and Thorn.

The old sea wolf made this more difficult for him by constantly changing his own pace and direction, and straying to within easy kicking distance of Stefan.

Whenever Stefan noticed, he would shy hastily away, then realize he was getting dangerously close to Lydia, and skip off in a third direction, sometimes taking shelter behind Stig or Ingvar, or one of the others. Whereupon Thorn would repeat his own action and set the whole sequence in train again.

Gilan noticed the wordless pantomime taking place and smiled quietly. He estimated that, by the time they reached camp, Stefan would have walked three times as far as anyone else in the party.

As they approached the entryway through the ditch and thorn-bush barrier, Kloof greeted them with a single, deep bark. Almost immediately, they saw a head appear over the barrier to one side of the entrance. Not Jesper, Thorn noted sourly, but Hal.

The skirl greeted them cheerfully as they entered. There was an air of suppressed excitement about him that Stig and Thorn had seen before. It told them that, whatever he had been working on, he had been successful.

"Where have you been?" Hal asked.

Stig gestured over his shoulder with his thumb. "We've been absorbing some culture at the theater."

Hal frowned. That didn't sound like his crew. "Why are you limping, Stefan?"

But before the mimic could reply, Thorn answered for him. "He had a problem," he said, smiling evilly.

"With his ankle?" Hal asked.

Thorn shook his head. "With his mouth."

"Oh . . ." Hal stopped as he digested that statement. It didn't really make sense, but then, Thorn often spoke in riddles. He decided to let the matter drop. He had more exciting things to discuss and to show them. "So," he said, pausing dramatically, "do you want to see what we've been up to?"

Stig and Thorn exchanged a quick glance. They had discussed this on the walk back from the theater. Hal's secretive ways could get to be too much after a while and they had decided it was time to take him down a peg or two.

Thorn pretended to consider the invitation, then shook his head. "Naaah. Not really."

Stig took his lead from the battle master. He feigned a huge yawn and stretched his arms out wide. "Think I'll get in a nap before supper. All that digging has made me sleepy."

And then they couldn't keep it up any longer. Hal's crestfallen expression was too much to resist. They both burst out laughing, the others in the group following suit.

"Of course we want to see!" Thorn said, clapping an arm around Hal's shoulders. "We've been wondering all day what you've come up with."

Lydia looked around the camp. "Where's Edvin?"

Hal gestured with a thumb toward the hippodrome. "He's just putting the finishing touches to the sail."

Stig looked at him in surprise. "The sail? You've been building a ship? Why?"

Hal grinned at the double questions, then answered them both.

"No and you'll see," he said. The cryptic reply left Stig more confused than before. But Thorn was also looking round the campsite.

"More to the point, where's Jesper? I left him on watch," he said, an ominous tone creeping into his voice. Hal shrugged easily.

"Oh, he was asleep when I came back about ten minutes ago. Kloof barked like mad, but she didn't wake him. He looked so tired I thought I'd let him sleep on."

Thorn's shaggy eyebrows came together in a scowl. "I'll let him sleep permanently when he wakes up," he threatened.

Hal turned his head to one side curiously. "That doesn't make a lot of sense," he said.

"Jesper will understand," Thorn replied. He walked to the pole where the ram's horn was hanging, took it down, then continued to the small tent where Jesper was curled up on his blankets, a cherubic smile on his face. "What lovely dreams he must be having." Then, raising the horn to his lips, he blew a shattering blast of noise.

To those watching, it appeared that Jesper levitated straight off his blankets, rising half a meter into the air. Then, suddenly wide awake, he scrambled round on all fours, feeling for the sword that lay beside his sleeping space.

"Alarm! Alarm!" he cried, his voice breaking with panic and surprise. "We're under attack! Alarm! Al . . . "

He trailed off as he realized that his friends were standing around him in a semicircle. He saw the horn in Thorn's left hand and understanding dawned on his face.

"Oh . . . ," he said. "You're back then? Just closed my eyes for a second—"

"We've been back five minutes," Thorn said cuttingly. "And Hal has been back for longer than that. But of course, you knew that."

"What? Oh . . . yes. Of course I did. Funny that Kloof didn't bark. Bad dog, Kloofy!" He turned to the massive dog, waving an admonishing finger at her. She rolled back her top lip in what could only be construed as a sneer. Hal looked at her, surprised. He'd never seen a dog sneer before.

"I left you on watch, Jesper," Thorn said. "Remember: *Oh yes, Thorn, trust me. I'll blow the horn to wake the dead.* Kloof did her job. But then, she has more brains than you." He regarded the dog quizzically. She wagged her tail. "And I never thought I'd use the words *Kloof* and *more brains* in the same sentence. If you ever sleep on watch again, you'll be the permanent bilge bailer for the next two years. Understood?"

Jesper hung his head in shame. "Understood, Thorn," he mumbled.

Thorn regarded him in silence for some seconds. He thought the message had got through—until next time, at least. Then he lightened his mood and turned back to Hal.

"Come on. Show us your latest invention."

Hal gestured for them to follow him and they all began to straggle along behind him. Jesper, after a moment's hesitation, joined in. But Thorn stopped him with a finger prodding into his chest.

"Not you," he growled. "You stay on guard. And stay awake!" The last two words were delivered in an angry shout.

Jesper flinched then nodded hurriedly. "Yes, yes! Of course, Thorn! Whatever you say! Tr—"

Thorn's eyes blazed with anger and he held that forefinger up in a gesture commanding silence.

Jesper had a vague memory that he might have said "Trust me" earlier. He hastily changed his statement. "Try and stop me! I'll be here on watch."

"You'd better be," Thorn told him. Then he turned and followed the others on the way to the hippodrome.

It stood in the center of the racetrack outside the stable room where they had discovered the chariots.

It was a large but rather spidery structure—a triangular frame some six meters wide by five long, built from springy bamboo trunks.

The central spine was made from the thickest piece of bamboo. At the rear end, two outriggers, each three meters long, angled out to either side. They were braced by two struts, bamboo again, running back to the other end of the spine. At the end of each outrigger was one of the chariot wheels. A third was placed at the front of the main spine. That wheel appeared to be free to swivel, with leather ropes running back to a rudimentary seat at the rear end of the spine.

A series of lighter struts connected the spine to each of the outriggers, creating a triangular platform at the rear third of the spine.

Rising high above the three-wheeled vehicle was a five-meter length of bamboo, secured at the forward end just behind the steering wheel, and braced by a backstay that held it in a slight curve. A triangular sail had been slipped over this mast—a sleeve sewn into one side of the sail for this purpose. At the base of the mast, a light boom ran backward, attached to the sail at several points.

A rope ran through two sets of pulleys—one on the spine and one on the boom—to allow the boom to be controlled by the person occupying the rear seat. Each of the outrigger poles was also fitted with a simple seat, with handholds and footrests, about halfway between the spine and the wheel.

For several moments, the group looked at this remarkable giant tricycle in awed silence. Finally, Stig asked the question they all had on the tips of their tongues.

"What is it?"

Hal smiled proudly and moved to stroke the wood near the central seat with a proprietorial air. "It's a land sailer," he said. "It'll sail across land rather than the ocean. The sail will catch the wind to power it—and there's plenty of that. The wheels will help it roll across the desert. I can steer it by the swiveling wheel at the front—just as I'd use a rudder to steer a ship. The bamboo is flexible so it'll absorb the shock of running on rough ground. I couldn't manage to rig a second yardarm like the one on *Heron,* so I've used a boom to control the sail at the lower side. It means a smaller sail, but it's simpler to handle."

Lydia was walking around the strange vehicle, staring up at the curving mast with something approaching awe.

"Will it work?" she asked quietly.

Hal smiled at her. "You mean *does* it work?" he replied. "And the answer is yes. Edvin and I have given it a test run here in the hippodrome. We're reasonably sheltered from the wind in here but it still managed a respectable speed. And it tacks and jibes quite nicely. I figure with a decent wind on our beam, it'll be about as fast as a cantering horse."

"Except it won't need to be rested and watered like a horse," Thorn said thoughtfully and Hal nodded, glad he'd made the point.

"Exactly. It'll keep running all day, rolling along hour after hour, eating up the kilometers. I estimate it should get us to the Amrashin Massif in a day and a half, instead of the three or four days we'd take walking. That way, we'll be there before the Shurmel knows we're on our way."

Gilan shook his head in wonder at the amazing contraption. The more he saw of Hal, the more he admired the young man's obvious genius for invention and improvisation.

"You keep saying 'we,'" he pointed out. "Who might that *we* be?"

"You, of course," Hal replied instantly. "You're the one who'll have to negotiate—or otherwise—with the Scorpion leader. I'll be the helmsman, naturally. And the third place will go to Stig."

Stig grinned at the news. But instantly there was an outcry from the others. The loudest protests came from Thorn, Ingvar and Lydia, who all wanted to accompany them to the Amrashin Massif and Scorpion Mountain. But Hal was adamant.

"There's only room for three," he said.

Thorn protested instantly. "I accept that you and Gilan have to go. But I could take Stig's place. You might need some extra muscle when you encounter these Scorpions."

Hal regarded him calmly. "Stig will provide plenty of muscle," he said. "You're both good fighters, but you're a better commander than Stig and I need you to lead the defense of the camp here. It'll be no use ending the *tolfah* against Princess Cassandra if we lose the *Heron* in the process."

Thorn subsided, grumbling quietly. But he could see Hal had a point.

Ingvar had a different outlook. "Leave them both here," he said. "I'll come with you. Now that you've fixed my eyesight, you know I can scatter those Scorpions like ninepins."

But again, Hal had an unarguable reason for his choice. "Without you, the Mangler will be useless, Ingvar," he pointed out. "And if the camp comes under attack, we're going to need it to bring the odds down."

And Ingvar, too, had to admit that Hal made sense. Lydia looked to be about to protest in her turn, but Hal cut her short.

"Same goes for you, Lydia. We might fit you on board. You're light enough, of course. But without Gilan's longbow, your darts will be our only long-range defensive weapons. You can carve up any attack with them. Plus you're the only other one trained to use the Mangler."

"Are you so sure there's going to be an attack?" she asked.

Hal eyed her for several seconds before he replied. "I'm convinced there is."

PART FOUR

SCORPION
MOUNTAIN

The sun had been up for forty minutes. As the temperature rose, the wind began blowing from the north, growing in strength with each minute.

The land sailer stood ready, outside the main gate of the hippodrome. Water skins, bedrolls, weapons and food had been loaded onto the triangular platform ahead of the helmsman's position. The sail was raised to its fullest extent, but so far was unrestrained. It slapped back and forth in the wind without any tension on the sheet to hold it in position. As it moved, the spidery structure swayed slightly and the boom rattled back and forth.

Hal adjusted his *kheffiyeh*, the Arridan desert headdress that Selethen had provided for the crew. He drew the trailing ends across his face and twisted one over the other to hold it in position. His face and head were now protected from the sun and the wind.

He climbed aboard the central seat, taking up the sheet that controlled the sail in one hand and the steering lines to the front wheel with the other. He glanced at his two companions, waiting to board. The rest of the crew stood in a half circle to see them off.

"Day isn't getting any younger," he said, and Gilan and Stig moved to their positions, climbing gingerly onto the outriggers, setting their feet in the footrests, and gripping the handholds. Hal smiled under the *kheffiyeh* as he noted they were gripping rather more tightly than might be required.

"Just relax," he called to them. "Don't try to fight the movement. Go with it."

They both nodded. Their faces were obscured by their *kheffiyehs* as well. But he could see there was no relaxation of the tension in their bodies. He began to draw in the sheet and the rope squealed softly through the pulleys, taking up the slack until it began hauling the sail in and tightening it against the wind.

There was the usual *whoomph* as the sail caught the wind and filled, forcing the boom out to port. Hal felt the tension in the sheet increase and hauled in a little more.

Creaking and rumbling, the land sailer began to move across the hard, rocky ground. Slowly at first, then with increasing speed as Hal heaved on the steering lines and brought the strange vehicle round to a position where the wind lay on their starboard beam.

As it began to move, the watching crew took an involuntary step forward, then another, keeping pace with the three-wheeled land sailer as it bumped and jounced over the rough ground. Then Hal hauled in tight on the sheet and the spidery craft accelerated suddenly, shooting ahead of the small group of onlookers, leaving them behind as it hit its pace.

Thorn and the others stopped, looking in wonder as the land sailer skimmed across the rough ground, bouncing and rattling as it gathered speed. Then, without anyone suggesting it, they all began to cheer.

Stig turned to wave at them, nearly lost his seat as the land sailer hit a bump, and snatched frantically at his handholds. The group cheered again.

Gilan, gripping tightly to his own handholds, turned to look at Hal, who was leaning forward eagerly, like a rider on a spirited horse. The analogy seemed appropriate, Gilan thought. He began to move with the motions of the land sailer, relaxing his muscles instead of fighting the movement by staying tense. Instantly, he felt more comfortable.

The rigging and mast groaned and the wheels rattled and rumbled, occasionally leaping over a larger than usual rock. The whole frame creaked alarmingly as it flexed over the uneven ground. All in all, the land sailer was making a considerable amount of noise.

"Does it always do this?" Gilan yelled. He saw Hal's head turn toward him. Even though only his eyes were visible above the *kheffiyeh*, he was sure the skirl was grinning in delight.

"How would I know?" came the muffled reply. "I've never done this before!"

He hauled in the sheet a little further and the sail tightened. The upwind strut, the one Gilan was sitting on, began to rise as the starboard wheel lifted from the ground, skimming the surface of the desert, coming back to rest every five meters or so. Hal gripped the steering lines and sheet in one hand and gestured with his other for Gilan to move farther outboard.

Tentatively, Gilan slid his rump along the flat wooden seat built onto the outrigger. There was another handhold farther outboard and he transferred his grip to it. As he moved out, the spar began to sink back to the ground again, until they were running on three wheels once more. The faster they went, he noticed, the smoother their passage became. It seemed that the impacts with the ruts and rocks and hillocks were smoothed out by their increased speed.

On his outrigger, Stig had noticed the same thing. He glanced down at the brown earth flashing past underneath them and grinned. Hal had estimated that they'd travel as fast as a cantering horse. But this close to the ground, with only half a meter separating him from the hard-packed sand and rocks, it seemed much faster. He looked up and glanced inboard at his friend.

"You've done it again," he said in admiration. But his words, muffled by the *kheffiyeh* wrapped round his face, were drowned by the rush of wind and the constant vibration of the speeding vehicle. A flash of movement out to their right took his eye and he craned round to see more clearly. A rider had burst from the concealment of the oasis and was galloping flat out to the south, paralleling their base course.

It was one of the observers who had kept an eye on them for the past two days. He heard Hal call and looked back inboard. His friend was pointing at the distant rider and Stig nodded his head emphatically to show that he had seen him.

"Off to warn the Shurmel," he said, although he knew Hal would never hear him.

He had begun to become accustomed to the swooping, soaring movement of the land sailer. Just as Gilan had used his horseman's instinctive movements, Stig employed his ingrained seaman's ability to match himself to the regular, plunging motion.

They careered on, moving faster and faster as Hal became more accustomed to the feeling of the land sailer and brought the sail in harder, always stopping short as a wheel began to lift.

Then Stig and Gilan heard him shout and they both turned to look at him. He had the reins and sheet in one hand and was making a circular motion over his head with the other. Then he jabbed a pointing finger out to starboard.

The meaning was obvious. He's going to come about onto the opposite tack, Stig thought, and took a firmer hold of the bamboo handles in front of him. Gilan did the same. Then Hal heaved on the tiller ropes and brought the land sailer's head round, releasing the sheet as he did so.

The speed dropped away as the land sailer's head came round, the wind driving the sail through the turn. Then Hal hauled in on the sheet again and the sail filled and tightened. The speed began to build up once more and, within a few minutes, they were flying again on the opposite tack.

"Just like a ship," Stig murmured. Now they were racing on the port tack, the frame rumbling and groaning and vibrating as loudly as before. Ahead of them, and a little to starboard, he could see the distant horseman, galloping frantically, his horse's hooves kicking up puffs of dust that were instantly left behind in his wake. The rider turned to look at them, then redoubled his efforts with his riding whip and the horse began to pull away from them once more.

"You won't keep that up all day," Stig said, echoing the thought Thorn had voiced about the comparative speeds of a horseman and the land sailer. He glanced astern—he couldn't help using shipboard terms in his mind—and saw they were leaving an impressive rooster tail of brown dust behind them. The buildings of Ephesa were fading into the distance. Only the tallest could still be seen.

"We're really moving," he said to himself. And once more, he shook his head in admiration of Hal's inventiveness.

After some time, they lost sight of the galloping horseman. They were traveling on slightly divergent paths, and in any event, the land sailer had to change direction back and forth in order to capture the beam wind that would give them their best speed. Stig sat on his outrigger, swaying to the motion of the land sailer, lulled by the repetitive rumbling, creaking, groaning noises of its passage. At one stage, he caught himself on the verge of falling asleep and jerked himself upright.

"All very well to relax," he told himself. "But don't overdo it."

The ground below him looked hard and unforgiving. If he fell off, he'd suffer bruises and abrasions, at the least. And he'd delay their passage to the Amrashin Massif. He shook off the sense of weariness and sat up straighter.

Then he became aware that Hal had released the sheet, spilling wind from the sail, and the land sailer was rumbling increasingly slowly across the rocky ground until it came to a stop. The sudden silence was remarkable. Stig's senses had become accustomed to the creaks and groans and rattles of wheels and rigging and the frame itself. Now there was just the constant sigh of the wind out of the south, and the occasional flapping of the sail as the wind tossed it from side to side.

Hal unwrapped the *kheffiyeh* from his face, letting the long ends fall down on either side of his neck. He stepped down from his seat and stretched himself, kneading his fists into the small of his back as he leaned backward.

"Let's take a break," he said. "My backside's killing me."

The others agreed wholeheartedly. Gilan stepped down stiffly from his seat and dusted himself off. Clouds of dust flew in the air around him.

"I feel like I've swallowed half the desert," he said, reaching for one of the water skins, taking a deep swig, then spitting it out on the dry ground. He watched with interest as the damp stain quickly disappeared from the superheated ground. He looked around. On all sides, the empty brown desert stretched away from them.

"How far do you think we've come?" he asked.

Hal shrugged. "Hard to tell. We're tacking constantly, so our progress as the crow flies is a lot less than the actual distance we've covered. I'd say we're about twenty or thirty kilometers from the coast. What do you think, Stig?"

Stig took the water skin from Gilan, rinsed his mouth, then took a deeper drink before replying. Then he nodded.

"I'd say that sounds about right."

Gilan had a further question, one that had been bothering him for some time. "The wind's behind us," he said. "Why don't we run directly ahead of it, instead of zigzagging back and forth?"

Hal acknowledged the question with a nod. "If we run dead ahead of the wind, I have no way of controlling our speed. We'd just go faster and faster until we were out of control. By slanting across it, I can slow down or speed up as I want to."

Stig was looking up at the sun, which wasn't yet directly overhead. "It's not noon yet. We've got at least four hours of steady wind coming this afternoon."

"And if we want to, we could keep going tonight once the wind shifts," Gilan said.

But Hal greeted the idea doubtfully. "Don't think I'd care to go careering around the desert after dark," he said. "If we hit a large rock or fall into a gully we'll be in big trouble."

Several times that morning he'd been forced to change course suddenly as they went hurtling toward large rock outcrops, and once they had nearly plunged into a dried-up watercourse—known as a wadi to the Arridans. It was a steep-sided gully that was nearly three meters deep.

Stig shuddered as he thought of what would have become of the frail land sailer had they gone over the edge.

"I hadn't thought of that," Gilan said.

Stig rubbed one buttock. He'd been sitting off center and he could feel a bruise forming there from the constant pounding movement of the land sailer.

"What about our friend from the oasis?" he asked.

Gilan considered the question, then replied. "If he has any sense, he'll stop for the night too. You can't keep galloping across country like this in the dark. His horse could break a leg or fall and roll on him."

"What if he hasn't got any sense?" Stig asked.

Gilan shrugged. "Then he'll either beat us to Scorpion Mountain or kill himself trying," he said. "My vote is for the latter."

Hal had moved to the triangular platform ahead of his steering position and was unpacking some of the supplies they had brought with them.

"Let's take a break now and eat," he said. "Then Stig and I can tighten up anything that's worked its way loose and we'll keep going till dusk. That should put us more than halfway to the Massif."

"And Scorpion Mountain," said Gilan, as he sliced a haunch of cold roast goat with his saxe knife.

Hal nodded. "And Scorpion Mountain," he echoed.

chapter thirty-eight

In a cave high inside Scorpion Mountain, the Shurmel gazed out over the brown, shimmering land surrounding the triple-peaked mass of rock.

The room was one of hundreds of caves and tunnels that honeycombed the mountain, providing accommodation, meeting rooms and worship areas for the Cult of the Scorpion, followers of the goddess Imrika. This particular cave comprised the Shurmel's personal suite of rooms. It was a huge, sprawling area, befitting his status as the leader of the cult and the High Priest of Imrika. A wide rift in the side of the mountain provided the view of the desert, letting him keep track of the comings and goings of his men— and other visitors to the Scorpions' lair.

Less than ten minutes ago, he had seen a rider approaching, spurring his weary horse across the last few hundred meters to the base of the mountain, where a large gallery provided access to the cave complex inside. Any moment now, the man should be reporting to him. The Shurmel had no idea what he might be going to report. But the rider's obvious haste, and the distressed state of his horse, hinted that it might be important news.

As he had the thought, there was a tentative knock at the door set into the stone walls of the cave. The Shurmel turned away from the rift in the side of the mountain and faced the door.

"Come in," he called softly.

His voice was deep and almost sepulchral. It fitted his physical appearance. He was a massively tall man, well over two meters in height and broad in the shoulder and body. His skin, unlike the swarthy, coffee-colored complexions of most of his followers, was pale and white. His head was clean-shaven and oiled and his face was adorned with markings of kohl, a black makeup compound often used by dancers and entertainers.

But there was nothing festive or entertaining about the markings the Shurmel had chosen. His eyes were surrounded by dark circles, giving them the appearance of the empty eye sockets of a skull. And his face was made up to accentuate the skull-like appearance as well, highlighting the cheekbones and deep-sunken cheeks.

He was dressed in a long, flowing black robe, with silver thread that depicted a scorpion in fighting pose, pincers raised to grip an opponent, sting poised to kill it.

In his left hand, he carried his staff of office—a two-meter ebony rod with a silver ferrule at the bottom, surmounted by a carved black scorpion in the same posture as the one on his robe, with eyes made from rubies.

The door opened and admitted a nervous desert nomad. He was dressed in a white tunic, marked by dirt and dust, and a dark green over-robe. His *kheffiyeh* was patterned in black and green checks. As he entered and stood before his lord, he hastily removed it, twisting it nervously in his hands.

The Shurmel, well aware of the man's nervousness, allowed the silence between them to stretch to an almost unbearable point. His dark brown eyes bored into the desert dweller, whom he recognized as a member of one of his vassal tribes. He called these tribes the *Ishti*. Literally, it meant slaves, although technically they had their freedom and the term was used more in contempt than in any accurate description of their roles. The Scorpion cult had long ago suborned the leaders of several local tribes, forcing them to provide soldiers and scouts for the Shurmel. His own trained assassins were too valuable and skilled for such lowly work. The *Ishti* kept watch over the surrounding lands for any sign of attack against the Scorpion cult. In such a case, they would fight the interlopers while the cult members silently melted away into the mountains, to any one of half a dozen different hideouts like the one the Shurmel was currently in.

He decided the man had spent long enough quaking before him. Naturally, no member of the *Ishti* would open a conversation with the Shurmel.

"You have news for me," he intoned in that same flat, resonating voice. It was not a question. If the man didn't have news for him, he had no business being here.

The scout stopped twisting his *kheffiyeh* for a moment and stammered a reply. "Lord Shurmel, there is a ship . . ."

The Shurmel raised one eyebrow and turned to look out the large opening at the desert below.

"Here?" he said, the sarcasm obvious in his voice. "Remarkable."

"No, no, lord," the *Ishti* hurried to reply. "Pardon my stupidity. The ship is at the coast, by the old city of the invaders."

Ephesa, the Shurmel thought. A slight frown touched his features but he dismissed it almost instantly. It didn't do for the Shurmel to show any sign of uncertainty or doubt. But inwardly, he wondered what a ship was doing at Ephesa. There was nothing of interest there. Anything of value had long ago been looted from the ruins by the Tualaghi or other nomad tribes.

There was, of course, the oasis. Perhaps the ship had landed to replenish its water supplies. That was possible, he thought. But it was second nature to him to suspect any new arrival or unusual event in the immediate vicinity of Scorpion Mountain.

"And what is this ship doing? Where is it from?"

The scout shrugged, a fearful expression crossing his face. He had left the coast as soon as the *Heron* had been sighted. He had no information other than the fact that she was there.

"Its crew came ashore, lord. I'm not sure where they're from. The ship is similar to those used by the pale northerners. I left two of my comrades there to continue to observe and came immediately to inform you of its arrival."

"And little else, unfortunately," the Shurmel said in a sour tone. "How big is this ship?"

Occasionally, Skandian wolfships had penetrated this far east. Some had gone even farther. If this was a wolfship, he would need to take notice. The pale northerners were savage fighters—although they rarely came as far inland as the mountains.

The scout wet his lips. He wasn't sure whether the ship would be classed as big or small. "There are perhaps a dozen in the crew," he said finally.

The Shurmel turned away and paced for several seconds, thinking. Normally, a northern ship could carry forty or fifty men. Obviously, this one wasn't a raider. But he didn't like strangers in his territory—or even near it.

"It's small then," he said to himself and the *Ishti* eagerly agreed, now that the size was established.

"Yes, lord. It's a small ship."

The Shurmel regarded him, his lip curled scornfully. "I don't need you to repeat my thoughts."

The *Ishti* bowed his head. "Pardon, my lord. I merely . . ." He was going to amplify the apology but, faced by the Shurmel's withering stare, realized in time that the Shurmel did not tolerate babblers. He let his voice tail away to silence. Eventually, the Shurmel looked away. He thought for a few minutes, then called to the guard outside his door.

"Fattah!"

The door opened to admit the sentry. "Yes, lord?"

"Notify the head of the guards that there is a foreign ship at the old city. He is to take . . ." He paused, thinking. The scout had estimated the crew's numbers as a dozen or less. ". . . a company of fifty men and destroy it."

"And the crew, my lord?"

"Destroy them also." The Shurmel had no idea what this foreign ship was up to. If they were, in fact, replenishing their water supplies, they would be gone by the time his men reached the coast. If they were still there, they were probably up to no good and should be disposed of.

"As you order, lord." The sentry saluted and left the room.

The Shurmel stood silently for some time. Eventually, he turned back to the nervous scout, who was still turning his headdress round and round in his hands.

"You're still here," he said.

The man nodded several times. "Yes, lord."

Again, that eyebrow was raised in an expression of surprise and disdain. "Why?"

The *Ishti* gulped and began to back toward the door. "Your pardon, lord. I'll go now. Imrika preserve you."

The Shurmel waved one languid hand at the man, shooing him out of the room. "I'm sure she will," he said. He resumed his position at the window, staring out over the desert, looking to the north as if he might see this ship. Behind him, the door closed quietly.

Zafir al Aban stirred as the morning sun finally traveled high enough to light his face. He turned his face away from the brightness and heat, muttering fitfully. Finally, he opened his eyes and looked around.

He was lying flat on his back on the rough desert ground. His body ached in several places and his head throbbed painfully. There was a sore point at the back of his skull and he touched it gingerly, his fingers coming away wet with blood. He tried to sit up and failed, the effort merely causing him pain in his body and head.

Carefully, making sure not to move too quickly, he rolled onto his side, then his stomach, and brought his knees up under him. He rose shakily to his feet, reeling a little and staring around himself through red-rimmed eyes, trying to reconstruct the events of the night before.

A few meters away lay the body of his horse, an inert mass that showed no sign of life. Already, scavenger birds were hopping around it, and one, bolder than the rest, was perched on the horse's side. As Zafir watched, it tore a strip of flesh away from the body. Zafir lurched awkwardly toward it and waved a hand to drive it away. The effort nearly sent him tumbling back to the ground. His knee was stiff and painful and there was a torn muscle in his thigh.

He stopped, wiping a hand over his face, feeling the clammy sweat there, and tried to remember what had happened.

The strange ship had landed near the old city. That much he remembered. He had been on patrol there with two companions and they discussed what they should do. Eventually, they decided to send one of their number back to the Shurmel, to alert him of the arrival of the ship. The remaining two would keep watch over the newcomers.

Now it came back to him. Three of the foreigners had left the city in a strange vehicle—a three-wheeled structure with a sail—that moved as fast as a galloping horse. They were headed southeast, toward the Amrashin Massif. Obviously, they were looking for Scorpion Mountain. Zafir had set out after them, hoping to outdistance them and warn the Shurmel of their approach. As night fell, he had a small lead over them. He elected to continue riding through the night, and that had been his downfall—literally as well as figuratively.

He had failed to see a hole in the ground—an animal's burrow, perhaps—and his horse had put one foot in it and somersaulted, throwing him over its neck to land on the rocky ground with a crash. He remembered hearing the sharp report of the animal's cannon bone fracturing. Then he hit the ground and everything went black.

Obviously, the horse hadn't survived the fall. Zafir had only done so because he had been thrown clear. He looked up into the glaring blue sky overhead. Already, more and more kites and buzzards were circling, ready to alight on the new source of fresh meat that lay on the desert below them.

Zafir limped the short distance to the horse. Thankfully, his water canteen was on the upper side, as was his scabbarded sword. He untied them both, slung the canteen over his shoulder and stood to contemplate his next course of action.

Originally, he had planned to warn the Shurmel of the approach of the three foreigners in the strange wind-driven vehicle. But now, without a horse, he realized he would arrive several hours after them. He would merely be confirming bad news, never a good thing to do with the Shurmel.

Shrugging, he came to a decision. There was a small tribe of nomads who frequented the desert some twenty kilometers to the west. He would join them and beg for their hospitality.

Anything to avoid the vengeance of the High Priest of Imrika.

chapter thirty-nine

H al brought the land sailer up into the wind and released the tension on the sheet.

The sail flapped back and forth as the force of
the wind was released and the three-wheeled vehicle
slowly trundled to a halt. The three companions sat silently for a
few seconds, staring in fascination at the massive, triple-peaked
mountain ahead of them.

It was part of the huge range of towering mountains that
stretched across the horizon. But it was separated from the rest of
the mountains, standing a little apart from the central spine of the
range.

"That has to be the place," Gilan said eventually.

Hal nodded. "It certainly looks like a scorpion." He squinted
his eyes and studied the three peaks.

The center peak was taller than the others, which were roughly the same height. All of them rose to pointed summits, and when viewed through half-closed eyes, an observer could make out the delineation of an angry scorpion. The two side peaks formed the raised pincers and the central peak took on the shape of the sting, poised high to pierce its prey. The mountain itself was black rock, which heightened the impression. There was a sense of foreboding about the place, a sense of evil, Then he shook his head and dismissed the fanciful notion. I'm reacting to the sinister name, that's all, he thought. If this were called Buttercup Mountain, I wouldn't have the same feeling.

His head agreed. His heart and his imagination thought otherwise.

Stig obviously agreed with the latter sentiment. "I don't like the look of this place," he said. "There's a bad feeling about it. The sooner we're done and out of here, the better I'll feel."

Hal glanced sideways at him. "A bad feeling?"

Stig nodded emphatically, his lips set in a tight line. "Some places just feel evil."

"It's just a pile of rock," Hal said, trying to convince himself as much as anyone. He was surprised when Gilan tended to concur with Stig.

"It's not the place itself," he said. "It's what goes on here. A cult like the Scorpions creates an evil atmosphere around it. And of course, it's not helped by the sinister look of the place."

Hal wiped dust from his face with the tail of his *kheffiyeh*. He rewound the ends to cover his face once more, then took hold of the main sheet and steering lines.

"Well, if we sit here much longer talking about it, we'll scare ourselves out of the whole idea," he said. "Let's go and meet this Shurmel person."

Stig stepped down from his seat and pushed against the outrigger he was riding on, swinging the land sailer so that the wind caught the sail, sending it bellying out. As Hal hauled in on the sheet, Stig, at ease now with the sailer's movement, stepped lightly back aboard and they began to trundle across the rough ground, gathering speed as they went. Once more, the familiar rooster tail of brown dust rose into the air behind it as Hal steered toward the black mountain that reared its three heads into the air ahead of them.

There was a flat, open area at the base of the central peak, rather like a military parade ground. They could see huts and tents set up around its perimeter. Dozens of dark holes pierced the side of the mountain, marking the entrance to caves. As their approach was noticed, men began to stream out of the tents, and from a large cave opening in the base of the mountain.

Hal eased the sheet, reducing the sailer's speed as they grew closer. He estimated there were about thirty men gathered in the open space between the tents and the large cave. Most of them were dressed in the traditional robes and headdresses of the desert tribes. But he could make out half a dozen who were bare headed, and wearing bloodred robes.

As they rolled up to the silent, staring group, Hal released the sheet and let the land sailer come to a halt once more. They had approached the mountain from due west, as a result of the long tack they had taken on the last leg of their journey.

For some seconds, there was an impasse. The nomads among the group were staring, openmouthed, at the remarkable craft that had just come sailing out of the desert.

The red-robed group all looked suspicious and unwelcoming. Not only were they bareheaded, Hal saw now, they were all shaven headed as well. And the red robes bore a black insignia—a scorpion in the now-familiar attack stance.

One of this group stepped forward, stopping ten meters away from them.

He said something in a foreign tongue. His voice was harsh and unfriendly. He addressed Hal, who spread his hands in a gesture of non-understanding.

The Scorpion spoke again, this time in the common tongue, but with a thick accent. "Who are you? Why have you come here?"

Hal pointed to Gilan, indicating that he was the one who would do the talking. The tall Ranger stepped down stiffly from his seat and raised his hand in greeting.

"*Saloom*," he said pleasantly. The word meant "peace" in the Arridan tongue and was the traditional way of greeting a stranger.

The Scorpion, however, waved the friendly overture aside with an angry gesture. "Never mind that! Why are you here? Who are you? Strangers are not welcome here!"

Gilan raised a questioning eyebrow. "Not even a stranger who wants to discuss a *tolfah* with the Shurmel?" he said mildly.

The Scorpion hesitated. He glanced around at his fellow cult members, not sure how to proceed. The stranger might be foreign, but he knew the name of their leader. And he knew about *tolfahs*. If he ordered him driven off or killed, the Shurmel might not be pleased. Such an action might even be taken as a blasphemy against Imrika.

He saw similar levels of uncertainty on the faces of the other Scorpions. The *Ishti*, of course, had no opinion on the matter. Most of them were still gawping at the land sailer.

Plus there was something else that made him hesitate. The number three was significant, verging on sacred, to the Scorpion cult. The symbol of their god was a scorpion—the two pincers and the tail forming a triple set of points. And now these three men arrived out of the desert with no warning, in a seemingly miraculous vehicle with three wheels.

So far, the members of the cult had heard nothing about the arrival of the foreign ship at Ephesa. That information was known only to the Shurmel himself. All they knew was that three men—obviously foreigners—had materialized out of nowhere in a three-wheeled conveyance that moved without benefit of horses or camels or other draft animals.

Antagonizing such men was not something that a rank and file member of the cult was willing to take a chance on.

And of course, there was the matter of the *tolfah*. The goddess Imrika loved *tolfahs*. They were bread and butter, meat and drink to her insatiable soul. They meant blood and death. Turning away, or harming, a supplicant who was willing to pay for a *tolfah* might well anger Imrika—and that was something no wise man did.

On top of that, the system of *tolfahs* was the reason for being of the Scorpion cult members themselves. They were highly trained assassins and they carried out the killing that a *tolfah* entailed. Without *tolfahs*, they had no purpose.

Of course, once the *tolfah* was in place, they could get rid of the foreigners with impunity. Then, it would be a compact between the Shurmel and the goddess. The men who had invoked the *tolfah* would no longer be of any significance.

"Let the Shurmel be the judge of this," one of his brother Scorpions said in a low voice.

The Scorpion who had spoken to them came to his own decision. "You may enter," he said, indicating the large fissure in the rock face behind him that marked the entrance to the cave complex.

Hal and Stig quickly lowered and furled the sail, lashing it in place. Hal unstrapped a water skin and a sack containing their food from the central strut of the land sailer. The Scorpion who had spoken to them frowned as he watched. Hal indicated the water skin and the haversack.

"We'll bring our own provisions," he said. "We wouldn't want to impose upon your hospitality." It was noticeable, he thought, that the Scorpions made no move to relieve them of their weapons. Then again, they were surrounded by dozens of warriors and the Scorpions themselves. Three men would hardly be expected to compete against odds like those.

"Follow me," said the red-robed man and led the way into the large opening at the base of the cliff.

It was cool inside, compared with the savage heat of the desert sun. There was a constant cool breeze blowing, emanating from the honeycomb of tunnels and caves that had been dug out of the mountain over the centuries.

He led them to a chamber on the ground level of the mountain and ushered them inside. It was quite large, lit by burning oil lamps set in brackets along the rough stone walls. There was a table to one side. Half a dozen tattered and grubby cushions were scattered on the rock floor around it. Aside from that, the room was unfurnished. There was no window, no way in or out other than the door by which they had just entered.

"Just as well we brought a snack," Stig said cheerfully.

The Scorpion scowled at him. Good humor seemed to have no place here. "Wait here," he said. "You will be summoned when the brothers are assembled."

"Thank you," said Gilan.

The Scorpion grunted at him and left the room, closing the door behind him. They heard the rattle of a bolt being thrown on the outside.

"Well, here we are," said Hal.

Stig grinned at him. "And here we stay, apparently, until *the brothers are assembled*." He managed a passable impersonation of the Scorpion's ominous, flat tones. "Wonder what he meant by that?"

Gilan shoved a cushion against the wall of the chamber with his foot and sat down on it, leaning his back against the rock wall.

"It sounds as if we have to plead our case to the entire cult," he said. "The one good thing about all this is that I'm not having the teeth rattled out of my head by that contraption of yours, Hal."

Hal grinned. "I can see it's made a big impression on you."

"It's made a deep impression—on my backside," Gilan said, shifting his behind on the cushion to a more comfortable position.

"So what do we do now?" Stig said. He was prowling around the room, taking stock of their surroundings. Not that there was much to take stock of. The walls were hewn out of rock. In places, the drill and pick marks were still clearly visible. Aside from that, and the half dozen oil lamps, there was nothing of interest in the room.

"We wait," Gilan told him. "Might as well make yourself comfortable." He indicated the cushions and Stig copied his actions, shoving a cushion against the wall, then placing another behind him as a backrest when he sat down. He shoved his legs straight out in front of him, splayed slightly apart, and studied his boots. After a few minutes, he shifted to a more comfortable position.

"Time these people were told about chairs," he said.

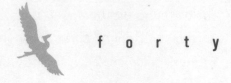
Thorn paced along the crescent-shaped thornbush barrier, frowning as he reached the western end, where the ditch and thornbush tangle reached the water's edge. He had chosen the spot for their camp carefully, picking a site where the shore dropped off steeply into the water. But still he felt there was a problem.

"Jesper!" he called sharply. The former thief, who had been relaxing on a flat rock, warmed by the morning sun, sighed deeply and rose to his feet.

"Coming, Thorn," he called, adding in a mumbled undertone, "Why is it always me?"

"Because you're the one who annoys me the most," Thorn told him briskly. Then he indicated the spot where the ditch and barricade reached the water's edge. "I want you to extend the thornbush tangle into the water," he said. "It'd be too easy for an attacker to simply go round the end and attack us from the rear."

Jesper frowned. "It'll just float away," he said. He was always ready with a reason not to do extra work.

Thorn looked at him patiently. "That's why I want you to weigh it down with rocks."

Jesper's frown was replaced by a pained look. "You mean I have to cut more thornbush, and drag it all the way down here and then carry a bunch of rocks as well?" he said plaintively. "That'll take an hour."

"Two hours," Thorn told him cheerfully. "I want you to do the same at the other end."

Jesper's shoulders slumped. "Why do I always have to do these things?"

Thorn seemed to relent. "You're right. Stefan!" he called, turning to where the mimic was watching with a smug look on his face. "You can give him a hand."

The smug look vanished. "Me? Why me?"

"Well," Thorn told him, with a deceptively pleasant expression on his face, "you're a talented mimic. You can impersonate Stig, Hal, me and Gilan and it will feel as if you have lots of people to help you. Many hands make light work, you know. Let's see if many voices do the same."

"I doubt it," Stefan said sourly.

"So do I," Thorn replied. He gestured to the water's edge. "Take it out until you're chest deep."

"Do you think that'll really stop a determined attack?" Lydia said from behind him. She was always interested to see Thorn's preparations for combat and this was a good opportunity to learn about defensive tactics.

He shook his head. "It'll do to stop the first attack."

She smiled. "Assuming somebody does attack us."

"Always assume someone will," he told her and she nodded. It made sense to expect the worst in potentially hostile territory. "I should think the first thing an attacker will do, after they've tried a frontal attack, will be to go round the end and hit us from the rear. They'll get tangled up in the thornbush, in chest-deep water. That'll make them an easy target for you. You'll be able to thin out their numbers."

She looked thoughtfully at the spot where Jesper and Stefan would be adding the extra entanglements of thornbush. In her mind's eye, she could see a group of hostile nomads, waist or chest deep in the water, already hampered by their long, flowing robes, and floundering in the almost impenetrable tangle of thorns and branches.

"They'll be sitting ducks," she said. She looked at Thorn with some admiration. He had an ability to envision what would happen in a battle. She guessed that came from long experience and she knew they were lucky to have him as their battle master. "You always think one step ahead, don't you?"

Thorn smiled at her. His expression was friendly, not the usual sly one he assumed when he was teasing her.

"I try to. It's something you should try to develop yourself. You'd be a good battle leader. Mind you," he said, a grin touching his face, "all too often, the enemy decides on a different step, and that can be embarrassing."

Lydia said nothing for a few minutes. She was a little taken aback by his statement that she'd make a good battle leader. Thorn was always surprising her, catching her off guard. Most of the time, he teased her and made jokes about her, then he'd suddenly come out with a compliment like that. She recalled Hal telling her that Thorn respected her and admired her fighting and hunting ability. The teasing was something he did to everyone he liked—it was actually a mark of affection. It was just that she always rose to it before she could stop herself.

Thorn had moved on, and was beckoning to Edvin.

"I want you and Wulf to bring the ship closer in to shore," he said. He turned back to where Lydia was still watching him, a bemused expression on her face. "The entanglements will only work once," he said. "We may need to fall back to the ship."

She looked around the camp. Jesper and Stefan were already at work farther up the beach, cutting great bunches of thornbush from a large, sprawling clump. Ingvar, unbidden, was carrying heavy rocks down to the water's edge for them to weigh down the underwater entanglement. It was typical of the big boy, she thought. He was always ready to pitch in and help. Edvin was launching the skiff, taking a mooring line out to the *Heron*, where she floated at anchor some thirty meters offshore. It seemed everyone had a task—except her.

"Can I do anything?" she asked Thorn.

He swept his gaze round the beach, taking in the distant oasis and the cluster of buildings in the deserted town.

"Keep a lookout," he said. "We've been here a couple of days. That's plenty of time for someone to organize an attack."

She nodded. Fetching her quiver of atlatl darts, she slung them over her shoulder and walked to the edge of the thornbush breast-work. Kloof, hearing her boots crunching on the coarse sand and fine pebbles of the beach, roused herself from where she was curled up snoozing in the sun and, stretching luxuriously, joined her. The spiny, tough branches were reinforced every meter or so with sharp-ened bamboo stakes driven into the ground and facing out at an angle. Lydia passed through the entry and found a rock where she had an elevated view of the surrounding area. She began scanning left to right, then back again, letting her eyes wander over the de-serted buildings of Ephesa, then the thick groves of trees in the oasis, then back again.

In most people, such a repetitive, unproductive action would have quickly led to drowsiness and inattention. But Lydia was a skilled hunter and she was used to keeping watch for elusive prey— for hours at a time if necessary. Behind her, she could hear the muted voices of the rest of the crew as they went about their tasks. Kloof sat beside her on the rock, the dog's head nearly at the same level as her own.

Idly, Lydia let her hand rest on the huge dog's thick ruff and scratched behind Kloof's ears. Kloof inclined her head in pleasure, yawned hugely, then turned to lick Lydia's hand.

"Get out of it," the girl said good-naturedly. She wiped her hand dry on the front of her jerkin. Kloof allowed her front legs to slide out from under her and sank to the ground with a contented *whuff!* of exhaled breath.

"Keep your eyes open," Lydia said quietly. The dog's ears pricked up at the sound of her voice. It was odd, Lydia thought, how she sensed the reason for their current activity. Normally,

Kloof would take any and every opportunity to snooze. But now she was alert, her head turning from side to side, her nose raised and sniffing the wind.

I guess she's taking her cue from me, Lydia thought. She was alert and on watch, and the dog could sense her level of attention and was able to match it.

"If anyone comes, you'll probably sniff them out long before I do," she said. Kloof continued to scan the surrounding countryside, her nose twitching.

Lydia craned round to see how work was progressing in the camp. Wulf was knee deep in the water, hauling on the hawser that Edvin had carried out to the ship. At the same time, Edvin, on board the little ship, was paying out a stern line attached to the buoy that marked the offshore anchor.

The *Heron* was now only a few meters offshore, in the deep water at the edge of the drop-off.

"That's close enough," Thorn called. She noticed that he'd taken pity on Jesper and Stefan and was helping Ingvar place heavy rocks to hold the underwater entanglement in place.

At the water's edge, Stefan surveyed the thick underwater tangle of branches and spikes, stretching out four or five meters into the water. It was a substantial obstruction, he thought. Then another thought occurred to him. He looked up to where Thorn was placing another rock.

"What happens when the tide goes out?" he called. If it went out far enough, there would be another section of exposed beach at the end of their carefully built obstacle. The old sea wolf looked up at him.

"D'you know why they call this the Constant Sea?" he asked.

When Stefan returned a blank look, Thorn jerked a thumb at Wulf. "You tell him, Wulf," he said.

Wulf looked equally blank, shrugging his shoulders.

Thorn rolled his eyes to heaven. "Did they teach you nothing in brotherband training?" he said in disgust.

Stefan thought it best to treat that as a rhetorical question. There was no answer he could give that didn't open him to further sarcasm.

When Thorn saw that that particular ploy wasn't going to work, he looked a little disappointed. He drew a long breath, then said, in very precise tones, "It's called the Constant Sea because it's unchanging. There are no tides here."

Stefan raised his eyebrows in surprise. "Really?"

"Really," Thorn replied.

Stefan tilted his head to one side as he considered that interesting fact. "Why's that?" he asked.

Thorn hesitated. It was all very well to make scathing comments about the boys' lack of knowledge. But now Stefan had asked a question to which Thorn had no answer.

"Do you expect me to tell you everything?" he asked now, and a knowing look came over Stefan's face.

"You don't know, do you?"

Thorn snorted. "Of course I do. But it's not my job to further your education, scant as it may be." He gestured toward the far end of the barricade. "Get that end started," he said shortly. When he heard Stefan's knowing snigger, he made a mental note to be dissatisfied with his work on the eastern end, and have him do twice as much there.

Wearily, calling to Jesper to join him, Stefan trudged out of the sea, water dripping from his clothes, and made his way to the prepared pile of thornbush at the far end of the campsite. Ingvar was already lugging rocks down to the water's edge and piling them there.

It took another hour for the work to be completed to Thorn's satisfaction. Contrary to his plan, he didn't insist on an extra effort from Stefan. The boys had worked well, if not willingly. In fact, after a decent interval, he joined in the work of piling the thornbush under the water's surface and weighing it down with rocks.

Lydia smiled as she saw him join in on the labor. "You're not as grumpy as you pretend, are you?" she said to herself. Beside her, Kloof rumbled a deep growl in reply. At least, that was what she thought the dog was doing and she tugged idly at the thick hair of her ruff. Then another growl resonated through Kloof's massive chest and Lydia took more notice. The dog was leaning forward, her attention riveted on the oasis. Following her line of sight, Lydia could see movement as a troop of mounted warriors picked their way through the trees.

"Thorn!" she called. "I think the guests you've been expecting have arrived."

chapter   forty-one

Hal had no idea how long they were kept waiting. Without any daylight visible to them, he couldn't judge the passage of time. For a while, he tried to relax like his two companions, but his impatience got the better of him and he began to pace up and down the chamber. The long wait didn't seem to bother Stig, who had the experienced sailors' ability to sleep anytime, anyplace the opportunity presented itself.

As far as Stig was concerned, the Shurmel would send for them eventually and there was no point in fretting about the fact. Better to snatch forty winks while he could.

Or eighty, if that's what it took.

Gilan seemed equally philosophical about the long wait. He sat with his back against the wall and his head tilted forward. His eyes were closed but Hal doubted that he was sleeping. That was borne out when there was a rattle at the door lock and the Ranger's eyes were wide-open immediately as his head snapped up.

The cult member who had conducted them to the chamber entered and looked around the dimly lit space, studying the three of them disdainfully. Stig, woken by the rattle of the lock and the squeaking of the door hinges, responded by yawning hugely at the scarlet-robed man.

Gilan rose gracefully from his sitting position against the wall. He did so without any need to set his hands on the floor. He simply unfolded his legs underneath him and came to his feet. Stig also stood, with a little less grace. He ran his hand through his hair and sniffed loudly. Hal, of course, was already on his feet.

"So," Stig said cheerfully, "I take it the Head Sherang is ready to see us?"

The cultist looked at him, not understanding. Stig decided to elaborate.

"The Big Bazoo," he said. "The Super Scorpion. The Sherbet."

The cultist glared at him. "The brothers are assembled," he said. "The Shurmel will hear your petition now."

"That's what I meant," Stig said, grinning.

The Scorpion member ignored him. He addressed himself to Gilan.

"All requests for a *tolfah* are heard in front of the full membership," he said.

Gilan shrugged. "That sounds reasonable," he replied and gestured for the cult member to lead the way.

They followed him out the door and along the low-ceilinged stone passageway by which they had come. When they reached the point where they had entered the cave complex, Hal managed to glance outside. From the length of the shadows cast by the sun, he deduced that it was early to mid-afternoon. They had been kept waiting for at least three hours. He wondered whether that was really how long it took to assemble the members of the cult or whether it was simply a matter of letting outsiders cool their heels at the Shurmel's pleasure. Probably the latter, he thought.

Their path veered away from the large opening in the mountainside, back along another passage cut through the rock. Lanterns set every ten meters or so cast a flickering, uncertain light on the corridor. The ground was rough and uneven and Hal stumbled several times. So, apparently, did Stig.

"Bit more light would be useful," he grumbled. Nobody said anything in reply.

Abruptly, their guide made a sharp turn to the right and they found themselves on a winding, ascending ramp leading up into the heart of the mountain. They passed passageways at two levels before they reached a third and followed their guide out onto yet another of the tunnels cut through the rock.

But now they could hear a noise above the soft patter of their feet on the floor. There was the subdued mutter of a large number of voices. The sound echoed off the rock walls of the narrow, winding corridor, becoming louder the farther they went.

Eventually, they rounded a corner and were confronted by a large, high-ceilinged cave, lit by dozens of torches set in brackets round the walls. The mutter of voices rose suddenly as they entered, then died away, and dozens of pairs of eyes turned toward them. Seated on individual rugs set on the floor were the members of the Scorpion cult. There appeared to be around fifty of them, all of them wearing the same scarlet robes as their guide, all of them clean shaven, all with dark circles of kohl around their eyes, giving them an ominous, deathlike appearance.

"I see they put on their makeup just for the occasion," Stig muttered.

Hal glanced at him. It wasn't really a time for levity, he thought. Their lives were balanced on a knife edge here. "Shut up, Stig," he said quietly.

Stig shrugged agreeably. "Whatever you say. Just trying to lighten the mood."

"I'll admit it could use some lightening," Gilan remarked. "But it might be better to do as Hal says until we learn a little more about what's in store for us."

Stig nodded. His hand touched the head of his ax, hanging in its belt loop. The Scorpions had still made no move to disarm them. Perhaps that was the convention for people who came to make a request of the goddess Imrika. Taking their weapons might be seen as a provocation. After all, people seeking a *tolfah* were hardly disposed to attack the cult. They were here to ask a favor.

The low-level murmur of voices had cut off as they entered the room. Now, as their guide led them to a position at the front of the chamber, the voices began again.

A giant oaken chair stood at the head of the room, on a raised wooden dais. Black drapes hung behind it, sectioning off the part of the chamber that lay behind it. The chair itself was plain, but was surmounted by the ubiquitous scorpion figure, a massive ebony carving nearly a meter high, with red-jeweled eyes. In the flickering torchlight, it appeared to be moving, a malevolent, threatening figure rearing above the back of the chair.

"Stand here," their guide told them, indicating a point in front of the platform. They complied. Stig and Hal glanced around the room, wondering what was to happen next. Gilan seemed unperturbed.

"*Kormella!*" the guide intoned in a loud voice and there was a rustle of movement behind them. Glancing back, Hal saw that the members of the cult had risen from their seated positions on the mats to kneel, facing the scorpion chair.

"*Imella,*" the guide said and, as one, the fifty members of the cult lowered their foreheads to touch the mats in front of them. The guide looked impatiently at the three foreigners, still standing.

"Kneel," he hissed and, as they all lowered themselves to their knees, he added, "Bow."

The two Skandians hesitated. It wasn't in their nature to prostrate themselves before anyone. But Gilan muttered out of the corner of his mouth:

"Do it."

Taking a lead from him, they inclined their heads, and bowed forward slightly from the waist. But by unspoken agreement, none of them assumed the full, forehead-to-the-floor pose of the fifty cult members behind them. The guide scowled at them, but realized this was as far as they were going to go, unless forced.

And he knew that it wasn't a good idea to use force on supplicants to the goddess. One never knew how she would view such actions, particularly if a large payment was involved.

The three friends remained with their heads bowed for some time. Behind them, they could hear the congregation of Scorpions beginning a low, ululating chant. As far as they could tell, it seemed to be wordless, merely a constant repetition of the sound *aaaaaaahhhhh.*

Hal also became aware of a sickly sweet fragrance wafting on the air in the cavern. He turned his head slightly, eliciting a warning hiss from the guide. Several of the cult members he could see had their hands to their mouths and their jaws were moving as they chewed something.

Gilan had apparently noticed the same thing. "It's some kind of drug," he said quietly. "Possibly a hallucinogenic or a relaxant to prepare them to confront their leader."

"Is he that ugly?" Stig asked. A ghost of a smile touched Gilan's face. He enjoyed Stig's irreverent approach to solemn occasions.

"Probably," he replied. Another warning hiss made them fall silent. More time passed, the chanting became more and more intense, and the volume rose. Finally, the guide stepped forward and swept out his arm, indicating the curtain to the left-hand side of the throne.

"*Imshavaaah!*" he cried, and the gathering echoed the cry, so that it rang around the walls of the vast cave.

Abruptly, the curtain was swept aside and a huge figure sprang through the gap, which instantly closed behind him. Now the cult members resumed their former single-syllable chant, but this time it rose to almost deafening proportions, echoing and reechoing off the stone walls of the vast cave.

The Shurmel was an impressive figure. Well over two meters tall, he was clad in a black cloak, with a silver rendering of the scorpion figure on his left breast. He was totally bald and his shaven skull had been polished and oiled so that it shone, reflecting the flickering torchlight.

In his right hand, he held his staff of office. It was a solid rod of ebony, two meters long. At the base, it was shod with a silver ferrule. On the top, it carried a carving of an angry scorpion—carved in shining black stone with red jewels inset for its eyes.

"I can see why they need to be drugged," Stig murmured. "That is a seriously ugly person."

Fortunately, his voice didn't carry to the leader of the Scorpion cult. But Gilan found his lips twitching as he attempted to control his expression, maintaining an air of suitable solemnity.

The Shurmel stepped forward to the front of the raised dais. He glared down at the trio of foreigners before him. In the dark circles of his eye sockets, the eyes glittered with malice. He addressed himself to Gilan, who was standing in the center.

"Are you the leader?" he asked. He didn't seem to be raising his voice, but it carried through the cavern to the farthest corner. It was a rich, deep voice. A sinister voice.

Gilan rose to his feet and took a half pace forward. "I am," he declared.

"And you have come here to the shrine of Imrika the Destroyer to discuss a *tolfah*?"

Gilan nodded.

"Then look around you at the followers of Imrika. The Assassins of the Scorpion Cult. These are the ones who will pursue your *tolfah*, until the subject you have named is dead. Look!" he repeated, sweeping his arm out to encompass the kneeling throng behind them. At his urging, Gilan and the others turned and studied the red-robed assassins, now swaying rhythmically in time to their underlying chant, as the Shurmel continued to talk.

"These are my elite. Each one of them is a skilled killer, trained until he is expert in the use of the stiletto, the crossbow, the javelin and the garrote. Each of them has a comprehensive knowledge of deadly poisons: venom from the sand viper that can be used to coat the tip of an arrow or quarrel. Poisons that can be secreted in a victim's food and will bring certain death, either long and agonizing or immediate.

"These are all implacable killers. Each one trains here for ten years to develop the skill that Imrika demands of her disciples. Only then can a Scorpion recruit expect to be assigned to a target, to carry out a *tolfah* for the goddess. Once a *tolfah* is agreed, the Scorpion killer will hunt and pursue his victim until death—either his own or that of the target. Nothing but death can stop them. And when one dies, another will assume his sacred duty until the *tolfah* is complete." He paused dramatically, arms thrown wide-open.

Interesting, Hal thought. He made no mention of any combat skills—no training with the sword or the ax or the spear. These men killed by stealth, not confrontation.

He caught Gilan's eye and made a slight shrugging gesture. The Ranger seemed to think some response to the Shurmel's declaration was expected.

"Fascinating," he said evenly.

The Shurmel glared at him, then continued. "So, tell us. Who is the target of your *tolfah*? Whom do you wish to have killed?"

The three interlopers, facing to the front once more, sensed a stirring in the kneeling crowd behind them. Hal glanced back quickly. The Scorpions were all leaning forward expectantly, their eyes glowing with anticipation. But Gilan was speaking, his voice conciliatory and apologetic.

"I'm afraid there's been a misunderstanding," he said. "I don't want to initiate a *tolfah*. I want to cancel one."

The commander of the *Ishti*, mindful of the Shurmel's orders not to let the strangers escape, had selected fifteen of his best mounted troopers and sent them ahead as an advance party.

"Observe only," he ordered their leader. "But if the foreigners try to leave, then do whatever you have to do to stop them."

The fifteen troopers had plunged ahead at a gallop, with the rest of the troop following behind at a trot. Perhaps it was the exhilaration of the speed, or the excitement of the hunt, but when they reached the oasis, their leader forgot, or ignored, his orders.

He carried out a quick reconnaissance, signaling his men to wait back in the concealment of the trees and moving forward on his own.

He could see the foreign ship anchored close to the shore. A makeshift barricade had been constructed on the edge of the water, looking like brushwood piled up in a semicircle. The troop leader laughed scornfully. A few flimsy branches wouldn't stop them, he thought. He was eager to earn the Shurmel's approval and he knew the Scorpion leader wanted these interlopers killed. No point in waiting for the rest of the party to arrive, he thought. He counted the people behind the barricade and could see there was only a half dozen of them. He had more than twice their numbers, and their makeshift stockade wouldn't keep him out.

In his haste, he failed to notice the sharpened bamboo stakes set every couple of meters, pointing outward around head height. That was understandable. They were set at a low angle and they tended to fade into the dark mass of the thornbush behind them. He also failed to appreciate that the brushwood tangle was set in a ditch more than a meter deep.

Truth be told, he wasn't the brightest of leaders. He saw what appeared to be an easy objective. He rose from behind the cover of the tree that had shielded him from view and scrambled into the saddle. Drawing his curved sword, he turned back to his men in the trees behind him and yelled an order for the charge.

He clapped his spurs into his horse's side and thundered out of the trees, his blood singing. Behind him, he could hear his men echoing his call, and hear the thud of their horses' hooves on the coarse sand beneath them.

He saw people behind the barricade running to get their weapons and take up defensive positions and he laughed out loud. There were too few of them, he thought. His horse would leap their puny barrier and he would be among them, striking to left and right, cutting them down.

Then his horse saw the wicked hedge of sharpened stakes directly ahead and swung wildly to the right, plunging and rearing to break his rider's controlling grip on the reins. The commander swayed in the saddle, nearly falling, and cursed the animal as it refused to confront those stakes.

He realized he could never force his mount into that hedge of sharpened points. He turned in his saddle as the horse pranced, terrified, in a circle.

"Dismount!" he yelled to the men behind him. "Dismount and attack on foot!"

He had begun to swing down from the saddle when Lydia's first dart arrived. It went into his upper arm, slightly above the small circular shield that he wore there, and penetrated through to his body. He screamed in pain and staggered, one foot still in the stirrup, one on the ground. His horse, thoroughly terrified by now, bolted, and he lost his balance, bumping and bouncing over the rocky ground as he was dragged behind it, one foot still firmly trapped in the stirrup.

His men took no notice, and made no attempt to save him. Truth be told, he was an unpopular leader—vain and stupid—and they were glad to see him go. But they were committed to the attack now and they dismounted in a more orderly fashion and swarmed toward the barricade.

Thorn, behind the thornbush entanglement, watched as the leader of the attack was struck down and disappeared along the beach, dragging behind his panicked animal.

"Good shot, Lydia!" he said softly to himself. The girl was truly a priceless addition to their crew, he thought. Her skill with the atlatl gave them a long-range striking power that always came as a shock to attackers. Unlike a bow, the weapon was difficult to see and recognize. The first most enemies knew of it was when a dart came hissing down out of the sky and transfixed them.

But now the *Ishti* were scrambling close to the barricade and Lydia dared not throw again for fear of hitting one of her comrades. She stood on the mound that had been built for her. A two-meter-high shield of wooden planks gave her cover from any return shots—although none of their attackers seemed to be armed with bows. They carried lances and swords for the most part.

The attackers were bunched up at the center of the defensive line. Still, she kept her eyes scanning to either side, waiting to see if any of them would try to break round the end of the barrier where it reached the lapping waves. So far, none had made the attempt. Secure in their superior numbers, and in the apparent frailty of the barricade, they were mounting a frontal attack, looking to overwhelm the small group of defenders behind it.

The first of them realized his mistake too late. As he tried to force his way through the tangle of brushwood, he felt the ground give way below him and he fell into the meter-deep ditch concealed by the thornbush. Trying to regain his feet, he found his progress halted by the clinging, penetrating thorns that held him prisoner.

Then, one of the defenders, a gray-haired, disheveled warrior who appeared to have only one hand, leaned forward and brought a huge, iron-studded war club down on his skull with crushing effect. The attacker's hoarse war cry was cut short and he fell facedown, suspended on the clinging thornbush.

The man next to him had no better luck. Warned by his companion's fate, he managed to stop himself from falling into the ditch, but the outer layers of thornbush tangled in his leggings, holding him prisoner on the edge of the barrier. He struggled to free his feet, becoming more and more entangled as he did so, and he never saw the long bamboo pole wielded by Wulf as it slammed forward into his chest. He was hurled back, his feet still trapped in the thornbush. He lay groaning on his back.

The rest of the group pulled back a meter or so, now more aware of the threat offered by the thornbush. They stood, facing the defenders, yelling threats and defiance. The defenders behind the barricade remained silent and watchful. There was nothing to be gained by wasting breath in threats and curses. They had the measure of their attackers. They were confident in their defenses and in their ability to hold the line. They needed no false boost to their confidence.

Their silence, their calm confidence, was unnerving. One of the *Ishti* studied the thornbush barrier more carefully. Then he leapt forward, slashing with his sword to clear a path through the branches and shouting for his companions to do the same.

His shouts were cut off as Ingvar's voulge darted forward like a striking snake. The attacker managed to bring his small shield up in time to block the weapon, but it was a vain attempt. The spearhead of the voulge, with all of Ingvar's weight and massive strength behind it, slammed through the thin outer layer of brass on the shield, shattering the wooden frame behind it. The *Ishti* warrior felt as if a galloping horse had slammed into his shield. He was hurled back several paces.

"Darn it!" snarled Ingvar, as the man sprawled on the beach. "I didn't have time to hook him."

"Next time don't hit him so hard," Thorn told him. Truth be told, he was a little overwhelmed by the change in Ingvar. He had always been a pillar of strength for the Herons. But now he was a roaring, rampaging one-man battle squad. His lunge had carried so much power behind it that the attacker was already flying back through the air when Ingvar tried for the follow-up hooking motion.

"I've created a monster," Thorn muttered. Then he grinned. "But thank the gods he's *our* monster."

Ingvar brandished the voulge at the attackers as they hesitated, just out of range. None of them were eager to face it. They had seen their companion come flying back through the air like a bale of hay from a pitchfork.

Once more, they withdrew a few paces, making sure they were well out of the reach of that vicious ax-headed spear wielded by the huge warrior behind the barricade. None of them was willing to take command. None of them seemed to have any idea how to break through to the interior. They milled together uncertainly, each of them waiting for someone else to take the lead, someone else to have an idea, watched all the time by the grim-faced Herons.

Then Lydia's voice rose clearly above the small battlefield.

"They're trying for the end!" she shouted.

From her elevated position, she had seen two of the *Ishti* break furtively away from their companions. Staying low so that the thornbush barricade might conceal their movements, they were sprinting for the western end of the barricade, where it reached the sea.

Thorn was about to order Wulf to come with him and block their path when he had a better idea. Let them all have another unpleasant surprise, he thought. That might be enough to break the back of this disastrous attack.

"Let them get caught up," he replied to Lydia, although he made sure he didn't call attention to her by turning toward her. "Then take care of them."

She nodded, licking her lips, which were dry with tension. It was unnerving to watch her companions do all the work in a fight like this, she thought. She was itching to play a part in the struggle at the barricade, but the enemy were too close for her to cast safely. Now she watched through slitted eyes as the two crouching figures reached what they thought was the end of the barricade and splashed into the water. They hesitated as they realized they were waist deep within a few meters, then hesitated again as the spiky, clinging masses of thornbush beneath the surface caught and held them, leaving them struggling against the water and the thorns, which penetrated their clothes in a score of places, tearing, ripping, then holding them fast, leaving them unable to progress any farther.

One of them turned to the other, gesturing down into the water beneath them.

"Use your sword!" he shouted desperately. "Cut a way through this cursed—"

He got no further as Lydia's first dart plunged down on a shallow angle. It cut cleanly through the mail shirt he wore under his outer robe and he fell backward under the force of the missile. The water around him was already beginning to stain red. His companion, horrified and panicking, struggled frantically to extricate himself.

In his struggles, he hurled himself to one side, his long robe tearing under the strain. His eyes widened in fright as a second dart hissed down into the water, in the spot where he had been a fraction of a second before. Panic now lent him strength and he dragged his clothes free of the underwater obstruction, reaching down to grasp strands of the thornbush and rip them free, cutting his hands in a dozen places, heedless of the pain.

He lurched backward into shallower water. A third dart just missed him.

Then he was back on dry land and running as fast as he could, desperate to leave the dreadful entanglement and the wicked darts behind him.

His hoarse cries of panic carried up the beach to his companions. They had been unaware of the abortive attempt to outflank the defenders until they heard and saw him retreating at top speed, then caught sight of his companion, half submerged, lying on his back a few meters off the beach, in water that was an ominous shade of red.

It was the last straw. The remaining members of the troop broke and ran, leaving their companions and their riderless horses behind them as they sought the concealment of the oasis.

For the first time, the defenders let their feelings show. A derisive cheer, led by Ingvar's massive voice, rang out above the small enclosure.

"That should see them off!" Stefan shouted exultantly.

Thorn shook his head. "From the way they fought—or rather, the way they *didn't* fight," he said, "they were the second team. There'll be more of them on the way—and they won't make the same mistakes next time."

Stefan was crestfallen. "They'll be back?"

Thorn nodded. "You can bet on it. We caught them unawares

this time. But these desert warriors aren't the kind to slink away in defeat. They'll be back."

"So what do we do now?" Lydia asked. She had left her observation point to rejoin them.

"Next time, they'll be ready for the thornbush barrier under the water," Thorn told them. "It's time we fell back to the ship."

Jesper looked woebegone. "To the ship? You mean we're going to abandon these defenses?"

"I plan to," Thorn said. "You can stay here if you want to."

"But I spent all morning digging and cutting and dragging thornbush into place! It hardly seems fair!" Jesper said indignantly.

"Perhaps you could stay here and explain that to them," Thorn remarked. "I'm sure they'll understand."

chapter forty-three

The Shurmel's brows drew together and his eyes glittered with anger. He took a pace forward, toward Gilan, but the slimly built Ranger held his ground. They were less than a meter apart and the massively built Scorpion leader had to stoop to face the foreigner eye to eye. Quietly, Hal and Stig rose to their feet behind the Ranger.

"Sacrilege!" the Shurmel roared. Gilan didn't flinch, although flecks of spittle flew from the Shurmel's mouth and landed on him. "There can be no cancellation of a *tolfah*! Once it is in place, it continues to the end!"

"Oh, come now. You're paid to put a *tolfah* in place. Surely I can pay you to remove one? I'm happy to pay extra. Perhaps twice the price of the original *tolfah*? That sounds reasonable to me." Gilan's voice was calm, in distinct contrast to the Shurmel's rage. The huge man drew himself up to full height and stepped back, throwing his arms wide.

"You cannot buy the consent of Imrika!" he shouted. The assembled Scorpions muttered in agreement. "Imrika's permission is not for sale!"

"Well, it certainly was when Iqbal paid her for the contract in the first place," Gilan said, and the Shurmel's eyes narrowed at the mention of the name.

"Iqbal?" he said. "Then we are talking about the *tolfah* against the western princess—the princess Cassandra?"

Gilan nodded and comprehension dawned on the Shurmel's face as pieces in a puzzle fell together. He'd been told these travelers had arrived from the west, not the north. As a result, he'd assumed they were from Arrida. Up until now, he hadn't connected them to the reports of the ship on the coast to the north.

"Then you are from the foreign ship that is anchored off the Old City?" he said. It was more of a statement than a question, but again Gilan nodded.

"That's right."

A malevolent smile twisted the grotesquely adorned face. "In that case, I regret to tell you that your comrades are no longer alive. I dispatched fifty of my best warriors yesterday to take the ship and burn it."

Hal felt the inevitable jolt of fear that strikes any captain who is away from his ship when danger looms. He forced himself to quell the rising panic in his chest, hiding it from the Shurmel.

"Only fifty?" he said, with forced nonchalance. "That might not be enough to get the job done." And as he said the words, he realized that they could well be true. Thorn was in command at the coast. And he was ably backed by Lydia and Ingvar, in his new capacity as a master warrior. Thorn was no fool and he would not easily be taken by surprise. At the first sign of trouble, Hal trusted him to simply up anchor and sail away.

The Shurmel glared at Hal, whose nonchalance and assumed confidence inflamed the big man's anger.

"Whether your companions live or die, the matter of the *tolfah* is already settled and we need discuss it no further. I assigned the mission to one of my best assassins some weeks ago. By now your princess is surely dead."

Gilan inclined his head and pursed his lips in disagreement. "Well, actually, no," he said. "That follower of yours wasn't very good at his job. He tried to kill her with one of those nasty little crossbows you people are so fond of." He paused, letting doubt flow into the Shurmel's eyes, then continued. "But he missed."

"Then he will try again!" the Shurmel spat out at him. "And he will keep trying until he succeeds."

"No-o-o . . ." Gilan dragged the word out deliberately. He was seeking to anger the Shurmel and goad him into a duel, where the massively built man would believe he could reassert his dominance over them by defeating him. "Actually, he's in a dungeon at Castle Araluen."

There were no dungeons at Araluen, of course, but the Shurmel could hardly be expected to know that. "Last I saw him," Gilan continued, "he was crying for his mummy."

The Shurmel's lip began to curl in disbelief.

"My dog chased him and frightened him," Hal added. "She's a very big dog."

And now doubt began to cloud the Shurmel's face and eyes. To followers of Imrika, dogs were unclean animals, beasts to be avoided at all costs. An encounter with such an animal would be a terrifying prospect for one of the Scorpion clan. Perhaps what they were saying was the truth.

"Matter of fact," Gilan added, "your man was the one who told us all about you, and this place." He waved an arm around the massive cavern. He didn't think it was necessary to add that they had been given more detail by Iqbal.

"Then he should have told you that what you propose is a sacrilege. It is an offense to Imrika and it is punishable by death. Your death!" The Shurmel's eyes bored into Gilan's. The Ranger seemed totally unaffected by the threat.

"Oh, come off your high horse," he said in a bored tone. "Your goddess accepts money to have you kill people. Why not accept more money to have you not kill someone? She wins either way. It seems perfectly logical to me, and there's a lot less effort involved in not killing someone."

"That's because you are a foreigner and an unbeliever. Imrika does not *accept money,* as you crudely put it. The money is a votive offering. It is incidental to the *tolfah.*"

"So you say. But I imagine a *tolfah* wouldn't last long unless there was some money involved." Gilan made a crudely venal gesture, rubbing the fingers and thumb of his right hand together in a universal sign of bribery.

The Shurmel snorted in disgust. "You have no concept of what constitutes a *tolfah.* It is a sacred contract between me and the goddess. The money we accept is not for the *tolfah* itself. It is to cover the expenses of our organization. Once a *tolfah* is agreed, the only thing that can negate it is death. The death of the subject of the *tolfah.*"

"I've heard there are two other possibilities," Gilan said quietly. "The death of the goddess, or *your* death."

A hush fell over the room. The low mutter of voices from the assembled cult members, which had counterpointed the discussion to date, suddenly fell silent. Even the Shurmel was momentarily taken aback.

"You would presume to challenge the goddess herself?" he said.

Gilan shrugged and affected to look around the room. "That might be a little difficult," he said. "She doesn't seem to be anywhere in sight, does she?"

The Shurmel took a pace forward, standing close to Gilan, towering over him, seeking to intimidate him with his huge size and threatening presence.

"Then you are challenging me?" he intoned. His voice had dropped to an ominous, low tone. For a moment, he reflected that leaving these men with their weapons had been a mistake. In the future, he would have to rectify that. But the thought of this man—this puny man—challenging him to combat was almost laughable. He was slim and athletic, but he would be no match for the Shurmel's massive strength. Even the well built third member of the group, the one who had said nothing so far, would be no match for the Shurmel. And he was much bigger and far stronger-looking than this strange, cloaked figure before him.

Again, Gilan showed a sign of reluctance.

"Well, only if I absolutely have to," he said. "I would much rather negotiate."

The Shurmel's scornful laugh boomed around the rock walls of the cavern.

"I am sure you would!" he declared. He looked around at his followers. "I am *sure* you would!"

There was an echoing ripple of laughter from the red-robed figures filling the room. The Shurmel considered for a moment. The foreigner posed no threat to him. The Shurmel had been the victor in a score of single combats. His size and strength and power had always been enough to overwhelm any who dared to face him. And it had been a while now since his followers had witnessed his invincibility in battle and it might well be time to let them see him in action once more. He had become aware lately of whisperings among his followers. One in particular, a scar-faced assassin called Taluf, had been a member of the cult for over fifteen years. He was beginning to gather support among its members and the Shurmel suspected that he was steeling himself to challenge for the position of leadership. Taluf was a skilled killer, as they all were. Of course, he was no warrior—Hal's earlier observation about the Scorpions' apparent lack of combat training was an accurate one—but if he gathered enough support, he might be emboldened to try a more devious method.

It might well be time for the Shurmel to demonstrate to his followers that he was not a man to be taken lightly. He was as skilled as any of them in the subtle arts of poison, of the stealthy attack with a stiletto, or with a small, single-handed crossbow and a venom-tipped bolt. But he had an extra dimension that they were lacking. He *was* a warrior.

Or at least, he considered himself to be one. And a demonstration of his combat skills might well set the others to thinking, and erode the growing support for Taluf.

All this passed through the Shurmel's mind in a matter of seconds. He smiled at the slim foreigner before him. Perhaps he was a blessing in disguise, he thought. He had provided an opportunity to dispel any thought of rebellion in the minds of Taluf and his wavering followers.

"No negotiation!" he said now, his voice deep and threatening. "Challenge me if you dare, and die for your impudence!"

He stepped back to the huge wooden throne behind him and leaned his scorpion staff against it. A massive two-handed long sword was secured in a scabbard behind the chair. He slid the long, heavy blade free of its scabbard with a *shringing* sound of steel on leather. As he did so, the violent movement disturbed the scorpion staff and it fell unnoticed to the floor.

Gilan unslung his quiver and passed it, with his bow, to Hal.

"Mind this for me, please, Hal," he said. He tossed his cloak back off his shoulders so that his arms were unencumbered, then his hand dropped to the hilt of the sword scabbarded on his left hip. It was smaller and shorter than the huge weapon the Shurmel was brandishing. But it had been forged and shaped by the armorers of the Ranger Corps, the men who fashioned the incredibly hard, incredibly sharp saxe knives that all Rangers carried.

Not that this was apparent in the way it looked. It was a simple, unadorned sword, with its hilt wrapped in practical leather, stained a little by perspiration from its owner's hand. The crosspiece was a slightly curved piece of brass and a heavy knob of the same metal made up the pommel. The blade of the Shurmel's sword was nearly half as long again as that of Gilan's. But whereas the long sword's blade was simple steel, the blade of the Ranger's sword provided the only clue to its superior manufacture. It was slightly blued, and the surface of the steel was patterned in faint, wavy lines for its entire length.

It was a blade that matched the hardness and purity of the *katanas* wielded by the warriors of Nihon-Ja, or those fashioned by the fabled sword smiths of the Dimascarene warriors.

But the Shurmel had no knowledge of either of those groups. He saw before him a small, simple, weak-looking blade in the hands of, by comparison to his own mighty size and muscles, a small, slim and weak-looking man. And he laughed aloud.

It was a cruel laugh. A laugh that embodied all his sadistic, brutal nature. It was a laugh that showed no sign of doubt as to the outcome of the approaching combat. The Shurmel knew he would win. He would vanquish this impudent foreigner, and expunge his sacrilegious ideas. And he would reinforce his position as leader of the Scorpion cult for years to come. Buoyed by the approbation he would win from the rank and file members, he might even take the opportunity to remove the rebellious Taluf and his immediate followers.

The more he thought about it, the more the Shurmel realized that this ridiculous foreigner offered him a wonderful opportunity. Truly, he thought, he was a gift from the goddess Imrika. He raised his eyes to heaven and uttered a silent word of thanks for this gift.

And in doing so, he forgot to consider that Imrika was the goddess of destruction and her greatest gift was, all too often, death.

He stepped down from the dais to face the puny figure before him.

"To the death!" he shouted.

Gilan shrugged, an infuriating gesture under the circumstances. "If you insist," he said.

Without further warning, the Shurmel leapt forward at Gilan, his sword swinging high over his head in a two-handed grip, then sweeping down in a stroke that would have split the smaller man from head to waist.

Had the smaller man still been in the same position.

Gilan had been expecting the Shurmel to try a surprise attack. His eyes narrowed as he saw the massive sword sweep up. It was an obvious, and clumsy, move and for a fraction of a second he wondered if it was a feint, a deliberately awkward action designed to give him false confidence. But his expert perusal of the man's stance and body language immediately negated the thought. It was a genuine attack, and not a very skillful one.

As the massive blade whistled down, Gilan simply swayed to one side, taking a half pace to remove himself from its path. His movement was barely noticeable, but none the less effective for all that. The sword cleaved the air half a meter from him, striking into the rock floor of the cavern with an echoing clang and sending sparks flying.

To the Shurmel, intent on delivering the last ounce of his strength and weight into the blow, it seemed that Gilan didn't move at all. But somehow, the huge, body-cleaving blow missed. He roared in frustration and swung the long sword back horizontally, then sent it whistling through at waist height.

At what seemed the last moment, Gilan's sword, propelled by his wrist, swung up and over in a half circle, slashing down onto the long sword, deflecting the immense power of the Shurmel's strike so that the blade dropped from its intended path and shrieked against the stone floor once again, the teeth-jarring sound accompanied by more sparks.

To the two Skandians, standing watching the combat, it seemed that Gilan had avoided or deflected the Shurmel's two overpowering strokes with an absolute minimum of movement or effort.

"He is seriously good at this," Stig said softly. Hal nodded, not saying a word, watching intently as the combat resumed.

Trying to take advantage of the superior reach of his weapon, the Shurmel launched a clumsy lunge at the Ranger, his right foot rising, then stamping down to impart more force to the blow.

A triumphant cry rose from the throats of the watching Scorpion cult members.

Only to die away in confusion as Gilan's sword, again propelled mainly by the iron muscles in his wrist, described a glittering half circle in the air, engaging the Shurmel's blade with his own and deflecting it clear of his body.

Meeting no solid resistance, the Shurmel staggered forward, off balance, and felt the razor-sharp point of Gilan's sword as it flicked up to touch his throat. A small runnel of blood came from the spot where it touched.

"We can stop this any time you like," Gilan said calmly. He had the measure of his opponent now. The Shurmel was strong, blindingly strong. And he was fast. But he was clumsy and relatively unskilled in swordsmanship, relying on his power and size to overwhelm an opponent.

Gilan's calmness, and the ease with which he had avoided injury so far, became a red rag to a bull. The Shurmel screamed in rage and frustration. With his left hand, he batted Gilan's sword to one side, then swung the long sword in a diagonal arc at the Ranger.

This time, Gilan chose not to avoid or deflect the blow. He blocked it with his own sword, the two blades ringing together like a hammer blow on an anvil, the sound of their contact striking echoes from the stone walls. Only Stig, watching closely with an expert warrior's eye, noticed how the Ranger's blade, in the last millisecond before contact, didn't simply remain static. Gilan's wrist launched it in its own countermovement toward the Shurmel's sword—traveling barely five centimeters, but building its own momentum to help counteract the power behind the Shurmel's blow. Then, at the last moment, the Ranger's grip tightened and created an unbreakable barrier.

A drawn-out cry of *aaaaah!* came from the watching assassins as the Shurmel struck. It died away in a cry of anguish as his blow was stopped by an iron-hard defense.

Stig whistled softly in admiration. It was an object lesson in technique and coordination, a simple movement that would have taken months or even years to perfect until it became instinctive.

"I thought these people could only shoot," he said to Hal.

The skirl shook his head. "Apparently not," he replied. "They're full of surprises, aren't they?"

For the first time, Gilan went on the attack. He flicked his own sword up and over, striking at the Shurmel between the shoulder and the neck. The huge man staggered back clumsily, only just managing to avoid the stroke. Then, before he could recover, Gilan's sword drove forward inside the other man's reach, darting like a snake for his midsection. Again, only a frantic, last-minute leap backward saved the Shurmel's life. The Shurmel's massive sword gave him an advantage in reach, but now that Gilan was inside that reach, its size and weight became a drawback, making it clumsy and slow to wield.

Watching his opponent's eyes, Gilan saw the first signs of doubt and fear. The Scorpion leader had expected a fast victory. He had planned to demolish his opponent with a few easy, devastating blows. But his best attacks had been met and countered, with almost contemptuous ease. The Shurmel had never faced a master swordsman before. Now, he realized, he was doing so for the first time.

Still concentrating on the big man's eyes, Gilan saw a light of cunning emerge behind the doubt. The Shurmel was planning something, he realized, and he waited to see what it might be. Any moment now, he thought, seeing the resolve harden in the Shurmel's expression.

The moment came. With a blinding flurry, the Shurmel described a bewildering pattern of movement with his hands, then, suddenly, he switched the massive sword to his left hand, instantly swinging it in a horizontal stroke from the new direction.

Gilan had been unaware what stratagem the Shurmel might attempt. But he knew from the man's eyes and face that he was planning something unexpected, so he was prepared. His sword blade hammered into the Shurmel's weapon, stopping it dead and leaving a deep notch in the long blade.

Again, those watching gave a great exhalation of despair. They had seen the Shurmel's rapid pattern of deception, saw the sword appear in his other hand and expected an instant killing stroke. But the stranger had calmly blocked the left-handed blow.

And now they watched as Gilan began to rain blows down on the Shurmel, who managed to block and parry desperately as he moved back away from his attacker. The blows came with lightning speed and from every direction, one flowing into the other as Gilan, reasoning that the Shurmel would be even less skillful with the left hand than he was with the right, forced him back across the cavern. The blows rang and reechoed in a constant clash of steel on steel, the sound never seeming to stop, the strikes and the echoes blending into one long, continuous, blood-chilling sound of ringing steel.

And then the Ranger paused momentarily, as if tiring, and the Shurmel seized the brief respite to return his sword to his more capable right hand. As he flicked the sword from left to right, he realized, too late, that the Ranger had drawn a long, heavy-bladed knife from his left hip with his left hand.

Gilan stepped forward and slammed the saxe into the Shurmel's unprotected ribs, driving the weapon in to the hilt.

The Shurmel's eyes mirrored shock, then disbelief, then pain, in quick succession. Then his knees gave way under him and his eyes went completely blank as he collapsed to the stone floor.

And lay there, still as the grave.

Once again, a cry of anguish and disbelief was torn from the throats of those watching. Gilan stepped quickly away from the massive form sprawled on the cavern floor. He re-sheathed both his weapons with quick, smooth movements and retrieved his bow and quiver from Hal's hands.

"Weapons, boys," he said softly, and the two Skandians complied, Hal drawing his own sword and Stig flicking his battleax from its belt loop.

The Scorpions were stunned for some moments. Then an angry muttering began. Gilan nocked an arrow to his bow, but left the weapon undrawn for the moment.

"Kill them!" a voice roared from the congregation. "Kill them now!"

Gilan's eyes swept the room and lit upon the speaker. He was a scar-faced man in the second row. The Ranger had been wondering who would try to take control of the Scorpion cult. In a group like this, there was always someone who aspired to the leadership. He reasoned that it would be the first man to speak. And here he was.

Several of the scarlet-robed assassins began to move forward. But they moved uncertainly, faced by the triple threat of the ax, sword and longbow. None of them was armed with anything larger than a stiletto.

"Stay where you are!" Gilan ordered.

The men who had begun to move forward halted, in some awe

of the stranger who had just defeated their mighty Shurmel. Now Gilan brought his bow up and drew the arrow back, aiming directly at the scar-faced man who had spoken.

"Try to take us," he said in a quieter tone, "and I estimate that at least a dozen of you will die before you do. Is there any glory in dying that way? It won't be for a *tolfah*. Your Shurmel chose to die for that, and the choice was his." Then he made direct eye contact with Taluf, the scar-faced man. "And I promise you that the first one to die will be you," he added.

He saw the sudden fear in the man's eyes, replaced by a look of animal cunning, and sensed he had guessed correctly. This was the man who would seek to take the leadership position.

"On the other hand, this is your opportunity to take over the leadership here. To become the new Shurmel. All you have to do is order the others to stand aside while we leave."

Now a new light came into the man's eyes: calculation and ambition.

"Your choice," Gilan said, driving home his advantage. "Let us go and you live. And you become Shurmel. Or you can order your men to stop us and you can die immediately."

Calculation and ambition vied with uncertainty and hatred. Taluf studied Gilan's calm face and saw no sign of hesitation there. He knew that if the Scorpions made a move toward the three men, he would die immediately. At this close range, the archer couldn't possibly miss.

On the other hand, this stranger had created the opportunity for him to claim the Shurmel's position. He had defeated the Shurmel in a fair challenge to end the *tolfah*.

It could be argued, and Taluf would argue this in the hours to come, that it had been Imrika's will for the Shurmel to die. And when that course of action occurred to him, he made his decision. He held up a hand to the other Scorpions. Their eyes were all riveted on him now.

"Let them pass," he said. "Imrika has shown us her will and your new Shurmel orders it."

chapter forty-five

Working quickly, and with one eye on the oasis, the crew cleared the campsite of their personal possessions and loaded them back aboard the *Heron*. The ship was moored with her prow dug into the sand of the beach. A long stern line connected her to an anchor set in the bay offshore.

When the campsite was cleared of bedrolls, spare weapons and foodstuffs, Thorn gave the order for Jesper to untie the beach mooring line while Ingvar and Wulf hauled in on the stern hawser, dragging the little ship back into deeper water. When he was satisfied that there was sufficient distance between the ship and the beach, Thorn gestured for Ingvar and Wulf to tie off the line. The onshore wind held the ship in position, so that her bow remained facing the shore. Thorn checked her position and grunted with satisfaction.

"We'll have to reattach the line to the bow when the wind veers at sunset," he said. "I want to keep the bow facing the beach."

"Why?" Jesper asked. "We're safe enough here, no matter which way we're facing."

Thorn regarded him patiently. "If the bow is pointing at the beach, so is the Mangler," he said, and understanding dawned in Jesper's eyes.

"Oh. Of course," he said. "I should have realized that."

"Perhaps if you ever actually *thought* for a second or two before you spoke, you might occasionally realize the obvious," Thorn said.

Lydia had remained for'ard, her eyes sweeping the oasis for any sign of their former attackers. But the *Ishti* were staying well under cover. They had seen the effect of her atlatl darts and, having no idea as to the actual range of the weapon, deemed it prudent not to expose themselves to further attacks. From time to time, she glimpsed a brief sign of movement within the trees. She had no doubt that the enemy was watching them, waiting for a chance to make another move.

She'd been surveying the trees for over an hour, slumped comfortably in a patch of shade against the mast. Her constant focus was eventually rewarded.

She heard a faint thud of hoofbeats on the sand—a large number of hoofbeats. And, rising above the trees of the oasis, she saw a drifting cloud of dust. Putting the two facts together, she called to Thorn.

"Reinforcements! There are more horsemen in the oasis now."

The shabby old warrior had been napping in the rowing well,

out of the sun. He wished Hal hadn't needed the canvas awning they used as a sun shelter on board the ship while she was at anchor, but it was the only material Hal could use as a sail for the land sailer. He rose now, buckling his belt and moving forward.

Not for the first time, Lydia wondered how such a bulky man could move so quietly when he chose to. He dropped to one knee beside her and she pointed at the oasis. The cloud of dust was dissipating now but it was still evident.

"They just rode in," she explained. "You can see the dust cloud they raised and I could hear their hoofbeats."

"Hmmm," said Thorn thoughtfully, tugging at the shaggy edge of his beard. "Any idea how many?"

She hesitated. "Quite a few," she said eventually. "More than a dozen, less than a hundred. But I'm only guessing there," she added.

Thorn pursed his lips thoughtfully. He had great respect for her tracking and observation skills. "Your guesses are usually pretty good," he said idly and, once again, she looked at him in some surprise. It always took her unawares when Thorn praised her. "Wonder what they're up to?" he asked.

The question was a rhetorical one, but Lydia answered nonetheless. "Want me to go take a look?" she asked. She pointed to a spit of rocks that jutted out from the beach about fifty meters to the south of the abandoned campsite. "I could swim to those rocks, then use them as cover to get to the oasis. Once I'm inside the tree line, there's plenty of cover I could use."

Thorn hesitated. All his instincts said it was a good idea. A commander needed all the information he could get in a situation like this—particularly when his forces were outnumbered. On the other hand, he'd be sending Lydia into considerable danger if he agreed to her suggestion, and he was loath to do that. He was genuinely fond of the girl.

Lydia, of course, misinterpreted the reason for his hesitation.

"I can do it, you know!" she said with some heat. "Even if I am just a girl."

Absently, he patted her wrist with his left hand as he strained his eyes toward the oasis, trying to pierce the dense screen of trees that hid the enemy from sight.

"I know you can. And better than anyone else, with the possible exception of Jesper." Jesper, of course, was a former thief and was highly skilled in the art of moving without being seen. At one stage, Thorn had heard someone say Jesper could slip between two raindrops and use them as cover.

"Well then?" Lydia said, a little mollified by his admission— although she didn't believe Jesper could do the job any better than she.

"It's . . . dangerous," Thorn said eventually. "We don't know where they are. We don't know how many of them there are. And we don't know what they're up to."

Lydia rolled her eyes at him when he said the word *dangerous*.

"All good reasons why I should go and take a look," she said. "As for dangerous, would that affect your thinking if Jesper volunteered to take a look?"

"Jesper hasn't volunteered," Thorn pointed out.

She sniffed disdainfully. "And you could grow old and gray waiting for him to do so."

Thorn smiled to himself, deciding not to point out that he was already old and gray. "True. But in Jesper's case, the fact that it's dangerous might influence me to send him."

She smiled in return, then the smile faded and she held up a hand for silence. From the oasis, they could hear a sudden noise— like metal striking wood.

"Are they hammering something?" Thorn asked.

Lydia didn't answer for a second or two. Then she pointed to where one of the tall bamboo trees was visible above the other trees. As they watched, it slid sideways and fell from their sight.

"They're chopping," she said. "They're chopping down trees."

Thorn nodded slowly. She was right. That was what they were doing. The next question was, why were they doing it?

"All right," he said. "Go take a look. But for pity's sake, be careful. I don't want to have to tell Hal that I've let you get yourself taken prisoner."

She laughed derisively. "You won't be letting me be taken," she said. "And I certainly have no plans to do it myself."

She unbuckled her belt and shrugged off her heavy, waist-length jerkin. Then she kicked her sealskin boots off as well, leaving herself barefoot and wearing only her light linen shirt and trousers.

"Go in over the stern," Thorn told her, "on the side away from the beach. Then swim underwater as far as you can. That way, if they're watching the ship, they may not see you go." She nodded, unclipping her atlatl from the belt, then re-donning it, so that her long, razor-sharp dirk hung by her side.

The other crew members became aware of her preparations. Ingvar approached her.

"What are you doing?" he asked, and she smiled at him.

"I'm going to see what the enemy are up to."

Ingvar began to shed his own outer jacket. "I'll come with you," he said immediately.

Lydia laughed out loud, laying a hand on his arm to stop him.

"Ingvar, I love you dearly," she said. "But you're simply not built for sneaking around and staying unnoticed. You're a very noticeable person."

He stopped, his face a mask of concern. "But if anything happens to you. If they catch you—"

She cut him off. "I don't plan on letting anyone catch me," she said. "But if anyone does, I'll feel a lot better knowing you're here to come and fetch me."

He paused, and looked steadily at her. "Count on it," he said.

She patted his arm again, then turned toward the stern bulwark.

"Now give me a hand over the side," she said.

Ranulf bin Shellah, the leader of the squad of fifty, crouched inside the tree line of the oasis and studied the enemy ship, sitting serenely on its own inverted reflection, fifty meters offshore. It might as well be fifty leagues, he thought bitterly.

He had sent fifteen men ahead to observe and make sure the foreigners didn't escape. Now the leader of those fifteen was gone—dragged by his horse out into the desert and probably dead—two other men were dead and three were badly wounded.

He was told of their failed attack on the campsite, and the unexpected barrier of thorns that prevented their breaking through the defenses. Now the ship floated defiantly, just out of his reach. Occasionally, he could see men moving on the deck, but for the most part there was no sign of life aboard her. He cursed the impulsive leader of his advance party, who had given away the advantage of surprise and made the enemy aware of their presence. At least, he thought, they would have no idea that the advance party had been reinforced. That could work to his advantage.

If only he could think of a way to reach that insolent vessel floating offshore.

He rolled onto his back, looking up into the trees, seeking inspiration. Then it came to him and he crawled back away from the edge of the tree line, into the main section of the oasis itself. He beckoned to his second in command and, when the man came to him, he pointed to the bamboo grove.

"Cut down trees," he said. "A lot of trees."

His subordinate touched his mouth, forehead and mouth in the strangely graceful gesture of greeting or acquiescence.

"Yes, Captain," he said. "And what shall we do with these trees?"

"We're going to use them to attack the foreign ship," Ranulf told him.

S lowly, keeping his bow half drawn and aimed at the group of red-clad men, Gilan began to move sideways toward the exit.

"Weapons ready, lads," he said in a quiet voice, and Hal and Stig moved in concert with him, ax and sword raised and leveled at the men watching them. Hal stumbled on something and, glancing down, saw that it was the Shurmel's staff. On an impulse, he stooped and picked it up, holding it behind him and masking it with his body to keep the action as unobtrusive as he could. All eyes in the room were on Gilan, and there was no sign that anyone had noticed what he had done.

The assassins moved a pace forward as the three interlopers reached the entrance. Gilan drew the arrow back a few centimeters and sought the eye of the man he had picked as the heir apparent to the Shurmel. He raised an eyebrow in warning.

"If they move," he said calmly, "you'll be the first one to die."

Taluf made a negative sideways gesture in the air and turned to his companions.

"Let them go," he ordered. "We have no further business with them."

Gilan breathed a silent prayer of thanks for overweening ambition. Still facing the fifty-odd men, he slipped backward out of the room into the rock-walled corridor. Stig and Hal followed him and they made their way back toward the ramp that led to the lower levels. Instinctively, they began to move faster and faster, until they were almost running. But Gilan held up a hand to slow them down. He was walking half-backward, watching the entrance to the gallery where he had confronted the Shurmel. So far, there was no sign of anyone trying to follow them, although he could hear the muted sound of Taluf's voice as he addressed his peers.

"Don't run," he cautioned them. "If they think we're running, they may come after us."

"So far, it's been easy," Stig said cheerfully, and Gilan turned a baleful eye on him.

"We're not out of here yet," he said. But as they reached the downward ramp and began to make their way down to ground level, there was still no sign or sound of any pursuit.

"I think we may have pulled it off," Hal said.

Gilan turned a mirthless grin on him. "What do you mean, 'we'?"

Hal nodded in acquiescence. "I stand corrected."

For the first time, Gilan noticed that Hal was carrying the Shurmel's scorpion staff. "What are you doing with that?" he asked.

Hal shrugged. "Thought it'd make a good souvenir."

Gilan shook his head. "It's the ugliest souvenir I've ever seen," he declared, and Hal smiled tolerantly.

"You've never seen our Oberjarl's stash of goodies," he said. "Some of the stuff he considers fine art would make a connoisseur throw up."

They reached the ground level and still there was no sign of any pursuit. Gilan guessed that the scar-faced man was too busy affirming his position of authority over the others to bother with such a thing. The three foreigners had been the concern of the Shurmel. Now there was a new man in charge and he was happy to divest himself of all his predecessor's problems.

There were several members of the *Ishti* idling around in the open space outside the cavern entrance. They glanced curiously at the three foreigners, but there was no sign of any antagonism.

"I think we can put our weapons away now," Gilan said, and the others complied. "Just keep that scorpion on a stick out of sight, will you? They might not take kindly to our walking off with it."

Hal grinned. He took off his *kheffiyeh* and wrapped the carved scorpion in it, concealing the staff's identity. Glancing round the open space, he saw the land sailer off to one side, its sail lowered and furled loosely along the boom. He started toward it but Gilan clicked his fingers, gesturing for him to stop. The Ranger then pointed a finger at one of the watching *Ishti*.

"You," he said. "Fetch our vehicle. The Shurmel has ordered it."

The soldier looked at him curiously for several seconds. He knew the three strangers had been in conference with the Shurmel and the members of the cult. Now they had obviously been released. It wasn't for him to question the Shurmel's orders. Beckoning to two of the other *Ishti*, he made his way across the parade ground to where the land sailer was standing. Carefully, taking pains not to damage the spindly vehicle, they began to push it to where the three waited. The loosely furled sail jerked back and forth as the wind caught it. Hal noted the movement with approval.

"Still a good breeze blowing," he said. "That should help us on our way."

Stig was looking curiously at the Ranger. "What was the point of that?" he asked, then elaborated, "Of making them fetch the land sailer for us."

A slight grin touched Gilan's features. "Always assume authority," he said. "It makes it easier for people like this to obey you. If we'd gone across and started raising the sail, they might have felt it necessary to ask what we were doing. Then they might have sent someone to check that we were allowed to leave. This way, they assume we have permission."

Stig nodded thoughtfully. "You're a cunning fellow at heart, aren't you?"

Gilan thought about the question for a second or two, then nodded. "I try to be," he said.

The nomads pushed the land sailer into position beside them. Hal checked the fittings and rigging briefly, making sure nobody had tampered with them while they had been kept waiting. Everything seemed fine so he seized the halyard and began to raise the sail. Stig lent a hand and the big triangle of canvas went up the mast in a series of swoops. As it was unfurled, it swung into the wind, setting the rigging creaking and the canvas flapping. Hal judged that it was sitting at a good angle to the wind and he wouldn't need the others to shove off. He stashed the concealed scorpion staff along the central spar of the sailer, then gestured for the others to board.

"Hold on," he said, then hauled in on the mainsheet, tightening the sail so that it bellied out with the familiar *whoomph!* of trapped wind. The wheels began to turn slowly, the axles creaking a protest.

There was the usual vibration of the wheels passing over the uneven ground, then the speed began to build up and the movement became smoother. Hal hauled on the tiller ropes and swung the land sailer toward the open desert. He glanced over his shoulder.

There was no sign of any of the red-robed Scorpions. But the *Ishti* who were assembled on the parade ground watched the sailer's progress with interest. It was a novel sight, a spidery, wheeled machine slipping across the desert with no apparent means of propulsion.

The speed built up until they were moving as fast as a horse could canter. The rumbling and rattling of the wheels on the ground settled into a constant low-pitched roar, and the familiar rooster tail of dust rose into the air behind them.

"I think we're in the clear," Hal said. He was craning round to look astern and he could see no sign of an alarm being raised. The *Ishti* troops had gone back to whatever they had been doing before the three foreigners had appeared. He glanced quickly at the sun for direction and brought the land sailer round on a course for the coast. The wheels roared and the frame of the vehicle flexed over the rough ground. Hal let his body move to the rhythm of the land sailer. From time to time, he would call a warning for the others to hold tight, and alter course to avoid the larger outcrops of rocks that dotted the terrain, or to steer round a gully or depression that seemed too large for the vehicle to negotiate.

They were running with the wind on their beam and he changed tack regularly, maintaining a base course back to the oasis and the ship. He felt a growing anxiety for the *Heron*'s safety now that they were clear of the Scorpions' lair. Fifty men, the Shurmel had said. Fifty men sent to destroy or sink the ship. And they'd be faced by a mere half dozen defenders. He glanced up at the sail, tightened the sheet a little and felt the upwind wheel begin to lift from the ground.

"Stig!" he called and his friend edged out along the outrigger, moving his weight outboard so that the errant wheel came down again, skimming the rough ground beneath it.

"Thorn won't let the *Heron* come to any harm," the muscular first mate called to him, sensing the reason for Hal's increasing the speed. Hal nodded, his expression masked by the *kheffiyeh*. After a couple of kilometers, he had brought the sailer to a halt and recovered his headdress, wrapping it firmly around his nose and mouth to protect his face from the flying dust and grit thrown up by the wheels of the land sailer. Reason told him that the *Heron* was in safe hands, with Thorn in charge. The old sea wolf wouldn't let himself be surprised by a band of desert nomads. He was too wily a campaigner for that.

But reason was one thing. Emotion was another, and Hal knew this gut-churning anxiety would be with him until he was striding the *Heron*'s decks once more, back in command.

They ran on throughout the afternoon. Every hour, Hal would

bring the sailer to a halt and they would get off to stretch cramped muscles and limbs. The constant need to hold on and balance the vehicle's movements left them tired and aching. After the second of these stops, Hal had a small inspiration and suggested that the two outriders should change sides each time they stopped. That brought fresh muscles into play in the effort to balance the little vehicle. Gilan and Stig reacted gratefully. For Hal, of course, there was no respite from the constant strain.

The grinding rumble of the wheels and axles, the creaking of the rigging and the groans from the frame as it flexed over the rough ground began to encapsulate their existence. The kilometers rolled under the wheels as the sun began to sink lower to the horizon in the west.

The shadows lengthened and it became increasingly difficult to make out the features of the land around them. Rocks and dry runnels in the desert became more difficult to make out with the low angle light, and on several occasions Hal had to shout a warning as he hauled the steering lines over at the last minute to avoid an obstacle. He became obsessed with the idea that he might shatter one of the wheels against a rock or in a gully. If that were to happen, they would be stranded. As the thought came to him, he berated himself for not loading a spare wheel onto the sailer. There had been several available when he'd stripped the old chariots.

"Look out! Go starboard!" Stig's shout dragged him out of his daydreaming. He heaved on the tiller, loosening the sheet, and the land sailer swung violently to port, barely missing the edge of a dried wadi that had loomed out of the late afternoon shadows into their path.

His heart pounding with panic, Hal let the sheet fly and allowed the way to run off the land sailer. Slowly, it lost speed, the roar of its wheels changing back to a series of dull bumps and thuds. Finally, it came to a stop facing the wind, with the sail and the boom slapping back and forth to either side.

"That was close," Gilan said. There was no sign of rebuke in his voice. He realized what a difficult task it must be to continue steering and controlling the sailer over this rough terrain in the failing light. All in all, he thought, Hal was doing a superb job.

The skirl slumped now in his seat, the sheet and tiller ropes lying loose in his lap. He pulled the *kheffiyeh* aside and pinched the bridge of his nose, then rubbed his red-rimmed eyes.

"Sorry," he said. "I just didn't see it. Good work, Stig."

Stig shook his head. "You're the one doing all the work. And it's getting tougher and tougher to see where we're going in this light. You must be exhausted."

Hal managed a tired grin. "I must admit, getting a faceful of dust and pebbles is a little different from the occasional bucketful of spray coming over the bows. Not half as invigorating." For the first time, he realized how tired he was. He glanced up at his first mate. "Do you want to take over for a while?" he said, but Stig shook his head immediately.

"Not me!" he said vigorously. "You've got the knack with this mad creation of yours. I wouldn't have the same feel for it."

Hal nodded. He realized that Stig was right. Perhaps he should have allowed the bigger youth to spell him earlier and get the feeling for the land sailer. But then, he realized, they'd been in a hurry both coming and going. There hadn't been time for Stig to acclimatize himself to the controls.

"We'll push on slowly for a few more kilometers," he said.

Then we're going to have to camp for the night. I can't risk travel-ing once the light's gone. It'd be too easy to wreck the sailer." He took a deep breath and rolled his shoulders to relieve the strain there. The land sailer was facing dead into the wind and they'd need to push her round. He gestured in the direction he wanted her turned.

"Push her round to port and we'll get going," he said.

"Slowly," Gilan admonished as he climbed down from his perch. Hal gave him a tired grin.

"Very slowly," he agreed.

chapter forty-seven

T he chopping went on for some hours, after which it was replaced by another sound—similar, but not quite the same. The Herons left on board puzzled over the sound.

"It's hammering," Jesper said, finally identifying it. "They've been chopping down trees and now they're hammering them together."

The noise continued as night fell and the wind shifted. They could see the reflected glow of several large fires in the oasis. The uncertainty began to play on all their nerves. Thorn was also becoming increasingly concerned about Lydia. She had been gone for some hours now. She should have had time to find out what was going on and report back.

"Do you think they caught her?" Ingvar asked. He had sensed what Thorn was thinking about. The old sea wolf shook his head.

"I doubt it. She's very good at what she does."

"But she should have been back by now," Ingvar insisted. He glanced to where his voulge was leaning against the mast. "I've a good mind to go and look for her."

Thorn rounded on him instantly. "No," he said and his voice was sharp, cutting off any discussion about that idea. He saw Ingvar draw himself up angrily and said in a more conciliatory tone, "Ingvar, you're big and you're powerful and since Hal made you those spectacles, as you call them, you've turned into one heck of a warrior. But the one thing you're not is stealthy."

Ingvar went to demur, then stopped. He had to admit that Thorn was right. The one-handed warrior went on.

"Let's say you go blundering around ashore and Lydia hasn't been discovered—which is most likely. They're bound to hear or see you and capture you. And then Lydia will feel obliged to help you. And then you'll both be caught. Is that what you want?"

"No. But—"

"There's no but to it. We have to trust Lydia's skill and her ability to move about the oasis without being discovered. If you go chasing after her, you'll only cause problems."

Somewhat surprisingly, it was Jesper who supported Thorn's position. He placed a hand on Ingvar's arm.

"Thorn's right, Ingvar. Trust me, I've done this sort of thing and it's a lot easier for one person to avoid discovery than for two. Particularly," he added with a small grin, "when the second person is a big muscle-bound oaf with the grace and stealthiness of a bull walrus on the prowl."

Despite himself, Ingvar couldn't help a smile touching his

mouth. Jesper's description of his way of moving was a graphic one.

"If you put it that way . . . ," he began, and Jesper nodded. He *did* put it that way. "Then I suppose it's better for me to remain on board. But that doesn't mean I have to like it."

Thorn nodded unequivocally. "None of us do. But I'm sure Lydia will be okay."

They heard a faint splash from the stern of the ship, and a hand appeared over the bulwark.

"Lydia will be fine," came the girl's voice, "if one of you will give her a hand back on board."

They all moved quickly to the stern. Ingvar leaned over the railing and, grabbing hold of Lydia's arm, hauled her bodily out of the water and deposited her, dripping profusely, on deck.

"Where have you been?" Thorn asked. He masked his earlier concern for her with a mock severity of tone. "What took you so long?"

She took a blanket that Edvin handed her. Once the sun set in the desert, the night quickly became chilly. She wrapped it round herself, using one corner to mop her face and towel her hair. She smiled her gratitude to Edvin before answering Thorn's question.

"I thought it best to wait until dark to swim back," she said. Thorn nodded, reluctantly accepting the good sense in that re-mark. She couldn't resist adding a little barb. "Seemed to work too. None of you saw me coming, did you?"

Thorn coughed and tried to ignore the question by asking one of his own.

"Well, did you find out what they're up to?"

"Yes. They're building rafts. Obviously, they intend to try boarding us in the morning."

There was a quick outburst from the assembled crew but Thorn held up his hand for silence.

"Rafts, you say? How many? And how many men are in the oasis now?"

"I couldn't get an exact count of the men, but I'd say between forty and fifty," Lydia said. There were exclamations of surprise and concern from the crew as they heard the number. "It looked as if they were working on five rafts."

"And what makes you think they'll wait till morning to attack?" Thorn asked.

Lydia shrugged. "They've got hours of work to do yet," she said. "And then they'll presumably need to rest. Plus they're cavalrymen, not sailors. I expect they'll want daylight before they try their luck on the water in an unfamiliar craft."

Thorn fingered his chin as he digested her words. "That makes sense," he said. "So we've got till dawn."

Lydia shrugged. "Well, I could be wrong. We'll need to keep a sharp lookout tonight." Then she couldn't resist adding, "Certainly a lot sharper than you kept while I was swimming back out."

"Yes. Yes. You've made your point," Thorn said, a little irritably.

Stefan was frowning as he considered Lydia's news. "Thorn, why don't we just up anchor and sail away? That would seem the simplest course of action."

Wulf and Jesper murmured agreement.

"Have you forgotten Hal and Stig and the Ranger are still ashore?" Thorn asked him. "What happens if we sail away and they arrive back, slap into the arms of fifty desert nomads?"

Stefan looked abashed at the reply. He shifted his feet uncomfortably. "Oh . . . yeah. I'd forgotten about that."

"Still," Thorn said, "we should be ready if we have to get away in a hurry. Edvin, buoy the end of the anchor rope so we can simply cast it off and get under way. Then we can always recover it later."

"I'll get on to it," Edvin said and turned to search for a suitable object with which to buoy the end of the anchor rope. Thorn looked around the others.

"We'll set a double watch. Wulf and Jesper, you take the first. Three hours, then wake Stefan and me. The rest of us better get some sleep. It's going to be a busy morning."

Hal let go the mainsheet and spilled the wind from the sail. The land sailer slowly trundled to a halt, its wheels rumbling and grumbling over the uneven surface of the desert. Not for the first time, he gave a mental vote of thanks to the chariot builders who had constructed those wheels to cope with this rough terrain.

He groaned softly as he straightened up, relieving the tension in his back muscles. The past hour had been an incredible strain, as he peered through the gathering dusk, trying to find a safe path.

Finally, he had to admit that it was time to stop. "I'll sail us off a cliff if I keep going."

Gilan had dismounted from his perch on the starboard outrigger. He studied the desert behind them long and hard, looking for some sign of pursuit. He could see nothing, but the failing light and the shadows cast by large rock outcrops could well have concealed riders coming after them.

"Can't see anyone," he said, at length.

"Whether you can or not, we're not going any farther tonight," Hal told him. "And if there's anyone riding after us, it'll be just as difficult and dangerous for them in this light."

"Of course," Stig put in, "there may be no pursuit. I think that scar-faced man was glad to be rid of us."

"That's true," Gilan agreed. "But we'd better set a watch none the less. Hal, you're all in. You've been doing all the work today. You get your head down. I'll take the first watch and Stig can take the second. That way, you'll get six hours straight sleep."

"I can use them," Hal said wearily. He dragged his bedroll off the land sailer, then went to lower the sail and furl it. Stig took the halyard from his hand.

"I'll do that," he said. "You get some rest."

Without argument, Hal spread out his bedding and literally fell onto it, rolling the blanket around him against the chill of the desert night air. Within seconds, he was asleep. Gilan regarded the still form for a few seconds, then looked at the spidery shape of the land sailer and shook his head once more in admiration.

"He's a remarkable young man," he said quietly to Stig.

The first mate nodded agreement. "We all look up to him," he said. "Funny, growing up in Hallasholm, he was something of an outcast. Half Araluen and half Skandian and nobody completely trusted him because of it."

"You did," Gilan pointed out. Thorn had told him a little about the background of the Heron crew, how they had all been outcasts and misfits, yet had gone on to become the champion brotherband of their year. Stig looked at him, his bottom lip pushed out thoughtfully.

"He saved my life," he said finally. "We weren't friends or anything at that stage, but he risked his life to save mine. There's nothing I wouldn't do for him."

The Ranger nodded. "That's a pretty good basis for a friendship." Then, changing the subject, he unpacked the last of their
meager rations. "Let's eat, then you get some sleep. I'll wake you for
the second watch."

Stig munched on a piece of stale flat bread, wrapping it round
some salted pork with just a hint of Edvin's precious pickles. He
nodded wearily.

"Amazing how good this can taste when you're hungry," he said.

Six hours later, Hal woke instantly to the gentle touch of Stig's
hand on his shoulder. His eyes shot wide open and for a moment
he lay still, not sure where he was or what he'd been doing. Then
the memory of the wild, plunging ride on the land sailer came back
to him and he sat up, rubbing his eyes. Stig handed him a beaker
of water and he drank deeply.

"No coffee, I'm afraid," the first mate said. "Gilan didn't think
we could risk a fire."

"He's probably right," Hal said, yawning. He drained off the
water, then tossed his blankets aside. Rising to his feet, he shrugged
on his sheepskin vest and buckled his sword belt around his waist.
The weight of the sword on one side and the heavy axe on the
other was strangely comforting.

Stretching, he walked to the slightly elevated spot where Stig
and Gilan had kept watch. It was a small outcrop of rocks and it
gave a wider view of the desert around them. He scanned the horizon through three hundred and sixty degrees but there was nothing
in sight. Yawning again, he settled down on the hard rock. Stig, he
saw, was already stretched out in his blanket. Hal wriggled his but-
tocks on the hard rock.

"No risk I'll fall asleep on watch," he reflected.

But he was wrong. In spite of the hard, sharp-edged rocks, he began to nod off after an hour. He jerked awake, got up and walked around. Eventually, deciding he was fully alert again, he sat down once more.

And within a few minutes, he was asleep.

He awoke with a jerk and looked around guiltily. Stig and Gilan were still sleeping peacefully. But in the east, the first red streaks of dawn were showing. Then a sound alerted him—the soft whiffle of a horse's breath. He swung round and his heart sank.

They were on an elevated piece of land, which afforded a good view of the desert around them. As he watched, a file of horsemen seemed to rise out of the ground behind their campsite, spread in a half circle to enclose them.

chapter　　　　　　　forty-eight

S tefan and Jesper had shared the last watch. Now, as dawn
began to break over the desert and the ocean, Stefan
reached out to shake Thorn's shoulder. The old sea wolf
was leaning against the base of the mast, his sheepskin
pulled up around his ears.

"I'm awake," he said, before the hand touched him. "Anything
happening?"

"Heard a bit of rustling and such a half hour ago," Stefan told
him. "And we thought we heard voices—sounded as if they were
trying to keep them quiet."

Thorn smiled grimly. "That usually ensures that people can
hear you," he said. He stood up and stretched, moving forward into
the bow. There was a water skin hanging from the Mangler. He
took it, rinsed his mouth and spat over the side. Then he peered
through the shadows to the beach.

"There's something there," he said, pointing. "See those dark shapes on the edge of the water?"

Stefan followed the line of his pointing hand. There were several dark shapes lined up on the beach but, in the dim light, he couldn't make them out.

"What do you think they are?"

"I'd say they're the rafts Lydia saw them making, and they're getting ready to launch them. Wake the others."

The sun appeared over the eastern horizon and seemed to shoot up into the sky. The light intensified and, within a few minutes, the objects on the beach took on hard lines. There were five of them, Thorn saw. They were approximately four meters long by three wide, constructed from large bamboo trunks. He heard the rest of the crew moving behind him.

"Get your weapons," he said quietly. He had moved back to his spot by the mast and was fastening his club-hand in place. His sword and saxe hung from his belt. For a moment, he considered donning his shield, then discarded the idea. He'd need both hands free in the coming fight.

The others gathered around him, all of them watching those five dark shapes on the water's edge.

"If it all goes wrong," Thorn said, "we may need to make a run for it. Edvin, be ready to cast off the anchor rope, then take the tiller. Stefan and Jesper, you stay ready to raise the sail and sheet home."

"What about me?" Wulf demanded truculently. It was normally his job to look after the mainsheet.

"You'll help Ingvar and me keep them off the ship," Thorn said. After himself and Ingvar, Wulf was the most skillful fighter aboard.

"Do you want me on the Mangler?" Lydia asked.

Thorn shook his head. "The Mangler's not very useful against bamboo rafts. It might smash a log or two, but the raft will stay afloat. Besides, I need Ingvar free to take care of any would-be boarders," he said. "He won't be able to load or train the Mangler for you. Use your atlatl and your darts. Take care of anyone who actually makes it on board."

Lydia frowned. "I've only got half a dozen darts left," she said. She had lost some of her store of darts in the previous battle.

"Then make them count," Thorn told her. He glanced around and saw Kloof, head on her paws, watching him intently. As usual when Hal was absent, she was tethered to a ring bolt in the deck. "Oh, and untie Kloof. If anyone makes it past us, she can be our second line of defense."

"That's some second line." Wulf grinned.

Thorn studied him for a few seconds. Wulf had been more cheerful over the past few days. He claimed that he could somehow sense that his twin brother was regaining his health and strength. Just as well, Thorn thought. He didn't want him distracted by concerns over Ulf in the coming battle.

"Thorn?" It was Edvin, peering at the beach. Instantly, Thorn swung to see what had caught his attention, the others following suit a second or so behind him.

"Here they come," said Jesper.

A dark line of men was advancing quickly from the shelter of the trees in the oasis, fanning out to run to the beach in groups of six.

"Stay quiet," Thorn ordered. "Let's let them think they've caught us napping."

The *Ishti* warriors reached the rafts and seized them, lifting them over the sand and launching them into the calm sea. Then they scrambled aboard—six men to each raft. They picked up paddles that had been left ready and began driving the clumsy craft out into the small waves that lapped against the beach. As they approached the ship, their courses began to diverge.

"Two to port. Two to starboard. One over the bows," Thorn said, judging their courses. One of the starboard-side rafts was pulling away from its comrades as its occupants paddled more skillfully. A mistake, Thorn thought. They should have made sure they all reached the boat at the same time to split the defenses.

"Wulf, Jesper, Stefan," he ordered. "You take the bow. Ingvar and Edvin, port side. I'll look after these characters to starboard."

The men on the rafts saw them moving and realized there was no further need for secrecy. They began to shout—whether it was war cries or calls of encouragement to one another, Thorn had no idea. He smiled mirthlessly.

"Go ahead and waste your breath," he said. He glanced back to the beach, where three men stood at the water's edge, urging on the paddlers.

"Attack! Attack!" shouted the one in the middle, obviously the commander. "Kill the invaders! Leave no one alive!"

His voice carried clearly over the water and his men responded with a hoarse chorus of cheers as they redoubled their efforts at the paddles. And, as so often happens in such cases, they lost their rhythm and technique and the paddling became ragged and haphazard.

"Faster! Faster!" screamed the man on the beach. "No prisoners! Kill them all!"

He spoke in the common tongue, which Thorn found a little strange. In fact, there was a good reason for it. The *Ishti* were recruited from half a dozen different tribes in the region, each with its own separate dialect. The common tongue was used for all battle commands, to avoid confusion.

Although, on this day, the opposite was about to happen.

The first raft bumped alongside the starboard side. An *Ishti* warrior seized the bulwark and dragged the raft closer. Then, as he began to heave himself up over the gunwale, he looked up in horror as Thorn appeared over the rail. The heavy club-hand swept down and smashed the man aside. He fell awkwardly, half in the water. The raft tilted crazily under him and one of his comrades went over the side. Spluttering and gasping in a panic, the man seized the raft's side and tried to haul himself back aboard, setting it rocking and plunging once more. Another would-be boarder, off balance from the violent movements of the uncertain platform beneath him, staggered wildly, windmilling his arms for balance. Thorn's sword caught him in the middle of the chest and he fell into the sea without another word.

The raft, listing badly to one side and not under control, drifted slowly away from the *Heron*'s side, the remaining four men on board searching frantically for their paddles.

But now the second raft was thudding into the *Heron*'s starboard side, and another had crashed heavily into the bow, where Wulf, Jesper and Stefan thrust and hacked at its occupants with sword and ax.

"Wait till they're almost on board," Wulf called to his companions. "Then hit them with everything you've got!"

Stefan and Jesper complied. There was a moment of opportunity as the boarders swarmed up onto the bulwarks—a split second where they were off balance and vulnerable. The three Herons took advantage of it and four of the boarders went over the side in quick succession. Two of them struggled to regain their position on the raft. The others floated clear, facedown, trailing ominous ribbons of blood in the water.

As the port-side rafts made contact, Ingvar let out a bellow of fighting rage and lunged with his voulge over the side. The blade stabbed in and out like a striking cobra, and three of the *Ishti* fell back from the ship in terror. But another raft had closed with the ship farther aft and two men made it unscathed to the deck.

One of them went no farther. A heavy dart flashed along the deck and thudded into his chest. He collapsed and crashed over onto the rowing benches. The second man took in his companion's fate and yelled a challenge to Ingvar, who was standing with his back to him, the voulge now flashing in a giant circle like an ax.

Ingvar didn't hear the challenge and didn't see the threat. But as Lydia was reloading with one of her dwindling supply of darts, a black, white and tan blur streaked along the deck and, leaping the last two meters, smashed into the *Ishti* warrior, driving him to the deck, screaming in fear.

"Good dog, Kloof!" Lydia shouted, lowering the dart she had been about to cast.

The man, miraculously disentangling himself from the snapping, snarling dog, wasted no energy in counterattack. He simply scrambled for the rail and heaved himself over it, hoping that there might be a raft below him.

There wasn't. The warrior was wearing a heavy mail shirt. He hit the water with a mighty splash and never resurfaced. Kloof, frustrated by his escape, stood with her paws on the rail, barking furiously at the roil of disturbed water where he'd disappeared.

The second raft on the port side was relatively unscathed. The senior man on board gestured toward the stern of the *Heron,* where there were no defenders, and yelled orders to his men. They dragged their clumsy craft along the side of the ship and swarmed over the rail, halfway to the stern. One of them instantly flew back over the rail again as a dart hit him. But the other four began to advance on Lydia, who stood defiantly, with only a dirk to defend herself.

Then the voice of their commander cut through the confusion, loud and clear.

"Retreat! Retreat! It's a trap! Back to the beach now!"

The four men hesitated. The girl was so close, and looked utterly vulnerable. Perhaps that's what decided them when their commander repeated his warning.

"It's a trap! Get out now!"

As one, they turned and scrambled back over the side onto their raft, and began paddling away toward the beach. The men on the other rafts heard the warning too. They disengaged and pulled away from the ship.

Thorn looked around, puzzled. "What the blazes just happened?"

On the beach, the commander of the *Ishti* was near apoplectic with rage as he saw his men withdrawing. "What are you doing? Attack! I tell you!"

Then, the same voice rang out again. "Retreat! Retreat! It's a trap!"

Thorn looked around wildly, then saw Stefan leaning against the bow post, his hands cupped around his mouth. Stefan shouted again, mimicking the enemy commander's voice perfectly.

"Back to the beach! It's a trap! Look out! Sharks!"

It was the last word that really tipped the balance. The men on the rafts redoubled their efforts at the paddles and drove their cumbersome craft back to the beach in record time.

Only to be greeted by their furious commander, who strode among them, slapping faces and striking out with the butt of his spear.

"Cowards! Idiots! What are you doing?"

Stefan watched the performance with interest, then shouted through cupped hands—once more in the commander's voice.

"Don't let him do that to you! He's an impostor! Stick a sword in him!"

Then he collapsed in laughter, Wulf and Jesper slapping him on the back triumphantly. Thorn strode over to the three of them.

"Nice work," he told Stefan. "I knew you'd come in useful one day."

Ingvar and Lydia joined the others in the bow. "That seems to have sent them packing," Lydia said.

Thorn nodded, frowning. "It won't work twice," he said. "That was a near-run thing. Next time, we'd better be ready to get under way."

For one wild moment, Hal considered flight. But the land sailer was secured for the night, its sail lowered and furled along the boom, and the ring of approaching horsemen would be on them before he could get it hoisted.

He cursed himself bitterly for falling asleep and putting his companions in danger.

"Gilan, Stig," he called, his voice bitter with the sense of failure. "Wake up. We've got company."

Stig and the Ranger woke immediately. They were experienced warriors and were ready to wake and fight at the slightest sound of alarm. They tossed their blankets aside and rose to their feet, seeing the silent ring of horsemen closing in on them. In one flowing movement, Gilan slung his quiver over his shoulder, selected an arrow and nocked it. His bow was already strung. In enemy territory, Rangers always kept their bows ready. In the words of his old mentor, *An unstrung bow is a stick.*

At the same time, Stig stooped to the ground beside his bedroll and seized his ax. He stood now with it held across his body, his left hand balancing the weight just below the gleaming head.

"Seems we were wrong about Scarface," he said quietly. Then he let a savage grin break over his features. "Well, if they try and take us, they'll end up a few men short."

Hal had been scanning the line of horsemen. They were now only a dozen meters away and still no word had been spoken. There must have been sixty or seventy of them and he realized that resistance was useless.

The horsemen stopped. Only the muted jingle of harness fittings and the creak of leather as their horses shifted their feet broke the silence. Their leader, in the center of the line, unwound the ends of his *kheffiyeh* and flicked them back over his shoulders so that he could speak.

"Who are you? And what are you doing here?"

Something about the voice struck a chord of recognition in Gilan's memory. He lowered his bow and stepped forward a few paces, peering intently at the rider. If he was one of the Shurmel's men sent to pursue them, why would he ask such questions?

In the growing light, he could see that the troop of horsemen all wore *kheffiyehs* that had a yellow-and-white-checked pattern. It was that detail that allowed his memory to click into place.

"Umar?" he said. "Umar ib'n Talud, *Aseikh* of the Khoresh Bedullin tribe. Is that you?"

The rider leaned forward to peer more closely at Gilan, then urged his horse forward a few paces. The riders flanking him began to move to accompany him but he waved them back, walking his horse forward alone until he was only three meters from the Ranger.

Hal, watching closely, could make out the man's features now. His nose was large and hooked, and at some stage had been badly broken. He wore a dark beard and his eyes were dark, almost black, and piercing. As Hal and Stig watched, the puzzled look on the rider's face vanished, and was replaced by a huge smile. His white teeth shone against the dark background of his beard.

"Friend Gilan!" he cried. "What are you doing here?"

He swung down from his horse and rushed to embrace Gilan. He was a big man and he literally swept the slim Ranger off his feet in a huge bear hug. He roared with laughter, then held Gilan away from him to study him more closely.

"Yes! It is you! May the almighty one be praised!"

Then Gilan, who had only just regained his breath, lost it all again in an explosive gasp as the Bedullin leader swept him into a crushing bear hug once more. The nomad riders behind him exchanged puzzled glances, although there were grins of recognition on the faces of several as they, too, recognized the Ranger.

Eventually, Gilan managed to disentangle himself and step clear of the Bedullin chief. Umar, however, overwhelmed with pleasure at seeing an old friend once more, kept making incipient attempts at another bear hug, which kept Gilan backing warily away. Eventually, the Ranger found the time to indicate his two companions, who were watching with rather mystified smiles on their faces.

"*Aseikh*," he said, using the Bedullin title for the leader of a tribe, "these are my friends, two Skandians by the name of Hal and Stig. Boys, this is Umar, leader of the Bedullins."

"Skandians!" Umar roared with delight as he shook hands with the two young men. "I know your Oberjarl well. Oberjarl Erak! A wonderful man! You know I rescued him from the clutches of the Tualaghi, all by myself!"

"You did?" said Hal, grinning. He had heard some of the details of Erak's capture and subsequent rescue.

Umar placed one hand on his chest, in a dramatic gesture. "I did! And I did it singlehandedly!" he declaimed.

Gilan coughed gently. "Perhaps with a little help, Umar?" he suggested.

The big Bedullin shook his head diffidently from side to side. "Well, surely, Ranger Gilan was there, and Rangers Will and Halt. Oh, and the mighty Araluen warrior Horace and the beautiful princess Evanlyn. And of course, your countryman, Svengal. But apart from that, I was all alone!"

"And apart from a hundred and twenty of your warriors," said Gilan, indicating the semicircle of riders, some of whom were openly grinning at Umar's wild exaggeration.

"Well, of course one hundred and twenty of my warriors!" Umar boomed. "But they were a ceremonial guard. No Bedullin *Aseikh* would think of traveling without a small retinue! But I stress, apart from those paltry numbers, I performed the feat entirely on my own."

"They still sing praises to your name in our home country," Stig said, a huge grin on his face. Umar bowed to him in mock modesty.

"As well they might, friend Stig. Tell me, how is your Oberjarl Erak?"

"A little overweight and very loud," Stig replied.

Umar fingered his chin thoughtfully. "Hasn't changed then?" he said slyly. He and the two Skandians exchanged smiles. Then he clapped his hands together, all business. "But tell me, my friends, what brings you to the desert? And what is this amazing vehicle you're traveling in?"

"We've been at Scorpion Mountain, dealing with the Shurmel of the Scorpion cult of assassins," Gilan told him. "There was a *tolfah* taken out against Princess Evanlyn." He used the name she had traveled under when she had led the mission to rescue Erak. "My King sent me here to have it rescinded."

Umar's brows drew closer together at the mention of the Scorpions. "A vile business. Who would threaten the life of such a beautiful and virtuous lady?"

"It was Iqbal, brother of the treacherous Yusal," Gilan said. "He wanted revenge for his brother and he dealt with the Scorpion cult to get it."

"But you say there was a *tolfah*? How did you manage to have it lifted? I thought once they were in place, they could not be altered."

"I killed the Scorpion leader," Gilan told him calmly. Umar regarded him for several seconds, then nodded repeatedly in recognition.

"That was well done, friend Gilan. The Scorpions are a blight upon our land. It's well past time that someone blunted their sting." He frowned thoughtfully. "But I understood the Shurmel was a mighty warrior?"

Gilan shrugged. "He was big. But not very skillful," he said dismissively. "But tell me, Umar, what brings you here? You've crossed the border out of Arrida."

Umar snorted disdainfully. "Borders are lines drawn on a map. True nomads like the Bedullin ignore them completely. We had heard talk of a wonderful machine that flew across the desert with no sign of anything to drive it." He nodded toward the land sailer, some meters away. "I take it this is that machine?"

Gilan smiled. "Indeed it is. And it was built by my young friend here." He indicated Hal. Umar regarded the young Skandian with interest and a degree of respect.

"Indeed? I must see it in motion later." He paused and his expression darkened. "There was another reason why we came here. My scouts told me that a large party of the Shurmel's warriors had left Scorpion Mountain and were crossing the desert."

His expression and the tone of his voice left little doubt as to his feelings about the Shurmel's *Ishti.*

"I take it you have no love for the Shurmel's men?" Hal said.

Umar nodded bleakly. "They are evil servants of an evil man. The Scorpion cult has been a thorn in our side for many years. But whenever we try to corner them, they melt away into their mountain labyrinth. We thought for once we might catch some of them in the open and teach them a lesson."

The three travelers exchanged glances. It was Gilan who replied. "Well, we happen to know where you might find them—and only a few hours away. They're at the ruined city of Ephesa, trying to capture our ship."

A slow smile spread over Umar's swarthy face. "So we are between them and their hideout?" he said. "How interesting. I think we might pay these people a visit, and let them see how unwise it is to show their noses too far from their evil mountain."

"We'd be delighted to accompany you," Gilan said.

Umar's expression changed to one of regret. "I'm afraid we have no horses to spare, friend Gilan. We'll need to travel fast and we have only those we ride and our remounts."

Gilan smiled and gestured to the land sailer. "We'll make our own way," he said. "And our transport doesn't get tired or need resting or replacing."

"Indeed?" Umar arched one eyebrow at them, then smiled. "I learned long ago not to doubt the claims you Rangers make. I can't wait to see this wonderful machine of yours in action."

"Just don't get too close behind us." Gilan smiled. "Our dust might sting your eyes."

A s the daylight strengthened and the land began to heat up, the wind veered. Edvin and Jesper transferred the anchor rope to the stern of the ship, keeping the bow pointed at the beach.

Thorn stood, one foot on the for'ard bulwark, watching events on the beach. Several of the rafts, which had been built in haste, had been damaged in the violent maneuvers that accompanied the first attack. Lashings had come loose and paddles had been lost. The *Ishti* warriors, under the scornful eyes of their commander, attended to these minor details, refastening the bamboo logs together and shaping new paddles from smaller pieces of bamboo.

There was a hangdog look to the desert riders as they went about their work. The foreign ship seemed to mock them, sitting placidly on the water only fifty meters offshore, unharmed and unaffected by their initial attack. Yet they had lost several comrades.

It was all very well for their commander to berate them and call them cowards and poltroons. But he hadn't faced the terrible wrath of the one-armed sailor with a giant club in place of his missing hand. Or the giant with the blackened, skull eye sockets who wreaked such havoc with his long half-spear, half-ax weapon. They understood now that they had been tricked into withdrawing from the fight. Truth be told, none of them regretted it, nor were they overeager to mount another attack. There might be only half a dozen of the enemy, but they were skillful and merciless fighters. Besides, there was also that monstrous devil of a dog, and the girl whose missiles had struck down their friends.

As a result, they dawdled over the adjustments to the rafts' lashings, even, on occasion, loosening them instead of drawing them tight. Their commander strode among them, checking their work suspiciously, and continuing to harangue them for their cowardice and slovenly workmanship.

But there was a limit to how long they could successfully stave off the inevitable moment. Late in the morning, their commander declared that the rafts were ready once more. He pointed to the water's edge and issued a curt command. Reluctantly, the raft crews seized hold of the awkward rafts and carried them once more to the water's edge.

"Here they come," Thorn called softly. "Edvin, stand by to let the anchor cable go, then get to the helm. Jesper and Stefan, you raise the sail . . ." He hesitated, glanced at the wind telltale and the direction in which the ship currently lay. "Make it the port-side sail. Wulf, stand ready on the sheets. Once they're in the water and fully committed, we'll get under way and sail in a curve to port. Then we'll bring her back. Lydia, Ingvar. This time, I want you on the Mangler. Smash up the rafts, cut down the crews. The ones you miss, we'll ram."

They all nodded silently. They had been over this plan while they had been waiting for the *Ishti* to make their move. As the first rafts were placed into the water, Lydia took her seat at the Mangler. Ingvar leaned past her and seized the cocking handles, drawing the bowstring back to full cock. They had already selected one of the shattering missiles for their first shot. He laid it now in the half-recessed track on top of the giant weapon. Then he seized the training handle and moved it back and forth on the swivel, making sure it moved freely and without obstruction.

Thorn moved aft, to a point astern of the mast, and peered over the starboard bulwark. The rafts were beginning to crab out from the shore. But they were moving slowly, a sign of their crews' reluctance.

"Ready, everyone . . . ," he called. Then he frowned. He saw Kloof suddenly sit up from where she had been lying beside the mast. Her ears were pricked and her head was canted to one side as she listened.

Then he heard it too: the drumming of horses' hooves on the hard-packed sand. And as he watched, a body of horsemen swept out of the oasis and headed for the beach. His heart sank as he saw there at least seventy riders in the tight-packed group.

"Reinforcements," he breathed.

Wulf turned to him. "We'll never be able to fight that many."

Both of them, and the others on board, were all too conscious of the fact that Stig, Hal and Gilan were still somewhere ashore. They would have no chance of reaching the ship through that mass of enemy riders.

Then Lydia was pointing to a spot to the left of the oasis. "Look! It's them! Hal and Stig!"

And they heard the whirring rattle of the land sailer's wheels over the rough ground as it came into view, traveling at full speed, canted up with its port wheel riding clear of the ground. They heard the wheel crash back to the ground as Hal heaved the strange vehicle through a tack, heard the slap of the sail as it filled with wind. Then it was arrowing back across the beach toward the suddenly panicking *Ishti.*

And that was when Thorn realized that the new arrivals weren't reinforcements for the Shurmel's men. They were attacking the *Ishti* warriors, driving into them at a full gallop, using lances and curved swords to spear them and cut them down. The Shurmel's warriors tried to regroup, but they were caught by surprise, with half their number on the rafts.

Thorn heard the ugly crash of the Mangler as the huge weapon released. He followed the path of the bolt as it sped toward the leading raft. It hit the raft at an angle, but the impact was enough to shatter the pottery warhead and send shards of hard clay whirring through the crew. The shaft itself cartwheeled, spinning just above the deck and taking the helmsman right near the knees. Men screamed and the water around the raft turned red with their blood. Ingvar was already loading another bolt into the Mangler. Thorn sighed and leaned on the hilt of his sword.

"Nothing much for me to do," he muttered. "Might as well watch."

At the controls of the land sailer, Hal scanned the beach in front of him as the little vehicle shot out into the open.

The *Ishti* warriors were running in all directions, and falling under the onslaught of Umar and his Bedullins as they carved a grim path through them. The enemy were taken completely by surprise. He saw a group of three men to one side, shouting and gesticulating, yelling orders at the disorganized rabble and at the rafts that were crabbing slowly away from the beach.

"Hang on!" he yelled to Gilan and Stig. They looked at him and saw the determination on his face as he swung the land sailer through a hard tack and hauled in on the sheet; the wheels skimmed the ground as he drove the vehicle across the beach, straight at the group of three, gathering speed with every meter they traveled.

The *Ishti* commander was intent on cursing his men and trying to rally them into a defensive circle. But those who hadn't already been struck down by a Bedullin lance or sword were throwing down their weapons and raising their hands in surrender. He screamed curses at them, then one of his companions plucked at his sleeve.

"Captain! Look out!"

The captain turned, saw the strange vehicle flying straight at him and froze in terror.

Seconds later, the land sailer plowed at full speed into the three men, hurling them to either side like so many ninepins. The impact was too great for the light timbers of the land sailer. The main spar shattered just behind the single steering wheel. The mast whipped forward under the sudden deceleration and snapped off halfway up, hurling the upper half forward, trailing a tangle of rope and canvas with it. Gilan and Stig spilled off the outriggers to the hard ground, rolling to lessen the impact of their fall. Hal was jettisoned forward, landing awkwardly beside the splintered central spar, his head missing contact with the iron-shod steering wheel by a matter of centimeters. As it was, the splintered end of the bamboo central spar tore a furrow across his forehead.

He rose to his feet, blood running down his face, and surveyed the wreckage of his land sailer. Gilan and Stig stood up stiffly as well. They moved to join him.

"You all right?" Stig asked. He looked worried and Hal regarded him, puzzled.

"Why?" he asked.

"Because your face is covered in blood," Stig told him.

Hal nodded groggily and wiped his face with the end of his *kheffiyeh*.

"Oh . . . so it is. I hadn't noticed. I think I broke the land sailer," he said.

"You certainly broke the *Ishti* command group," Gilan said, indicating the three still bodies scattered by the crash.

Hal shrugged. "I'm sure they had it coming."

The fight on the beach was over. A third of the *Ishti* fighters had been killed or wounded in that first wild charge. The others wasted no time in surrendering. The clumsy rafts were slowly returning to shore, their occupants throwing their weapons aside as they waded onto dry land. Fifty meters offshore, Hal saw four oars run out on the *Heron*. As he watched, they began to rise and fall, driving the little ship slowly toward the beach. As her prow touched, Stefan jumped ashore with a beach anchor and made her fast. The rest of the crew followed him in rapid order, running up the beach to their prodigal shipmates. Kloof, forgotten in the rush and excitement, barked furiously, then hurled herself overboard and swam ashore. Pausing to shake several gallons of seawater from her coat, she then bounded up the beach and reached Hal before any of the others, sending him flying with her rapturous, saturated welcome.

As he picked himself up, he saw Umar approaching, a huge smile of satisfaction on his face.

"Wonderful!" he enthused. "We have finally taught these people a lesson they won't soon forget." His eye landed on Kloof and he hesitated.

"What is this?" he said. "Is it some kind of Skandian horse?"

"It's my dog, Kloof," Hal told him. Kloof, sensing that Umar was a friend, moved forward, her damp tail swishing, and licked his hand.

"She likes you," Stig told the Bedullin leader.

Umar looked doubtful. "It's more like she's tasting me," he said. "What does this . . . horse-dog eat?"

Stig, Hal and Thorn, who had arrived in time to hear the question, exchanged grins and answered in unison:

"Anything she wants to!"

Hal embraced the old sea wolf, then made introductions as the rest of the Herons arrived. They regarded the Bedullin leader with interest. All of them, with the exception of Lydia, had heard the tale of Erak's rescue from the Tualaghi, and the role played by the Bedullin tribe in the battle that ensued.

Lydia hesitated, standing halfway between Stig and Hal, and made an awkward gesture with her hands. Not knowing which one to embrace first, she chose to embrace neither, but said in a subdued tone:

"You're back. You're safe." Then, noticing the blood running down Hal's face from under the improvised bandage he had fashioned from the *kheffiyeh*, she went a little pale. "Are you all right?"

Hal hesitated. He had been about to say something along the lines of "It's nothing. Just a scratch," as wounded heroes always said, but he stopped himself just in time. Instead, he let out a pitiful groan and clasped his hands to his head.

"No! It hurts! Oh, it hurts!"

For a moment, Lydia was taken in. She stepped toward him, then saw the irrepressible grin breaking through the dried blood on his face and withdrew in anger.

"Oh, go cry to your mummy!" she snarled and stalked off, followed by the laughter of the others.

Umar was sizing up Thorn, taking in the shabby old sea wolf's heavy chest and thickly muscled arms and legs.

"Now this one looks like a real Skandian!" he declared. "This one looks like Erak."

"No," said Thorn, "I'm a lot prettier than him."

Umar hesitated, eyeing him with his head tilted to one side. "You Skandians have a strange idea of pretty," he said at length.

Gilan had been surveying the defeated *Ishti* cavalrymen, being mustered into a group under the watchful eyes of Umar's warriors. The prisoners' hands were bound and their legs hobbled to prevent their running. He took Umar's arm and led him to one side.

"Umar, you say you've tried to attack the Scorpions' den in the past," he began.

The *Aseikh* nodded vigorously, showing his frustration. "True. I have wanted to teach that evil band a real lesson for years. But they always disappear into the tunnels and caves of the mountain before we can get close. I'd give a lot to take them by surprise one day. The world would be better off without the Scorpion cult."

"I agree. And it occurs to me that this might be your opportunity."

Suddenly he had Umar's undivided attention. The Bedullin chief leaned forward eagerly. "How's that, friend Gilan?"

Gilan gestured at the disconsolate prisoners, sitting on the sand. "Well, it occurs to me that the new Shurmel will be expecting these men to return sometime soon. And you have their cloaks and *kheffiyehs* . . ." He let the sentence hang uncompleted, and saw understanding dawn on Umar's face.

"If we wear their robes and *kheffiyehs,* the Scorpions will think we're their own men returning. We'll catch them by surprise before they have a chance to fade away!" he said triumphantly.

"At least, you'll catch some of them," Gilan said. "In that mass of caves and tunnels, some will probably escape."

"But we'll almost surely put them out of business for years, if not permanently," said Umar. "And that is something that we would all be glad to see." He seized Gilan's hand and pumped it enthusiastically. "Gilan, my friend, you are as wily as your friend Halt. And even more devious than Will Treaty!"

"I'll take that as a compliment—I think," Gilan said, smiling a little uncertainly.

"Will you join us on this expedition?" Umar asked. "We have plenty of extra horses now." He indicated the horses that the *Ishti* had been riding, but Gilan shook his head.

"We've done what we set out to do," he said. "My princess is safe from the *tolfah* now. And I think my wild Skandians are anxious to leave this desert behind them. Beautiful as it is," he added.

"Then I wish you godspeed. It is best if we get moving as soon as possible. You never know who's watching in the desert, and we need to strike swiftly."

Umar gripped Gilan's hand once more, then turned abruptly, shouting orders for his men to gather round. Gilan smiled after him. With Umar, he realized, to think was to act.

He turned back to the Herons standing nearby. "Anybody want to go home?"

Ulf was waiting on the jetty as the *Heron* glided into Tabork harbor.

"He looks healthy enough," Hal observed dryly.

Ulf was literally dancing from one foot to the other in anticipation of seeing his shipmates. He shoved one of the dock-yard workers aside to grab the mooring line that Stefan threw ashore, and set himself to the task of hauling the little ship along-side. He grimaced once, clasping his side, as the strain came onto the rope, then the local laborers took hold of the mooring line to assist him.

As the *Heron* bumped alongside, fenders squealing and grinding between the hull and the stone jetty, Wulf was the first ashore. He bounded up from the ship's rail and dashed to meet his brother, embracing him in a gigantic hug, and actually lifting him several centimeters from the ground.

"Careful!" Ulf said, his face covered with an enormous grin. "My side's still a bit tender."

Wulf instantly released him, his own face showing concern. "Are you not healed?"

Ulf hastened to reassure him. "I'm fine," he said. "Just a few muscles left to recover fully. It's so good to see you!" he added.

Wulf put his arm around his twin's shoulder. "I knew when you woke," he said. "I felt it somehow."

Ulf nodded eagerly. "I knew you could feel it!" he said. "I sensed your thoughts as well!"

"Amazing!" Wulf said. Then he seized his brother again, this time more carefully.

Ulf, looking over his shoulder, saw their shipmates gathered by the ship's rail, watching them with smiles on their faces. Such a show of affection between the twins was highly unusual, to say the least. He coughed, and muttered in his brother's ear.

"The others are watching."

Wulf turned quickly, releasing his grip. He too saw the row of grinning faces along the side of the ship. He turned back to Ulf and said in a loud, accusatory voice, "Didn't you ever learn to duck? Didn't anyone ever teach you that?"

"Duck?" said Ulf indignantly. "I was busy stopping a warrior who was about to split your skull."

"And you forgot to duck!" Wulf finished for him. "You nearly caused me to tell our mam that her second favorite son had got himself filleted."

"Second favorite?" Ulf challenged. "What do you mean, second favorite?"

"Least favorite, then. I was being polite."

"I'll have you know, Mam told me that I'm her favorite, by a long way," Ulf told him.

Wulf shook his head patiently. "Of course she did. She had to do that precisely because you *are* her second favorite. She knew you'd feel challenged and inferior. Whereas I have no need for such false praise. I *know* I'm her favorite, and because I know it, she doesn't have to lie and tell me so."

"So you admit she'd be lying if she did tell you?" Ulf challenged instantly.

"The point is, she *didn't* tell me. Which makes you her second favorite son. Or rather, since that's a little too flattering for you, her least favorite."

As they argued, they had been moving farther away from the ship. Wulf, without looking, spoke in a lowered tone. "Can they still hear us?"

Ulf shook his head. "No. They've gone back to stowing the gear."

Wulf nodded several times, then he placed his arm around his brother's shoulders again. He felt Ulf's arm go round his waist.

"It's good to see you on your feet again. I thought you were going to die," Wulf said, with a slight catch in his voice. Ulf said nothing, but momentarily increased the pressure of his arm around his brother's waist.

Selethen was still in Tabork, overseeing the new administration of the city and working on the recruitment of new troops for the garrison. He planned to leave some of his more experienced officers to take over the defense of the city. It was a good opportunity to promote those who had served well in the retaking of Tabork from the Tualaghi.

Once *Heron* was secured, Edvin began the task of restocking her with provisions and replacing any lost or damaged equipment. Foremost on his list was an item from Thorn—a large piece of canvas to replace the weather awning over the deck. With this task under way, Hal, Thorn and Gilan tidied themselves up and marched down the jetty to call on Selethen.

They found the *Wakir* literally up to his elbows in paperwork. Parchments and forms and requisitions of all kinds were piled up on his temporary desk. Aides rushed in and out, each one with a new set of questions and requirements. He looked up gratefully as the three foreigners walked into his office. Glaring distastefully at the mass of paper littering his desk, he shoved the lot onto the floor and glared at one of his secretaries.

"Take care of this lot!" he ordered. "And bring coffee for four."

He ushered them to cushions set around a low table by the open doorway that led onto the terrace overlooking the harbor. He eyed them all keenly.

"I take it you've settled the matter of the *tolfah?*" he said quietly.

"Permanently," Gilan said.

Selethen raised an eyebrow, obviously wanting more detail. Hal supplied it.

"Gilan challenged the Shurmel to a duel and killed him," he explained.

Selethen nodded several times. "That's a good result. The world will be a better place without him."

Gilan nodded, but added a qualification. "The cult did elect a new leader," he said. "But he might not enjoy the position too long." He described the battle at Ephesa and their encounter with Umar and his tribe of wild nomads. At the mention of the *Aseikh*'s name, a smile touched Selethen's lips.

"Umar is a good ally to have. And his men are great fighters."

"When we left Ephesa," Gilan told him, "he was planning an attack on Scorpion Mountain."

Selethen shook his head sadly. "A fine idea, but doomed to failure, I'm afraid. Their lookouts can see across the desert for miles. At the first sign of an attacking force, they all withdraw into the labyrinth of caves under the mountain."

"Except they won't see an attacking force," Hal pointed out. "They'll see what they assume are their own troops returning from Ephesa. Umar and his men will be in disguise and the Scorpions will actually be expecting to see their own troops returning."

A smile spread slowly across Selethen's face.

"Now that is a cunning idea." He assumed a mock frown of thoughtfulness. "Although cunning is not a word I would associate with Umar. Was this his idea?"

Gilan looked at the ceiling.

Thorn let out a brief, explosive laugh. "It was Gilan's idea. He's as cunning as a sea snake, he is!"

Selethen smiled again. "I might have known it. Cunning *is* a word we associate with Rangers."

Thorn slapped Gilan on the shoulder and nearly sent him sprawling across the coffee table. "This lad has cunning he hasn't even used yet!"

Gilan recovered and glared at the old sea wolf. "I wish you'd be a little less effusive, Thorn," he said.

Thorn shrugged happily. "No idea what the word means!"

Selethen concealed his own smile. "I trust you'll dine with me tonight?" he said. "Your entire crew." He addressed the invitation to Hal, who nodded his thanks.

"We plan to sail for Araluen tomorrow," he said. "But we'd be honored to be your guests tonight."

"We'll try not to be too effusive," Thorn added.

Gilan cast a sidelong glance at him. "That'd be a first," he muttered.

The return voyage down the Constant Sea was uneventful. The weather was fine and the winds were favorable. All in all, it was much like a pleasure cruise.

Even when they sailed through the Narrows and out into the Endless Ocean, the fine weather stayed with them, and *Heron* rolled the kilometers under her keel day after day. Eventually, the green shores of Araluen could be seen on the horizon as they entered the Narrow Sea. They sailed past the reefs and shoals where Tursgud had so nearly trapped them. This time, Hal stayed well to seaward of the treacherous stretch of water.

Lydia, Hal and Stig stood by the steering position, enjoying the rhythmic lift of the ship over the succeeding swells, and the constant groan of timbers and cordage as she rolled and pitched gently. There was a companionable silence about them, then Lydia, her face turned to the wind, said, "I can see why you love this. It makes up for all the bad weather and gales and salt water drenching everything. This is wonderful!"

"You're becoming a real deepwater sailor." Stig grinned and she nodded happily.

Hal, who was steering, had a sudden impulse. "Would you like to steer her?" he asked.

Lydia's eyes went wide open. "Could I?"

He gestured to the tiller. "Why not? I think you've earned a turn at the helm."

Gingerly, she took the tiller, feeling the vibration of the water running past it. As she took hold, she unwittingly released the pressure Hal had kept on the tiller and allowed the rudder to straighten. The ship instantly tried to go downwind. She felt a moment of panic.

"Meet her!" Hal said briskly and she frowned at him. She had no idea what that meant.

"Push the tiller away from you," Stig explained. She did and the bow swung back upwind. But now it went too far and she saw Ulf and Wulf turning to stare at the steering platform.

"Back!" said Hal, and as she did the bow swung to port again.

"Now center the rudder," Stig added. "That's it! Hold her there."

"Bring it up a little," Hal said quickly.

"But not too much. That's enough!" That was Stig again.

"Remember, if you want to go to port, you push the tiller to starboard," Hal said.

She glanced at him, concentrating fiercely on the tiller. "Why?"

He shrugged. "That's just the way it is. A little to port."

"Now ease it," said Stig.

Lydia laughed. They were like two mother hens with their precious chick of a ship, she thought.

"It's not as simple as you make it look," she said. The two

friends looked at each other and smiled. Lydia felt a great sense of contentment. She felt that she truly belonged with this ship, and particularly with these two young men. And as she had that thought, she felt the same old confusion. A part of her was saying that, one day, she would have to choose between them, but another part was telling her that she never wanted to have to make that choice. She twitched the tiller once more and laughed as the ship responded to her command.

"I thought you just held it in one position the whole time," she said, indicating the tiller.

"No," said Hal. "The sea is moving constantly and you have to constantly make little adjustments to keep it all going smoothly. You can't take it for granted."

"Just like a friendship," she said, smiling. And Hal nodded.

"Maybe that's why the word ends in *ship*," he said.

Lydia continued to steer, gradually getting the feel for the ship, until they sighted Cresthaven Bay. Then Hal took over and they sailed into the anchorage with a sense of homecoming.

They were surprised to see a wolfship moored alongside the jetty. She was one of the older models, still fitted with a square sail.

"That's *Wolfcall*," Thorn said, "Rugen Cloudseeker's ship."

The crew on the other ship called greetings to them and hurried to take mooring lines and bring *Heron* alongside. As the two hulls bumped and ground together, the skirl of the other ship moved to its waist.

"Permission to come aboard, Thorn?" he called out.

Thorn frowned. Rugen had always been a tactless dolt, he thought.

"Ask the skirl," he said bluntly.

Rugen made an apologetic gesture. It was sometimes hard to remember that a man as young as Hal could be a skirl.

"Sorry!" he said. "Permission to come aboard, Hal Mikkelson?"

Hal shook his head at Thorn. Sometimes his old friend could be a little too prickly on his behalf. He gestured to the other skirl to board and Rugen stepped lightly across the gap between the two ships. He strode aft and clasped Hal's hand, then Thorn's.

"Welcome back," he said. "Was it a successful voyage?"

Hal smiled wearily. So much had happened in the preceding weeks. They seemed to have been gone for an age.

"Yes," he said eventually. "Yes, it was. But tell me, Rugen, what are you doing here?"

Rugen was a tall and cadaverously thin man. His long, bony face creased in a smile.

"We're your relief," he said. "Your tour as duty ship is finished. You're going home."

E p i l o g u e

eron sailed through the breakwater into Hallasholm
harbor.

She bore the marks of her long voyage. Her hull
was stained with salt, and the seawater had stripped away sections
of the paintwork on her planks and mast. Her sails, once snowy
white, were stained and gray now, and the port sail showed a large
rectangular patch, where a sudden gale had blown it out after they
rounded Cape Shelter into the Stormwhite. Her rigging was worn
and frayed and had been spliced in a dozen places.

But if the *Heron* looked tired, her crew was anything but. They
lined the sides of the little ship as Hal brought her up into the
wind, then allowed her to drift downwind to the jetty. Eager hands
onshore sent mooring ropes sailing out over the gap between shore
and ship and hauled her in tight against the stone wall, quickly
looping the hawsers around bollards to hold her fast.

Heron had been sighted some time ago and word had gone
round the town. Consequently, the crew's families had all gathered
on the jetty to greet their sons. As the crew piled ashore, scram-

bling over the bulwarks and leaping onto dry land, the jetty became the scene of a dozen excited encounters, with everyone talking at once as mothers, fathers and siblings all plied their young men with questions, seldom waiting for the first to be answered before asking another.

Most common was the request for reassurance. "Are you all right? You're not hurt, are you?"

Ulf and Wulf's mother went pale with anguish as her sons tactlessly described Ulf's brush with death.

"I thought we'd lost him for sure, Mam," Wulf said enthusiastically. "One of the tribesmen stabbed him with this great knife and cut him from here to here." He demonstrated the extent of Ulf's wound, exaggerating more than a little. "There was blood and gore everywhere!"

His poor mother grabbed Ulf into her arms. "But you're all right now?" she said anxiously.

Ulf shrugged off her concern with all the careless impatience of youth. "Of course I am, Mam. I mean, it was only a knife wound!"

His mother turned away, shaking her head, wondering how many more of her hairs had gone gray in the last thirty seconds.

Karina was one of the first to the jetty. She waited until her son stepped ashore—last to leave the ship, as usual. Then she stepped forward and embraced him, holding him far longer than he expected her to, hugging him to her, too full of emotion for words. When she finally released him and stepped back, her eyes were moist.

"Loki's beard," she exclaimed. "I swear you've grown five centimeters!"

Hal laughed. Stig, who was close by and had a strong affection for Karina, asked her, laughing, "How about me, Hal's mam?"

The diminutive woman looked up at him before replying.

"You've grown at least ten, you gawky lout," she said fondly.

Stig laughed, hugged her, then pushed through the crowd to where he could see his own mother, as always, standing back from the crowd. Karina watched him go, a little sadly.

"I hope there'll come a day when she forgets about her husband's shame and enjoys the fame her son has gained," she said. Hal nodded agreement. Then Karina turned to regard Thorn, who was standing expectantly by. She took in his clean, albeit crumpled, linen shirt and roughly combed hair and beard.

"So, how are you?" she said coolly. She eyed his wooden hook. "Did you lose anything this time?"

Thorn grinned and placed his wooden hand over his chest. "Only my heart, to a beautiful Araluen girl!" he declaimed dramatically.

Karina's face darkened with fury. She stepped back from him, her hands on her hips, every inch of her bristling with anger.

"What Araluen girl?" she roared, her voice carrying over the general sounds of rejoicing and reunion on the wharf, and stilling all those around her. "Who is she? Where is she?"

Hal stepped forward and laid a calming hand on her shoulder. He could feel the tension and the rage in her body.

"Mam, I think he means you."

Karina looked at him. Looked at Thorn, who was smiling artlessly at her, and the rage went out of her like air out of a punctured bladder.

"Eh? Oh . . . then why didn't he say?"

She stepped primly toward Thorn and held up her cheek to be kissed. When he tried to turn her face to kiss her on the lips, she resisted.

"That can wait till the wedding," she said.

Thorn looked around in surprise. "Oh? Is someone getting married?" He recoiled in pain as Karina's elbow jolted into his ribs.

"Someone had better be," she said grimly.

He nodded quickly. "Oh, yes, of course." He sought Hal's eyes and shrugged helplessly.

Hal rolled his eyes at the shaggy old sea wolf. "You're a silver-tongued charmer, aren't you?"

Thorn opened his mouth to reply, realized there was nothing he could say, and shut it again. He was saved by Svengal's voice bellowing from the back of the crowd.

"Make way for the Oberjarl! Make way for the Oberjarl!"

Erak swept through the crowd as they parted before him like minnows fleeing a shark. Truth be told, he had no need for Svengal to announce him that way and he suspected that his old first mate only did it to annoy him.

The burly Oberjarl stopped, facing Hal. "Welcome back. I trust it all went well?"

Hal nodded. He noticed that Erak had carried out rather crude repairs on the beautiful staff that Kloof had destroyed. He had mounted the silver knob and ferrule on a rather crooked branch that he had found on the foreshore. Erak had never been much of a craftsman.

The Oberjarl let his gaze travel around the crew, who all nodded cheerfully at him.

"I see you've still got that dog," he said. Kloof was lying on the jetty, her nose on her paws, her tail swiping the air behind her.

"Um . . . yes. I see you've repaired your staff," Hal said.

Erak looked at him coldly. "And my ax," he said. "That boy spent days diving for it in the harbor. Thought I might need it if that dog of yours ever came back."

"Ah, well, actually, I brought you something from Arrida," Hal said.

Erak stopped pretending to be angry. In spite of his pretended irascibility, he had a soft spot for the *Heron* and her motley crew of misfits. And he loved getting presents.

"Arrida? What were you doing in Arrida?"

But Hal brushed the question aside. "It'll all be in my report." He turned. "Jesper, bring the staff, please."

Jesper stepped forward, bearing the scorpion staff that Hal had taken from the Shurmel's cave. He passed it to Hal, who presented it formally to Erak. The Oberjarl's eyes glowed as he let his crooked branch staff fall to one side and ran his hands lovingly over the smooth ebony shaft, touching the grotesque scorpion figure with reverence.

"Well now, isn't that something?" he crooned softly. "It's a real work of art!" Erak fancied himself as a connoisseur of fine art, it has to be said. "It's beautiful."

Hal shook his head. "It's something, all right," he said quietly. "But I'm not sure if the something is beautiful."

Standing apart from the noisy throng, Lydia watched proceedings with a sad little smile on her face. It was times like these when she missed her grandfather most. The Skandians were such noisy, demonstrative and family-oriented people. Apart from the other Herons and Karina, she had no strong attachments in Hallasholm and she didn't want to intrude on her shipmates' family reunions. Quietly, she collected her gear and made her way unnoticed to the house in town where she stayed with a kindly widow.

Several hours later, her landlady found her, sitting on the porch, looking at the sun setting over the ocean. The widow, Agathe by name, was a motherly type. Her own daughter had moved away to another town when she had married recently and she enjoyed having this quiet, reserved girl staying with her.

"What's this? Not dressed for the party?"

Lydia looked up. "What party is that?"

"There's always a party to welcome home the duty ship," Agathe told her. "And seeing how you're one of the crew, you'll be one of the guests of honor. Now get yourself bathed and dressed and I'll brush your hair and make you beautiful."

Lydia gave her a wan little smile. "Not sure if that's possible," she said and Agathe looked at her for a few seconds, her head on one side.

"You really mean that, don't you? You have no idea how stunning you can be with that olive skin and those dark eyes and that beautiful glossy hair."

The younger woman flushed slightly. "I don't have anything to wear," she prevaricated.

Agathe smiled. She had been expecting that response. "Aaah, yes you do. I bought a beautiful yellow dress for you at the market last month. You'll be the star of the party, believe me!"

And she was. An hour later, as she walked into the square where tables and casks of ale were set up, and three lambs were roasting on spits, every head turned to watch her.

"Lydia! Good to see you!" said a familiar voice. She turned to see Rollond, prepared to gently discourage any overtures he might make. She was surprised to see an attractive black-haired girl holding his arm, most possessively.

"Have you met Frieda, my fiancée?" he asked.

Lydia smiled sweetly at the girl. She didn't know why, but she felt a sudden pang of jealousy. It was all right for her to rebuff Rollond's advances. But for him to find another girl was not quite so easy to take. Rollond and Frieda exchanged a few words with her, then moved off to the food tables.

She stood awkwardly for a moment, feeling a vague sense of loss and looking for the familiar faces of her shipmates, when suddenly she was engulfed by half a dozen girls her own age.

"Lydia!" they cried excitedly. "Come and join us! You look fabulous! How do you do your hair that way?"

She found herself being dragged toward the girls' table, where she was plied with questions and compliments. Truth was, Lydia had become something of a celebrity among the young women of Hallasholm. She was a woman who did things her own way, who joined with her men friends in an adventurous, dangerous life. She was a skilled hunter and tracker. She had fought in battles and was regarded as an equal by the young men who were her shipmates. She had even been inducted into their brotherband—being referred to as a "Sister of the Brotherband."

In her hometown of Limmat, she had been regarded as something of an oddity. Limmatan girls spent their days primping and doing their hair and makeup, not stalking game in the forest. Skandian girls, however, were more inclined to adventure and the outdoor life and to them, Lydia was a shining beacon, a living example of what a woman could achieve if she set her mind to it. She realized, as they continued to fetch her food and drinks and ask if she could teach them to use an atlatl, or to field dress a deer, that she had made a group of good friends. Looking around their open, welcoming faces, she finally felt that she belonged here. And she felt happiness stealing over her.

As the night wore on and more ale casks were broached, the revelers began to look for Stefan and Jesper. Eventually, the two Herons were propelled toward a table in the center of the square.

"A saga!" the crowd demanded. "Let's hear a saga about your trip!"

"But we didn't prepare anything . . . ," Jesper said, his face a mask of innocence.

"Oh really," Hal muttered, rolling his eyes. He'd seen them with their heads together over the past week, as they noted down lyrics and ideas, foreheads knotted in frowns as they strove for a rhyme or a colorful expression. This mock reluctance was too much, he thought. The crowd howled at Jesper, refusing to accept his excuse. Eventually, with a great show of reluctance, he and Stefan allowed themselves to be hoisted onto the table.

Erak, his new scorpion staff in his hand, shoved his way through the crowd to stand at the table. He had a full tankard of ale in the other hand and those nearby, knowing what was to come, quickly cleared a space around him.

"Come on!" he roared. "Let's hear the saga!" Erak loved a good saga. He even loved a bad one, as a matter of fact, which was just as well.

Jesper and Stefan grinned at each other and began to sing.

The Herons! The Herons!
The mighty, fighting Herons!
No other brotherband you'll see
is even half as darin'!

Hal raised his eyes to heaven. "I had hoped they might have improved that part," he said. But after the first two words, the crowd had joined in enthusiastically. They stopped as the boys launched into their first verse.

We sailed away from Hallasholm, we had to be real quick,
for Kloof had eaten Erak's ax and chewed his walking stick.

"Oh, very tactful indeed," Hal said, as Erak turned a baleful eye upon him. Erak still hadn't totally forgiven Kloof for the destruction of that walking stick.

We sailed across the Stormwhite and we struck a mighty storm.
We had to wear our woolly caps to keep us nice and warm.

As they sang those lines, both of them produced their distinctive woolen watch caps and pulled them on. The crowd cheered. Several mothers nodded their approval of such wise behavior while at sea. Then it was time for a repeat of the chorus and this time Erak, his anger at Kloof dispelled by the occasion, joined in, singing and beating time with his tankard and staff. People around him were suitably drenched. One had his toe thumped by the staff crashing to earth. He howled and collapsed.

Jesper and Stefan had agreed to leave all references to Tursgud out of their song. The renegade still had family in Hallasholm and they had no wish to embarrass them.

> *We sailed around Cape Shelter and then south to Araluen.*
> *We called upon the people there to find out what was doin'.*

"Oh, that's very good!" Erak shouted. "Great poetry. *Araluen* and *doin'*. That's genius, sheer genius."

"The man has a strange idea of genius," Hal said quietly. But the rhyming continued to go from bad to execrable.

> *We chased an evil slaver to the market in Socorro.*
> *"We can't rescue them tonight," said Hal. "We'll get them out tomorrow."*
> *Lydia and the Ranger burned the market to the ground.*
> *The rest of us, we freed the slaves then headed out of town.*

> *The Herons! The Herons!*
> *The mighty, fighting Herons!*
> *No other brotherband you'll see*
> *is even half as darin'!*

> *The slave master named Mahmel was a nasty kind of thug,*
> *so Stiggy dropped a rock on him and squashed him like a bug.*

The crowd cheered and Stig waved cheerfully to them. After

another staff-thumping, ale-spilling chorus, the saga continued.

We sailed back to Cresthaven and we set the captives free.
King Duncan said, "Well done, my lads, you're just the boys for me.
My Ranger Gilan has to go and hunt down some assassins
So go along with him and give these wicked types a thrashin'."

"Oh, spare me!" said Hal. Erak shushed him angrily.

"You just don't appreciate the arts," he said. "On the other hand, I'm something of a patron."

Hal eyed the grotesque scorpion staff that the Oberjarl was so proudly waving and shook his head.

A pirate galley barred our way. We quickly overtook 'em.
And Ingvar led the charge aboard to stab and chop and hook 'em.

More cheers, for Ingvar this time. Sheepishly, he acknowledged the crowd's applause.

We beat the Tualaghi and the Scorpions as well.
The Ranger stuck his saxe into their leader, the Shurmel.
When all of the assassins threw a fit of wild hysterics,
Hal grabbed up the Shurmel's staff and brought it back for Erak.

Erak cheered at that and brandished his dreadful staff above his head. The crowd roared. They joined in for two more choruses, agreeing totally that no other brotherband was even half as darin'.

Hal closed his eyes with a shudder and gave thanks when the song was finally over. Erak grabbed him in a huge bear hug and led him round the square, showing him off to all those assembled as the hero of the hour.

Half an hour later, the Oberjarl was still expounding on Hal's wisdom and courage and ingenuity when he suddenly stopped and looked around.

"Where's my new walking stick?" he said.

With a sinking feeling, Hal realized that the scorpion staff, which Erak had laid to one side, was nowhere in sight. Neither, he realized, was Kloof.

"And where's your dog?" said Erak, following the same train of thought.

"He's . . . uh . . . he's on the ship, guarding it," Hal said nervously.

Erak's brows drew together. "Where's my ax?" he said threateningly, looking round for the weapon. Then Svengal's cheerful voice rang across the square and Hal felt a huge rush of relief.

"Here's your spider on a stick, chief!" called Svengal, brandishing the scorpion staff, which he had found under a table. Gratefully, Erak reclaimed it, smiling forgiveness at Hal.

"Sorry I even thought it," he said. "She's a good dog."

"She is," Hal agreed. He moved away, smiling and greeting people who came up to congratulate him on a successful tour as the Araluen duty ship. After a while, his eyelids began to droop and he staved off several yawns. He realized how tired he felt. It had been an exhausting, emotional day to complete an emotional, exhausting tour of duty, and he just wanted to be on his own for a while. He slipped away into the shadows around the town square and left the sound of revelry behind.

Walking back to his mother's house, he passed a thicket of bushes and heard another sound, an all-too-familiar one.

It was a crunching, grinding sound, overlaid by Kloof's soft growls of contentment as she worked her jaws on something hard and solid. He pushed the bushes aside and froze in horror at the sight that confronted him.

"Oh, you great, hairy idiot!" he said. The dog whuffled unrepentantly, wagging her tail as she continued to chew the object she grasped in her front paws.

The party went on until long after midnight. Gradually, people made their way to their homes and, one by one, the lights of Hallasholm went out.

Save for the light in Hal's workshop.

It burned long into the small hours of the morning as he labored to fit a new handle to Erak's grandfather's ax.

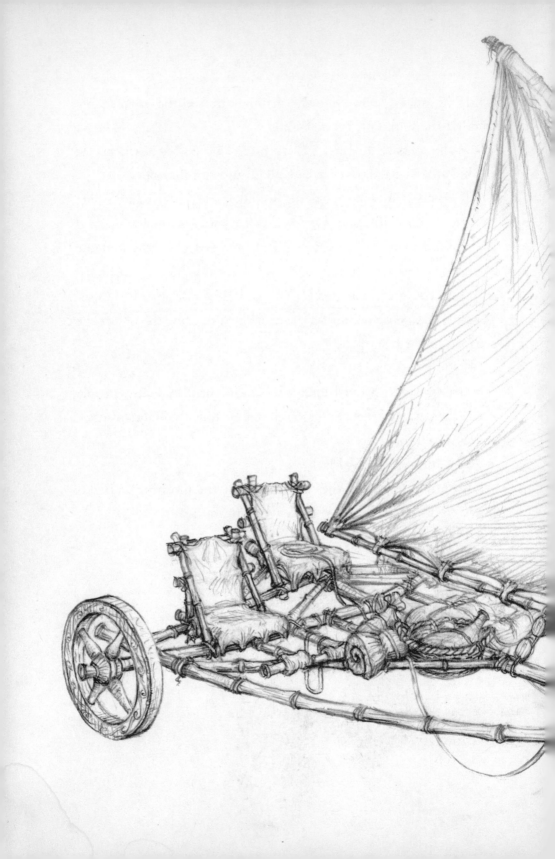

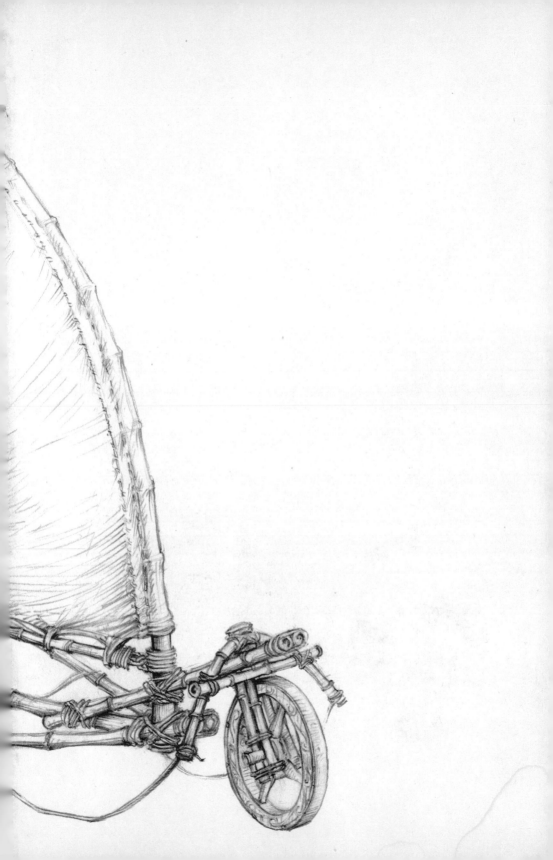